PRAISE FOR DIANE DUANE'S
THE DOOR INTO SHADOW

"A rousing trumpet voluntary for Diane Duane's THE DOOR INTO SHADOW. A fine tale of daring, caring and sharing, of self-revelation and self-sacrifice, with a superbly realized religion, integrated into a civilization at risk to the evil side of that religious ethos. The Duane dragon Hasai is a 'gentleman' to be reckoned with and of special interest to me!"

—Anne McCaffrey, bestselling author of *Moreta: Dragonlady of Pern*

"This fantasy sequel of *The Door into Fire* is energetic and features several original twists, some good ideas and lots of excitement . . . different and above average."

—*The Kirkus Reviews*

"To my way of reckoning, this is an even stronger story than the first. . . . I found it absorbing—the kind of book one reads in gulps and cannot put down. . . . Her talent is outstanding in a field in which there are so many excellent craftspeople. I found her heroine one I could feel with and for . . . She is to highly complimented on the wgole book —which I hope will at least bring her a Hugo. This is one of those volumes one can read over again and find new points of interest in every reading."

—Andre Norton, author of the *Witchworld* books

Other books by Diane Duane

THE TALE OF THE FIVE, Volume 1:
†*THE DOOR INTO FIRE
SO YOU WANT TO BE A WIZARD?
THE WOUNDED SKY
†DEEP WIZARDRY

*Published by Bluejay Books
†Forthcoming

THE DOOR INTO SHADOW

DIANE DUANE

BLUEJAY BOOKS INC.

A Bluejay Book, published by arrangement with the Author

Copyright © 1983, 1984 by Diane E. Duane

Cover and fold-out art (jacket and endpaper art in the collector's edition) by Susan S. Collins

A portion of this book appeared in slightly different form in *Fantasy Book* magazine

Manufactured in the United States of America

First Bluejay printing: April 1984

Book design by Rhea Braunstein

LIBRARY OF CONGRESS CATALOGING IN PUBLICATION DATA

Duane, Diane.
  The door into shadow.

  (Epic tales of the five; v. 2)
  I. Title. II. Series.
PS3554.U233D6 1984   813'.54   84-2948
ISBN 0-312-94111-0
ISBN 0-312-94110-2 (pbk.)

For Harlan Ellison:

for Michael and Charlene,
who were in at the kill:

for Jim and Joan,
who waited and waited and waited:

and (at last)
for Edward David Duane,
with love

The Wound is healed
by the sword that deals it;

the heart is knit
by the pain that breaks it;

the life is made whole
by the death that starts it;

the death is made whole
by the life that ends it.

(Hamartics, 186)

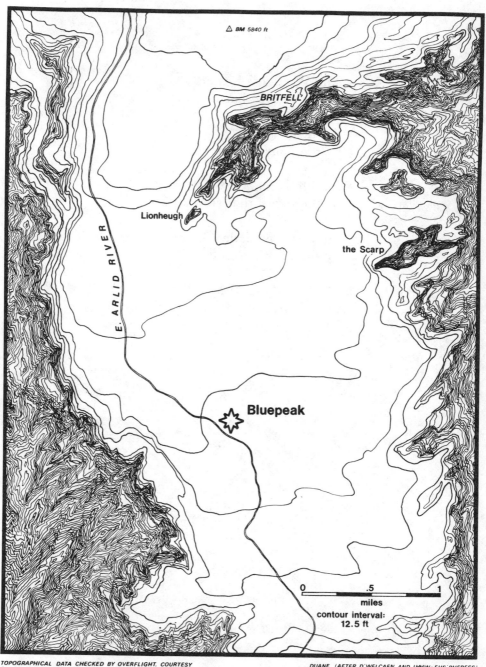

△ *BM* 5840 ft

BRITFELL

Lionheugh

the Scarp

E. ARLID RIVER

✺ **Bluepeak**

0   .5   1
miles
contour interval:
12.5 ft

TOPOGRAPHICAL DATA CHECKED BY OVERFLIGHT. COURTESY
OF THE MARCHWARDERS-GENERAL. ONOLÍ·TÁTH·LHHW'HAD

DUANE (AFTER D'WELCAEN AND LHHW·EHS'PHERESS)

Four lands hemmed in by mountain and waste and the Sea—those were the Middle Kingdoms: and the greatest of them, Arlen and Darthen, were in peril of destruction. For seven years Arlen's throne had been empty of the royalty needed to keep the land fertile and the people at peace. And Darthen suffered as a result of Arlen's lack, for the Two Lands were bound together by oaths of friendship and by joint maintenance of the royal sorceries that kept their lands safe from the ever-present menace of the Shadow.

In those days there appeared a man with the blue Fire—not just the spark of Flame that every man and woman possesses, but enough to channel and use to change the world around him. His lover was the child of Arlen's last king, heir to his usurped throne. In the Firebearer's relationship to Freelorn, King Ferrant's son, many later saw the Goddess's hand. She had been working quietly, so as not to alarm Her old adversary the Shadow.

Her hand seemed visible elsewhere too. Freelorn had taken companions with him into his exile. They lived as outlaws and bandits, stealing what they needed when they had to—though none of their hearts were in it. One of them in particular would certainly have been elsewhere, if she had had a choice. Swordswoman and sorceress, trained in the Silent Precincts and in every other place in the Kingdoms that dealt in the use and mastery of the blue Fire that some women bear, Segnbora d'Welcaen tai-Enraesi was a spectacular and expensive failure. She had the Fire in prodigious quantity, and couldn't focus it. On her way home from one more school that couldn't do anything for her, chance threw her together with Freelorn's people one night. Bitterly frustrated with what seemed a wasted life, desperately needing something useful to do, Segnbora swore fealty that night to the rightful heir of the Arlene throne, and fled with him and his people into the eastern Waste where Freelorn's loved, Herewiss, awaited him.

The children of House tai-Enraesi traditionally had a talent for getting themselves into dangerous situations. There in the Waste, in an ancient pile built by no human hand—a fortress rising gray and bizarre out of the empty land, skewed and blind-walled and ominous—she started wondering whether even the tai-Enraesi luck would do her any good. There were stories about this place, about soul-eating monsters that guarded innumerable doors into Otherwheres. Even the mildest of the stories were gruesome. Fear gripped her, but her oath gripped her harder. She stayed with Freelorn and his people.

And there in the Hold, fulfilling her fears, the stories she had heard came true—even the one of how nothing good would come out of this terrible place until (ridiculous improbability) a male should focus his Fire.

On the night Herewiss declared his intention to use his newly gained Fire to replace Freelorn on his throne, Segnbora lay in the darkness and considered the old rede that spoke of her family's luck. That luck would run out some day, when the last of her line died by his or her own hand, in a time of ice and darkness. But that hardly had anything to do with her. She wasn't the last of the tai-Enraesi, and anyway her luck was holding splendidly. She would be riding out of here with three good friends, a sometime lover, a prince about to retake his throne, a fire elemental, and the first man in a thousand years to focus his Fire. So maybe, maybe just this once, everything was going to turn out all right. . . .

One

Sirronde stared at the Goddess. "Are You saying, then, that You were wrong to make heroes?"

"Indeed not," She said. "But I should have warned them— if you save the world too often, it starts to expect it."

*Tales of the Darthene
South,* book iv, 29

When she was studying in the Silent Precincts, the Rodmistresses had warned her: If you're going to look for meaning in a dream, first make sure it's your own. Any sensitive is most sensitive in her sleep; and others' dreams can draw you in and fool you. Now, therefore, Segnbora held quite still in her sleep so as not to disturb whoever else was dreaming the landscape into which she had stumbled. It wasn't often, after all, that one was privileged to see the Universe being created.

The Maiden was working, as She always is, while the other two Persons of the Goddess, the Mother and the Eldest, looked on. Young and fair and preoccupied was the Maiden, as She worked elbow-deep in stars and flesh and dirt. She was so delighted with the wild diversity of Her creation that She never noticed the Mother and the Eldest desperately trying to get Her attention. They saw what she did not: the shapeless, lurking hunger that hid in the darkness at the Universe's borders.

Finally the Maiden, satisfied that Her world was complete, cried out the irrevocable Word that started life running on its own and sealed the Universe against any subtractions. And the instant She had done so, Death stood up from where it had been hiding, and laughed at Her.

She had locked the doors of the world, and had locked Death in. Slowly it would suck the Universe dry of life, and She could not prevent it. Nor could She prevent Death's darkness from casting shadows sideways from Her light—rogue aspects of Her, darksides, bent on destroying more swiftly what was already doomed. The Maiden was grief-stricken, and took counsel with Her otherselves to find some way to combat death. Among Them, They invented first the heart's love, and then the body's—lying down together in the manner of woman with woman, and becoming with child.

The Maiden, becoming the Mother now, brought forth twins—sons, or daughters, or daughter and son; the ambivalence of the dream made the Firstborn seem all of these at once. Swiftly They grew, and discovered love in Their Mother's arms—then turned to one another and discovered it anew. But in the midst of Their bliss, surrounded by the blue Fire that was Their Mother's gift and Their pride, the Death stood up again. It entered one of the Lovers and taught that one jealousy.

The shadowed Lover slew the innocent One—and in the same act destroyed Its own Fire, which had been bound by love to the Other's. Cursing, the Dark Lover fled in a rage into the outer darkness, where It would reenact Its murder and loss and bereavement for as long as the Universe should last. It was not a Lover anymore, but the Shadow.

In the dream Segnbora wept, knowing all along what was going to happen. She knew that mortals would be reenacting this tragedy in their own lives forever. The dream broke, then, and gradually re-formed as an image in water does when a stone is thrown in.

She saw a scene skewed sideways, as if her head rested on someone's shoulder. Much of the great room where she stood was dark, but in her hand—which had become a man's hand —she held a core of blinding white light, wreathed all about with flames as blue as summer sky. Herewiss, she realized. Last night.

His weariness was so terrible he could barely stand. He had banished the hralcins, the soul-eaters, yet he was too tired to exult in the focus he had forged—the unfinished sword he would call Khávrinen. He was the first man in a thousand years to focus the Fire, and he knew what difficulties lay ahead. The Shadow would not long tolerate him, or any man who enjoyed the Power It had cast away. It would deal with him quickly, before the Goddess had time, through him, to consolidate newly regained ground.

We must move more quickly, then, the dream said. *For look what the Shadow has planned.* Segnbora shuddered in her sleep at the sight of a whole valley suddenly buried under mountains that had formerly stood above it. *Dead,* a voice said soundlessly. *She's dead.* Snow whirled wildly down onto a battlefield, turning red as soon as it fell. Monsters gnawed the dead. Elsewhere a wave of blackness came rolling down out of murky heights, crashed down onto a leaping, threatening fire, and smothered it.

The air was thick with the feel of ancient sorceries falling apart, fraying. Grass forgot how to grow. Grain rotted on the stalk and fruit on the bough. Plague downed beasts and people alike, leaving their blackened corpses to lie splitting in the sun. Even the scavenger birds sickened and died of what they ate. It was happening. The royal magics were failing. If they weakened enough to let the Shadow fully into this world, into Bluepeak, this was what would happen.

The soundless voice of the dream spoke urgently. *Freelorn must see to the Royal Bindings quickly. This is his job, he's the Lion's Child and heir to Arlen. Go with him, Herewiss, in the full of your Power. Use the Fire to the utmost. He'll need assistance.*

But I just got the Fire, Herewiss said, terrified. *It takes time to master it.*

There is no time. What must be done needs doing now. The Other is coming.

And she could feel it, that throbbing of hatred in the background, getting stronger by the minute. As she watched, the sky grew dark. The snow blasted about them, in that place to which they would have to go to reinforce the Royal Bindings. Herewiss's Fire, for so long a blaze within him, was now faint under a blanket of oppressive power. Just in front of him, Freelorn started to stand up. The whole dream focused then on the sight of Freelorn's back, with a three-barbed, razor-sharp Reaver arrow standing out of it.

Sagging, Lorn sunk back slowly against Herewiss. Then there was a deeper darkness, and the two of them stood together before a Door in which burned the stars that would never go out. Freelorn, his face in shadow, was pulling his hand gently out of Herewiss's grasp, turning away toward death's Door . . .

No!

Do what you must to come to the full of your Power. There's no time! Her voice was almost frightened. Herewiss had never believed She could sound that way.

But if I do—and we get there—then Lorn—

It must not be prevented.

But—

You must not attempt to prevent it!

I—

Hurry!

NO!!

The scream tore through her throat as she sat bolt upright in the bedroll, sweating—still seeing against the darkness the long ruinous fall of an entire mountain, still hearing the crash of it, first note in a song of disaster.

In the great main hall of the old Hold, people fumbled frantically for their swords—the memory of the hralcins' sudden arrival the night before was very fresh. The fire in the firepit rose up too, putting several broad curves of flame over the edge and leaning anxiously out to see what was the matter. As a fire elemental, Sunspark had not had much experience with fear, but after last night it was apparently taking no chances.

Segnbora lifted a hand to her pounding head and found that she was holding her sword, Charriselm. Evidently she had drawn it while she was still half-sleeping. Beside her in the bedroll, blond Lang was still blanket-wrapped, but nevertheless he had found his graceknife in a hurry. Lying propped on one elbow with the knife in one ham of a hand, he blinked at her like an anxious owl. A few feet away, big swarthy Dritt and lanky Moris were sitting up back to back, looking as panicked as Segnbora felt. On the other side of the firepit, Harald was attempting simultaneously to string his bow and brush the brown hair out of his eyes. All of these looked at Segnbora as if they thought she was crazy.

"A bad dream?" Lang said.

She nodded, sliding Charriselm back into its sheath and looking across the room toward the firepit and the bedrolls laid down there.

Herewiss was sitting up, bracing himself with one hand, rubbing his eyes with the other. He took the hand away from his face, and Segnbora was shocked to see his terrified expression. Lorn was holding Herewiss tight and peering worriedly into his face. Under other circumstances it could have been a touching and humorous sight—the little, dark-mustachioed, fierce-eyed man comforting someone who, judged by his slim hard build and shoulder musculature, might have been the village blacksmith.

"Are you all right? What happened?"

"It was a dream," Herewiss said, his voice anguished.

"Shh, it's all right."

"No, it's not." Herewiss rubbed his eyes again, then glanced around him with frightened determination. He started searching in the blankets for his clothes. "We've got to go."

"What?"

"We have to hurry."

Herewiss grabbed one bunched-up blanket and impatiently shook it. A sword fell out and clattered to the floor—a hand-and-a-half broadsword of gray steel that would have seemed of ordinary make except for the odd blue sheen about it. He reached out for it, and at his touch his Power ran down the blade: blinding blue Fire, twisting and flurrying about as if in bright reflection of his distress.

"It was—there was—the mountain fell down, just like that. And there were thousands of Fyrd, and bigger monsters too —and a wave came down over everything, and Sunspark went out—"

(I did *not!*)

"Loved, slow down so I can understand what the Dark you're talking about—"

"So much for a whole night's sleep," Lang muttered under his breath. Putting his knife away under the rolled-up cloak that was serving them as pillow, he lay down again. "Wake me up when they're finished?"

"If necessary," Segnbora said, rubbing his shoulder absently. The gesture was more for her comfort than for his. Her underhearing was wide awake, bringing her the hot coppery blood-taste of Herewiss's fright as if it were her own.

Herewiss was talking fast. He had yanked a shirt out of the blankets and was struggling into it, while in his lap Khávrinen kept on blazing like a torch.

"It's angry as anything," he was saying. "And It's going to work the worst mischief It can, by putting pressure on the Royal Bindings that have been keeping It in check." He started feeling around for his britches. "For seven years no one's reinforced the Arlene half of those Bindings, and they're wearing thin—"

Freelorn glanced away from Herewiss. Segnbora put her hands behind her and leaned back, closing her eyes and bracing herself against the gut-punch of grief and anger she knew would come from Lorn. When his father had died on the throne, and the Minister of the Exchequer, Cillmod, had taken the opportunity to seize power, Freelorn had fled for his life with a price on his head. Now Lorn would wonder again whether staying in Arlen to see to the bindings, and possibly getting killed as a result, might not have been the more noble course.

It was an old midnight pain that Segnbora had come to know as well as the arthritis in Harald's right knee, or Dritt's self-consciousness about his weight. Indeed, no Precinct-trained sensitive could have helped underhearing her surroundings as Segnbora did. It was the gift she would have been happiest to lose when she gave up her studies. She had enough trouble dealing with her own pains. Those of others were an unwelcome burden.

"Lorn, enough," Herewiss said, catching Freelorn's anguish himself. "The fact remains that if the Shadow leans Its full strength against the Bluepeak bindings, we're done for. The Kingdoms will founder. I saw the southern passes full of Reaver armies. And the plains full of Fyrd. There were storms and earthquakes, and where the earth opened a whole town fell in. And that cliff at Bluepeak—" Herewiss broke off.

Freelorn, still holding him close, looked puzzled. "But it was just a dream!"

"Oh no," Herewiss said, shaking his head emphatically. "I saw."

"He's dreaming true," Segnbora said quietly.

Freelorn's frightened eyes flicked to her.

"He's focused now," she said hurriedly. "It's to be expected."

"What about the cliff?" Freelorn said to Herewiss.

Herewiss closed his eyes and sagged back on his heels, looking tired. "It was snowing—"

"A month and a half before Midsummer's? You call that dreaming true?"

Segnbora held her face still as Herewiss saw again that image of Freelorn turning away from him, away from love and life toward death.

"Lorn," Herewiss said. "I was shown a lot of things. I don't know what they all meant. I don't think most of them have happened yet. But some of them will, unless they're prevented." He swallowed hard. "I have to assist in the process. I was given all this Power. Now it has to be used, fully, and I won't be able to to take my time about its mastery, either."

Freelorn looked askance at his loved, getting an idea and not liking it. "But what other way is there, but to work into your Power slowly?"

"The Morrowfane, Lorn."

Freelorn looked grim. "I've done a little reading on the subject," he said.

It was a great understatement, for among the responsibilities of a throne prince of Arlen was the curatorship of rr'Virendir, the Arlene royal library, and that meant intimate knowledge of nearly every extant writing dealing with both mundane sorcery and more elevated matters of Power.

"All the sources say you can't go up there without coming down changed—"

(What's the problem with that?) Sunspark said from the firepit. The reaction was understandable; change was a fire elemental's chief delight. (Just yesterday Herewiss changed—quite a bit—and you didn't mind.)

Lorn glanced with annoyance at Sunspark, and the elemental threw back a smug feeling. During the time Herewiss had spent in the Hold forging Khávrinen, Sunspark had come to be his loved too. Lorn, not yet at peace with the situation, was still subject to occasional twinges of jealousy.

"I don't mean shapechanges," Lorn said with exaggerated patience. "Soul-changes. Great alterations in personality. Madness and other brands of sanity that human beings don't usually survive."

"The change needn't be harmful," Herewiss put in. "Remember, the place is a great repository of Flame. All the legends agree on that. Those who climb the Fane are given what's needed to do what they must do in a life."

"Then why do so few people go up it?"

"For one thing, you need focused Fire, and enough of it to keep the Power of the place from blasting you," Herewiss explained. "For another, very few people *want* what they need. . . . Lorn, listen. This is necessary. It's part of getting you back on your throne. If we don't get to Bluepeak by Midyear's Eve, so that you can aid in restoring the bindings, there won't be a country left for you to rule."

"But I was never Initiated into the Mysteries. If I had been, we wouldn't have these problems—I'd be King, and that slimy bastard Cillmod would be out looking for a situation."

"True, but you know the royal rites, don't you? You have to do it."

"Who says?"

"Whom do you think?" Herewiss said, very gently. "When you dream true, Whom do you think sends the dream?"

Lorn held very still, and most of the fierceness faded out of his eyes. "There's another problem. You know the money I removed from the Arlene treasury in Osta? Well, Bluepeak's in Arlen too. Cillmod's probably pretty annoyed about that missing money, and if we go back to Arlen so soon, and he hears about it. . . ."

Herewiss said nothing.

After a moment or two, Freelorn shrugged. "Oh, what the Dark! If the Reavers and the Shadow are going to come down on Arlen, Cillmod hardly matters. I suppose I have no choice anyway. I swore that damn Oath when I was little. 'Darthen's House and Arlen's Hall—' "

" '—share their feast and share their fall,' " Herewiss

finished. "If Arlen goes, so does Darthen. And after them Steldin, North Arlen, the Brightwood. . . ."

Freelorn laughed, but without merriment. "Why am I even worried about Cillmod at all? The Shadow is a far greater danger. It can't afford to leave you alive now, can It? You're the embodiment of the old days before the Catastrophe, when males had the Power. The time of Its decline. . . ."

Herewiss shook his head and smiled, an expression more of grim agreement than of reassurance. "We'll both be careful," he said. "That is, if you're coming with me? . . ."

Reaching down, Freelorn gently freed one of Herewiss's hands from Khávrinen's hilt, and held the hand between his own. "No more dividing our forces," he said. "From now until it's done, we go together."

Herewiss held his peace and didn't change expression. Segnbora had to drop her eyes, seeing again that image of one hand that let go of another's, the face that turned away.

All at once Freelorn was thumping on the floor for attention. "Listen, people—"

Segnbora nudged Lang. He rolled over under his covers. "Whatever you say, Lorn, I'll do it," he said, and pulled the blanket back over his head.

"There's a man who follows his liege oaths too well," Freelorn said with a grimace of affectionate disgust. "On his own head be it. But for the rest of you—I can't in good conscience ask you to go on this trip. The Shadow—"

"The Shadow can go swive with sheep for all I care," Moris said with one of his slow grins. "I haven't come this far with you to stop now."

"Me either," Harald said, stubbornly folding his huge bear's arms.

"You're not listening," Freelorn said, in great earnest. "Your oaths are a matter of friendship and I love you for them. But it's not just Cillmod we're playing with now. It's the Shadow. Your *souls* are at stake—"

"The things that were in here last night ate souls too," Dritt said calmly, putting his chin down on his arms. "Herewiss did for *them* all right."

(I helped,) said the voiceless voice from the firepit. Eyes

looked out of the flames at the company, then came to rest with calm interest on Freelorn. (I'm coming too.)

The building rumble of irritation in the room, combined with so much unspoken affection, was making Segnbora's head ache; the walls of this place, opaque to thought, bounced the emotions back and forth until the undersenses were deafened by echoes.

"Look," she said, shaking free of her own blankets. "If we've got to get an early start in the morning—" She glanced at Herewiss. "—it *can* wait until morning?"

"I suppose so," he said.

"Good. Then I want some sleep. But if this argument keeps up any longer I'll have to sleep outside." She went over to Freelorn in her shift and offered him Charriselm hilt-first, about an inch from his nose. "Do you seriously want your oath back?" she said. "That whole 'my-lordship-shall-be-between-you-and-the-Shadow-while-in-my-service' business?"

Lorn glared up at her, fierce eyes going fiercer. "*No!* Are you crazy? What makes you think I'd—"

"What makes you think *we* would?"

Freelorn held absolutely still. His anger churned wildly for a moment, then fell off, leaving reluctant acceptance in its place.

"Good night, Lorn," Segnbora said, and went back to her bedroll. She was careful not to smile until her back was turned.

Sunspark pulled itself back down into the firepit, and soon the darkness of the hall held no sound but Harald's cloak-muffled snoring.

It took Segnbora a little while to get enough of the blankets unwrapped from around Lang to cover herself. That done, she lay on her back for a long while, gazing up at the smoke-shaft in the ceiling, through which a few unfamiliar stars shone. Her underhearing, sharpened by all the excitement, brought her the faint dream-touched emotions of those falling asleep, and the physical sensations of those asleep already —breathing, the slide of muscles, muted pulse-thunder.

It's a gift, she told herself for the thousandth time. Truth, however, reared its head. It was a nuisance. If her Fire was focused, as Herewiss's was, she wouldn't be having this problem. . . . *If.* She exhaled sharply at her useless obsession with what she couldn't have. It wasn't focused. It would never be. She had given up. Other things had become more important now. Oaths, for example . . .

It had been a long time ago. *All of a month,* she thought—a busy month full of desperate rides, escapes, sorcery, terror, wonder. All started by a chance meeting in a smelly alley, when she had stumbled on a dark fierce little man losing a swordfight to the crude but powerful axework of a Royal Steldene guard. The small man looked as if he was about to be split like kindling. She had intervened. The guardsman never saw the shadow who stepped in from behind.

Over the course of the evening, she found she had rescued family; though the tai-Enraesi were only a small poor cadet branch of the Darthene royal line, and strangers to court, the Oath of Lion and Eagle was binding on them too, and a king's son of Arlen was therefore a brother.

The relationship got more complex with time, however. On the road Segnbora had shared herself with Freelorn, as she sometimes did with the others, for delight or consolation. But before that, more importantly, came friendship and the oaths. *Before Maiden and Bride and Mother I swear it, before the Lovers in Their power, and in the Dark One's despite: My sword will be between you and the Shadow until you pass the Door into Starlight.*

She exhaled quietly. Her determination was set.
There has to be a way.
There has to.
You're not going to get him. . . .

After a while, as she lay at last near the brink of sleep, Segnbora sensed something shining. She opened one eye. Across the room sat a form sculpted of darkness and deep blue radiance—Herewiss, cross-legged, shoulders hunched wearily as he gazed down at the sleeping Freelorn. Across his lap lay his sword, wrapped about with curling flames the color of a twilight burning low.

She lay unmoving, and regarded him. Eventually the

thought came, tasting as if it had been soaked in tears and wrung out.

(You know, don't you.)

(Yes.) She felt sorrow still, and now a touch of embarrassment. (Sorry. You know how it is with dreams.)

(No matter. I've been in a few others' dreams myself.)

(The scales are even, then.)

He nodded. Herewiss didn't look up, but his attention was fixed so intensely upon her that no stare could have been more discomfiting.

(You understand what you're getting into?) he said. (It may not be just Lorn heading for that Door. Probably me too. Maybe all of us will have to die so the Kingdoms can go on living.)

(Those who defeat the Shadow,) Segnbora said silently, (usually die of it. It's in all the stories.)

(*Defeat!*) Now he raised his head. His look was pained at first, then incredulous.

(I love him too,) she said.

(You're as crazy as the rest of us,) Herewiss said. The thought was sour, but there was a thread of amusement on it like the bright edge of a knife.

He threw her a quick image of herself as she had been the night before, when the air in the hall had been full of the stink of hralcins. As the monsters had come shambling across the floor toward them she had stood, driven to the brink of panic, unable to do even the smallest sorcery. Hands upheld, shaking all over, she cowered before the advancing, screaming horrors and made blinding light—a byproduct of her blocked Fire—until even that guttered out and left her exhausted.

Segnbora bit the inside of her cheek, annoyed even though Herewiss had been compassionate afterward.

(What we're facing,) he said with gentle sarcasm, (is the father of those things, and worse—the Maker of Enmities, the engenderer of the shadows at the bottoms of our hearts, Who can overturn the world in fire and storm. You have some new defense that you've come up with since last night? A strategy sufficient to stop a being so powerful that to be rid of it the Goddess Herself can only let the Universe run down and die?)

(I plan to win,) she said. (What are *you* going to do?)

He looked across the room at her for a while, still not moving. (I'm glad you're here,) he said finally. (I can't tell *him* about this—) A quick thought, a flicker of the shape of an arrowhead, passed between them. (I hope you won't either.)

(Of course not.)

He straightened, laid Khávrinen aside. Away from its source, the Fire in the blade died down to the merest glow. Only in his hands did a little Flame remain burning. Looking down at Freelorn, Herewiss absently began to pour it from hand to hand. Like burning water it flowed, the essence of life, the stuff of shapechanges and mastery of elements and magics of the heart, the Goddess's gift to the Lovers and to humankind, the Power that founded the world, that the Shadow had lost and caused men to lose.

And there's nothing It hates more, Segnbora thought to herself. *Though love probably comes close.*

She closed her eyes to the light of Herewiss's hands, shuddered, and went to sleep.

TWO

... ere the Dark could spredde so far as to kyll all Powre and
thought . . . there fled to Lake Rilthor that was holie, the men
and womyn gretest of Fire att that time. And of theyre greate
might and Powyre, that those whoo came after the Darke
should learn agayn the wrekings of those auncient daies,
those Wommen and Men did drive their Flame down intoo the
mount at the Lak's heart; and all dyed there, that Fyre might
bee spared from the Darrk for those to comm after. Therefore
it ys called Morrow-fane. . . .

> (Of the Dayes of Travaile, ms.
> xix, in rr'Virendir, Prydon)

In the long west-reaching shadow of the glittering gray walls that rose a hundred fathoms high, fourteen figures stood: seven riders, and six horses, and a creature that looked like a blood-bay stallion, but wasn't. Dawn was barely over, and the morning was still cool. The vast expanses of the Waste all around—sand and rubble and salt pans—was sharp and bright in the crisp air. But behind them the Hold from which they had departed wavered and shimmered uncannily, as if in the heat of noon.

"Be glad to be out of here," Lang muttered from beside Segnbora.

She nodded, yanking absently at her mare Steelsheen's reins to keep her from biting Lang's dapplegray, Gyrfalcon. The Hold unnerved her too. The Old People from whom the humans of the Middle Kingdoms were descended had wrought with their Fire on an awesome scale. Within those slick and jointless towering walls, odd buildings reared up: skewed towers, blind of windows; stairs that started in midair and went nowhere; steps staggered in such a way as to suggest that the builders had more legs than humans; more rooms inside the inner buildings than their outer walls could possibly contain.

And worst of all, or best, the place was full of doors—entrances into other worlds. Likewise, there were entrances to other places in this world, and doors into areas not even classifiable as worlds or places. People could go out those doors and return. People, or things, could come in them, as the hralcins had. Segnbora shuddered.

"You sure you can pull this off?" Freelorn was saying nervously to Herewiss.

"Mmmph," Herewiss said. He was standing with Khávrinen unsheathed, and seemed to be minutely examining a patch of empty air three feet in front of him. The Fire that ran down from his hand flooded the length of Khávrinen, leaping out from it in quick tongues that stretched out and snapped back, reflecting his concentration.

Behind Herewiss, Sunspark extended its magnificent head to nibble teasingly at the sleeve of Freelorn's surcoat, leaving singed places where it bit. (You have to be careful, doing worldgating inside a world,) it said, sounding smug. (Don't distract him.)

Freelorn smacked the elemental's nose away and got a scorched hand for his pains. "He could have used one of the doors in the Hold. Now he's got to use his Flame—"

(It's simpler doing it yourself,) Sunspark said. It knew about such things, having been a traveller among worlds before love had bound it to Herewiss's service. (Those doors are complex; it would have taken quite a while to figure them out. Don't complain.)

"I'm *not.*"

Segnbora felt like laughing, but restrained herself. Sunspark had done perhaps more than any of them to save their lives two nights before, holding the hralcins off until Herewiss could break through into his Flame. It had done so specifically because it knew Herewiss loved Freelorn and would have been in anguish if he died. But Sunspark seemed determined not to admit his motives to Lorn—and Freelorn, if he knew, was at best ambivalent about them.

Herewiss was now scowling at the air he had been examining, or whatever lay beyond it. It was dangerous, this business of opening doors to go from one place to another. Gates, when opened, tended to tear as wide as they could. A person doing a wreaking had to maintain complete control, or risk ending up in a world that looked exactly like the one he wanted to journey in, but with minor differences—a differing past or future, say, or familiar people missing.

Segnbora was not happy that one man was trying to pull off a gating by himself, and in such an unprotected place. All her previous experiences with worldgates had been in the Silent Precincts, where safe-wreakings bound every leaf about the Forest Altars. Always there had been ten or twenty senior Rodmistresses on call to assist if there was trouble, and never had a gate been held open long enough for so many to pass through. She hoped Herewiss knew what he was doing . . .

Herewiss didn't move, but from where Khávrinen's point rested against the ground, a sudden runnel of blue Fire uncoiled like a snake and shot out across the sand. It put down swift roots to anchor itself, then leaped upward into the air. The atmosphere prickled with ruthlessly constrained Power as the line of blue light described a large doorway as tall as Herewiss and equally as wide. When the frame was complete the Fire ran back along its doorsill and reached upward again, this time branching out like ivy on an unseen trellis, filling the doorway with a network that steadily grew more complex. In a few breaths' time the door became one solid, pulsing panel of blue.

Sweat stood on Herewiss's face. "Now," he said, still unmoving.

The blue winked out, all but the outline. From beyond the door a wet-smelling wind struck out and smote them all in the face. Lake Rilthor, their destination, lay in the lowlands, a thousand feet closer to sea level than the Waste. Through the door Segnbora saw green grass, and a soft rolling meadow leading down toward a silver-hazed lake, within which a hill was half-hidden.

"Go on," Herewiss said, and his voice sounded strained. "Don't take all day."

They led their horses through as quickly as they could, though not as quickly as they wanted to, for without exception the horses tried to put their heads down to graze as soon as they passed the doorway, and had to be pulled onward to let the others through. At last Segnbora was able to pull through the reluctant Steelsheen. She was followed closely by Herewiss and Sunspark, behind whom the door winked out with a very audible slam of sealed-in air.

Segnbora turned to compliment Herewiss and found him half-collapsed over Sunspark's back, with Freelorn supporting him anxiously from one side. He looked like a man who had just run a race; his breath went in and out in great racking gasps, and his face was nearly gray.

"I thought there would be no more backlash once you got your Fire!" Freelorn said.

Herewiss rolled his head from side to side on the saddle, unable for several moments to find enough breath with which to reply. "Different," he said, "different problem," and began to cough.

Freelorn pounded his back ineffectually while Segnbora and the others looked on.

When the coughing subsided, Herewiss rested his head on the saddle again, still gasping. "—open too wide," he said.

"What? The gate?"

"No. Me."

Confused, Freelorn looked at Segnbora. "Do you know what he's talking about?"

She nodded. "In a worldgating, the gate isn't really the physical shape you see. The gate is in your mind—the 'door' shape is just a physical expression of it. When you open a gate, you're actually throwing your soul wide open. Anything can get out. And anything can get in. It's not pleasant."

"I can't hear anything," Dritt muttered, wondering what all the discussion was about.

"Swallow," Herewiss said. "Your ears'll pop." At last, his strength returning, he looked around with satisfaction. "You're better than I am with distances, Lorn. How far from Lake Rilthor would you say we are?"

Freelorn shaded his eyes, looking first at the Sun to orient himself. "It's lower—"

"Of course. We're sixty leagues west."

Freelorn looked southwest toward the lake, and to the mist-girdled peak rising from its waters. "Four miles, I'd say."

"That's about what I wanted," Herewiss said, pleased. "Not bad for a first gating."

"It's so quiet," Harald said, looking around suspiciously.

"It's a holy place," said Moris, unruffled and matter-of-fact as always.

Segnbora looked around at the silent green country, agreeing, opening out her undersenses to the affect of this place.

Like most fanes or groves or great altars, Morrowfane had a feeling as if Someone was watching—Someone who would only speak using the heart's own voice. Yet the feeling was less personified, more awesome, than any she had experienced before. Above everything hung a waiting silence like the one when the hawk sails high and no bird sings. Below the silence was a slow, steady throbbing of incalculable power, as if the world's heart beat nearby. A ruthless benevolence slept at the center of Lake Rilthor, she sensed, and slept lightly. It was no wonder that there wasn't a town or a farm or even a sheepfold for miles around.

—It was not a smell, or a feeling, or a vision precisely, that started to creep up on her. Segnbora stood up straight, glancing around at the others. None of them sensed what she had. Herewiss and Freelorn were leaning against Lorn's dun, Blackmane, together, speaking quietly; Moris and Dritt had walked off a little way to look southwest at the Fane; Lang was rubbing down the perpetually sweaty Gyrfalcon; Harald was seeing to yellow-coated Swallow's cinches. Sunspark had disappeared on some mysterious errand of its own.

She turned and looked east, her hand unconsciously dropping to Charriselm's hilt. There it was again, another flash of sight—vague and odd, focus bizarrely rounded, colors all awry. And smell too, acrid, terrible, enraging. *That's familiar, I know that*—Then the memory found her: that one time in the Precincts when the novices, carefully supervised, were allowed to shapechange and feel what a beast's body was like.

"Herewiss!" she said, turning to him in alarm.

He put his head up to the wind, gazing eastward as she had, but saw nothing.

"You just did a wreaking," she said. "You may still be overloaded. *Taste it!*"

The fear in her voice brought unease to his eyes. He closed them and reached out his undersenses. She did too, standing swaying in the long grass, and caught the impression again, stronger this time. Now there was something even more unnerving added to the flash of skewed viewpoint: *thought*, stunted and twisted and bizarre, but thought. And it was all of hate.

The mind she touched bounded above the whipping grass for a moment. It saw forms on the horizon, the source of a maddening stench.

She heard a cough, opened her eyes to see Herewiss choking briefly. His empathy must have been more profound than hers, for the remembered shape of the runner's throat was not letting his words out.

"Fyrd!" he managed to croak, and pushed away from Blackmane, unsheathing Khávrinen hurriedly.

The word took Segnbora by surprise. "But that was thinking! Fyrd are Shadow-twisted, but they're just of dumb animal stock. They don't *think!*" She let the rest of her protest drop then. There was no mistaking what she had felt.

"My move was anticipated," Herewiss said bitterly. He swung Khávrinen sideways, whipping a great brilliance of Fire angrily down the blade. "It's a step ahead of me—and mocking me, too."

Segnbora understood. At Bluepeak, long ago, the Shadow had driven down that first terrible breed of thinking Fyrd into the Kingdoms. Far more dangerous than the noxious things It had twisted out of the beasts of ancient days, these Fyrd had the cunning of warriors. It had taken the Transformation, in which Earn and Héalhra burned away their very forms and their mortality, to exterminate that breed. And now, for Herewiss, here they were again—

Steel scraped out of sheaths all around as movement became visible in the high grass to the east. Segnbora's undersenses brought her more and more clearly the experience of their hungry rage. They knew their quarry was human, and they hated them. They had come to murder.

"Dammit," Herewiss muttered, "Sunspark, where are you when I need you?!" But no answering thought came, and Herewiss hefted Khávrinen grimly. Only two days forged, and already the sword would be tasting blood.

There was little time to prepare. One moment the dark backs were jolting through the tall grass and the next, with a wave of grunts and screeches, the Fyrd were upon them. Segnbora found herself holding her blade too high to guard against a maw that was suddenly springing at her throat. She threw herself sideways. Jaws went *snick!* above her, in the air where she had been. She hit the ground, rolled, found her footing and sprang up again. The maw hit the turf where she had been. For a moment it tore the ground with teeth and talons, its hunched back to her. That was all she needed. Chosing her spot she swung Charriselm up, sliced through thick flesh to the shock of bone. The maw writhed and screamed once, as its half-severed head flopped into the grass. She paid it no more heed, simply whipped the blood off Charriselm and swung around to find another foe. There were certain to be plenty—

—More maws, five or six of them, broad and round with piggish, wicked eyes; several keplian, horse-looking things with carnivores' teeth and three razory toes on each forefoot; other shapes less identifiable. The standard Fyrd varieties had been twisted further away from the animals they had anciently been. She forgot about specifics and dove away from the spring of one maw, took another one across the chest with a two-handed stroke and was knocked down by its momentum. *Move, move, as long as you're moving you're safe!* she remembered her old sword-instructor Shíhan shouting at her.

Off to her left she heard Steelsheen scream in defiance and crash into a Fyrd, followed by the flat brittle sound of a skull being crushed by hooves. At the same time she got a pinwheeling glimpse of Khávrinen, Herewiss's sword, being jerked up after a downstroke. Then a half-seen form came at her low and sideways—she chopped at it, a poorly aimed blow that slid off hard smooth plates. Hissing, the nadder's gigantic serpent-head rose up before her, then struck; she danced desperately aside and chopped off the head at the neck.

Segnbora turned away and looked around. Khávrinen was striking downward again, and as it struck both Herewiss and the keplian he had killed moaned aloud. The Fire wavering about those parts of the blade not yet obscured illuminated Herewiss's face. *Crying?* Segnbora thought, surprised, but not too much so. Khávrinen was more of a symbol than a weapon. Herewiss was no killer—

Steelsheen trampled another maw, and Moris nailed the

last one to the ground with a two-handed straight-down thrust. Finally everyone was standing still, panting, sagging, wiping blood out of their eyes.

"More coming!" Segnbora said, groaning aloud at the feeling of yet another of those hot, hating minds heading their way.

She looked northward. It was a hundred yards away, and it showed much more of itself above the grass than had the other Fyrd. Segnbora's heart constricted in terror as she recognized it. She had never seen one of these, but if the stories of the creatures' endurance were true, this one could afford to take its time.

"Oh Goddess," whispered Freelorn from beside her. "A deathjaw!"

"With the Fire," Herewiss said between gasps, "possibly—" He lifted Khávrinen again, but there was no great hope in the gesture.

Deathjaws were so fearsome that there was only one way to successfully hunt them: stake out a human being as bait, and hide a Rodmistress close by to do a brainburn when the thing got close enough. *We've got plenty of bait, but he doesn't know the protocol for a brainburn. If he did, he would be doing it.*

The shambling form came closer.

"Run for it," Herewiss said, sounding very calm.

Everyone hesitated.

"I mean it!"

Lang turned, and Moris, and Harald, but they were slow about retreating. Freelorn didn't move from beside Herewiss.

"Lorn—"

"Big, isn't it," Freelorn said. His eyes were wide with fear, but his voice was as steady as if he was discussing a draft horse.

"Lorn—!"

"Shut up, Dusty," Freelorn said. "Do whatever you're going to do to that thing. I'll watch your back."

Segnbora stepped up behind them as they set themselves. "I don't know how to burn it," Herewiss said to her. "The eye, though, that's possible—"

—Put a longsword into that little eye, and hope to hit the brain?

Segnbora thought, and didn't laugh at the idea. The deathjaw was close—shaggy-coated, brindled, the size of three Darthene lions. Shiny black talons gleamed on its great catlike paws. The deathjaw opened its mouth just a little, showing two of its three lines of fangs above and below. Then it began to run, its face wrinkling into a horrible mask.

Herewiss swung Khávrinen up with elbows locked and let it charge—his only option, for running was as hopeless as a slash-and-cut duel would be. *The blade into the eye,* she heard him thinking, *and Fire down the blade, enough to blast the brain dead.*

He never used his plan. While still twenty feet away the deathjaw screamed horribly as fire suddenly bloomed about it, eating inward through flesh and muscle and sinew quick as a gasp. The still-moving skeleton burned incandescent for a moment more before the swirling flames blasted bone to powder, then ate that too. The deathjaw was gone before its death shrieks died.

And Sunspark appeared—a brief bright coalescence like a meteor changing its mind in midexplosion—and paced casually over to the three. It was exuding a feeling of great pleasure, its mane and tail burning merrily as holiday bonfires. (You called for me?) it said to Herewiss, who was breathing hard now with delayed terror.

"I believe I did," he said.

Sunspark looked at Freelorn with an expression of good-natured wickedness and said nothing.

"Thank you," Freelorn said, courteous enough; but there was a touch of grudge in his voice.

Sunspark snorted. (Gratitude! Next time I'll choose my moment with more care . . . a little later.)

"*Choose* the moment—!"

(So that you'll appreciate me.)

"You mean you *watched* those things attack us and you didn't—!"

"Lorn, enough," Herewiss said. "It doesn't think the way you do. Luckily for us. Loved," he said to the elemental, "did you notice any other wildlife in these parts while you were having breakfast?"

(Singers,) it said, looking to the northwest. (The ones with fur.)

"Wolves? Perfect." Herewiss glanced down at Khávrinen, which blazed just long enough to burn the blood off itself. "We won't be climbing the Fane until sunset, since a Summoning there works best at twilight. But damned if I'm going to put up with any more Fyrd in the meantime. I'll go have a word with the wolves and see if I can work something out. Now, how do I manage this—"

He frowned, closed his eyes. Fire swirled outward from Khávrinen, hiding both sword and wielder. The pillar of brilliance shrank as it swirled, and sank close to the ground. When the blue Flame died away it left behind a handsome cream-white wolf with orange-brown points and downturned blue eyes.

(Not bad,) Sunspark remarked, (for a beginner.)

(Hmp!) Herewiss said, grinning a wolf-grin. (Stay close till I get back, loved, just in case the Fyrd try again. I won't be long.)

The wolf bounded away through the long grass. Watching him go, Segnbora dug down in her belt-pouch for a square of soft paper, with which she began cleaning off Charriselm's blade. When she had finished, she looked thoughtfully at the Fane. It seemed to gaze back, calm and blind and patient, waiting for something. *Fyrd so close to this place—that's unheard of. All the rules are changing. After this nothing is going to be the way it was. Not even me.*

She shook her head uneasily, not entirely understanding the thought.

"You going to stand there all day?" someone shouted at her. Freelorn and the others were in the saddle, getting ready to ride down to the Fane. Segnbora swung up into Steelsheen's saddle and went after them.

She sat underneath an old rowan tree near the lakeshore, her back against its trunk, and watched the long shadows of men, horses, and trees drown in slow dusk. The Fane, a half mile away across Rilthor's water, shone golden as a legend where its heights still caught the sunset. The mirroring water

lay still in the breathless evening, the mountain's burning
image broken only by the wakes of the gray songswans gliding
by. *Truly it's not so impressive,* she thought, stretching. The
Fane's mountain was a little one, no more than a half mile
wide at the base, broad at the bottom and flat at the top,
stippled roughly with brush and scrub pine.

But for all the seeming plainness of the landscape, their
camp that day had been abnormally quiet. Freelorn had been
pacing and frowning most of the afternoon. Herewiss had
come back from his parley with the wolves, reporting success
—and a sore throat from much howling. Now he sat under an
alder with Khávrinen flaming in his lap, meditating; for hours
he hadn't moved, gazing across at the Fane with an expression
that was half wonder and half fear. Harald and Moris had been
keeping so close to one another that one might have thought
they had been lovers for only a week or so, rather than several
years. Dritt and Lang had become almost obsessive about
caring for their horses, and the otherwise fearless Lang had
been looking over his shoulder a great deal. Even Sunspark,
while in its horse-shape, had been cribbing quietly at an elm
tree, leaving small scorched places bitten out of the bark.

She laughed at herself then, a mere breath of merriment.
*And me. All this time on the trail, all this time I've been a hunted
woman—look what kind of watch I'm keeping. My back turned to open
country, where Goddess knows what could be coming up from behind
—and me sitting here staring at this silly hill as if it's going to jump
out of the water and come after me!* Yet that silent benevolence
kept watching her, kept waiting.

She shivered with expectation. Practically at the same moment, a clear melodious sound like the night finding its voice
rose up in the distance—then was joined in the long note by
another voice wavering downward a third, and yet another,
higher by a fourth. The unsettling harmony sent a delighted
shiver down her spine. The wolves were on post as their
rearguard, singing to while away the watch.

The Goddess's dogs, she thought, the old affectionate name
for them—votaries who sang to Her mirror, the Moon,
through all its phases, silent only when She was dark and
dangerous. *Where is the Moon tonight,* Segnbora wondered,

glancing upward. It had not yet risen. But she was distracted, as always, with the sight of the first few stars pointing through the twilight, and the memory they always recalled. *How old was I?* she wondered, but wondering was vain. Very small, she had been—small enough to still be wearing a shift instead of a kilt, but large enough to push open the front door of the old house at Asfahaeg and escape at bedtime.

She had gone out into the dark, unsure just what she was looking for, then had glanced up and found something, a marvel. Not just sunset, or dusk, or dark, but a sky burning with lights, every one solitary and glorious; and she knew, small as she was, that somehow or other she and those lights were intimately connected.

Now she knew them as stars, knew their names, knew about the Dragons that had come from among them, and about the Goddess Who had made them. But the wonder had never left Segnbora: that desire to get closer to those lights that called her—and, eventually, closer to the One Who had made the stars. When the Rodmistresses tested her at the age of three and found the Fire, she had been overjoyed. Everybody knew that when you had the Flame, you often got to talk to Her.

But years of study had failed her; school after school had been unable to provide her with a focus strong enough to channel the huge outflow of her Power—and so there had been no breakthrough, and no truedreams in which She walked. After much bitter time she had admitted the truth to herself, that she was one of those who was never going to focus. She might as well give up sorcery and lore and Flame and all the other timewasting for something useful, as her father had always said.

So it was that she had met the Goddess at last. She was good with Charriselm; she went looking for a job as a guard in a little Steldene town called Madeil—and found Freelorn in the mucky alley behind a tavern. Later, fleeing from an old keep in which the aroused Steldenes had laid siege to them, the group had come across a little fieldstone inn on the border between Steldin and the Waste. It was strange that there should have been an inn out there at the very edge of human habitation, but the innkeeper had put them all at ease. Finding that they were short of money, she offered to share herself with one of them to settle the scot. A common enough arrangement, and Segnbora had won the draw for the privilege.

It had been a sweet evening. The innkeeper had been fair, but there was more to her beauty than that. A long while they sat together by the window of Segnbora's little room, she and a white-shifted shadow veiled in hair like the night, talking and breathing the apple-blossom scent while the full Moon went softly up the sky. The talk drifted gradually to matters that Segnbora usually kept deeply hidden—old joys, old pains —while the brown-and-beige-banded pottery cup went back and forth between them, filled with a wine like summer wind running sweet under starlight.

I'm talking a great deal, Segnbora had thought, not so much frightened by the intimacy as bemused. *The wine*— But the wine was not intoxicating her; she was seeing and feeling, if anything, more clearly than usual. Shivering with delight at the feeling of magic in the air, she drank deep of the cup, deeply enough to drain it . . . and found it still three-quarters full. *Two hours we've been drinking from this cup,* she realized, *and she only filled it once.*

She looked across at the other, then, and realized Who had come to share Herself with her, as She comes to every man and woman born, once before they die. Not Mother now, as she had been at dinner, feeding them all and gossiping about the Kingdoms, but the aspect of the Goddess she loved best —Maiden about to be Bride, Creatress about to create something as beautiful as the multitude of stars. Back and forth a few more times that cup went, while Segnbora drank deep of building joy and anticipation, and named the Other's name, and saw her joy reflected a hundredfold, a thousandfold, incalculably.

Then she went to bed. And was joined by warmth that enfolded, and lips that spoke her name as if she was the only thing in creation. She was intensely loved; and was given to drink of that other cup that brims over forever, the endless source. She drowned, eternally it seemed, in the deep slow bliss of her own deity, and the Other's. . . .

The bark against her back was hard as she blinked, glanced down from the sky. *Oh, again,* she thought, *someday again.*

. . . Though the odds of that were slight. Once in a lifetime in *that* manner, one might expect the Goddess. Otherwise, only at birth did one see Her, in one's own mother—quickly forgotten, that sight—and at death, when the Silent Mother, the Winnower, came to open the last Door.

She glanced across the lake, at the Fane standing silent, watching her, surrounded by the constellations of early summer. *He'll be ready soon,* she thought. Somewhere to northward the wolves began singing again.

Someone came lurching along toward her in the darkness, walking loud and heavy as usual. *Oh, Lady, not now,* she thought with affectionate annoyance, as Lang plopped down next to her. "Are we waiting for Moonrise?" he said.

He smelled of unwashed horse and unwashed self, and Segnbora wrinkled her nose in the dark—then wrinkled it more, at herself, for she had no call to be throwing stones on *that* account.

"Just full nightfall," she said. "I guess the theory is, if you're crazy enough to climb the Fane, then exercise your madness in the dark, as the Maiden did. 'Out of darkness, light; out of madness, wisdom—' "

Lang nodded. "How crazy are you?"

His tone was very uneasy. Her stomach knotted, hearing in his words a reflection of the nervousness she had been trying to ignore. Worse, she didn't feel like talking. Segnbora wished for the thousandth time that Lang weren't thought-deaf.

She plucked a blade of grass from beside her and began running it back and forth between her fingers. "I think I told you about my family, a little," she said.

She could feel his confusion, typical of him when she chose to come at a question sideways. Lang rarely understood any approach but the head-on kind. "Tai-Enraesi," he said. "Enra was a Queen's sister of Darthen, wasn't she?"

Segnbora nodded. "I'm related to a lot of people who've been up that hill. Béorgan, and Béaneth, the doomed Queens. Raela Way-Opener. Efmaer d'Seldun. Gereth Dragonheart . . . " She trailed off. Then, after a while, "To be where they were . . . I don't know how I can pass the Fane by—"

Lang slouched further down against the tree, his face calm,

but his heart shouting, *Yes, and look what happened to* them! *Béorgan and Béaneth dead of the Shadow or of sorrow, Raela gone off through some door and never heard of again, Efmaer dead in the mountains or worse in Glasscastle—*

Segnbora twitched uneasily, resettling her back against the rowan's trunk. She heartily wished there was something else to try, but over twenty years she had exhausted the talents of instructors all over the Kingdoms.

"I thought I might talk you out of it," Lang said, very low. "I like you the way you are."

The words came a breath too late. She had chosen. "I don't," she said.

"But if you go up there there's no telling what'll happen to you—"

"I know. That's the idea!"

Lang pulled back, pained.

"Look," she said. "Twenty years of training, and I'm Fire-trained without Fire, I'm a sorcerer who doesn't care for sorcery and a trained bard who's too depressed to tell stories. It's time to be something else. *Anything.*"

"But, 'Berend—"

The use of the old nickname, which Eftgan had coined so long ago, poked her in a suddenly sensitive spot. She laid her hand on Lang's, startling him out of his frightened annoyance. "You remember the first time we met? You tried to talk me out of joining up with Lorn, remember?"

"Stubborn," Lang muttered, "you were stubborn. I couldn't stand you."

She glanced at him humorously. "Maybe change isn't such a bad thing, then?"

They traded gentle looks through the dark, and he squeezed her hand. "Care to share afterwards? If you haven't turned into a giant toadstool or some such, of course."

Her heart turned over inside her. When Lang made such offers, there was always more love in his voice than she could answer with, and the inequity troubled her. It had been a long time since her ability to share had been rooted in anything deeper than friendship. "Yes," she said, hoping desperately he would be able to lighten up a little. "You disturb me, though. You have a prejudice against toad-stools? . . ."

Lang chuckled.

"You two ready?" said another voice, and they both looked up. Herewiss was standing beside them with Khávrinen sheathed and slung over his shoulder. Freelorn was with him, arms folded and looking nervous.

"What do you mean 'you two'?" Lang said. "I prefer to die in bed, thanks."

Segnbora squeezed his hand back and got up, brushing herself off. "You found the raft, I take it."

"It was hidden in the reeds," Freelorn said. "In fact, the reeds were growing through it in places. Evidently not many people come this way."

"Just the three of us are climbing, then." Herewiss said. "Still, it's probably better that we all go across—in case any Fyrd get by our rearguard."

Lang nodded and got up, and the four of them went off to join the others by the lakeshore. Dritt and Harald and Moris were standing at a respectable distance from the raft, for Sunspark was inspecting it suspiciously.

(You really want me to get on this thing?) it said to Herewiss as he came up. (That water's deep. If I fell in there—) It shuddered at the thought.

"So fly over," Herewiss said, stepping onto the raft from the bank.

Sunspark gazed across at the Fane, its mane and tail burning low. (There's a Power there, and in the water,) it said. (I'm not sure I want to attract Its attention. . . .)

"Then come on."

Three

The Goddess's courtesy is a terrible thing. To the mortal asker She will give what is asked for, without stinting, without fail. Nor will She stop giving until the gift's recipient, like the gift, becomes perfect. Let the asker beware. . . .

(Charestics, 45)

They all climbed onto the raft. Sunspark came last, picking its way onto the mossy planks with the exaggerated delicacy of a cat. But it stood quite still in the midst of them as Herewiss and Freelorn poled the raft. No one broke the silence. On the water the feeling of being watched was stronger than ever.

The raft grounded, scraping and crunching on a rough beach of pale pebbles. Herewiss stepped off, Freelorn behind him, and each of the others in turn. Everyone winced at the sound of their footsteps. Segnbora, second-to-last off, thought she had never heard anything so loud as her light step on the gravel. Sunspark, behind her, got off and made no sound at all. It was carefully walking a handspan above the ground.

They were not only watched, they were *felt*. There was no mistaking it. There was no threat in the sensation; the regard running through them was patient, passive. But whatever fueled it was immeasurably old, and huge. The others looked at one another wondering, as the Power reached up into them, and found old companions suddenly strange.

Segnbora, feeling what they felt, understood the sensation as most of her companions couldn't. The Fire within her, that had dwindled over the years and was now nearly dead because of her lack of focus, was suddenly leaping up as wildly in her as if a wind had blown through her soul. The Power pushed at her, urging her upward toward the mountain. At the same time it looked through her at the others, and looked through them at her, determining what changes would be made—

Oh Goddess, she thought, *this is what I've needed.* There was no mistaking the Source of what stirred here, though this half-slumbering immensity of calling Flame was only the least tithe of Her Power.

And I'm terrified—

Herewiss and Freelorn were standing transfixed, keeping very close to each other. She could not see their faces, but Freelorn's arms were unwound from around Herewiss for the first time since the morning. Khávrinen in its back-sheath was blue-white with Fire. Its light shone through seams in the scabbard, and the hilt blazed like a torch. "There's the trail," Freelorn said quietly, looking upward.

"I'll race you," Segnbora said, just as quietly. She slipped past them and started climbing.

The trail wasn't too difficult. Part of it followed old gullies or slide-paths; part of it seemed to have been cut into the hillside, but only lightly, so that rockfall or deadwood frequently blocked the way. The hill was no more than five hundred feet high, but in the starlight it was hard to see where to put one's feet. Each of them fell and slid at least once. By the time they reached the flattened hilltop, they were all bruised, and breathing hard.

But the gasping for breath didn't last. It was replaced almost immediately by a sensation of being anchored, centered, secured past any dislodging. Freelorn and Herewiss stood as still as Segnbora, feeling their pulses become tranquil, their breath come more gently. The three of them stood poised at the apex of the world's Heart. The Universe swung around them, slow and silent, waiting. After a few moments Segnbora sank to one knee, bending to touch the gullied ground with one hand, the ground where Raela and Efmaer and Béorgan had stood. She could feel the Power, bound, waiting, alive. Her own Fire strained downward to reach it, and, unfocused, could not. But that seemed unimportant as she knelt there, feeling the ages run through her. This place was more important than the needs of any one human being.

Freelorn turned to Herewiss. "Loved," he said, his voice uncertain, "something's strange inside me—"

"Of course there is." Herewiss reached out to Freelorn and drew him close, not so much in compassion as in exultation. "It's your Fire. You have a spark of it like everyone else; here at the heart of Fire, how could you *not* feel it? The Fane is reaching up to you."

"I thought so." Freelorn sounded almost in pain. "It wants me. But I don't know what to do."

"Listen to what it has to say to you," Herewiss said. "Just feel it. Few enough people ever do."

Herewiss let go of Freelorn with his right arm, then stretched slowly upward and felt behind him for Khávrinen's hilt. He drew the sword from the back-scabbard slowly, with relish and ease and much tenderness, as he might have drawn himself from his loved after passion spent. The sword swept effortlessly over his head and downward before him, Fire trailing behind the blade. Even now, before the wreaking had begun, the Flame was too bright to look at directly.

"So much," Lorn said, soft-voiced, blinking and tearing in the light. "You can do *anything* now. . . ."

"Yes. For the moment." Herewiss laughed gently at Freelorn's puzzled look. "Lorn, how did you think I was able to destroy those hralcins? Under normal circumstances twenty Rodmistresses, fifty, couldn't have done it. I was in 'breakthrough,' as they call it in the Precincts, and I will be for maybe another tenday or so. After that the Power begins to drop to more normal levels. That's surely why She wants me to hurry."

He gazed down at the Flame-flowing sword in his hand.

"I'll give back some of what was given to me," he said, resting Khávrinen's point on the ground. The Flame about the blade burned brighter, lighting the hilltop more brilliantly with every breath he took. "It's going to cost me, Lorn. But it will be worth it."

His words failed him, then, but his Fire did not. The light was becoming like an otherworldly Sun now, a blaze of determination and joy that dazzled the mind as much as it did the eyes, transfiguring what it touched.

Segnbora had a brief vision through the brilliance of a young god raising His arms, offering His loved, across His two hands, the thunderbolt He wielded. In her vision the other, blasted by the overpowering magnificence into another shape, yet somehow still unchanged, reached out hands to lay them, fearless, in the Fire—

For long seconds Segnbora did not move, could not. Once not too long ago, when Herewiss had been away and Lorn had seemed to need consoling, she had entered a little way into the relationship between these two—sharing herself with Lorn, offering her friendship. At the time she had thought her motives benevolent enough. But recent events had made her suspect that, in fact, she had been the one in need of consoling. Now, by this light, in which any untruth withered and fell away, she clearly saw the shape of her own loneliness and sorrow. Likewise she saw the essential *twoness* of Herewiss and Freelorn—something even Sunspark had perceived more clearly than she did. *No more interference,* she thought. There was no sadness about it. The decision came almost triumphantly, with a feeling of celebration and release.

This was Herewiss's moment, and Lorn's, not hers. Unsteadily—for the forces being freed on the hilltop had made her a bit light-headed—Segnbora turned her back on the ferocious glory raging there. By the time one of the Lovers began speaking Nhaired in invocation—*"Ae, hn'Hláfedë, ir untáye Lai—"*she was descending from the hilltop, sliding and stumbling down the path.

Dear Goddess, Segnbora thought as she reached the end of the steepest part of the path. *The first wreaking he tries is the Naming of Names? I wish I had his faith. If some dark power should slip close enough to hear—*

The possibility so unnerved her that Segnbora lost her balance. She had to grab at brush to catch herself. An inner Name was a powerful commodity even after its owner's death, useful to lend power to various spells and wreakings. The Names of great Rodmistresses, for instance, were passed down through generations. In Segnbora's own family, Queen Efmaer's ancient Name was preserved, though the Queen herself was long lost.

Segnbora exhaled in sudden amusement at the notion that someday sorcerers and Rodmistresses would probably pay great treasures for the true Name of one Herewiss—a slim

dark young man with a tendency toward creative swearing in
dead languages—

The path went right out from under her. It was not her
own clumsiness this time, but the Morrowfane itself trembling under her feet. Segnbora looked up. The blaze on the
hilltop, hidden till now by the bulk of the hill, was hidden no
longer. A narrow, sword-shaped core of blue-white Fire
swung up into view, and then a light of impossible brilliance
broke the night open from end to end. Like lightning burning in steel, it turned the dark into sudden day and extin-
guished the stars. The Fane shook to its roots as outpoured
Firelight smote into everything, illuminating every leaf and
tree trunk and stone with fierce clarity. On the surface of the
shivering lake, the light shattered into countless knives and
splinters of dazzle.

Blinded, Segnbora turned away and rubbed her eyes. When
they saw clearly again, she started once more down the trail.
She had no trouble finding her way; the Fane was lit like
midmorning. At one point she paused for breath, looked
around, and saw something she had missed in the dimness on
the way up—a huge crevasse or cavern around on the southern face of the hillside, an opening into darkness that even
Herwiss's Fire didn't illumine. *How about that. The World's
Heart has a secret in it*—

Above her Herewiss's Flame dimmed and faded, leaving
her looking at where the cave entrance had been. *He's taking
a rest, I suppose. I bet I could have a closer look at that before he
starts shaking things again*— Once piqued, Segnbora's curiosity would never give her peace until it was satisfied, and she
knew it so she gave in. Scrabbling up off the trail, she used
scrubby bushes and trees to climb toward the area she had
seen. It took a few minutes to climb up a ravine that ran
down between two folds, but finally the cave opening
loomed huge before her, dark as uncertainty. There Segnbora halted, uneasy. Her undersenses were still blunted
from the onslaught of Power and joy at the top of the hill,
but not so much so that she couldn't catch an odd mental
flavor that grew stronger the closer she came to the cave-
mouth. *Something hot. Metal? Stone?*

She drew Charriselm with a whisper of steel that suddenly

sounded very loud indeed. Very carefully she stepped over and around the boulders that lay about the great cave entrance, and slipped a few feet inside where she paused to listen again.

Nothing. I must have been imagining that feeling. Cautiously, keeping her left hand against the cave wall, she took another step in. The faint crunch of her footstep echoed away into the dark. She took another step. This one echoed too. The place was huge, filling most of the mountain from the sound of it. Another—

A voice spoke, and Segnbora froze, clenching Charriselm. Her heart pounded. For a moment she thought the cave was about to fall in on her. The voice was huge, and incredibly deep. It thundered, rumbling, shaking the air; yet there was music in it, a slow and terrible song of pain. Hair stood up all over Segnbora. She could make nothing of the words the voice seemed to be speaking. At the end of the sentence, the silence that fell was waiting for her answer.

She swallowed hard. "I don't know that language," she said, her voice sounding amazingly small despite all the echoes it awoke. "Do you speak Arlene or Darthene?"

There was a long pause; then the voice spoke once more. It used Darthene, but the timbre was that of a storm on the Sea. "You were a long time coming," it said. "But you're thrice welcome nevertheless."

Segnbora leaned against the wall of the cave, bewildered. Her eyes were getting used to the darkness, and in the faint starlight from the doorway she could make out a great lumpy mass lying on the floor of the cave before her. The hot stone smell she had noticed before was coming from it, though there was little actual warmth in the place. "I don't understand," she said. "What are you?"

"Lhhw'ae," the voice said, a rumbling growl and a sigh.

Segnbora gripped Charriselm even tighter, for that word of the strange language she *did* understand. A *Dragon*—

The voice began to speak again, and was suddenly choked off. Rocks cracked and rattled about in the cave, rolling, shattering. The Dragon had abruptly started thrashing around. Segnbora leaped for the doorway, as afraid of being attacked as of a cave-in; but after a few moments the uncontrolled motion subsided and the immense half-seen bulk of the Dragon lay quiet again. She stared at it fearfully.

"I am about to lose this body," the Dragon said, an anguished-sounding melody winding about the words. "That is the cause of my seizures."

"You're dying?" Segnbora said, and then had to grab for balance once more as another convulsion threw rocks in all directions. When the Dragon had settled again, she saw that it was looking at her from great round eyes, each of which was at least four feet across, globed and pupilless. Segnbora shuddered as she realized how big the rest of the beast must be, and was glad she couldn't see it.

"Going *rdaheih.*" The Dragon whispered the word, but even its whisper sounded like a thunderstorm. "My time came upon me."

The pain in its voice confused Segnbora. No one but Marchwarders—the humans who lived with Dragons in their high places—knew much about Dragons, but the one thing everybody said about them was that they never died. Even more confusing was the undercurrent of joy that ran under the Dragon's pain, growing stronger by the moment.

"No matter." it said. "You are here. At last, what was, *is*—"

The words had an ominous sound to them. For an instant she considered running away, but did not. She had been curious about Dragons ever since the first and only time she had seen one, at the age of seven, soaring over the blue Darthene Gulf. Now that old curiosity was raging, and it overcame her fear.

Slowly Segnbora sheathed Charriselm, then began to pick her way toward the Dragon's head among the fallen stones, watching carefully in case another seizure should occur. Lying flat on the rubble, the head from lower jaw to upper faceplate was twice her height. Above it, the spine in which the shielding faceplate terminated speared up into the gloom for another ten or fifteen feet. Segnbora reached out gingerly and touched the edge of the plate between nose and eyes. It was hard and rough as stone, and warm. The eye on that side regarded her steadily, but she couldn't read its expression. It looked dimmer than it had—

"Are you sure you're not just ill?" Segnbora said.

"I know my time," said the Dragon. "I welcome it. I always have."

She shook her head. With her hands on the Dragon, she could feel its weary sorrow as if it were her own—but also that perplexing joy, both sober and expectant at once.

"Is there anything I can do for you?" she said.

The Dragon's eyes flared brighter, and a tremor ran up and down its body. *"Arhe-sta rdaheh q'ae hfyn'tsa!"* the Dragon whispered in a great rush of fulfillment, as if its last fear had been lifted from it. "If you truly ask," it said in Darthene, "don't let me—die—uncompanioned."

Segnbora shivered, having misgivings. Again she considered running away, but only briefly. "I'll stay with you."

"Yes," the Dragon said. The light of its eye ebbed again. "You always did."

That was when the last, and worst, convulsion happened. Walls shook. Stone chips and splinters rained from the ceiling. The floor danced. There was nothing for Segnbora to grab for support but the Dragon's head. A brief feeling of hot stone—

—and the next moment, her head burst open from the inside. Segnbora knew how it felt to share her mind with another consciousness, but this was nothing like her experiences in the Precincts; those decorous, sliding melds of one Rodmistress-novice with another, each always wary of disturbing the delicately balanced economy of the other's mind. This was like a boulder dropping into a bucket—a brutal invasion that smashed her against the borders of her self and threatened to smother her.

Strangling, agonized, she flailed about inside for room to think. There was none. Her inner spaces were crowded with *otherness,* a multitude of ruthless presences straining and seething in intolerable confinement—minds that beat at her, buffeting her like wings; thoughts that gnawed at her like alien jaws; strange memories that stalked through her past, promising her a horrifying and incomprehensible future. The Dragon's imminent death—

No! Segnbora screamed. She pushed desperately away

without knowing for sure what she was pushing back from, but ready to do anything, even die, to avoid it. She fell and fell, yet the images followed her inexorably as a doom, becoming more and more real. *I don't want to remember!* she screamed, but the words wouldn't even come out right. Instead, a white-hot burning and a strange language took her by the throat, twisting the plea into a wracking curse: *'sta, taueh-sta 'ae mnek-kej, mnek—!*

A roar of condemnation went up in he stifling, crowded darkness; the damp cold dirt rushed toward her face. Then mercifully the fall ended in a pain-colored flash that killed the presences, and the memories, and, Segnbora hoped, her too. . . .

Four

"Are you going to kill me?" said the child to the Dragon.

"Kill you?" The Dragon smiled at him. "Certainly not until we have been introduced."

Tales for Opening Night,
Nia d'Eleth

The darkness tears wide, splitting as hewn skin does when the sword strikes.

This is Etachnë field, all one gloomy sodden mass of misery —lead-gray above with clouds that have been pouring rain for three days now, dun and black and red below with the scattered bodies of the slain. The stench is incredible. Those who fight do so with their faces wrapped, and fall as often to the sick miasma of the air as to Reaver arrows. Fyrd are harrying the fringes of the battlefield, devouring the dead. A few hundred feet away, a maw and a horwolf and a nadder are busily dismembering a fallen woman. Her surcoat was once Darthene midnight blue. Now it is mostly red-brown.

She gulps down sourness for the hundredth time and stares across the misty valley. Somewhere over there the Reavers have retreated into cover, regrouping for the next attack. There are only about a thousand of them left, but those are more than enough to break the Darthene defense at the other end of the valley and let them out into the open lands. Once that happens they'll begin pillaging at Etachnë and leave the country burning behind them as far as Wendwen. Around her the Darthenes holding the gap are huddled, soaked through, hungry, outnumbered, waiting.

The Rodmistress is dead, so they have no idea when reinforcements may be coming. Segnbora is the only sorcerer left, and over the past few days her sorceries have been going progressively flatter—a starved sorcerer is good for very little. It was all she could do yesterday to stop the miserable rain for a little while; today her head still aches with the backlash. *Oh, food,* she thinks. *Just oatcakes and milk—* She stops herself, does a brief mind-exercise to calm down.

It doesn't work. Her partner Eftgan has been gone for three days now, ridden off for the reinforcements; and the Goddess only knows whether she lives or not, for there's a great silence where her mind used to be. *Oh, Tegánë, loved, be all right, please—* She winces away from the painful thought, opening her eyes on the Fyrd again. The sickness comes up in her throat as she sees them tugging at the limbs of the woman in Darthene blue. Then sickness turns to rage and she throws her sodden cloak off savagely and stands up in the rain, fists clenched.

"Irn maehsta irn aehsta," she whispers, *as within, so without,* and begins a bitter poem in Nhàired, shaping in her mind a construct. Anger-fueled sorcery is dangerous, she knows, but anger and terror are all she has left. Her desperation fuels the sorcery, scansion shapes its skeleton, meter sets the beast-shape, filling it out. Words link in sliding musculature, the hot pelt of intent furs it over, angry purpose glares like eyes beneath a shaggy mane of verse.

Uncaring of the backlash to come, she grips the shape of words and wraps it round her like a cloak—then drops to all fours in the rain and leaps roaring at the Fyrd—

—and the darkness falls.

(—*they all do that, we've watched them do that since we first came. Yet while they feel for one member of their kind, they still do murder on others. Stihëh-stá annikh'é—*)

(*We don't understand it either. What about this one—*)

Here's the last rise before home, with the little rutted track that serves for road. Steelsheen quickens her pace a bit, sensing road's end. The air is full of the smell of salt: beach-grass hisses incessantly on either side of the track. She makes the top of the rise—and there it is, spread out blue and wrinkled, glittering and lovely, the Darthene Gulf. The Sun is beginning to pierce through from a silver sky; the black beach glistens as the waves slide back; sandpipers dance daintily after them, poking for whelks in the bubbling crevices and tide pools. She looks across at the lonely stone manor-house built on the headland—*Home!*

Steelsheen breaks into a canter. *They'll be so proud. My master has never before given live steel to anyone so young. And Tegánë has spoken for me to see if I can be in the royal household. To live in Darthis, in a town with walls! And Sheen, Father will be so proud when he sees her. A real Steldene, a* silverdust *Steldene, and I broke her myself with all the tricks he taught me!*

She punches the mare into a gallop and rides into the demesne, under the old stone arch with the tai-Enraesi arms, lioncelle, passant regardant, sword upraised in the dexter paw. Chickens scatter in all directions. Dogs scramble to their feet and bounce around her, barking, as she rides in to the dooryard with a great clatter of hooves. She dismounts. A yellow cat on the doorstep opens one eye at the noise, says a rude word and closes the eye again.

Segnbora laughs as she pulls off Steelsheen's saddle, drops it on the ground, fends off various dogs with pats and scratches, and bends to chuck the cat under the chin. Three weeks she has been on the road from Darthis. Three weeks of lousy weather, an attack by bandits and a case of the flux. One cat, however grumpy, isn't going to spoil this splendid homecoming.

"Mother, Father, I'm back!" she shouts, shoving open the front door and swaggering in.

She walks through the little main hall with its benches and carvings and hangings and firepit. Secretly she's a little shocked by the shabbiness of the place; it never looked this run down before she went to the city. Her father's old complaints about failed crops and the sorry state of family finances suddenly begin to disturb her—

"Mama?"

No answer. *She's in the kitchen, then.* Through the hall and out into the big stone-paved kitchen and pantry. Her mother is just stepping in the far door with a string of onions from the buttery shed outside. Close behind is her father, who carries a newly dispatched chicken.

"Hi!" she shouts.

" 'Berend!" says her mother, and "Don't shout," says her father, both at once.

She trots over, embraces them both in a huge hug, and pulls her sheathed sword out of her belt to show them. "Mama, look, I named it Charri—"

"How is your Fire coming, dear?" her mother interrupts. Her father says nothing, waiting for the answer, holding himself aloof.

And suddenly it's all wrong. *Don't they think if I had finally focused, I'd have come in here streaming blue Fire from every orifice? Why don't they—*

"Mother," she says, "can't you ever ask me about something else?"

Her mother looks surprised. "What else is there?" she says; and, "Don't talk to your mother in that tone of voice," her father says.

"I have to rub down my horse, excuse me." She bites the inside of her cheek hard to keep from saying anything else, and walks out the way she came—

—and then darkness again.

She staggers about, lost in the darkness of her self, and begins to understand madness.

(Stihëh, stihëh-stá annikh'é-!) rumbles the voice of storm again. It's joined by more voices, all intoning the same rushing phrase, a litany of incomprehension and curiosity. They won't go away. They bump and jostle her roughly when she stumbles into them in the dark, feeling for a way out.

The place where she walks is walled and domed and floored in adamant, built that way long ago to protect her inner verities. There her memories are stored. Some have been buried by accident, some she's sealed in stone on purpose; many stand about smooth and polished from much handling.

It's the buried ones that chiefly interest her invaders. Stone means nothing to them, it being one of their elements. Cruel claws slice down effortlessly. White fire burns and melts. Delicate talons turn over exposed thoughts—old joys like polished jewels, razory fragments of pain.

(Khai'rae tachoi? Sshir'stihé-khai?)

(No, this moment's fairer far. Look. I hadn't thought they sang—)

—it's quite dark, but she needs no light to know that the slab of marble is a handspan from her nose. The sound of her breathing is loud beneath it, and the condensation from her breath drips maddeningly onto her face. The sarcophagus-

shaped Testing Bath is full of icy water, and Segnbora, naked
as a fish, is submerged in it up to her face. Her hands are
bound to her sides. On her chest rests a ten-pound stone.
Above her is the three-inch-thick lid of the Bath, open only
at the end behind her head, just enough to let in air and
Saris's voice.

This is the final test of a loremistress-Bard, which will deter-
mine whether three years of training will desert her under
extreme stress. There's no telling which of the Four Hundred
Tales she'll be required to recite faultlessly tonight, or what
song, or poem, or legend. When the lid is removed in the
morning, she'll be expected to take up the kithara and extem-
porize a poem in tragic-epic meter on the forging of Fórlennh
BrokenBlade.

"Sunset to sunrise?" she had said to Eftgan this morning, before the last of the orals. "I can do that standing on my head."

Now she's not so sure. She feels like she's been in this cold,
wet tomb forever. She suspects it's more like two hours.

"The Lost Queen's Ballad," Saris says from outside the
Bath.

Segnbora closes her eyes, hunting for the memory-tag she
uses to remember that ballad, and finds it. She sings softly, in
a minor key:

> "Oh, when Darthen's Queen went riding
> out of Barachael that day,
> she rode up the empty corrie
> and she sang a rondelay;
>
> and the three Lights shone upon her
> as on Skádhwë's bitter blade,
> and she fared on up that awful trail
> and little of it made;
>
> She stood laughing on the peak-snows
> with the new Moon in her hair,
> and she smiled and set her foot upon
> the Bridge that isn't There;

> She took the road right gladly
> to the Castle in the Sky,
> and Darthen's sorrel steed came back,
> but the Queen stayed there for aye. . . ."

She lies there expecting to be asked for the rest of the history—the suicide of Queen Efmaer's loved, and her journey up to Glasscastle, where suicides go, to get her inner Name back from him. *But no, that would be too easy.*

"Jarrin's Debt," says Saris.

Segnbora sighs. "As long ago as your last night's dreams, and as far away as tonight's," she begins, "the Battle of Bluepeak befell. . . ."

—and the darkness in the Bath is suddenly the darkness inside her mind.

Damn you! Damn you all to Darkness! Get out of here!

—the courtyard is fairly large, but its size is no help; there's nowhere to hide from Shíhan's sword, which is everywhere at once.

She dances back and swings her wooden practice sword up in a desperate block—a mistake, for no conscious act can possibly counter one of Shíhan's moves. He strikes the practice sword aside with a single scornful sweep of Clothespole, then smacks her in the head with the flat in an elegant backhand—a blow painful enough to let her know she's in disgrace. Segnbora sits down hard with the shock of it, saying hello to the hard paving of the practice yard for the millionth time.

"Idiot," Shíhan growls. He is a Steldene, black-haired, dark-skinned, with a broad-nosed face, a bristly mustache, and fierce brown eyes. He stands right over her—a great brown cat of a man; lithe, muscular, and dangerous-looking. He is utterly contemptuous.

"When will you learn to stop *thinking!*" He glares at her. "Save thinking for your bardcraft and your sorcery and the Fire you keep chasing, but don't bring it here! Sweet Lady of

the Forges, why do I waste my time on walking butchers'
meat?"

She gets up, slowly, resheathes the practice sword in her
belt and settles into a ready stance: one hand gripping the
imaginary sheath, the other at her side, relaxed. She's seething, for the other advanced students, starting to eat their
nunch, are watching from the sides of the courtyard. Maryn,
around whom she danced with insulting ease this morning, is
snickering, damn him.

Even as her eyes flick away from Maryn, she sees Shíhan
drawing. She draws too, spins out of reach as she does so,
comes around at him from his momentarily undefended side
and hits him—not a hard blow, but so focused that his whole
chest cavity seems to jump away from it.

Quite suddenly, to her absolute amazement, Shíhan is on
his left side on the ground, with the point of her practice
sword leaning delicately against his ribs. Shíhan's eyes close
with hers like steel touching steel, and bind there, a bladed
glance. All around the courtyard people have stopped chewing. No one in her class has ever downed Shíhan. Segnbora
starts to tremble.

"Good," Shíhan says in a voice that all the others can hear.
"And wrong," he adds more quietly, for her alone. "Come
and eat."

They step off to the far side of the courtyard, apart from the
other students, and settle under the plane-tree where Shíhan's nunch-meal lies ready—blue-streaked sheep's-milk
cheese, crumbly biscuits, sour beer. Shíhan silently casts a few
crumbs off to one side and spills a few drops of beer as
libation to the Goddess, then starts eating.

"Was it your anger at Maryn that caused you to stop thinking?" Shíhan asks.

"Yes, sir."

"*Feeling* when you strike is all right," says her master. "First
time I've seen you do that. There may be hope for you yet.
Provided," and he glances up with a frown, "that it's the right
kind of feeling."

She sits quiet while he eats.

"Listen," Shíhan says. "Don't try to figure this out: just

hear it, let it in. When you strike another, especially to kill, you're striking yourself. When you kill, the other takes a little part of you with them, past the Door. If you do it in anger, what they take is the part of you that feels." Shíhan wipes his mouth on his sleeve. His eyes burn with the intensity of one imparting a sacred mystery to a fellow initiate. "Kill in anger often enough and your aliveness starts running out too. Soon there's nothing left but a husk that walks and speaks and does skillful murder. Were you angry at *me?*" He shoots the question at her sudden as a dart.

"Master! No."

"But *I'm* the one that anger struck down. See how easily it used you?"

Segnbora stares at the ground, her face burning.

"Shíhan, I didn't think—"

"I noticed," he says, for the first time smiling. "Keep that up."

She shakes her head, confused. "Master, in killing in war or in self-defense, if I'm not supposed to feel angry—what *should* I be feeling?"

He looks at her. "Compassion," he says, gruff-voiced. "Anguish. What else, when you've just killed yourself?"

(-*ae'wnh khai-phaa ür'ts'shaóinëh rahiw?*)
(*I don't know for certain; all I felt there before was a memory of cold dirt. It must be something interesting. See how thick the stone is over it? Several of us will be needed—*)
OH NO YOU DON'T!

—maybe it was the momentary burst of outrage that let her briefly out into the light again.

Whatever the reason, suddenly the world was bright and clear, though it seemed very small, and the creatures that moved through it were earthbound and crippled of mind.

She was not in the Morrowfane country anymore. This was some twilit camp under the lee of a hill. She could feel the warmth of a fire against her side. She lay on her back, her limbs aching so much that she couldn't move.

To her left sat Lang, warm in the firelight, gazing down at

her with a bleak, helpless expression. Her distress at her im-
mobility fell away at the sight of him. Lang *mattered:* He was
stability, normalcy, all embodied in one stocky blond
shape.

In all her life before this terror she had never cried for help
but once, and that time help had been refused. She had never
asked since. But now she had lost her mind, and surely there
was nothing else to lose. *Oh Lang,* she tried to cry, *I'm crazy,
I'm scared, I can't find my way out, but I'm here—*

But the words caught on a blazing place in her throat, got
twisted out of shape and came out hoarse and strange.
"R'mdahé, au'Lang, irikhé, stihé-sta 'ae vehhy't-kej, ssih haa-hté—"

Not far away Herewiss and Freelorn lay together with their
backs against a rock, holding weary conversation with the
campfire that burned between them and the place where she
lay.

(—indeed not,) the campfire was saying. Sunspark's eyes,
ember-bright in the flickering fire, threw a glance of mild
interest in her direction. (There aren't that many things in this
bland little corner of the Pattern that can bother my kind. But
we used to come across other travellers among the worlds,
and some of them told of being unseated in heart or mind
after coming to a world too strange for them to understand.
They lost their languages, some of them—)

"Did they get better?" Freelorn said. His tone indicated
that he desperately wanted to hear that they did.

"Lorn," Herewiss said gently, putting his arm around his
loved and hugging him, "we're going to have to leave her
somewhere safe. She can't ride, she can't talk, she can't take
care of herself. The arrow-shot she got from that last batch
of bandits would have been the end of her if I hadn't been to
the Fane first and learned what to do."

Freelorn didn't answer.

"I went as deep as I could last night," Herewiss said. "I
couldn't hear anything but a confusion of voices, and if I can't
reach her there's nothing more we can do. Look, tomorrow
afternoon—tomorrow night, maybe—we'll be riding through
Chavi to get the news. We can leave her there; they'll be glad
to have her. She'll take her time, get better, and follow us

when she can. Face it, Lorn, the Shadow's after us. We can't care for an invalid from here to Bluepeak."

"She saved my life," Freelorn said, his voice breaking harshly out of him. He wasn't angry at his loved, but at the unfairness of the Morrowfane, which had done this to her and left him untouched. "Several times . . ."

"She knew what she was doing, all those times," Herewiss said. "She knew what she was doing when she went up the Morrowfane. Lang told us so. And she'll know why we're doing what we're doing, and understand."

But there was little hope in his voice—

—the blackness swallowed her again. All around her the rush and swell of inhuman voices was beginning, faintly, as if for the first time the sources of the sound were at some distance from her. But soon enough they would drown her resistance beneath their implacable song, close in on that one untouchable memory, rip it untimely from beneath the rock and make it come as real as the others.

She shuddered violently. No, oh no. And in any case I won't be left behind at the next inn as if I were a lamed horse!

Her bruised and battered pride got up one more time from the hard floor to which it had been knocked, and made itself useful. I am a tai-Enraiesi. If my ancestors could see me they would laugh me to scorn! And I'm a sensitive trained in the ways of the inner mind, Fire or no Fire. I won't stand inside here and do nothing!

Off to one side, distantly, she could still hear Freelorn and Herewiss talking. Gulping with terror, Segnbora turned her back on them, concentrated as best she could, and began making her way toward the huge voices, deeper into the dark . . .

Five

Offer an enemy a false show of hospitality in order to damn him, and the fires will fall on *your* head, not his. Give him the truth with his meat and drink, and trust it not to sour the wine. . . .

s'Jheren, *Advice unasked,* 199

It was a long walk, full of halts, hesitations, and confusions, for the voices seemed to grow no nearer as she walked. Then abruptly she discovered that she had a seeming-body again, by walking into a wall, hard. She staggered back from it, momentarily seeing white with pain—then stepped forward with arms outstretched, and bashed her fingertips into the wall. She pushed close to it, spreading her arms wide, embracing the familiar roughness; she laid her face against it and squeezed her eyes shut against tears of vast relief. At last this place was beginning to behave as it should.

Any trained sorcerer has an inner milieu into which he or she retreats for contemplation or preparation of sorceries. This, at last, was hers—not an abstraction of blackness and things buried, but the old cavern a mile down the seacoast from the house at Asfahaeg, her favorite secret place as a child.

Long ago the coast dwellers had broken a thirty-foot hole through the cavern's high, domed ceiling, turning it into a rude temple where they performed wreakings and weather-sorceries to the sound of the waves crashing just outside. As an adult sorcerer Segnbora had made its image part of her, a great airy cave full of sunlight or moonlight and the smell of the ocean.

She opened her eyes again, pushed back cautiously from the wall and looked up, trying to find the shaft-hole in the ceiling. After a moment she located it, though the shaft was distinguishable from the rest of the ceiling only by two or three faint stars that shone through. Odd. The cavern had never been this dark before . . . She turned and looked the other way, trying to get herself oriented somehow. The faint rumble of the Sea bounced all around her, difficult to localize, but at last she thought she detected a slight difference in sound right across from her, a deadness that might mean the cave's opening onto the beach. She stepped cautiously away from the wall, then started to walk.

She touched something. It wasn't the wall. It was smooth, and dry, and *hot.* In her shock she stumbled forward instead of jerking back, and the something clamped down on her outstretched right hand, hard.

She cried out wordlessly in rage and horror at the frightening violation.

"It seems rude to put your hand in the Dragon's mouth and then scream before you know whether you've been injured," said a huge, slow, deep bass viol of a voice, from right in front of her.

Whatever had been holding her hand released it. Segnbora backed away and stood there rubbing the hand, which had been held tightly but not hurt. She was bitterly angry at herself for having shown fear. "What the Dark are you *doing* in here?" she yelled.

"We were invited," said the voice, puzzled. "Your accent is poor," it added. "Speak more slowly."

"Accent—" She stopped and realized that she hadn't been speaking Darthene, or any human language, but the odd and terrible one that the voices in the darkness had been using. "Never mind that! You can't be in here, this is *me!*"

"What is 'me'?" the voice said without curiosity. "Rather, say 'We are here.'"

There was a pause.

"May we ask why you keep it so dark in here? Were you keeping it so because the place where we met was dark?"

"I can remedy that," Segnbora said, annoyed. She lifted a hand, called up a memory of noon sunlight pouring in through the shaft—

—and nothing happened.

"You are leaving us out of the reckoning," said the deep, slow voice as calmly as before.

"Perhaps you would assist me then," Segnbora said, annoyed and uneasy. She concentrated again. "Sunlight . . ."

This time the light came, streaming down through the shaft from a sky that seemed bluer and deeper than usual. Segnbora looked down and away from the blinding light—and was blinded instead by the intruder.

The rough dark textures of the face she had touched in the Fane were dark no longer. The sunlight spilling down from above shattered and rainbowed from scales like black sapphires, every one with its shifting star. The Dragon blazed and glittered like a queen's ransom, his every breath and movement creating a shower of dazzle around him.

Now, Segnbora thought in wonder, *I begin to understand that old story about Dragons spending their time lying on piles of jewels. . . .*

His head hung above and before her, no longer an inert, half-perceived shape as it had been in the Morrowfane cave. It was an elongated head: sleeker and more slender than a snake's. Its mouth was a beak, like that of a snapping turtle. It was the point of the beak, at the very end of the immense serrated jaw, that had closed on her hand.

Her gaze travelled upward. From the beak to the place where the jaw met the neck was twenty feet at least. The eyes were great pupilless globes filled with liquid fire, blazing a brilliant white even in the full sunlight. In the iron braziers of the nostrils the same light glowed though not so brightly

The Dragon was watching her with no less interest. "Casting one's skin for the last time is always a nuisance," it said, "but it's still one of the more pleasant things about going *mdahaih.* You like this body better than the one you saw in the cave?"

"No!" Segnbora started to say, but the thought snagged on the new language living in her throat, and wouldn't move. The Dracon tongue, she realized then, put a great emphasis on accuracy of expression, and her one, bald, angry word was therefore insufficient.

"You look absolutely beautiful," she said at last, "and I wish to the Dark you'd go away."

"It wasn't my idea to become *mdahaih* in a human, believe me," the Dragon said. "Nor was it that of the rest of the *mdeihei.* They've been making a great deal of noise about it."

She had never heard the words before, and she understood them instantly. *Mdahaih:* indwelling within a host body and mind. *Mdeihei:* the indwellers, the souls of linear ancestors, the thousand-voiced consensus, the eternal companions.

The thought made Segnbora's hair stand up. She realized then that the sound she had been hearing in the background was not the Sea. It was other voices, like that of the Dragon. *It's a pleasant enough sound,* she thought. A single Dragon sounded like a bass viol talking to itself—a deep breathy voice full of hisses and rumbles and vocal bow-scrapes. But Dragons in a group seemed to prefer speaking together, and had been doing just that ever since she walked back into her cavern. The result was a constant quiet mutter of seemingly sourceless voices: scores of them, maybe hundreds, coiling together words and meaning-melodies in decorous, dissonant musics.

Now they were growing louder. They didn't approve of Segnbora, of her clumsy gropings and her rudeness to them in the darkness into which they had been thrust. Nor did they approve of the abnormal singleness of her mind, and they said so, in a dark-hued melody that sounded like a consort of bass instruments upbraiding its audience.

"I don't much care whose idea this whole thing was," Segnbora said. "But won't you creatures please—" She fumbled for the right word, but there was no word for undoing the *mdahaih* relationship. "Won't you just go away?" she said finally, feeling uneasy about the vagueness of the term.

"Where?" the Dragon said, puzzled.

"Out of *us!*" She stopped, then, annoyed. In this language there seemed to be no singular pronouns. The only singular forms in the language were for inanimate objects, and human beings, and other such crippled, single-minded entities.

"That is impossible," the Dragon explained patiently. It had lowered its voice into its deepest register, the one used for addressing the very young. "You are *mdeihei,* and will be until you die."

The word it used was *res'uw:* lose-the-old-body-and-move-into-a-new-one. Segnbora rubbed at her aching head in bewilderment.

"Listen," the Dragon said, "if you were one of us, you'd bring about hatchlings in time, and the soulbond between you and them would be established once they broke shell. The bond would grow stronger in them as they grew, and weaker in you as you became old. Finally, when you left your body, you would be drawn into them: become *mdahaih*. And so it would be with their hatchlings, on through the generations, forever . . ."

"Forever," Segnbora whispered, feeling weak. "But all those voices—they can't *all* be your ancestors. . . . we wouldn't be able to hear for the noise!"

"The ones furthest back are hardest to hear. They fade out in time—which may be as well. The *mdeihei* are for advice, among other things, and what kind of advice can someone gone *mdahaih* fifty generations ago give to the *sdaha*, the out-dweller? The strongest voices are the newest, the first four generations or so."

Segnbora sat down on the floor, miserable. The great head inclined slightly to watch her, causing another brief storm of rainbows.

"What happens," she said eventually, "if I die, and there are no children, and no one is close by to accept the linkage, the soulbond, as I seem to have done for you?"

She could see no change of expression in the iron-and-diamond face, but the Dragon's tone went grave. "A few have died and gone *rdahaih*," he said: not "indwelling" or "out-dwelling," but "undwelling." "They are lost. They and their *mdeihei* vanished completely, and from the *mdeihei* of every Dragon everywhere. They cease to be . . ."

Segnbora shuddered.

The Dragon's wings rustled in its own unease. "Your people have a word," he said. "A Marchwarder taught it to us: 'immortality.' He said that humans desire it the way we desire doing-and-being. We have 'immortality' already; only rarely do we lose it. Had you not come to the Fane, we would have gone *rdahaih*. Mercifully the Immanance at the heart of what-was-and-is saw to it that you were there."

I'll never get married, then, Segnbora thought, heavy-hearted. Humans had a Responsibility: They had to reproduce themselves at least once, and until the Responsibility was fulfilled she was not free to marry any man or woman or group. She couldn't take the chance of passing this curse along to a child. She couldn't! It was going to be hard to die without knowing whether she would see the Shore—

"O *sdaha*," the Dragon said quietly, "since we're going to be together for a long time—regardless of your plans for hatchlings—perhaps we might know your name?"

She stared upward, angry again in the midst of her pain. "I don't remember asking you to listen to me think!"

"Among *sda'tdae*, there's no use in asking for permission or refusing it," the Dragon said. "One hears. You'll find there's little I will hide from you. Nor do I understand why so many of your memories are lying here sealed in stone, though doubtless answers will become plain in time."

The pattern of notes the Dragon wove around them said plainly that he considered her something of a disappointment. Still, there was compassion in the song behind the words, and amusement mixed with wry distaste at the situation he found himself in.

Segnbora rose slowly. She was finding it difficult to be angry for long with someone so relentlessly polite—especially when he was so large. She was also getting the uneasy feeling that all the courtesy and precision built into the Dracon language was there to control a potential for terrible savagery.

"Segnbora d'Welcaen tai-Enraesi," she said, giving him the eyes-up half bow due a peer.

"Hasai s'Vheress d'Naen s'Dithe d'Rr'nojh d'Karalh mes'-en-Dhaa'lhhw'ae," the Dragon said, giving his name only to the nearest five generations.

The named ancestors sang quiet acknowledgment from the shadows beyond the sunlight. Hasai lowered his head almost to the floor and raised his wings in greeting, spreading them fully upward and outward in an awesome double canopy. Membranes like polished onyx stretched between batlike finger-struts, and the sunlight was blocked suddenly away.

Her breath went out of her again in sheer amazement. "Oh, my," she said, awed, "you *are* big. May I look at you?"

"Certainly."

Segnbora walked around to her left, putting some fifteen yards between herself and Hasai so she could see more of him at once. Fifty feet of jeweled neck led down to two immense double shoulders, from which sprang both the backward-bent forelimbs, now folded underneath Hasai, and the first "upper arm" strut of the wings. Each of these struts ended at the first bend of the wing in a curved crystalline spur, as sharp as the diamond talons on each forelimb's four claws, but much longer.

Segnbora walked the length of the Dragon, out of the shadow of his wings, past the great corded hindlimbs, which were taloned as the forelimbs were. Slowly she walked along the crystal-spined tail, scaled in sapphires above, crusted in diamond below—and walked, and walked, and walked. Finally she came to the end of it, where the sapphires were small enough to be set in an arm-ring, and the last crystalline barb, sharp as a sword, lanced out ten feet or so from the foot-thick tailtip.

She looked back up the length of the body between the wings. It was like looking at a hill wrought of gems and black metal. Even supine on the stony floor, the slenderest part of Hasai's body, his abdomen, was at least fifteen feet high and perhaps forty around. His upper shoulders were at least thirty feet across. There was just too much of him.

"I can't understand how you fly," Segnbora said, starting back up the other side.

"The proper frame of mind," Hasai said, arching his head backwards to watch her. "After all, our people aren't built like the flying things you have here. We are light. Observe." Hasai lifted up the last ten feet of his tail and dropped it on her.

Reflexively, knowing she was about to be crushed, Segnbora threw her arms up to ward the tail away—and found herself supporting it on her hands. It was very heavy, but not at all the crushing weight she had expected.

"See?" Hasai said, flicking the tail away to lie at rest again.

Segnbora shook her head in wonder. The rough under-crusting *looked* like diamond, the scales *looked* like sapphire— "What are you made of?" she said, starting to walk again.

"Flesh, bone, hide. And you?"

Segnbora blinked. "About the same. . . ."

"You're not quite as tough, however," the Dragon said, sounding mildly rueful. "I remember the beast you will be riding, biting you there—" The glittering tail snaked up at Segnbora again, prodding her delicately in the chest. "You will be bleeding, and wishing for hide more like mine, that the beast would have broken its teeth on—"

As politely as she could, Segnbora undid the tailspine from her surcoat's embroidery, where it had snagged. She was wrestling with an unease that was no longer vague. She had noticed before, while fumbling for words, that in Dragon language there seemed to be several extra tenses for verbs. Now they all became clear. They were *precognitive* tenses—future possible, future probable, future definite. Dragons, she realized, remember ahead as well as back.

She shuddered, wanting to reject the possibility of ever doing that herself.

"We're not *built* to remember everything that happens to us," she said then to Hasai, resentfully. "Not consciously, anyway. Listen . . . I can feel the *mdeihei* back there remembering everything that ever happened to them, every sunset and conversation and breath of wind. We don't *do* that."

"It makes sense that you would reject ahead-memory," Hasai said. "You do not have it, the warders tell us. You even have trouble dealing with what *is*. But to reject our past-memories as well—"

Segnbora shrugged. "What good are fifty generations of Dragon memories to a human?"

"But you're not a human," Hasai said calmly. "Not totally. Not anymore." He looked away from her, a Dragon shrug, matching hers. "Sooner or later you will look and see. Doubtless not soon."

Segnbora went narrow-eyed with anger at the Dragon's cool dare—and at the realization that this situation was completely out of her control.

"Show me now," she said.

Hasai bent his head down beside her and dropped his jaw slightly in an expression of mild amusement. His action gave

Segnbora a frightfully clear view of diamond fangs as long
and sharp as scythes, and of the three-forked smelling-tongue
in its recess beneath the blunt one used for speech. Worst of
all, she could see the fulminous magma-glow of the back of
the throat, where Dragonfire seethed blindingly.

"Well," Hasai said, watching her calmly as a sleepy volcano,
"will you put your hand in the Dragon's mouth willingly this
time?"

"Why not," Segnbora said, nervous, and irritated for being
so. "Here, take the whole arm—"

Without giving herself time to hesitate, she went over to his
great toothy table of a lower jaw and thrust her arm up to the
shoulder between two huge forefangs, resting the forearm on
the dry hot tongue. Slowly and carefully Hasai closed his
mouth, holding Segnbora's arm immobile but not hurting it.

(Comfortable?) he said wordlessly, his inner voice sounding, if possible, bigger than his outer one.

"Yes, thank you."

(Well, then . . .)

Without warning, Segnbora found that her body felt wonderful. Her eyes could suddenly see colors she had been missing: the black reds, the white violets. She felt for the first time
the curves and planes of the energy flows that were as much
a Dragon's medium as the currents and flows of atmosphere.
Her muscles slid lithe and warm beneath gemmed skin. Her
eyes held light within them as well as beholding it without. An
old, yet delightful burning banished the cold from her throat
and insides. Power was there, and strength—the dangerous
grace of limb and talon and tail. She felt reborn. She also felt
hungry.

(We'll eat,) she heard one of her selves suggest.

Agreeing, she crouched and coiled her way over to the door
of the cavern, folded her wings carefully and slipped out.

(Wait a moment—that door's only a few feet wide!)

(That was your memory,) said one of the mdeihei, a strong
voice, fairly recently alive. (This is mine.)

Out they went into the brilliant light of noon at Onolí. (This
isn't my beach, either!)

(No, my old one.)

Immediately she spread her wings right out to their fullest, to feel the sunfire soak into the hungry membranes and run through her like white-hot wine. She basked, drinking her fill of the light, lazing while the strange-familiar thoughts of a Dragon's day-to-day life flowed through her.

The *mdeihei* rumbled lazy assent, a placid rush of low voices blending with the sound of the waves. She got up after a while, raising her wings, feeling with them the flows of all the forces that Dragons manipulated and took for granted, as fish accept water or birds the air. It was an old delight: the chief joy of the Dragonkind, dearer even than speech.

(What else are we for?)

The wings were hands. She grasped the currents she felt moving about her, pulled herself upward, sprang and flew.

The first leap took her high over the shore, and she watched with amazement and delight as she gained altitude. Boulders dwindled to pebbles and the huge crash of the breakers shrank to a soft-spoken crawl.

(Inland, perhaps?) said the *mdaha* who had spoken, her song calm with her own joy.

(Oh please!)

She wheeled, catching currents of air and fields of force with her wings and her mind, gaining more altitude and speed as she soared south and west over northern Darthen. Below them the sunlit headlands of Síonan and Rûl Tyn lay patched and quilted with small field-squares. There were threads of brown road, and toy houses like a child's carved playthings. Southward stretched wilder, emptier lands, tree-stippled hills, forests like green shadows on the fields.

She leaned up toward the sky and gained more height, watching the sunlight flash on a river-strung series of little lakes. Upward still she dove, through a furry fog of cloud-cover, and saw the Darst below go pewter-shadowed. More distant lakes and rivers seem to hover unsupported in the haze below. She dipped one wing, stretched the other up and out in a bank. Over her the patterned sky turned as if on a pivot, wheeled like a starry night about her center . . .

The higher and farther she went, the lovelier it all became. Thick clouds as white as drifting snow rose up before her, balzing in the sunlight. Bounded by these mountains of the sky, drowned far down in the depths of air, the land lay dim and still. Pacing her above the silence, the white Sun rode, swimming soundlessly in an unfathomable eternity of blue.

Still higher she climbed. Above her the sky went royal blue, then violet. Her wings lost the wind entirely and began to stiffen in the great cold above the air. She stopped beating them and fixed them at full soaring extension. Her mind was doing all the work now, manipulating fields and flows, triggering the shutdown of some body functions, the initiation of others which would protect her in the utter cold of the Emptiness.

The sky went black, and the stars came out, the winter stars that summer daylight hid, burning steady as beacons. In the same sky with them hung the ravening Sun, unshielded now by the thick cloak of the world's air. It was a searing agony on her membranes but an ecstatic heat within. Quite suddenly the *mdaha* whose memory this was flipped forward, tumbling end for end—

Had she been breathing, breath would have gone out of her. Below her, she saw an impossibility. The flat world was *curved.* The black depths of the Mother's night rested against that curvature, holding it as if in a careful hand. The whole great expanse of the Middle Kingdoms, from Arlen in the west to the Waste in the east, could be seen in a single glance. Beyond them were unknown lands, unsailed seas—the whole of human experience and possibility held under a fragile crystal skin of air.

Awed, she spread wings and bowed her head to the wonder. Surely this was the way the Dragons had seen the world on the day they came falling out of the airless depths: a jewel, a treasure, *life*—

(Perhaps you understand now,) Hasai said, his voice hushed with old love, old pain, (why we decided to stand and fight for a home.)

She hung there, unmoving in the silence beyond all silences, and understood.

(Not that we've forgotten what we left,) said the other *mdaha.* (Turn and see—)

Something happened to the Sun hanging behind her back. It felt suddenly strange, but welcome, like the touch of a friend coming up from behind. She turned and found that it *had* changed, was bigger, hotter, pinker. Close beneath her hung the memory of the ancient Homeworld, red-brown and dry; a harsh place, a birthplace, dear and dead.

A great mournful love for the lost lands where her kind was born rose up in her at the sight. But the mournfulness turned to something deeper and more piercing as she looked off to one side. Suspended there, seeming to cover half the endless night, was a great swirled pattern of stars. They seemed frozen in midturn—a whirlpool spraying drops and gemlets of rainbow fire, its arcs sinuous and splendid as the curve of a tail, its heart ablaze like the memory of the Day of Dawning, when the World's Heart beat its first.

Oh, My Maiden, my Queen, they know You too—

She could find no other thought. Thinking was driven out of her by the immensities. After a while she realized she was leaning against Hasai's face, her cheek resting on the great sapphired one, her left arm holding the Dragon close and her right in his mouth up to the shoulder. And her face was wet. She straightened up, abashed.

Hasai let her arm loose, and Segnbora spent a few moments brushing herself off and trying to find some composure. Hasai watched her gravely, waiting.

"It felt real!"

"And so it was."

"But that happened a long time ago!"

"Certainly. And it happened again, right then."

"But it was a memory," Segnbora said, confused. "If I had tried to change what was happening, I couldn't have."

"Of course you could have changed it," Hasai said, politely. "We wondered that you didn't try."

She shook her head again. Perhaps she was just not thinking well in this language yet.

"It was very beautiful," she said after a pause.

"We thank you, *sdaha.*" There was nothing in Dragon life more important than memories, and the sharing of them. "It's well that you find value in who we were, and are, for we cannot

leave. Henceforward, you will have to deal with us as we are
—as we shall deal with you."

Segnbora looked up in sudden anger at the immense face
above her. "Who are you to dictate terms to me in my own
mind?" she cried.

"You say 'your own mind'," Hasai said. "You imply owner-
ship—or at least control. Prove your claim. Leave this 'mind'
and then come back. Or better still, remove *us.*"

There was a long silence, during which Hasai watched her,
and neither of them moved.

"We cannot leave, either," said Hasai.

Baffled, Segnbora shook her head.

"Now what?" she said finally.

"Now," Hasai said, "we sue for pardon of wrongs done in
haste."

He bowed to her, his wings going up again, and his great
head sinking low; lower than ever, this time, till it almost
touched the floor. Those eyes as tall as her body were below
her own.

"I am—sorry—about the *mdeihei.*" The words came out of
him oddly; to a Dragon this was like apologizing for breathing. "They were trying to find out what kind of place they
were in. That can be very important. We are large as your kind
reckons size, true enough; and well armed, and long-lived.
But we have our fears too."

Segnbora became conscious that the rustling in the shadows had stopped, and that many eyes were gazing out of it at
her with a frightening and alien directness.

"I am aware of your dislike for others delving in your
memories. I will keep the *mdeihei* out of your past—though
you are of course welcome to ours. But I don't know what I
can do about your future—"

"Neither do I," Segnbora said, with a rueful laugh. "The
present is giving me enough problems already." Suddenly she
was thinking about Lorn, and Lang, and the others. Had they
left her in Chavi as planned? She had to get out and see where
she was . . .

"Since you are us now," Hasai said, sensing both the joy
and danger her liege represented, "you must be more consci-

entious in safeguarding your body. There is more than just one of you to go *rdahaih* if you're careless."

"And you of course will take care of *me* for the same reason—"

"We would take care of you anyway, shared mindspace or no," Hasai said. "Life is the Immanence's gift, not to be thoughtlessly cast away even when it is alien—or angry."

Segnbora bit the inside of her lip, ashamed of herself. *I did ask for a change at the Fane,* she thought after a moment. *The request has certainly been granted! But it's just like the old stories: If you don't specify what you want when you wish for something, you may get a surprise. . . .*

"I must go." Segnbora turned and headed for the little low door of the cavern.

"Sehe'rae, sdaha," said the huge viol-voice from behind her: *Go well, outdweller.*

Segnbora paused. *"Sehe'rae—"* she said, and tasted the next word. *"—mdaha."* *Mindmate.*

The *mdeihei,* pacified at last, settled back into the song of the ages, the litany of all their memories, all their lives. Segnbora threw a last glance at Hasai, burning in iron and diamond in the light from the shaft. Then she turned and ducked through the door—

—to stare at the dawn from her blanket-roll. The Sun hadn't yet climbed over the edge of the world, and gray mist lay low over the grassy lea in which the camp was set. Off to one side the horses stood together, stamping and quietly snorting their way toward wakefulness; three or four feet in front of her, the campfire was down to ashes and embers.

"Thank You, Goddess," she tried to say; but her throat, after some days of disuse, refused to do anything but squeak like the sparrows trying their voices all around. She was about to try clearing her throat a bit when the fire before her flared up wildly.

(*Took* you long enough!) it shouted, annoyed and delighted. (*Herewiss!*)

From behind her came hurried rustling: blankets being thrown aside, wet grass whispering as someone came quickly through it. Then Herewiss was down on his knees in front of her, staring at her.

"Are you sure? The last time it was just a coughing spell—"

Segnbora looked up at Herewiss and very distinctly croaked a rude word in the oldest of the dead Darthene dialects, a word having to do with one of the less sanitary habits of sheep.

"*Now* I'll cough," she said, and she did.

A thump occurred during the coughing spell, and Freelorn was beside Herewiss. He grabbed Segnbora by the shoulders and shook her. "Are you all right? Are you?"

"I will be when you stop that. . . ." she gasped. As Lorn helped her sit up, she looked around at the approaching morning with appreciation too great for words. "Can I have a drink?"

Herewiss got water for her and sat with Freelorn staring at her while she drank, as if at someone returned from the dead. "How long was I out?" she said between sips.

"Six days," Herewiss said. "We thought we'd have to leave you in—"

"I know. I heard you. I would have done the same thing."

Freelorn and Herewiss glanced at one another in relief. To the sound of more rustling, Lang dropped to the grass beside them. He stared at Segnbora and said nothing; but her under-hearing woke up as if it had been kicked, bringing her a flood of worry, not nearly as relieved as that of the others.

She took another drink to gather her composure, and then looked at Lang and said quietly, "You told me so. . . ."

He shrugged and looked away.

"Here," Freelorn said, "you ought to see—" He got up, went off and rummaged around in his bags for a moment, then came back with a small square of polished steel, a mirror.

Segnbora looked at herself. The same old face—prominent nose, pointed chin, deep-set eyes with circles smudged a bit darker than usual. But her hair wasn't the same: It was coming in shockingly silver-white at the roots. "Oh dear," she said, and couldn't find anything else to say.

Lang got up abruptly and went away.

Segnbora handed Freelorn back his mirror and looked at

Herewiss. "I had quite a night. Can I sleep a little more? Then I'll be able to ride."

Herewiss nodded. "Rest," he said. "Chavi is still a day away, and we're not in such a hurry that you can't recuperate a bit."

She nodded back, suddenly very weary, and lay down, gratefully wrapping her blankets around her. Some time after she closed her eyes, she realized that neither her liege-lord nor his loved had moved, but were still watching her, wondering.

" 'Berend," Freelorn said very quietly, "the thing that happened to you at the Fane— What was it?"

"Not 'it'," she sighed, without opening her eyes. " 'Them.' "

This time the darkness was only sleep, and she embraced it.

Six

If you'll walk with kings and queens, well; but take care. For
the Shadow aims ever at them—and though It often misses,
It doesn't scorn to hit the person standing closest.

Askrythen, 14, xi

It was an odd riding that someone standing on the old diked road to Chavi would have seen approaching through the evening. Indeed, maybe it was better that no one was there to witness it.

Between the tall hawthorn hedges in the fading light came, first, two men in country clothes, one on a sorrel, one on a bay. Their horses flinched and shied occasionally, for their riders were juggling stones, and dropping them frequently. A third man on a black palfrey was repeatedly plucking a single string on a lute, trying to elicit the same note twice in a row from his tone-deaf companion. Then came a young slim woman in a worn brown surcoat, riding a Steldene steeldust mare. She spoke occasionally to the empty air, like a madwoman, with a hoarse voice; and frequently raised a hand to brush back hair that was oddly pale at its roots and part.

Behind her, bringing up the rear, rode a tall dark man on a blood-bay stallion and a short dark man on a black-maned chestnut. The small man was waving his arms and arguing about something; his tall companion nodded gravely at most of what he said, glancing occasionally over to his left, where a hundredweight boulder was floating along beside him in the air.

"Look at them. *Look* at them! They'll never manage a juggling act with people watching them! Dusty, I love them, but they can't juggle *air!*"

"They'll do all right. They're just out of practice. It's been seven years since they juggled for a living, after all."

"Yes, but—"

"Lorn, they'll do all right. So will you, and so will Moris and

Dritt and the rest. Most of the entertainers on the road are only mediocre anyway. And it's not as if gleemen's immunity depended on whether we're good or not. No one's going to suspect anything. This is the middle of nowhere."

"Mmmmf. . . ."

(Hah!) Sunspark said suddenly from beneath Herewiss. (For one lousy penny I'm supposed to cut off my legs?)

Segnbora tried to put her head under her wing in token of mild exasperation, and found she couldn't. She made a face. "The punch line usually comes at the end of the joke," she said.

(Oh. Well, there's this beggar—)

"That one won't work now. We know the ending. Start another."

(All right.) It thought a moment, and Segnbora shook her head, bemused.

While she had been busy with Hasai, Dritt had made the mistake one day of trying to make friends with Sunspark by telling it a joke. Since then it had decided that joking was a vital part of human experience, and had been demanding everyone to teach it the art, on pain of burning them when Herewiss wasn't looking. As soon as she was in the saddle again, Sunspark had accosted Segnbora. In no mood for joking, she had suggested that it tell *her* jokes, and thus learn by doing. She'd had no peace since.

(—so there are these two women, they go into an inn and the innkeeper comes to their table, and one of the women says, 'Bring us the best red wine you have, and be sure the cups are clean!' So the innkeeper goes off, and comes back with a tray, and says, 'Two red wines. And which one asked for the clean cup?')

Herewiss closed his eyes and laughed. "Not bad."

(I made it up,) said Sunspark, all childish pride. It did a quick capriole out of sheer pleasure, and almost unseated Herewiss.

"Oof! Watch that, you. On second thought, maybe we should increase your part in the act. We could use another jester."

"*Mnh'qalasihiw, Hhír*—" Segnbora cleared her throat. The

Dracon language was beginning to fascinate her, and her desire to master it sometimes caused it to get out of her mouth before Darthene did. "I mean, Herewiss, there's only one problem with that. What happens if an audience doesn't laugh?"

Sunspark threw a merry glance at its rider. (If they don't laugh, we get rid of them and bring in a new audience.) The thought "get rid of them" was attached to plans for the same sudden-death fire that had been the end of the deathjaw.

Freelorn glanced up at the sky, no doubt to invoke the Goddess's protection on their next audience. Herewiss looked hard at his mount.

Sunspark laid back its ears and showed all its teeth around the bit, then subsided somewhat. (They *will* come back,) it said, sulkiness showing in the thought, (you *told* me so!)

"They will. But there's no reason to hurry people out of this life."

"Don't be hard on it," Segnbora said. "It learns quickly. Another few months and I dare say the audiences will be safe."

Freelorn and Herewiss exchanged unconvinced, humorous glances, but Segnbora didn't notice.

She was feeling hot—but then, these days, she felt hot most of the time. She closed her eyes to glance back, in mind, at Hasai. Through this day and the day before he had been stretched at ease in the seaside cave, looking out of her eyes, silent for the most part. He stayed out of her thoughts except to ask an occasional question. The rest of the time the rumble of his private thought blended with the bass chorus of the *mdeihei*, a sound Segnbora found she could now start to ignore, like the seashore when one lives nearby.

She looked down into herself now and saw Hasai sunning himself in the noon light that splashed down through the cave's shaft. His wings were spread out flat like a butterfly's, lying easy on the floor; his neck was curled so that his head lay under one of them in the position Segnbora had tried to achieve before.

"That one is insolent," Hasai said, referring to Sunspark. "Is it not?"

In Dracon the question was rhetorical, and Segnbora had no answer for it. She turned away from Hasai without further thought and opened her eyes again on the evening. There was a sweet sharp hawthorn scent in the air.

" 'Berend, did you hear me?" Freelorn said.

"No, Lorn, I was talking to my lodger." She reached out and picked a white blossom off the hedge past which they were riding, held it to her nose.

"Oh. Sorry. What are *you* going to do tonight? Pass the purse?"

"She can sing," Herewiss said.

"You can? Well, that's news! You know many songs?"

"A few," Segnbora said. She reined Steelsheen back to ride abreast of Herewiss and Freelorn, suddenly feeling the need for company more normal than that she carried inside her. "I'm best with a kithara, but I'll do all right with the lute."

Herewiss was still being paced by that boulder. It was easily half Sunspark's size, but he showed no sign of strain, and at the same time was keeping Khávrinen from showing so much as a flicker of Fire. His control was improving rapidly.

"You won't have any trouble with your part of the act, that's plain," Segnbora said.

Herewiss shrugged, waving the rock away with one hand. It soared up over the hedge like a blown feather and dropped out of sight, hitting the ground in the field on the other side with an appalling thud.

"It's easy," Herewiss said. "Even the ecstatic part of the Fireflow—those overwhelming sensations of pleasure you experience during a wreaking—are under control since we climbed the Fane."

Freelorn looked thoughtful. "You know, I wonder whether the Goddess installed that ecstatic aspect of the Fire on purpose, to keep people from doing large wreakings casually; as a sort of control—"

"More likely as a reward, to make sure the Power's used. But in either case, I'm as free of the ecstatic part of the flow as I desire." He paused, then went on nervously. "It's a little dangerous, though. The first time I picked up that rock, I had to be careful that the whole field didn't come with it . . ."

Lorn laughed, and reached out to squeeze the hand of his loved.

After a while, at a turn in the road, they could make out a low huddle of squared-off silhouettes against the horizon. Lamps burned like yellow stars in each window.

"Your guest—" Freelorn said abruptly to Segnbora. "You said 'they' before . . ."

"*Hh'rae nt'ssëh,*" she said, and corrected herself with a smile. "It *is* they. But it's also he. Mostly he."

Freelorn's expression was impossible to read. "Are you— still you?"

Oh Goddess, Lorn, if I only knew! she wanted to cry; but she kept her voice calm. "I'm not sure. Oh, Lorn, let it lie . . . when we have time, I'll take you and Herewiss inside and introduce you. I'm me enough to function, at least."

Freelorn hastily cast around for something else to talk about. The lane had widened into a road of a size to drive cattle down, and was well tracked and rutted. "Been a lot of traffic here, I'd say."

"For this time of year, yes." Segnbora gazed up at the town. "How many days in Spring this year?"

"Ninety-three," Herewiss said. "A Moon and a day till Midsummer. Why?"

"Just wondering. . . . Used to be my mother and father would start up for Darthis now, to do Midsummer's in the city with the rest of the Houses. We used to pass this way. But we haven't done the trip since they built the inn at Chavi. My father started having trouble with his legs. It was arthritis, and he couldn't take the long rides anymore." Suddenly she missed him terribly, in spite of the poor understanding he'd had of her.

"You know this place, then," Herewiss was saying. "That's a help."

She nodded, blinking back unexpected tears. "They'll be glad to see players. Not many come down here, especially after the bad weather sets in. They probably haven't been entertained since last summer." She glanced at Freelorn. "If things are as bad in Arlen as they are here. . . don't overcharge them, okay? From the look of the fields, this year's harvest isn't going to be any better than the last."

Freelorn nodded. Good harvests were a king's responsibility. Bad ones were a sign of trouble—like the empty throne in Arlen.

"I'll see to it," he said.

Segnbora nodded, pleased. Lorn was changing. In most respects he was still the same brash, adventure-hungry prince whom she loved so dearly, but increasingly he was overcome by thoughtful silences. When he spoke, there was a new sobriety in his tone.

She could sense why. The land through which they travelled was his by right, and its plight was desperate. The fields were dry and dusty; the people, over-taxed, were in rags. What prince could see this and fail to feel his heart swell with outrage, fail to feel his sword-hand itch for justice? There was a cause growing in Freelorn's mind, and it excited her.

Nevertheless, they were a long way from restoring him to his throne. They were so few, after all, and had been away so long. . .

Indeed, it was months since they had heard any news of the kingdom. The usurper's authority would be well established by now. It was for that reason that Lorn had chosen the inconspicuous town of Chavi for their first real foray into civilization. Here, disguised as entertainers, they could gather intelligence without arousing suspicion.

(How about this?) Sunspark said. (The Goddess is walking down the road and She sees a duck—)

They rode up to the town's rough fieldstone-and-mortar walls and were readily admitted. Chavi was much as Segnbora remembered it. The town's central square was stone-paved, surrounded by earth and fieldstone houses with soundly thatched roofs. A few, though, still had turf roofs, with here and there a scamp flower growing. Men drying their hands on dishtowels and young women with floury hands came to the windows, attracted by the sound of hooves on cobbles.

Up at the front of the line of riders, Dritt unslung his tim-

brel and began banging it earnestly, calling their wares:
"Songs and stories, tall tales! Shivers and chuckles, sleepless
nights, horrors and heartthrobs, deaths and delights! Mim-
icry, musicry, tragedy, comedy—"

A small crowd began to gather. Dritt began juggling two
knives and a lemon, breaking the rhythm occasionally by
catching the lemon in his mouth, and making puckery faces
when he let go of it. Harald was strumming changes on Segnbora's lute, and angling it so the torchlight from the cressets
by the inndoor would catch the mother-of-pearl inlay.

Herewiss dismounted, pulled the saddle off Sunspark, and
snapped his fingers. The stallion disappeared, replaced by a
great white hound of the kind that runs with the Maiden's
Hunting. The fayhound danced once about Herewiss on its
hind legs—bringing *oooh*s and *aaaah*s from the audience, for
upright it stood two feet taller than he did—then, at his clap,
it sat up most prettily and begged. At another clap it bowed
to the audience, grinning with its huge jaws. At a fourth clap
it changed to a tree that creaked and groaned as if a wild wind
tore at it; then to a huge serpent that coiled around Herewiss
and tried to squeeze the life out of him, and finally to a buck
unicorn.

A delighted cheer went up from the crowd, the kerchiefed
ladies and dusty-britched men applauding such illusion as
they had only heard of before. Man and unicorn held their
tableau, while Moris turned handsprings on the stones, and
Freelorn went inside to dicker with the innkeeper for the
night's room and board.

Not long afterward Lorn emerged, and gestured to the
crowd for silence. He was wearing the very slight crease of
frown that was all he allowed himself when disturbed in pub-
lic. "Kind gentlemen, good ladies," he said, "we'll begin our
evening's entertainment an hour after sunset. Please join us,
one and all."

The crowd in the street, murmuring appreciations, began
to disperse. Herewiss stood up and dusted himself off.

"Everything all right?" he said to Freelorn, noticing that
faint crease of worry.

"Yes," Freelorn said, in the same tone of voice he would
have used to say "no." "The innkeeper worries me, though."

"He's stingy?"

"No. We hardly had to bargain, he gave right in. It's something about his manner—"

"Maybe he was busy."

Freelorn shrugged. "Could be—the place is lively inside. Come on, I want a bath before dinner."

They stabled the horses, including Sunspark, who wanted to indulge its fondness for oats but promised to follow later.

The inn itself, the "Yale and Fetlock," was a long, low, battered-looking place of fieldstone with a weedy turf roof and a rammed dirt floor. The main room was smoky and full of people, all in the linens and woolens of townsmen. Some sat eating at long rough tables starred with rushlights. Others stood eating at sideboards, sat drinking in the middle of the room, or simply milled around. All were talking at the top of their lungs.

(Sweet Immanence,) Hasai said, sitting up in alarm behind Segnbora's eyes and looking out at the jostly drinkers' dance, (what's being decided here?)

(What?)

A—memory now surfaced, but of a sight she had never seen. In a stony deserted vale, Dragons, a great crowd of them, moved among one another in a precise and graceful pattern. It was *nn's'raihle,* Convocation—sport and ceremony and family fight and celebration all at once, the form of disagreement and resolution that Dragons found the most elegant and delightful.

(Oh,) Segnbora said, seeing the likeness to *nn's'raihle* in the tense movement in the room. (No, *mdaha,* this is social. They'll talk about whatever's happening, but they won't be making any decisions here.)

(How can they all abrogate their responsibility like that?) Hasai said, uneasy. (You all live here; how can you not act to run the world?)

(Uh—) Segnbora stalled, watching Freelorn. He had somehow already found a mug of ale, and was shouting in an old man's ear, "Ei, grand'ser, what's all the pother for?"

"Reavers!" the gaffer shouted back, and started telling of incursions to the south in Wasten and Nestekhai.

(Well?)

She breathed out, wondering what to say. (Uh. Hasai, most humans are empowered only to make decisions regarding themselves—or those close to them. They don't sit down, have an argument about something and then make a decision by which all humans will be bound. They would never all agree—)

(Then how do you get this world to work? How do you get anything accomplished?) Hasai said, bewildered.

Segnbora shook her head. "Done" didn't translate well; "do" and "be" seemed to be the same word in Dracon—*stihé.* (That will take time to explain . . .)

(Never mind, then. I see that there are more important matters to be concerned with. These incursions by the Reavers . . . are they close by, do you think?)

Segnbora made a face. (Too close. I wish we were farther north. But we dare not be; we would arouse too much curiosity there. Excuse me, Hasai. I've got to get ready for our show—)

(Certainly.)

She found the innkeeper. He was a knifeblade of a man, all grin and nervous energy. Segnbora could see that he would have made a quick business of the dickering. She got a mug of rough cider from him, and went to her bath.

Scrubbed and dressed in her worn but serviceable black gown with the tai-Enraesi crest on one shoulder, she went back to the common room and began talking to the patrons, assessing their mood, asking for requests. Just the sound of their voices gave her pleasure. They spoke in the old reassuring South Darthene accent that had been her mother's. It was a rich speech, slow, broad and full of archaisms. "Maistress," the slow-smiling, staid-faced townsfolk called her. "Aye, gaffer, tha'st hit it," she would drawl back, and they would laugh together.

She found Freelorn and Herewiss and the others at the best table by the central hearth, and sat down with them to a meal of aggressively garlicked lamb and buttered turnips, baked bannocks, and a soft, sharp sheep's-milk cheese to spread on them.

Freelorn, reviling the vintage of the cool white potato wine that had been brought up for them from the ice-cellar, nevertheless drank off three cups one after another, and by mistake almost drank the Goddess's cup as well. Lang gave Segnbora a nudge, and they traded glances. Freelorn had been in a mood like this the night he had gotten them all chased out of Madeil, the night Segnbora ran across him.

"It's all right, I think," she whispered.

Herewiss took the wineflask gently away from his loved and forestalled his protests by saying, "Who's performing first?"

This started the predictable argument, punctuated with exclamations of, "I need more practice!"; "You are *too* in good voice, I heard you in the outhouse!"; "Oh, don't be a coward!"; "I'm a coward, huh, then *you* go first!"

Segnbora groped under the table for the lute, causing more exclamations. She winked at Lang and pulled her chair over by the hearth. Behind her, as she tuned the lute's slack ela-string, the fire leaped, roaring up the chimney. There was a momentary hush close to the hearth, then intrigued whispers. The fire had acquired eyes.

"Thank you," she said, stroking the lute. "This is how it was," she said. That had been the storyteller's opening line from time immemorial. The quiet spread far back in the room. "There was a queen who would not die—"

It was a relative's story, and an old favorite of hers: the tale of Efmaer d'Seldun tai-Earnési, the first woman to be both Queen of Darthen and a Rodmistress.

In the fourth year of Efmaer's reign came an outbreak of lunglock fever. Efmaer did what she could to treat those of the royal household who were ill, but the Fire was of no avail. Soon she caught the malady herself. There was bitter mourning then, for under Efmaer's rule the land had prospered as never before. When finally she fell into the unconsciousness that precedes death, her attendants stole weeping from her rooms, leaving her to die peacefully in the night.

But none of them knew their Queen's determination. It wasn't yet her time to die. When she suddenly found herself standing before the open Door into Starlight, and felt the forces at her back pushing her toward it, Efmaer rebelled. She caught at the black doorsills and hung over the starry abyss by ten straining fingers. Peace and the last Shore awaited her

at the bottom of the darkness, but Efmaer would have none
of them. She hung on.

When her tearful attendants slipped into her bedchamber
in the morning to prepare her body for the pyre, they found
her not dead, but sleeping. She looked drawn and fever-
wasted, but the sickness was broken. In her hand, clutched
tight, was a long sharp splinter of darkness—a broken-off
piece of the Door.

Later, when Efmaer was well again, she wrought the splinter into a sword. Skádhwë, it was called in Darthene, "Dark-
harm." It would cut anything, stone or steel or soul, and many
were Efmaer's deeds with it across the breadth of Darthen and
down the length of her reign. And if anyone spoke in fear to
Efmaer because she had cheated Death at its own Door, the
Queen would laugh, unworried, certain the Shadow would
never bother avenging so small a slight.

Whether she was right no one could surely say, for Efmaer's
loved, Sefeden, killed himself, and his soul passed into Meni
Auardhem, into Glasscastle, to which go suicides and those
weary of life.

Then Efmaer grew frightened, for Sefeden knew her inner
Name; and therefore his soul could bind her to this world
when it was time to pass onward and be reborn. In haste
Efmaer rode to Barachael, and climbed Mount Adínë, above
which Glasscastle appeared at times of sunset and crescent
Moon and Evenstar.

There was at that time no way for one still in the body to
cross to the castle. The souls of the dead and the minds of the
mad found their way across with no need of a physical road.
It would have been easy for Efmaer to attempt the crossing
to Glasscastle in a bird's shape, or as a disembodied soul, but
she was no fool. The terrible magics of the place would have
warped her own wreaking out of shape and killed her. Yet she
had to get into Glasscastle; yet she could not get into Glasscastle.

For some people this would have been a problem. But
Efmaer waited for the time of three Lights, when the castle
faded into being. When it was fully there, she drew Skádhwë
and smote the stone of Adínë with it, opening a great rent in

the mountain, like a wound. With her Fire, Efmaer brought about the chief wreaking of her lifetime, singing the mountain's blood out of its wound, drawing out the incomparable iron of the great Eisargir lodes, tempering it in Flame and passion, hammering it with ruthless song into a blue-steel bridge that arched up to the Castle, fit road for a mortal's feet.

When had she wrought the bridge, she climbed it. She came to the crystal doors of Glasscastle and passed them, searching for Sefeden to get her Name back from him. But she did not come out. And at nightfall Glasscastle vanished into its eternal twilight, until the next time of three Lights in the world . . .

"And from that day to this," she said at last, unnerved to feel the tears coming, "no one has been so bold as to say they have seen Efmaer d'Seldun among the living or the dead. With her, Skádhwë passed out of life and into legend; and in the years since the Queen's disappearance, cheating Death has gone out of style. . . ."

The applause embarrassed her, as usual. She was glad to get out of what was now a very hot chair, and give place to Dritt and Moris and their juggling. Someone pushed a cup of cold wine into her hand. She took it gratefully and made her way to the back of the room, wiping her eyes as surreptitiously as she could.

"Smoke," she said to Lang as she came up beside him.

"Mmm-hmm."

Together they held up the wall awhile, leaning on one another's shoulder and watching Moris and Dritt juggle objects the audience gave them: beerpots, platters, clay pipes, truncheons, rushlight holders. Nothing fell, nothing at all.

"I can't believe it!" Lang whispered. "Did all that practicing actually pay off?"

"Not a chance," Segnbora whispered back. "I smell Fire. Herewiss threw a wreaking over them. I doubt they'll be able to drop even a *hint* until it breaks."

Freelorn came toward them through the crowd, with another cup of wine in his hand.

"Lorn," Segnbora said softly as he joined them, "just you watch it. Don't get sozzled."

"Yes, mother."

Segnbora settled back against the wall again and went back to watching the jugglers, particularly poor Moris, who had just been handed a full winejug to add to the other objects being juggled. He was giving it a look such as the King gave the Maiden when he had come to beg one of the hares She was herding. Glancing back at Lorn to see his reaction, Segnbora saw that he wasn't paying attention. He was watching someone off to one side, out of the hearthlight, eyes wide with admiration.

A blocky man moved and Segnbora could see over his shoulder. Past him, there, a small figure slipped out of her cloak, accepted a cup from the passing barmaid and raised it to her lip, looking over the rim in Freelorn's direction. She was a short woman with close-cropped hair of a very fair blonde, small bright eyes like a bird's, a mouth that quirked up at one corner—

Segnbora froze for a breath, two breaths, watching the light from a wall-cresset catch in the butter-blonde hair, giving its owner a halo. (Tegánë,) she said silently, fighting hard to keep her delight off her face. Her loved from those long-ago days at the Precincts—here! (You're a long way from home: is Wyn keeping supper hot for you?)

('Berend? Are you here!) The face across the room didn't change a bit, but Segnbora heard the old familiar laughter, sounding all the more real for being silent. (Now I see! 'Berend, you—!)

(Me what? What are you doing here?) She bowed her head over her cup, needing the darkness to hide the smile that wouldn't stay in.

(I was told to come. I dreamed true last night. She told me, 'I know your troubles and your questions. Go quickly to Chavi and you'll find answers.' I used the Kings' Door, and a mile away I smelled so much Fire that—oh 'Berend, I'm so glad for you!)

(Not me, Tegánë.) She flicked a mind-glance at Freelorn. (It's this one's loved.)

(You mean—) Eftgan's emotions swung rapidly from embarrassment to incredulity. (Then that uproar in the Power we all felt last week *was* someone donating to the Fane! And that story I got from the Brightwood people about a *man* focusing—)

(It's true,) Segnbora said, and leaned back against the wall, weak from the backwash of Eftgan's excitement.

Moris and Dritt finished their juggling, amid much applause. There was no opportunity to go to Eftgan, however, for at that moment Herewiss walked in through the door from the stableyard and took his place by the hearth. The room quieted.

Herewiss didn't bother with the lengthy introduction that some sorcerers used to assure that their illusions would take root in the spectators' minds. Nor did he bother with spells. He just sat back in the chair, one arm leaning casually on his long sheathed sword. "My gentlemen, my ladies," he said, "a little sorcery."

It was a great deal more than that, but since no Fire showed there was no way for the audience to tell. They chuckled appreciatively when tankards and plates engaged in a stately aerial sarabande in the middle of the room. They clapped when one empty table shook itself like a sleepy dog, got up and began stumping around the room on its legs. They hooted with pleased derision when the big rough fieldstones in the fireplace all suddenly grew mouths and began talking noisily about the things they had seen in their time, some of which made for very choice gossip.

When finally all the flames in the rooms shot up suddenly, swirled together in the empty air and coalesced into a bright-feathered bird that hung upside down by one foot from the chandelier and croaked, "I've got it! The Goddess is walking down the street and She meets this duck . . ." the storm of laughter and applause became deafening.

Not even Eftgan's composure remained unshattered. "My Goddess," she whispered, and from clear across the room Segnbora could feel her smothering down the Flame that was trying to leap from her Rod in response to the Fireflow Herewiss was letting loose.

A good sorcerer would have had no trouble producing such effects by illusion; but these were actual objects moving around, briefly alive and self-willed. Normally it would have taken two or three Rodmistresses working in consort to produce even one of the transformations taking place—but there sat Herewiss all by himself, looking like a child enjoying a new toy.

The table had sneaked up behind one tall woman and was nibbling curiously at her tunic, like a browsing goat. The stones had begun singing rounds. Sunspark had forgotten by now that it ought to have been holding onto the chandelier, and was simply suspended upside down in midair, getting laughs for jokes without punch lines attached.

(How is he *doing* that?!) Eftgan said, bespeaking Segnbora very quietly, so as not to distract Herewiss.

(Most of these things were alive once,) Herewiss said silently, not moving or looking up. (It's just a matter of reminding them how it was. Mistress, I can taste your Fire but I can't place you—though there's something familiar about your pattern. You know my loved, perhaps?)

(The pattern might be familiar prince) the small woman said, as two chairs put their arms about each other and begin dancing in a corner, muttering creaky endearments, (because you and I have met. At Lidika fields you jumped in front of a Reaver with a crossbow and took the quarrel for me while I was having trouble with a swordfight—)

The hearthstone snorted as if in great surprise, then settled into a bout of ratchety snoring. (Eftgan! The Queen's grace might have given me warning!)

(I didn't want to disturb your concentration, prince, though it appears I worried for nought. But pardon me if I leave off complimenting you for the moment. I have business here, and you're part of it, I've been told. If I rework the wreaking on the Kings' Door, can you come with me to Barachael tonight?)

(Depends on Freelorn, madam.) All the candles on tables and in sconces tied themselves in knots and kept on burning. (We're on business of our own, and I have oaths in hand that may even supersede the oaths of the Brightwood line to Darthen.)

(Oh, *that* business. I think your business and mine will go well enough together.)

(Then we'll talk when I've finished.)

At that Lorn quietly left the shadow of his doorway, heading across the common room—ostensibly to get another drink—and "noticed" Eftgan in what appeared to be the fashion of one potential bed-partner noticing another. He paused beside her, bent toward the pretty woman, and with a smile that any onlooker would have found unmistakable, said in her ear, "Since it's *my* throne we're talking about, madam, and *my* country, I'd best be there too. Don't you think?"

Eftgan smiled back, the same smile. "Sir," she whispered, "that sounds good to me."

The room had become such a merry hurly-burly of laughter and clapping that saying anything and having it heard was becoming impossible. Freelorn went off for his drink, leaving Eftgan to say silently, and with some diffidence, ('Berend, have you taken a mind-hurt recently? There's a darkness down there that didn't used to be. Is there anything I can do?)

(Dear heart, I don't think so,) she said silently. (I'm told the change is permanent.)

(You mean *She*—)

(No. Well, not directly. If you want to take a look . . .)

(Yes.)

Across the room, their eyes caught and held, then dropped again as their minds fell together in that companionable meld that had always come so easily.

Segnbora saw and felt, in a few breaths' space, a rush of images that were Eftgan's surface memories of the past four years. Initiation into the royal priesthood, her brother's death, and her own investiture as Queen. The hot morning spent hammering out her crown in the great square of Darthis, alone and unguarded, wondering whether someone would come out of the gathered crowd to kill her, as was her people's right if they felt her reign would not be prosperous. Worries about Arlen and the usurper who sat in power there, making raids on her borders. Marriage to her loved, Wyn s'Heleth. Childbirth, midnight feedings, Namings, ceremonies, the rites of life, all tumbled together with the lesser and greater drudgeries of queenship: mornings in court-justice, evenings spent in the difficult wreakings that were necessary to buy her land temporary reprieve from the hunger and death creeping toward its borders.

There was more. Border problems. Reavers gathering in ever greater numbers on the far side of the mountain passes, pouring through them almost as if in migration. The loss of communications with numerous villages in the far south— suggesting that their Rodmistresses were dead. The loss of one of her best intelligencers here in Chavi, some weeks back. The sudden, urgent true-dream that showed Eftgan plainly the reason for all the Reaver movements of late. This last discovery had been more shocking than anything the Queen had been willing to imagine.

She had been so shocked, in fact, that she had not once, but several times, opened and used the Kings' Door, the dangerous worldgate in the Black Palace at Darthis. She had done so tonight, and so here she sat in faded woolens and patched cloak and embroidered white shirt, like any countrywoman with a pot of beer. Yet her eyes were open for trouble, and for the answers she had been promised. Her Rod was sheathed and ready at her side.

Segnbora touched lightly on all these things, meanwhile letting Eftgan do what she didn't trust the *mdeihei* to do: turn over her memories one by one. When they were done, Segnbora saw Eftgan stare down inside her at a shape burning in iron and diamond. Hasai stared back up, bowed his head and lifted his wings in calm greeting, then went back about his own concerns, singing something low and solemn to the rest of the *mdeihei*.

When their glances rested in one another's eyes again, Segnbora and Eftgan both breathed a sigh of relief at the end of the exertion.

(He's very big,) Eftgan said. (And how many others are in there?)

(Maybe a couple hundred. I tried counting and had to give up. They don't count the way we do, and I could never get our tallies to agree. Tegánë, what's bringing all these Reavers down on us? You saw something—)

(I did.) Eftgan was profoundly disturbed inside. (Part of the reason is storms. Their weather is worsening. It was never very good to begin with, and now the Reaver tribes farthest south are faced with a choice. Either they move north or freeze even at Midsummer. The tribes already close to us are feeling the pressure. There are more people hunting those lands than the available game can support. Thinking Fyrd are driving them too. But worse than that—)

(What could be worse!)

(Cillmod is in league with them,) Eftgan said, sour-faced, (and the Shadow is directing them all.)

Segnbora stared, then took a long drink to hide her nervousness.

(There's worse yet to come,) the Queen said. (My Lady tells me that a great shifting and unbalancing of Powers is about to occur in the area around Barachael during the dark of the next Moon. On one hand, Reavers are gathering on the far side of the Barachael Pass, as if for a great incursion. On the other—) The Queen took a drink. (On the other, we're due for a night of three Lights shortly. And that means that Glasscastle will appear. Now, what might go into Glasscastle doesn't concern me. What might come out of it *does*. Unhuman things, monsters, have been summoned out of there before by sorcerers of foul intent—)

(But who in the Kingdoms would do something like that? That whole area is soaked with old blood! Nine chances out of ten, a sorcery would go askew—)

(No one in the Kingdoms would attempt such a thing,) Eftgan said. (But I have other news. The dying thought of a certain Rodmistress managed to reach me, even though her bones had just been turned to flour inside her.)

"What!" Segnbora said aloud, in utter shock. She drank again to silence herself.

(The Reavers have got sorcerers now. Apparently someone has gotten a few of them over their fear of magic. It is that individual, who surely has no knowledge or concern for sorcerous balances, who worries me. Think what horrors he might call forth from Glasscastle! He could easily protect the Reaver incursion and destroy our defense—what then?)

Segnbora thought of Herewiss's dream, of mountains falling on mountains, and blood on the Moon, and said nothing.

(I need him,) said Eftgan, catching the images, which were in agreement with those in her own true-dream. (I can't be in all the places I must be, just now. One of my other spies tells me that Cillmod and some of his mercenaries are about to attack my granaries at Orsvier. I must be there to lead the defense. But Glasscastle and Barachael also have to be protected, and it will take Fire of an extraordinary level to manage that. Up until now, I thought I was the only one in Darthen who had achieved that level. Now—) She looked over toward where Herewiss stood by the hearth, grinning at the applause he was receiving for his "sorcery." (I can't tell you how glad I am to be surpassed,) Eftgan said. (Especially at a time like this, when everything seems to be happening at once.)

(Queen,) Segnbora said, (you say that everything's happening at once . . . well, he's one of the reasons.)

Eftgan nodded, understanding. Then, as Herewiss stepped away from the hearth, she crossed glances with him, a "let's-talk" look.

(I'll see you later, Tegánë,) Segnbora said, putting her drink aside, and headed for the door that gave onto the back of the inn.

Lang was hurrying in as she stepped out.

"You on now?" Segnbora said.

"Uh-huh. Wish me luck."

"You won't need it. Except maybe to keep yourself from being knocked unconscious by the money they'll throw."

Lang smiled. "Where're you headed? —Oh, my Goddess," he said. Before Segnbora could say anything about either the Queen or her own increasingly urgent need to find a friendly bush, Lang had spotted Eftgan. "*She's* here? After seven years, she finally tracked down poor Dritt and Moris!"

"Ssssh. Tell the two of them to keep mum; something's on the spit, I'm not sure what yet."

Lang said nothing, only touched her shoulder gently as she went past, out into the alley and the cool air.

A shiver went down her back. It was more than just a reaction to the coolness outside, after the heat and smoke of the inn. *Cillmod in league with the Shadow?* She drew up her gown to keep it off the wet ground, and went down the alley behind the inn, looking for a drier spot to take care of her business. The alley ended in a cobbled street that led to the town's fields through an unguarded postern gate.

Quietly Segnbora walked down the street, patting Charriselm once to make sure it was loose in the sheath, unbarred the gate, and slipped out. She relieved herself in the shadow of one of the ubiquitous hawthorn hedges, then stood stretching awhile, listening to the night and letting herself calm down. Far behind her, the sound of Lang's baritone escaped through the inn's back door, following the lighter notes of the lute through the reflective minor chords of "The Goddess's Riding":

> ". . . But if I speak with yon Lady bright,
> I wis my heart will bryst in three;
> Now shall I go with all my might
> Her for to meet beneath Her tree. . . ."

"Tegáně," Segnbora whispered, smiling. *Moon-bright,* the nickname said in Darthene. Eftgan had liked it; she had never been terribly fond of her right name. In fact, she had returned the favor, turning *segnbora,* "standard-bearer," into *'berend,* a verb. It meant "swift-rushing": impetuous, always in a hurry, sometimes too much of one—as when the Maiden had let Death into the worlds by accident.

And as their names, so they had been together while they were in love: Eftgan swinging slow and steady through her moods, like the Moon, waxing and waning, giving and withholding; Segnbora pushing, hurrying, urging, not sure what she wanted but not willing to wait long for it.

The senior Rodmistresses had paired them off to work together in hopes that Eftgan's Fire, unusually intense for a sixteen year old, might influence Segnbora's enough to make her focus. They expected the play-sharing that usually took place between work partners to make the two novices' patterns match more closely. No one, however, had expected these two, who were so unlike—one a tall, loud, spindly daughter of hedge-nobility, the other a small, compact, quiet daughter of the Eagle—to fall in love. . . .

Segnbora thought of the day Eftgan had had to leave the

Precincts. It was sudden. Her brother Bryn had been killed by Fyrd while hunting.

"They're going to make me be Queen," Eftgan had said, bitter, standing in the green shade with her face averted from Segnbora. She had been trying not to cry.

"Tégané—"

" 'Berend, you can't do anything for me. Any more than I've been able to do anything for you, all this while. Perhaps its better that I'm leaving now. You can't focus, and I can't be happy around you using the Fire and watching you suffer while I do wreakings. If this kept on much longer, we'd be hating each other."

This was the truth, and it reduced anything Segnbora could have said in reply to a meaningless noise. The two of them stood in the shade, hardly able to look at one another, and made their good-byes. Each laid a kiss in the palm of the other's hand, the restrained and formal farewell between kinsfolk of the Forty Houses.

Then Eftgan turned away and vanished among the green leaves of the outer Precincts; and Segnbora went in deeper, and didn't come out till her soul was cried dry, a matter of some days. . . .

Now Segnbora stood bemused for a moment, then realized that a dark head seemed to loom just over her shoulder, though of course there was nothing between her and the stars of late spring.

(When you forget me, when you let us be one, it can be this way,) Hasai said, dispassionately. (Do you prefer discomfort, apartness?)

She almost said yes, but held her peace. "It was a very private memory," she said quietly.

(*Sdaha*, you still don't understand. You must be who you have been to be who you are.)

Segnbora shook her head, weary. *Every time I think I understand the* mdeihei, *I find I don't at all.* . . . She looked out across the field into which she had ducked when she came through the hedge. It was tall with green hay that whispered in the starlight. On an impulse she tucked her robe up into her swordbelt and started across it, wading waist-deep, enjoying the sensations: the rasp and itch of the hay against her legs, the darkness, the cool wind.

Hasai said nothing, his mind resting alongside hers, tasting the night as she did—

She stopped short in the middle of the field. Something teased at her undersenses, a whiff of wrongness that was out of tune with the clean night. She stood there with eyes closed to "see" better—

—and *there,* sharp as a cymbal-clash, came the clear perception of a place just to the east that felt like an unhealed wound. A hidden thing meant to stay that way, and failing.

(Hasai?)

(I'm here. I feel it also.)

(Come on.)

Seven

"You are cruel," Efmaer said. "More cruel than any legend has ever told."

"No more cruel than humans to themselves, who keep hope as a precious jewel."

Then the Shadow vanished, and Efmaer filled the air where It had been with curses, and rode away after the soul of her loved . . .

(*Efmaer's Ride,* traditional: part the Second)

Segnbora unsheathed Charriselm and went off eastward through the standing hay. Another hedge loomed up before her, without stile or hedge-gate. With Charriselm she cut an opening, making certain that it would be too small for a cow to escape through in the morning, and squeezed through.

The sour mind-stench she had smelled got stronger by the second, becoming so terrible that Segnbora wondered how she could have missed it from fifty miles away, let alone from the town. At the edge of the field the ground under her feet seemed to be burning with it. Her inner hearing buzzed and roared as if two powerful hands were choking her. She stopped and held still, forcing herself not to gag. The stench was coming from beneath an old yew with peeling bark and drooping branches.

She walked under the tree and went to her knees. The fallow ground had been plowed almost up to the tree trunk. The furrows lay neat and seemingly undisturbed, yet when Segnbora thrust her hands into the still soft ground and turned it over, she sat back on her heels, sick to her stomach and sicker at heart. There is no mistaking the smell of a grave, especially a shallow one.

Nor was it the only grave. When she found strength to stand again, the death-taint led her to four others scattered around the edges of the field. All were deeper and better concealed, and all were older: the oldest perhaps three months old, the newest about three weeks.

So much for Eftgan's messenger, Segnbora thought, standing over the last grave. From the intelligencer's grave and three others, the souls were long flown, despite the brutality of their deaths. But from the one under the yew tree came a sensation of vague, scattered, helpless loss. There were two souls trapped there, shattered by their murder, trying to coalesce in time to find the Door into Starlight before the strength to pass it was lost.

Segnbora swore bitterly, torn with pity for the struggling dead and her own inability to do anything for them. Sorcery has no power over the opening or closing of that final Door. She knew the protocols for the laying of the dead, but without Fire they were useless to her. But Herewiss, or Eftgan—

She headed back for town at a run, pausing outside the postern gate to remove the sticktights and hay blades from her clothes. The inn's common room was, if possible, noisier than it had been. There were perhaps one hundred people there, laughing, joking, singing—Segnbora's hair stood up at the thought that any one of them might be a murderer several times over.

She found Freelorn relieving the barmaid of another bottle of potato wine, and swung him aside. "Lorn, where's Herewiss gone?"

"He's still out talking to—" Lorn stopped short of saying the Queen's name, then looked more closely at Segnbora. "You're shaking!"

"Lorn, never mind. Smile! There's something very wrong and we're not supposed to know about it. Take your time but find Herewiss—"

"—so if the others agree, we'll go to Barachael," Herewiss's voice said suddenly as he came up behind Freelorn from the other side. "It's as good a place to hide as any, and it's a lot closer to Arlen than we are now . . . What's wrong?" he said, looking at Segnbora. His underhearing brought him an answer that made his eyes go wide with shock. "Show us," he said. "Lorn, go out the front way. I'll take the side. By the postern gate?"

Segnbora nodded and went out the way she had come, doing her best to take her time. Lorn and Herewiss were through the postern and into the hay ahead of her. She tied up her gown again and hurried after.

"Eftgan's gone to readjust her Door," Herewiss said when

she reached them. "It may take her a little while—seven people, six horses, and Sunspark are a larger group than usually uses that gateway." He lowered his voice. "I think she's ready to back Lorn against Cillmod, openly. She'll give us the details tomorrow, at Barachael."

"That's wonderful," Segnbora said, "but with the problems she's been having she's hardly in a position to leave Barachael for a campaign in Arlen."

"True. However, I believe I can help her, and thus free her to help us in return. You see, the Reavers are pouring through Chaelonde Pass, and it's a simple enough matter to close that avenue—"

"But the Queen's Rodmistresses have been doing illusion-wreakings there for years," Segnbora objected. "They're no longer strong enough. People have been dying in that pass for centuries, and the built-up negative energies are enough to ruin even the best Rodmistress's work."

"Oh, I'm not planning mere illusions. I'm planning something more powerful, and less subtle: a sealing."

"You mean physically closing the pass?" Freelorn said, stunned. "Shaking down a few mountains?"

"That's right."

"You call that *simple*?"

"Simple, yes. And dangerous, too. It will require much Power, but then it's also less likely that something will go wrong . . ."

They slowed as they approached the spot Segnbora had sensed before. Herewiss looked at her as he let drop what he had been saying. A long moment passed.

"How long have the people in the grave been dead?" he asked her.

"*Grave?*"

"A week or so, I think. They're weak. They were getting along in years, I believe, and the shock of their death was considerable. You have the protocols—"

"I have them."

"Protocols, *what* protocols?" Freelorn said.

"For raising the dead," Herewiss said. "Stay close, Lorn, I'm going to need you . . . Oh, sweet Mother," he added as

the sour smell of murder hit him. Segnbora was already tearing—the psychic residue of violence became not easier, but
harder to handle with exposure.

"Goddess, what *is* that," Freelorn said, and coughed.

Both Segnbora and Herewiss looked at him, surprised.

"You smell something?" Herewiss said.

"Don't you? Like a charnel pit." Freelorn coughed again.

Herewiss looked most thoughtful, for the graves were covered and the night air was sweet even here; the stench was
purely a matter of the undersenses.

They came to the yew tree, and stopped. Quickly, for the
smell was now overwhelming, Herewiss reached over his
shoulder and drew Khávrinen. Its Fire, suppressed all
through the evening, now flared up, a hot blue-white.

Concerned, Segnbora threw a look over her shoulder at the
walls of Chavi.

"Only our own people and Eftgan will be able to see the
Fire," Herewiss said, quiet-voiced, slipping into the calm he
would need for his wreaking. "Now then . . ."

The wavering of Flame about Khávrinen grew less hurried
as its master calmed, yet there was still a great tension in every
curl and curve of the Flame. With the tip of the sword, Herewiss drew a circle around the tree, the graves, Freelorn, and
Segnbora. Where Khávrinen's point cut the fallow ground,
Fire remained, until at the circle's end it flowed into itself, a
seamless circle of blue Flame that licked and wreathed upward. Finally, when the three of them had stepped inside the
circle, Herewiss thrust Khávrinen span-deep into the soft dirt,
laid his hands, one over the other, on the sword's fiery hilt,
and began the wreaking. *"Erhn tai 'mis kuithen, ástehae sschür;
úsven kes uibren—"*

The words were in a more ancient dialect of Nhàired than
any Segnbora had been taught. Even in Nhàired, which held
within it many odd rhythms, the scansion of this wreaking-
rhyme was bizarre. Freelorn was fidgeting, watching his loved
with unease as Herewiss reassured the trembling yew and the
murder-stained earth that he was about to end their pain, not
make it worse. He stood and called the Power up out of him,
sweating. The circle's Fire reached higher, twisting, wreath-

ing, matching the interlock of word with word, of thought with rhyme—

Herewiss poured out the words, poured out the Flame, profligate. Power built and built in the circle until it numbed the mind, until the eyes saw nothing anywhere but blue Fire, and a man-shaped shadow at the heart of it, the summoner.

Segnbora was overwhelmed. She did the only thing safe to do—turned around inside herself and fled down to the dark place in search of Hasai. *His Power, he has too much! No one can have that much!* she thought. Once in her own depths she could see nothing but burning blue light, but at last she stumbled into Hasai and flung her arms around a hot, stony talon. Concerned, the Dragon lowered his head protectively over her.

Outside, after what seemed an eternity of blueness, tension ebbed. Segnbora dared to look out of herself again and saw the pillar of Fire that wreathed about Herewiss diminish slightly as he released his wreaking to seek outside the circle for the fragments of the murdered people's souls. He spoke on, in a different rhythm now, low and insistent, urging outward the unseen web the Fire had woven of itself, moving it as an ebb tide pushes a thrown net away from shore. When the web had drifted across the entire field, he reversed the meter of his poetry and began pulling it in again.

Segnbora swallowed hard. Light followed the blue-glittering weave; dusts and motes and sparkles drifted inward, small coalescing clouds of pallid light. They drifted inward faster now, coiling into two separate sources; they grew brighter and brighter, tightening to cores of light that pulsed in time with Herewiss's verse. A last sharp word from Herewiss, a last burst of blue light, dazzling—

The Fire of the circle died down to a twilight shimmer, though about Herewiss and Khávrinen, Flame still twined bright. Segnbora found herself looking at two solid-seeming people—a man, shorter than herself, middle-aged, stocky, with a blunt, worn face; a woman of about the same age, still shorter, but more slender for her height. They both looked weary and confused. Segnbora gazed at them pityingly in that first second or so, seeing strangers—

—and then knew them.

She could not move. " 'Kani, what happened? We were in bed . . ." the man said, looking at the woman with distress.

His voice, the voice that had frightened her, praised her, laughed with her. The woman turned to him. *Her* face. The sight of it made Segnbora weak behind the knees, as if struck by a deadly blow.

"Mother," she whispered.

"Hol, no," Welcaen said. "The innkeeper woke us up, he said the horses were loose—" She broke off, horrified by the memory. Segnbora was stunned. That beautiful, sharp, lively voice was dulled now, like that of anyone who died by violence. "They tricked us into coming out here," the voice continued, finally. "He had an axe. His wife had—"

Her husband's eyes hardened, a flash of life left. "Why did they bother with such illusions? We have no money—"

Herewiss stood without moving, although through her shock Segnbora saw him swallow four times before he could get his voice to work. "Sir," he said, "madam . . . It was no illusion that was wrought upon you."

"Hol," Segnbora's mother said, stepping forward to get a better look at Herewiss. She moved like a sleepwalker. "Hol, this isn't one of them—"

Holmaern looked not at Herewiss's face, but at his sword. "That's impossible. Men don't have Fire!" The words came with a flash of disbelief and scorn. Segnbora remembered too well his bitterness over the fact that, despite all the money he had spent, she had never focused.

"This man has it," her mother said, a touch of wonder piercing the sleepy sound of her voice. "Sir, did you save us?"

"Lady Welcaen," Herewiss said. "I didn't save you. Of your courtesy, tell me what brought you to the inn here."

"Reavers," she said, dreamy voiced, as if telling of a threat years and miles gone. "They came down through the mountains at Onther looking for food, and overran the farmsteads. We and a few of our neighbors had warning. We got away north before the burnings, and told our news here, to the innkeeper, so he could spread it among those of this town. And tonight he woke us up—"

Holmaern turned to his wife, slow realization changing his expression to a different kind of dullness. " 'Kani," he said. He reached out to touch her, but it was plain from his expression that she didn't feel as he expected her to. " 'Kani, we're dead."

Segnbora saw her mother's eyes go terrible with the truth. "Oh . . . but then . . . where is the last Shore?"

Herewiss stared down at Khávrinen, and Segnbora felt him calling up the Power again, a great wash of it. This time it took a strange and frightening shape, one she didn't know.

"I am the way," he said, speaking another's words for Her.

He let go of Khávrinen and lifted his arms, opening them to her mother and father. They gazed at him in wonder. Freelorn, across the circle, went pale. Segnbora trembled at the sight of him. Herewiss was still there as much as any of them, but within the outlines of his body the stars blazed, more brilliant than they had been even in Hasai's memory of the gulf between worlds.

Herewiss trembled too, but his voice was steady. "Who will be first?" he said.

Holmaern held Welcaen close. "Can't we go together?"

Herewiss shook his head sorrowfully. "I'm too narrow a Door," he said. "Besides, even at the usual Door, everyone goes through alone. . . ."

Husband and wife looked at one another. "We have a daughter," her mother said after a moment. She glanced around the field, but saw nothing. "Will you send her word—?"

Segnbora's heart turned over and broke inside her.

"Segnbora d'Welcaen tai-Enraesi is her name," her father said, and even through the dullness it came out proudly. "She was eastaway in Steldin last we heard. Please tell her . . . tell her that we love her."

"Come on, Hol," her mother said then. "We've got time to go."

Herewiss opened his arms. Welcaen moved into them, throwing a last glance at her husband on the threshold of true death. "I'll wait for you," she said.

Herewiss embraced her, and she was gone.

Next Holmaern stepped slowly forward. When he was still one pace away, however, he paused, a last glimmer of earthly concern showing in his eyes. He spoke to Herewiss. "Sir, you will tell her, won't you? She is my daughter, and although I have been slow to say so, she is very dear to me."

"Your message has already reached her," Herewiss assured him.

Holmaern looked relieved. With a nod of thanks, he gathered Herewiss close, passed through, and was gone.

Khávrinen's Fire went out, and the circle faded to a blue smolder and died. Beside his now-dark sword Herewiss went slowly to his knees, and sobbed once, bitterly.

"That's not the way it is supposed to be." He gasped again. "Lorn, it was supposed to be *life* I give—"

Freelorn went to him, and held him close. "And what kind of life would they have had, dead and on the wrong side of the Door?"

Segnbora stood still, seeing behind her eyes, with the immediacy that came of Hasai's presence, old lost times: summer mornings in Asfahaeg, rich with the smell of sunlight and the Sea; winter nights by the old hearthside in Darthis; afternoons weaving with her father, riding with her mother; laughter, anger, argument, joy, the sounds of life. She turned and walked away, back toward town.

The purpose behind her stride caught up with her at about the same time that Freelorn and Herewiss did, in the middle of the hayfield. They stopped her, looked at her as if expecting her to lapse again into a state of madness like that she had experienced after the Fane.

"Well? What's the problem?" she asked, her anger hot and quick.

"What are you going to do?" Freelorn asked warily.

Charriselm's grip was sweaty in her hand as she thought of the innkeeper—hurried, merry, sharp-faced, with eyes that wouldn't meet hers. "I'm going to kill someone," she said, and shook out of their grasp.

" 'Berend—" Freelorn said.

She ignored him, hurrying off through the hay. Didn't he realize that it wasn't only because of her parents that she had to do this? Lorn's people might easily have been the next victims, bringing—as might be thought—news from the South. She at least would have to be killed, since she wore the same arms as two others who were silenced, and was thus probably in search of them.

Behind her she could feel Fire stirring again. Herewiss had begun another wreaking. She understood why. He was a strategist. He would count it folly to kill a spy, and thus alert the spy's superiors to the fact that that someone had discovered the game they played. He was building around the innkeeper a wreaking that would later cause the man to believe he had murdered those whom he was duty-bound to murder, when in fact they would go on their way, unnoticed and unharmed. It was all perfectly sensible, and Segnbora despised the idea.

(My way is more efficient,) she said, silent and bitter. (He won't know what's happened to him until a second after I hit him, when he tries to move and falls over in two pieces. And as for his wife—)

She went quietly through the postern, expecting an empty street. Instead, Moris and Dritt were there. So was Harald, standing about silently with their horses. Lang had just joined them, along with Eftgan, who had her cloak about her shoulders and her unsheathed white Rod in her hand.

Segnbora would have brushed past the Queen to take care of her unfinished business in the inn, but Eftgan's hand on her arm, together with her look of deepening concern at the taste of Segnbora's mind, stopped Segnbora as if she had walked into a wall.

" 'Berend? *What happened?*"

Segnbora looked down at Eftgan's brown eyes, so like her mother's, and flinched away, unable to bear it.

"Oh, my Goddess," Eftgan said. "Herewiss?"

A breath's worth of silence sufficed for Herewiss to show Eftgan what Segnbora had found, what he had done for her parents, and the dream-wreaking he had woven and implanted in the innkeeper, and afterward in his wife.

"Can we get out of here now?" he said, sounding deadly tired. Sunspark paced to him in its stallion shape, and Herewiss leaned on it, sagging like a man near exhaustion. It looked at him in concern.

"Done," said the Queen, and gestured with her Rod at the ground where she stood. The wreaking she had been maintaining until they arrived leaped upward from the stone and wove itself on the air, a warp and weft of blue Fire that outlined a small squarish doorway. The doorway flashed completely blue for a moment and then blacked out—but the black was that of a different night, a long way off. The Door sucked in air. On the other side they could see smooth paving, a better road than that of the damp cobbles of Chavi.

"Hurry up," Eftgan said. "It's a strain to hold it for this many, and the Kings' Door is unpredictable."

One by one they went through, each leading a horse. Eftgan stood to one side of the Door, Flame running down her Rod and keeping the lintels alight. Lang stepped through before Segnbora, his eyes on her, looking worried. Numb, she followed him. The one step took her from the wet lowland air of Chavi, air stinking of death, into air colder, purer, but not entirely clean of the taste. Her ears popped painfully.

The night was perhaps an hour further along here; the stars had shifted. In one part of the sky they were missing entirely. She looked around the paved courtyard where Freelorn's people milled, among horses and men and women in the midnight blue of Darthen. Over the low northward wall she could see faintly, in the starshine, the valley where she had sometimes lived as a child, with the braided Chaelonde running through it. Many a time she had stood down there looking up at the place where she stood now—Sai khas-Barachael Fortress, the black sentinel perched on an outthrust root of one of the Highpeaks.

Dully, she looked southward to where the stars were blocked from the sky. Looming over khas-Barachael, shadowy dark below and pale with starlight above, the snows of Mount Adínë brooded, impassive and cruel.

"It's late," Freelorn was saying. "We'll meet in the morning, all of us. Meanwhile, does the Queen's hospitality extend to a drink?"

Segnbora saw to Steelsheen's stabling and made sure her

corncrib was full, then followed Lang (who seemed to be beside her every time she turned around) to a warmly lit room faced in black stone. There was hot wine, and she drank a great deal of it. The explanations went on and on around her, but she was never as dead to them as she wanted to be.

Snatches of conversation and random thoughts faded in and out of hearing, as they had when she had first come down from the Morrowfane. She would have welcomed Hasai's darkness to flee to again, but she couldn't find it. He and the *mdeihei* were, for once, *too* remote. They wanted nothing to do with her, the *mdeihei*. She was too familiar with the kind of death to which they couldn't admit. She was carrier of a contagion of terror and impossibility. The more she tried to approach, the more they fled her, afraid of any death in which one could lose oneself.

Somehow she found her way off to the tower room they had given her, and to bed. Lang was there too. He held her, and she clutched him, but she found no comfort in his presence. Her thoughts were full of graves, bare dirt, eyes that looked right through her. Her mind talked constantly, again and again making the most terrible admission a sensitive could make: *I never felt you die. I never felt it.*

Tears were a long time coming, but they found her at last; and Lang, more hero than she had ever been, held her and bore the brunt of her blows and cries and impotent rage. Bitterness and a shameful desire for vengeance; they were all still tangled in her at the end, but she knew at least she would be able to sleep. For tonight.

Over the bed and the room and the fortress, like a great weight, loomed the thought of Adíne, and a line from the old family rede, which now might have a chance to come true: *There will come a time of ice and darkness, and then the last of the tai-Enraesi will die. Flee the fate as you may, you shall know no peace until the blade finds your own heart, and lets the darkness in. . . .*

Darkness. That was the key. One Whose sign and chosen hiding place was darkness was coming after Herewiss and Freelorn. She had chosen to ride with them, and to defy It. And It hated defiance, and never failed to reward it with pain of one kind or another.

She could leave Lorn now, and her troubles would cease, or she could stay with him, and they would almost certainly get worse. The Dark One obviously had it in for her. But what could be worse than a head full of Dragons, and to suddenly find oneself orphaned, she couldn't imagine.

Beside her, Lang turned over and started to snore.

She lay there for a long time with the tears running down the sides of her face into her ears. And chose again.

Shadow, she thought at last, *it's war between us from now on. I'll die soon enough. But You won't get Lorn—or anybody else, if I can help it.*

The darkness about her teemed with silent, derisive laughter. She turned her back on it and went to sleep.

Eight

Kings build the bridges from earth to heaven. But it is their subjects' decision whether or not to cross—and if they do, there is no guaranteeing the nature of the result.

On the Royal Priesthood,
Arien d'Lhared

People who live in the Highpeaks find it easy to believe the old story that the Maiden creates the World anew, every day, for the sheer joy of it. Astonishing dawns come there. Later, the face of a mountain changes as the shadows swing across it, revealing a new countenance every quarter hour. Still later come sunsets that run blood down cornices of snow, or light a whole range as if from within, until it all seems one great burning opal. Then twilight dissolves everything, leaving only shadows where peaks have been; cut-out patches on the sky, from which the mischievous Maiden has removed the mountains so She can rework them for the next day.

Huddled in her cloak, Segnbora leaned on her elbows on a battlement of Sai khas-Barachael at dawn, watching the mountains come back. The Sun was up, though not yet visible past the eastern peaks. Beneath her Barachael valley was still hidden in shadow and morning mist. The valley was nearly circular. The walls broke only at the far northern end, where a quarter-arc of the circle was missing and the land sloped down northward toward the rest of Darthen. Khas-Barachael fortress stood on the northernmost spur of high ground, on the western side of the break, commanding a view of both the Darthene plains and the valley.

Segnbora gazed across the gap, though which the little braided Chaelonde River ran down from its glacier, toward the mountains that reached long spurs to each other and made the rest of the ring. First came Aulys, right across the gap, like an eagle with bowed head and drooping wings. South and west of it Houndstooth reared, smooth and polished-looking, and armed with avalanches. West of Hounds-

tooth, between it and the next mountain, was a shadowy spot
—the north end of the Eisargir Pass, through which Reavers
had been raiding for food and metal since time immemorial.
Then Eisargir himself, like a great stone rose unfolding with
his down-spiraling spurs. Westward again lay a low col or
saddle between mountains, over which looked red Tamien.
Then came rising ground that grew into the long northeast-
pointing Adínë massif.

Segnbora looked over her shoulder, scanning the long crest
line. It was scarred on both sides with old glacial cirques;
scraped-out bowls of stone. One such bowl was still full: the
South Face cirque beneath the lesser, southern peak of Adínë.
Ice spilled over from it to feed the glacial lake which in turn
fed the Chaelonde. Every now and then the morning stillness
would be broken by a remote groan or a huge crashing snap,
made tiny by distance, as the glacier calved off an iceberg into
the lake.

Above the glacier, and above the eminence of Sai khas-
Barachael two thousand feet above the valley floor, Mount
Adínë loomed like a crooked, ruined tower. Its greater peak
stood two miles higher than khas-Barachael and a sheer
league above town in the valley's depths. Segnbora shuddered, though whether from morning's cold or a feeling of
threat she didn't know. A breath later, the Sun rose through
the gap between Aulys and Houndstooth and touched on the
lesser Adínë summit. There, tiny and sharp, a line of something silvery glittered; the Skybridge, bright even against the
blinding white of the peak on which it stood.

Segnbora shuddered again, this time knowing why. Unconcerned, Hasai said from inside her, (We thought about living
there, once . . .)

(Under the bridge? I thought Dragons didn't care to live
where the shadowed powers are.)

(We don't. When we saw what happened at certain times of
year, we abandoned plans to make a Marchward there. Also
there are weaknesses in the valley, and we were afraid we
would disrupt the land if we worked as deep into that main
massif as we normally would.)

(This was how long ago?)

Hasai looked at his memories and counted the passing suns backward in his mind. (Fifteen hundred years or so.)

(That long . . .)

Segnbora moved away from the wall and walked along it, southward, to a corner where she could better see the Eisargir Pass. The increasing light was already revealing the reddish tinge to the rocks where they were bare of snow. There under Eisargir lay the oldest mines in Darthen. From them came the finest iron in the Kingdoms; iron from which the people of Barachael made the matchless Masterforge steel. Goddess only knew how many times Barachael had been raided, burned, and razed by the Reavers, who came down the Eisargir Pass again and again on their forays into the Kingdoms.

Those forays had been one of the deadlier aspects of life in the South for a long, long time. No one knew much about the Reavers; their language was utterly different from any spoken in the Kingdoms. But prisoners taken in battle had revealed a little of their lives. The countries overmountain were short of iron. Indeed, one had merely to examine the Reaver bodies on any battlefield to see that: Their weapons were largely flint-tipped spears and arrows. Some were not tipped at all, but were mere sharpened sticks blackened and hardened in fire. Because of their lack of metal the overmountain tribes were small and poor. In the high cold South few crops grew and little game could flourish. So it had been until twelve or thirteen hundred years before, when some desperately hungry Reaver tribe had followed a game migration northward instead of southward . . . and had discovered the Eisargir Pass, and Darthen, and steel.

Those first Reavers were no fools. They saw that the richness of the farmland below them was not all to the credit of the warmer climate. They discovered the plow and the sword. They stole as many of both as possible, and fled back overmountain with them to change their world.

The tribes that followed grew swiftly in power, becoming more successful as both hunters and warriors. In no time the old balance of power was upset. Tribes skirmished, merged, conquered, or dominated one another, grew more numerous, extended their hunting grounds. Game became scarce as they overhunted their lands. Their agriculture languished, as it usually does in lands where war has become a profitable pastime.

Already a nomadic people during their short summer, the Reavers took wholeheartedly to a raiding lifestyle in order to survive in their unbalanced world. When the weather broke in the spring and the passes opened, they would raid northward, spending the spring and summer raiding for loot and cattle, but most of all for steel to use in their endless tribal quarrels. Time and again Barachael was attacked, looted, and burned—

Again and again the town was rebuilt, too. Neither the stubborn smith-sorcerers who lived there, nor the Darthene crown that ruled them, would give up the Eisargir mines. Sai khas-Barachael was built on the northernmost Adínë spur to keep an eye on the Eisargir incursion route, but even its formidable presence did not deter the Reavers. They continued to raid, though more circumspectly, and in greater numbers, so that the battle for the Chaelonde valley was never over. Only Bluepeak had ever seen more blood shed on its behalf.

The thought of battle, of blood, was not a welcome one that morning. Segnbora turned her back on the southern prospect and walked north along the wall. But that view held no comfort for her either. Northward the highlands fell away to the green and golden plains. On the plains, far out of sight but clear in her mind, was Darthis, her family's formal home, and the only one remaining, now that Asfahaeg was sold and Wasten Beeches sacked by Reavers.

There in Darthis, on Potboilers' Street just outside the old second wall, stood the little stone house with doors and windows shuttered blind, and the tai-Enraesi lioncelle carved over the passage to the horseyard. Her mother wouldn't be singing in the armory anymore, her father wouldn't be rehanging the bedroom shutter that was always falling down. There was only one person left to carry the lioncelle; and how long even that one would survive she couldn't tell. *Ice and darkness.* . . .

(Those who sired you?) Hasai said diffidently, (is that ques-

tion what concerns you? Since last night there's been a—
I don't know what you would call it—an opening in the
depths—)

She blinked back sudden tears, and her mouth was grim.
(*Mdaha*, forget it, they're *rdahaih*. They're gone and I'll never
see them again, not till I pass the last Door. Maybe not even
then.)

She felt him turn his head away, a gesture of shock and
sorrow at her hard words and her pain. (Their souls live yet,
don't they?)

(They do. It might have been otherwise if we hadn't found
them in time.) Her rage at the murdering innkeeper, which
had been gnawing at her like an ulcer all the night before,
flared up hot again. She turned her back to the wall, to the
wind.

After a long time Hasai said, (We didn't understand this
business—or believe it.) In his voice there was distress. Far
back in her inner darkness, the *mdeihei* were singing a mournful bass cadence, both dirge and apology. (You humans throw
yourselves so willingly into strifes and dangers that we
thought surely you must go *mdahaih* somehow. Otherwise it
seemed a madness—)

(We don't get the same life twice. Or know the same people
twice. So in this life we fight for what matters. Herewiss fights
for Lorn, and Lorn for his kingship. All of us fight for our own
happiness, as best we can. Once past the Door, it's done
forever.)

Hasai fell silent again. The same fear, of not-being, and
not-remembering, was at the heart of the terror of going
rdahaih, and nothing could frighten a Dragon more. She
heard Hasai wondering what would become of him and the
mdeihei when her time came to change bodies. Perhaps this
human *death* would be more final and terrible, in its way, than
going *rdahaih*. Segnbora's pain turned to sorrow for the fear
she had planted in him.

(*Mdaha*,) she said, (I'm sorry. But you and I, we're an exper-
iment, it seems. If it'll make you feel better, I intend to put
off my death as long as possible.)

His low rumbling sigh of agreement mingled with the
sound of steps on stone. Segnbora looked southward along

the wall. Eftgan was coming, not in country clothes, this
morning, but dressed for battle: boots and britches, jerkin
and mailshirt, and the Darthene midnight blue surcoat bla-
zoned with the undifferenced royal arms—the White Eagle in
trian aspect, wings spread, striking. Eftgan's sheathed Rod
still bumped at her side, but she was carrying another weapon
over her shoulder. It was Fórlennh BrokenBlade, Earn's
sword, without which no Darthene ruler went to war.

Eftgan was a fair sight, and even a little funny, bumping
down the parapet toward Segnbora with a sword over her
shoulder that was almost as long as she was. Segnbora
remembered the days when Eftgan had been her wreaking-
partner in the Precincts. Back then she had refused to wear
any gear more complicated than a belt for her tunic, or maybe
a ribbon in her hair. Evidently queenship had brought some
changes. Segnbora smiled, and wiped her nose as Eftgan
came up and leaned on the parapet beside her.

"Fair morn, your grace."

"Oh, don't be formal," Eftgan said, making a sour face. "I
have enough problems today. Your friends are looking for
you, 'Berend."

"I dare say. I needed to get away from their watchful eyes
for a while."

Eftgan looked somber. "I didn't say it last night—you were
getting drunk and I didn't want to interfere—but I share your
grief, dear."

"May our pain soon be healed," Segnbora said. They were
words she had thought she wouldn't have to say for years yet.
She sighed and gazed down at Barachael town with its moat
and ditches and star fortifications. "Where are you off to?"

"Orsvier, as soon as I'm finished here. A force of Reavers
and mercenaries is forming there to raid the granaries. There
will be a thousand or more gathered by nightfall. They'll
attack tonight, or tomorrow morning perhaps."

"Goddess," said Segnbora, disturbed. "More mercenaries.
. . . Where is Cillmod getting them all?"

"Most of them are Steldenes. Some are even Steldene regulars; evidently King Dariw sold their services to Cillmod at a
discount to make up for letting Freelorn get away."

Segnbora went cold at the thought of what might have

happened had she not stepped into a certain alley in Madeil one night. She shook her head. "How do you stand?"

"A thousand foot, five hundred horse, thirty sorcerers, and the right is on our side. Whether that'll be enough, I don't know." Eftgan let out a tired breath and fell silent.

Segnbora thought of Herewiss standing on the Morrowfane, an open challenge to the Shadow. Obviously It had taken up the challenge. These latest incursions by the Reavers were too well timed, and too well organized, to be coincidence.

"Have any suggestions for me?" Eftgan said.

Segnbora put an eyebrow up. "The Queen's grace hardly needs to discuss battle tactics with an outlaw."

"With an outlaw, no. But with the head of one of the Forty Houses—"

Segnbora winced.

" 'Berend, I'm sorry," Eftgan said, "but you had better face up to it. You're now *the* tai-Enraesi, and I have the right to require your advice as such."

"For what it's worth."

"Your present position makes it worth more than old Arian's, say, sitting up north on his moneybags. Stop thinking of yourself as 'landless' and 'poverty-stricken,' and tell me what I should do about Freelorn."

"You should ask him that," said Segnbora. "Or Herewiss."

"I have. And they've been very cautious and polite. But that doesn't tell me what to do, really. Consider my position . . . even if we put down the present incursion, Darthen is still suffering worse and worse harvests, things are coming over the borders of the Waste that shouldn't be, Arlen is yapping at my western border, the Oath that made those borders safe is in pieces, and the Reavers are coming out of every bolt hole like rats out of a burning granary." Eftgan sighed.

"Arlen needs someone on that throne who'll enact the royal rites again, and restore one of the Two Lands to normal. And, lo, here's the Lion's Child, sitting right in my lap, wanting his throne back. The question is, if I spend Darthene blood to put him on his throne, will he fulfill his responsibilities as King, or just sit there collecting taxes and parading around in silks and furs, looking royal?"

Segnbora looked her old loved in the eye, reluctant. "I've known him for all of a month—"

"You have underhearing. Better underhearing than mine, if things are the same as they used to be. You *know* them." She poked Segnbora in the ribs, not entirely out of humor. "The Queen requires your advice, tai-Enraesi. Stop stalling."

She wanted no responsibility for advising Eftgan on such a decision. But she had no choice. "I think Lorn will make a good king," she said. "Better than some who've had long quiet reigns and never been in trouble. He loves his land, and he loves his people . . . perhaps too much."

"What do you mean?"

"If you made him King one week and halfway through the next told him that the royal sacrifice was necessary, he'd tie *himself* up in the fivefold bond and tell you to hurry with the knife. He has an unfortunate fondness for death and glory stands, you see. Luckily, he's got Herewiss to advise him. *He's* as conservative as they come."

Eftgan looked at her squarely. "Does 'Berend, the 'swift-rusher,' say this?" she said. "Or does the tai-Enraesi?"

Segnbora shook her head. "Tegánë, after just a month I could tell you endless stories of the noble things he's done. But they'd be just that—stories. What I *know* about Lorn is that although I could have hired my sword to any number of high-paying rulers in the Four Kingdoms, he has something that moved me to swear liege-oath to him."

Eftgan simply kept looking at her. "Loyalty can be blind," she said.

"So can love," Segnbora said, "or so I hear. Tegánë, what else can I tell you? I'm fresh out of proofs. But the truth is that he's my liege, and my friend, and once or twice a bit more. And if I go to my death in his service, that's as good a death as any other I'm likely to find." She swallowed. "Segnbora says that, Queen. The standard-bearer. *His* standard-bearer, for the moment. Will that answer your question?"

Eftgan looked away from her, gazing down the vale, north-ward toward the rest of Darthen. She let out a quiet breath of decision. "Yes," she said. "So be it. And we'll hope that the famous tai-Enraesi luck will stick to him too, just this once. Now, shall we have breakfast?"

"Absolutely."

They went together from the wall to the great inner court. Halfway down the stairs, Segnbora suddenly lost her footing and brought up hard against the wall to the left. "Sorry!" she said, and then realized that the wall itself was jittering, and all around them a low mutter of vibration ran through the fortress. It subsided after a few seconds.

Eftgan let go of the wall, which she also had been holding for support. "Just a little shake," she said.

Segnbora gulped as they continued down the rest of the stairs.

"Does it do that often?"

"Two or three times a week, they tell me. Better a lot of little quakes, though, than a big one that would bring the mountains down on the valley. . . ."

They went across the huge paved court, where men and women in Darthene blue were grooming horses and practicing at the sword or bow or lance. The court, like the walls that surrounded it, lay in a square around khas-Barachael's central tower. Eftgan led the way in, through a high-roofed hall and up a stair that climbed along one wall. In a smaller room on the next story a table was set under the south-facing windows. Freelorn, Herewiss, Lang, and the others sat there breaking their fast with several of Eftgan's officers.

"Sit here," Eftgan said, and pulled out a chair for her between Lang and a Darthene officer.

Segnbora sat down and reached for an empty cup, glancing up and down the table. To her surprise and slight discomfort, she saw that around Lang's left arm, and Dritt's and Moris's and Harald's and Freelorn's, and even Herewiss's, was bound the white cord of mourning. All up and down the table, eyes rested on her with concern. She swallowed hard.

"Wine?" Lang said, reaching for her cup.

Her head throbbed at the thought. "Dear Lady, no. Is there barley-water with mint in it, perhaps?"

There was; Harald passed it up.

"Segnbora," Eftgan said, "you haven't met Torve, I think. He was raised here."

She turned to the man on her right. He was young, of middle height and build, with dark hair and beard and a slightly reticent smile. His downturned gray eyes, however, smiled even when his lips did not.

"Torve s'Keruer," Eftgan said as the two of them touched hands in greeting, "the Chastellain-major. He runs this place."

"You were raised *here*?" Segnbora said.

Torve nodded. "My mother was the last Chastellain. But she got tired of the long winters and retired to the lowlands. The Queen was good enough to confirm me in her place."

"Anything you need, he'll give you," Eftgan said.

"Thank you, Queen."

"Pardon," Dritt said, and reached across the Queen for the butter.

Eftgan raised a tolerant eyebrow. "His manners haven't improved any," she said, looking with wry amusement at her former court musician. "He used to do that at court too. My father thought sending him to Arlen might put some polish on his manners. But then what does he do but leave his post there, and not send word for seven years...." There was mild chuckling over that. "Of course," Eftgan said, "his liege seems to have done the same thing, and taken the long way home as well."

The laughter was more subdued this time; Lorn shot Eftgan a quick look. Herewiss was suddenly very busy with his porridge.

"Freelorn," the Queen said, helping herself to bread and holding out a hand for Dritt to return the butter plate, "we've already talked a great deal since last night, but I still have a few questions to ask you."

"Ask," Freelorn said, sounding unconcerned.

"What on earth do you want to be a king for?"

He looked at her in shock. He took brief refuge in his mulled wine, then said, "It's what I was raised to be."

"Rubbish," Eftgan said merrily but with force. "That's like saying that a slopman's child should spend his life carting slops because his father before him did."

Freelorn stared at Eftgan, his shock growing greater by the moment.

"Look at this," the Queen said, gesturing around the room. It was comfortable enough, on a bright summer morning, but definitely not luxurious. "If I'd had the sense to marry out of the royal line young, I could be spending my day sitting on silken cushions in some mansion in Darthis, eating roast ortolan and botargoes on toast, taking lovers, going to the races in the daytime and to parties at night. But instead I let them make me Queen."

Segnbora took a long drink of her barley-water, to hide her rueful smile.

"I had to be Queen," Eftgan said again, "and now look what I've got for my troubles. Battlefield food and soldier's quarters, five days out of the ten. Back home in Darthis are three children I hardly ever see, because by the time I'm finished meeting with my ministers all morning, presiding over court-justice all afternoon, and receiving visits—I should say, 'complaints'—from the various members of the Forty Houses all evening, it's long past the children's bedtimes. I say nothing of *my* bedtime. My husband has to have a separate bedroom so that my reading won't keep him awake all night. In the daytime he has to throw people out of his wineshop because they don't want to buy his wine, they want to buy appointments with *me*. Even he aches at the end of the day."

Freelorn had at this point just gotten around to closing his mouth.

"So do I," Eftgan said. "Sometimes I do more than ache. I get wounds, too. A Queen has to be first in every charge and last in every retreat. . . ." She pulled aside the shoulder of her surcoat, looking under it with a momentarily abstracted air. "I was knifed here, once— No, of course you remember that; you were there. Herewiss stopped the crossbow quarrel, but I got the knife of the Reaver before that one." She pulled the surcoat back in place and spent a moment looking around her plate to find the butterknife. "Bad enough to have to put up with that kind of thing from your enemies. But sooner or later it comes from your own people . . . in Darthen, at least. One day when you're hammering out your crown in the Square, somebody whose crops failed last year comes out of the crowd and runs you through. Or worse, the rains won't come, and all the wreakings and all the royal magics refuse to work. Then there's only one thing that will save the land from famine." She looked down and began slowly buttering her bread. "So you take the knife, and call the person who loves you best in the world to witness the ceremony; and pierce the sky's heart by piercing yours, and cause it to shed rain by shedding blood, and bring the breath of the stormwind by breathing out your last. . . ."

Eftgan's tone all this while had been light, almost matter-of-fact. Now she looked up at Freelorn and, in the profound silence that had fallen around the table, said, "This is a stupid job to go hunting for, Lorn. You were smart to stay away from it as long as you have."

Segnbora listened hard and could have sworn that people were holding their breaths. Only Lorn looked at all normal. The amazement had worn off him; his face was set.

"Eftgan," he said, "I ran away from Arlen because I was afraid of being tortured to death. I still am. But I notice that I'm not running in the opposite direction."

At that Eftgan paused to bite into her bread. She chewed reflectively, and swallowed. "You've had a lot of help."

"I have," he said, with only the swiftest glance to one side at Herewiss. "What is it they always say about lovers? That they usually know your mind better than you do." It was Freelorn's turn to pause now, looking around the table for honey for his porridge. He pointed, and Lang passed it to him. "Herewiss always knew what I wanted—what I *really* wanted—better than I did. It's a good thing, too. If he had been one of those spineless anything-you-say-dear types, I'd probably be peacefully dead in a ditch somewhere now. Instead I'm here, with Fyrd and Reavers on three sides and the Shadow on the fourth."

That got a smile out of Eftgan.

"You're right to question my motives and intent." Freelorn ate a spoonful of porridge. "Yes, Herewiss called the tune. And yes, I followed his lead toward kingship because it was convenient, and I was confused. But the confusion isn't so much of a problem now." He took another spoonful, throwing a quick glance out the window at the great silent mass of Adíne. "Dusty will probably still be the strategist of this group's business, the brains. But I'm this group's heart. I've forgotten that, once or twice, I know. A prince gets used to having things done for him. But in the past couple of weeks I've seen my loved almost die for me—for my cause, rather —three times. I suspect I'm done being a prince. It's my turn to be a king." Lorn took a long drink of mulled wine. "And as for you, Eftgan . . . if you don't like your job, you should abdicate. Maybe afterward you could take up carting slops."

Eftgan, who was also drinking at that moment, spluttered and choked—then, when she had finished choking, began to whoop with laughter. "Oh Goddess!" was all she managed to say for a while. When she was calmer, she wiped tears of merriment out of her eyes. "I guess I left myself open for that. Freelorn, your hand! Keep this sort of thing up, and we'll do very well together."

They reached across the length of the table to touch hands.

"Truth," Lorn said, sounding rueful, as if the speech had cost him something, "and beauty. A perfect match."

"Flatterer."

"Now, what about that news about the Reavers that you promised us?"

"Well . . . let's take this in order. There's more news than just of Reavers. When you left Arlen, Lorn, what was your understanding of the way things stood with the Lords-Householders, the Four Hundred, concerning your succession to the throne?"

"Mixed. There would've been no question of the succession if I had been Initiated, taken by my father into the Lion-hall on the Nightwalk. But he put off the ceremony, until finally it was too late. When he died, the Four Hundred split on the issue. I had been spending a lot of time out of the country, helling around, and there was some question about whether I'd be a fit ruler. The army split on the issue too, and with Arlene regulars assigned to each household the situation quickly became volatile, as you can imagine. No one wanted a civil war, so the Householders hesitated . . . which gave

Cillmod time to step in with his mercenaries and make the whole question moot."

"Yes, and when he made you an outlaw, you and Herewiss and the rest fled the country." Eftgan sat back in her chair.

Segnbora knew much of the rest of the story, and listened with only half an ear as Eftgan filled in details for Freelorn. Cillmod had done well enough for several years. He took the throne and bore Stave, though he didn't go into Lionhall. Likewise, he reaffirmed the Oath with Eftgan's father, who was still alive and ruling then. It was around the middle of his fourth year that the crop failures began. The next year the crops were worse, and the next year worse still. Then the failures began spreading into Darthen as well. The royal sorceries, and the Great Bindings, were wearing thin.

Eftgan's father had been unwilling to help Cillmod beyond the reaffirmation of the Oath: He was among those who hoped that an uprising would eventually bring Freelorn back. But by the time of Eftgan's first crowning the situation was unbearable. Unaware of Freelorn's whereabouts, Eftgan wrote to Cillmod and offered to repair the Royal Bindings herself. Amazingly, he refused.

Segnbora looked up from her food in surprise at that, as did the rest of Freelorn's company.

"He said that inquiries were being made in Arlen for a surviving heir to the Lion's Line," Eftgan explained. "He had put about the story that you had died, did you know that?"

"No!"

"Later there was even proof of it: a mangled head sent from the torture chambers of Dariw of Steldin, whom you eluded at Madeil."

"Hmmm . . . Do ghosts eat? No? Then there must have been a mistake."

"Must have been. Anyway, Cillmod was apparently unsuccessful in finding any other children in the Lion's Line. Which is fortunate, since I'm sure he would have killed any that he found. Another question, Lorn: Do you have any children outside of Arlen?"

Freelorn shook his head sadly. "I only fulfilled the Responsibility once," he said. "My daughter died in infancy."

"Well enough." Eftgan chewed some bacon. "I ask because Cillmod's search for an heir took some strange turns. For example, some of the searches were conducted by large groups of mercenaries who crossed the Darthene borders and went after our granaries. It was the only way Cillmod could forestall a revolt by the Four Hundred and their starving tenant-farmers. Anyway, to continue: There were also reports for some time of sorcerers and Rodmistresses visiting Prydon. More sorcerers than Rodmistresses, of course. There's one sorcerer in particular—"

"Someone who either claimed to be of Lion's Line," Freelorn guessed, "or who claimed he could get Cillmod into Lionhall without dying of it, and show him how to reinforce the Bindings."

"Exactly. The second was what this sorcerer claimed. Rian, his name is. But then something peculiar happened. The man never went into Lionhall at all, as far as my spies can tell. Neither did Cillmod. Nevertheless, starting about a year ago Rian became a fixture at what now passes for the Arlene court." Eftgan took a drink of barley-water. "Other odd things—the Four Hundred have become very quiet recently. When you robbed the treasury at Osta, for example, it became apparent then that you weren't dead after all. Naturally there was a clamor for your return. But it died down very quickly."

"Why?"

"I believe because the families who called loudest for your crowning were suddenly beset by Fyrd—the thinking variety."

Mutters of distaste were heard round the table. "Rian," Segnbora said, very quietly to herself.

The Queen nodded. "I have no doubt that we're dealing here with a person whom the Shadow occasionally inhabits and controls. The man has a past and a family just as he should, but he's the center of too many odd occurrences. Where his influence appears, Cillmod's neglect usually breaks out into full-fledged malice."

Lorn, who had finished his porridge, set down his spoon. "What else has friend Rian—or rather, the Shadow—been up to?"

"You know the problems the Reavers have been having with the weather, their crops, and their game? How they are being forced northward? That's obviously the Shadow's work. There's something else, too. Starting about six months ago, it seems that emissaries—mostly mercenary captains—were sent over the mountains in to Reaver country to strike a bargain. In return for making incursions into the Kingdoms when ordered, some of the hardest-pressed Reaver clans were promised loot, cattle . . . and land in Arlen in which to settle."

All around the table, there was silence.

"The Shadow's purpose is apparently to keep Darthen busy with war until something special happens," Eftgan said. "My guess is that 'something' is the collapse of the Royal Bindings."

The silence in the room erupted into cries of disbelief. The end of the Royal Bindings was unthinkable. Such a calamity would turn the Shadow loose in the Kingdoms as It hadn't been loose in centuries, since the Lion and the Eagle first bound It.

Lang looked at Freelorn. "I can't believe anyone would knowingly do this to his own country! Can it be Cillmod doesn't know what the failure of the Bindings will mean?"

"Could be," Lorn said. "After all, he's not trained in the royal sorceries. Perhaps the true nature of the destruction that would follow is being hidden from him somehow. In any case, if this is the Shadow's purpose, it must not be allowed."

The firmness of his resolve sent a dart of sharp pride through Segnbora. The others, equally moved, quieted. Eftgan nodded her approval.

"First of all, what are we doing about the Reavers locally?" Freelorn asked.

"I've spoken to Herewiss about the possibility of closing off the Chaelonde incursion route with a sealing," the Queen said. "That would cause the Reavers a great deal of trouble right away. Without it, they'd have to go as far east as Araveyn or as far west as Bluepeak itself to get into the Kingdoms. Araveyn is practically in the Waste; they wouldn't bother. And Bluepeak is in Arlen, meaning that Cillmod would have to march Reavers all the way through his own country to attack

Darthen. Tactically, a sealing is a good idea. The question is whether it can be done."

"It can," Herewiss said. "But right now the timing's bad. I wouldn't dare try it with Glasscastle imminent; we'll have to wait until it passes. Which brings us to another problem—sealing off the peak of Adíně so that no sorcery of the Shadow's, or anyone else's, can bring anything down out of Glasscastle onto our heads. That, too, I can do; and I'll do it tonight. My only fear is that the sudden removal of access to a place where our mortal world and another world touch might cause Power imbalances. In a place as delicately balanced as Barachael is, with its years of warfare and piled-up negative energies, that can be dangerous."

"I know," Eftgan said. "But it can't be helped. My true-dream made it plain that the next time someone passed into or out of Glasscastle, so great a disturbance would follow that the Kingdoms might not survive."

Herewiss looked gravely at Lorn, and then back at the Queen again. "I'll do what I can, madam," he said. "I hope it'll suffice."

"It's more than I could have done, that's for sure...." Eftgan pushed her chair back from the table. "I leave the matter in your capable hands. I should be back from Orsvier tomorrow, and we can worry about sealing the pass itself then. As for you, Arlen—" She fixed Freelorn with a hard, smiling look. "I stand on the Oath. As soon as I get this unfought army off my right flank, and yours, then it's 'the Eagle for Arlen and the Lion at bay.' I trust you two will be willing to deal with this flank, should it become necessary today."

"Darthen," he said, returning Eftgan's look without the smile, "you know how my loved has been handling this so far. And I agree with him. I'd prefer not to shed blood, Arlene or Darthene."

"Cillmod's had no such compunctions," Eftgan said. "Neither have the Reavers, and right now there are Reavers coming here, and Reavers at Orsvier. You two clear this flank, I'll clear the other. Then we'll have leisure to consider what to do about Arlen. When we campaign there I'll be guided by your judgment; you know your land best."

Freelorn nodded, looking solemn. Eftgan turned to the corner and picked up something that stood against the wall —a big old iron fireplace poker, its haft studded with rough white diamonds. It was Sarsweng, the battle-standard of the Darthenes. "I have to get my work done," the little fair woman said. "My husband hates it when I get home late. The Lady be with you all 'til I get back—"

"And with you," those at the table said.

Eftgan shouldered Sarsweng and strode out, the sunlight flashing on the poker's gemmed haft as she passed through a bar of light falling down the stairs.

At breakfast's end Harald, Moris, Dritt, and Lang went off with the Darthene officers to look the place over. Herewiss sat quietly in his chair, drinking spiced wine and looking thoughtful, while Freelorn stared out the window at the towering Adínë massif.

On her way to the stairs, Segnbora stopped beside him. Her underhearing was prickling with his unease. "You all right?" she said. "You look green."

Freelorn shrugged, not looking at her. "The change in altitude," he said. "It didn't agree with me. I had a bad night."

He was lying, she knew. His eyes were fixed on Adínë, and on the lesser peak, where a tiny glitter of silver bridgespan caught the morning Sun. Freelorn said nothing more aloud, but she caught his thought: *If only my dreams weren't so bad!* And behind the thought lay the sure conviction that something he had recently seen in dream was no baseless vision, but a foreknowledge of reality. A reality that he could avoid if he chose—

Freelorn swung around and leaned on the table. "Are you going to sit there drinking all day," he said to Herewiss, "or are you going to get up and get Eftgan's business out of the way so we can tend to our own?"

Herewiss's glance was much like Freelorn's—all mockery above, and love below . . . and underneath that, a breath of fear very much suppressed. "Hark to the early riser," he said, "who pulled me back into bed twice this morning when I would have gotten up. Come on, you can help correct my scansion. This wreaking tonight is going to be difficult . . ."

Their easy laughter faded down the stairs behind them. Segnbora sat down on the windowsill, gazing up in turn at the terrible blind walls and cruel precipices of Adíně. The mountain cared nothing for human life. With such an audience before her, and the empty room behind, Segnbora took what was likely to be her last opportunity for a while, laid her head against the windowframe, and mourned the dead.

An hour or so before sunset, the seven of them took to horse at khas-Barachael gate to begin the ascent of Adíně.

While they were saddling up, Torve came out of the stables leading a little rusty Steldene gelding. "Of your courtesy," he said to Herewiss, "perhaps you'd take me as guide. I've ridden this trail a number of times, and climbed to the summit too."

Herewiss looked at the young man, suppressing a smile. There was no need to read Torve's thought, for it was plain enough: He was staring at Khávrinen, which was slung over Herewiss's shoulder, like a small child staring at what the Goddess had left him on New Year's morning.

"With all these other spectators," Herewiss said, glancing around at Freelorn's band, most of whom were along only for the ride, "certainly we can use one person who'll earn his keep on the way. Come and welcome."

They headed out over the half-bridge that reached out from Barachael, on its two-thousand-foot pier of stone, across to the spur of Adíně proper. The sorcerer-architects who built the place had carved a hundred foot gap right through the spur, so that with the drawbridge up the fortress stood unassailable, one great corner-shoulder turned to the spur.

Once across, a causey wide enough for ten horsemen abreast wound downward through several switchbacks. On both sides the road was overshadowed by cliffs, the shattered faces of which made it obvious that invaders had occasionally tried to come up that way against the defenders' wishes, and had had large rocks dropped on them for their trouble.

"They've tried a few times to shuck this oyster," Torve said cheerfully, "but even Reaver horses can't charge straight up."

At its bottom the paved road gave out onto a narrow saddle-corridor between khas-Barachael rock and Swaleback, a flattened, marshy little spur of Adínë. Torve led them eastward and out into the valley proper, then southwestward along the skirts of the Adínë massif. Past two minor spurs they went. The ground was rocky, and every now and then the mountain, cooling from the warmth of the day, would let a little reddish scree slide down at them.

Under Adínë's lengthening shadow they turned due westward into a long shallow rampway scoured out by an ancient glacier, and picked their way carefully among the boulders that lay scattered about. Some fifteen hundred feet up the mountain's flank, the ascent became too steep for horses.

"We'll leave them here," Torve said, dismounting.

(Not all of them,) Sunspark said mildly.

Torve glanced up in great surprise from the hobbling of his gelding, and noticed that Herewiss's mount was calmly standing a foot above the ground. "Sir," he said, addressing Sunspark with the slight bow due a fellow officer, "we haven't been introduced."

"Torve, this is Sunspark," Herewiss said, dismounting. "Firechild, be good to him, he's on our side. Torve, if you ever need a fortress reduced on short notice, Sunspark is the one to talk to. He eats stone for breakfast."

Torve nodded. Having seen a man with the Fire he looked as if he was now ready to believe anything. "Up this way," he said, and led them up the side of the cirque to a trail that led along its top, under the shadow of the great Adínë summit.

They rounded the east-pointing scarp, moving quietly under the great out-handing cornice of snow that loomed a thousand feet above them, and so came to face the north side of the lesser summit ridge. The ridge stood up sheer as a wall, overhung in places, itself at least seven hundred feet high.

"Don't worry, it's not an expert-level climb," Torve said, looking up the walls of rock and ice with relish. "Beginners could handle it—"

Freelorn, who had done extensive climbing in the High-peaks of Arlen as a child, made a wry face.

Herewiss gazed up the cliff. "This trail is exactly as the song

describes it," he said. " 'Awful.' Torve, I hope you won't tell
the Queen's grace on me, but I'm no climber. Maybe we
Brightwood people have been down from the mountains too
long. Sunspark?"

(Who'll go first?) Sunspark said, with an anticipatory grin.
Freelorn's band blanched and began deferring to one another.

It took Herewiss and Freelorn and Torve first, managing
the thousand-foot ascent to the summit ridge in a single leap.
When Segnbora swung herself up into the saddle, Sunspark
looked around at her with a naughty light in its eye. (Nervous?)

She gave it a threatening look in return and said nothing,
while inside Hasai laughed at her. (Afraid of heights! Oh,
Immanence within us, what kind of *sdaha*—)

(Well enough for *you* to laugh. You've got wings . . .)

Hasai continued laughing, a deep rough hiss. Segnbora did
her best to ignore him and made very sure of her seat. A
moment later she was glad of her care, for Sunspark shot up
to the summit, trailing bright fire like a newborn comet and
going at least twice as fast as it had the first time. It came down
fast, too, landing on the snow with a hiss of steam and an
incongruously light impact.

Shaky-kneed, Segnbora scrambled down.

(Well, that was probably the high point of your day,) Sunspark said, genially malicious.

"Mmmnh," Segnbora said, slapping it familiarly on the
flank, and burning herself. "The others are waiting."

It gave her a final look, walked off the precipice and
plunged down out of sight.

She picked up a fistful of snow to cool the burned hand and
walked over to join the others. They stood around the base
of the Skybridge where it rooted into the stone, some thirty
feet broad. The bridge had no look of a made thing about it,
for there were no rivets, no marks of tools anywhere to be
seen. Drawn from the mountain's heart by Fire, the metal had
the light uprising grace of a growing thing about it, as if Adíně
had put up stem and flower. There were actually a number of
stems—three lower ones, anchoring the main spans to con-

secutively lower points on the side of the peak. The angle of
the bridge itself wasn't steep: It gained perhaps a foot in
height for each three of length.

Herewiss held Khávrinen out and touched the bright silvery
metal of the bridge with the point—then jerked his arm back
quickly as a blue spark jumped from bridge to sword. "Firework, all right," he said, rubbing his arm as if it stung. "And
a life-wreaking. No wonder poor Efmaer never came back.
She either died of this wreaking or didn't recover enough
Power to fight her way out again before Glasscastle vanished
and took her away forever."

"You're going to have to do a life-wreaking too, to seal it
off." Freelorn looked uneasy.

Herewiss stood with one hand on his hip, staring at the
bridge the way a carpenter stares at a tree he must fell. "Well,
the sealing has to be done whether I survive it or not. Don't
worry, though, Lorn. Merely sealing it won't cost me the kind
of effort building it cost Efmaer. I'll lose a month or two of
life, and my head'll hurt tonight, but that's all."

Sunspark came up with Moris, whose great bulk left no
room for other passengers, and then with Harald, Dritt, and
Lang. Finally it paced over to Herewiss, peering over his
shoulder at the bridge. Herewiss reached around its neck,
patted it, then turned as if he had noticed something disturbing. "You all right, loved?"

(It's *cold* up there,) Sunspark said.

Herewiss looked shocked. The others glanced at one another: they'd never heard the elemental say anything like *that*
before. It pawed the ground uneasily, melting snow.

(All this water,) it said. (It's uncomfortable. And there's
something else . . .)

Segnbora turned her face away and considered what she
felt coming from Sunspark: a cold that had nothing to do with
the bone-chilling wind whispering about the summit. Up near
the end of the bridge, something was pouring down a cold of
the spirit that grew stronger as twilight grew deeper and the
mountains less distinct. All of them were shivering, but the
looks of foreboding and concern on their faces were far more
disturbing.

Herewiss stroked Sunspark's neck. "We'll be down soon enough, loved. This won't take long. Shall we?"

It turned, offering him the stirrup. Herewiss mounted and sat looking at the bridge for a moment. It was a dark silhouette against the crystalline clarity of the golden mountain sunset. Abruptly he sent Fire down Khávrinen, lighting the whole mountaintop, and nudged Sunspark with his heels. The elemental walked off the cliff on the east side and stood on the empty air two thousand feet above the southface cirque.

"Down a bit," Herewiss said. Sunspark sank leisurely through the air, as if sliding down a stairway banister. "Torve," Herewiss called up to the peak, "where are the usual accesses?"

"East face," Torve said, "and northwest. But a climber with stepping-spikes and a rope could go up about anywhere. As for the suicides, the Queen said they find themselves on the summit without climbing."

"Thanks," Herewiss said. "It's got to be the whole thing, then." He reined Sunspark close to the sheer cliff that fell down from the summit, and touched the ice and snow with Khávrinen. Despite her trouble with heights, Segnbora crowded close to the edge with Torve and the others to watch the wreaking.

Blue Fire lanced from Khávrinen's point, melting snow and striking into the bare red rock of the mountain, which heated from red- to yellow- to white-hot and finally to an azure incandescence. Flame leaped up from the kindled stone, though the tongues were small and sluggish, like those of an ordinary fire upon wet wood.

Sunspark moved around the peak, staying within arm's reach, and as elemental and rider progressed the bright line of blue melted itself into the stone behind them. Around the southeast spur they went, and out of sight. Most of Freelorn's band went around to watch the work on that side, but Torve stood by the cirque-facing cliff with Lang and Segnbora, shaking his head.

"This is a marvel," he said. "And strange. He's not what I expected a man with the Fire to be . . ."

"The Rodmistresses in the Precincts agreed with you, I'm

afraid," Segnbora said absently. For the moment her mind wasn't on Herewiss. For all her uneasiness with heights, something different was stirring in her now: a desire to lift wings and fall out into that glorious gulf of darkening blue air beneath her. A smile crossed her face at the realization that Dragons, like any of the more common soaring creatures of the world, preferred to drop from a height rather than to work for altitude.

(And why not,) Hasai said, stretching wings lazily inside her and admiring the view himself. (Why waste energy, or manipulate field, when you don't have to? This is a fine height. Not as high as the Éorlhowe, to be sure, but a respectable height—)

"There it is," Torve said, his voice very quiet. Segnbora glanced up from the glacier.

High to the west, above the vista of Adínë peak behind them, past Esa and Mirit and the long sleek flank of Whitestack, had risen a slim crescent of Moon. To its right, and lower, a point of light glittered: the Evenstar. Quickly Segnbora looked upward along the silver-blue curve of the Skybridge . . . and forgot to breathe.

It had come out as silently and suddenly as the Moon. The Skybridge, half of a curve before, was whole now. The new part of the span *did* look to be made of the sky—cerulean blue, transparent, yet very much there. And at the span's end rose Glasscastle.

It was like a castle in an old story, a place built for pleasure rather than defense, fanciful and wide-windowed and fair. Halls and high towers pierced the upper air; slender spires were bound together by curving bridges and fairy buttresses. Everything, from the wide-flung gates at the end of the bridge to the highest needle spire, was built of the same airy crystal as the bridge.

The evening sky could plainly be seen through walls and towers. The fading hues of the sunset—rose, gold, and deepening royal blue—were reflected from them, pale and ghostly. Yet there was nothing fragile about the place. Glasscastle stood as immovably founded on the air as if on rock. It reflected the sunset colors, the icy light of the Moon, and even the frozen gleam of the Evenstar, but cast no shadow.

"Not a moment too soon," Herewiss said, his voice hushed, as Sunspark stepped up to the peak again, completing their circuit of the mountaintop. All around the barrel of the peak burned a line of blue, the circle within which the spell would be confined. Herewiss dismounted and stood for a moment with Khávrinen in his hand, gazing up at the crystalline apparition.

"Beautiful," he said. "But from now on, that's all it's going to be." He struck Khávrinen's point down into the snow at the foot of the bridge, and looked up the curve of metal, raising his arms—

—and stopped, squinting upward. "Who's *that?*" he said.

Everyone looked. Segnbora's stomach constricted at the sight of the lone dark figure approaching the end of the metal part of the span, a tiny shadow against the twilight.

"I don't believe it," Herewiss said, in the voice of someone who *does* believe it, and wishes he were wrong. "I don't— *LORN!*"

Nine

"It's dangerous to invoke the Goddess as you conceive Her to be," said Tav, "and more dangerous still to invoke Her as She truly is."

"Right enough," said Airru. "Breathing is dangerous too. But necessary . . ."

Tales from the South,
x, 118

Herewiss's anguished shout came back as echoes, but had no effect on the small dark silhouette that hurried purposefully up the bridge. Herewiss swung Khávrinen up two-handed, pointing at Freelorn, and the sword spat a blinding line of Fire that ran upward toward him—but whatever wreaking he had in mind came unraveled before it ever touched Lorn. Many feet short of the bridge, the Fire hit some unseen barrier and splashed in all directions like water thrown at a wall.

Freelorn kept walking. Another twenty paces would see him up onto the phantom portion of the span. Herewiss wasn't waiting; he ran up the bridge after his loved, swearing frightfully in an ancient Arlene dialect, Khávrinen streaming frantic Fire behind him. Sunspark went galloping up after, unable to leave his loved.

"Damn!" Lang said, and followed.

"Torve, wait here!" Segnbora said, unsheathing Charriselm as she headed after Lang.

"Are you joking? The Queen would . . ." Torve began to say as he followed her and the others onto the bridge.

They didn't run long—the altitude saw to that. Only Torve could run fast enough to catch up with Herewiss. In addition, the bridge was longer than it looked: an eighth mile, perhaps, to the point where it truly became sky. Far ahead of them, Freelorn's small figure slowed in its stride, hesitating only briefly. He put one foot on the phantom bridge, found it would support him, and went on as before, in a confident but hurried walk.

Damn! Segnbora thought as she ran. She clutched Charriselm harder than necessary, for her hands and face were numb from the chill. That other, more inward cold was pouring down more bitterly than before, yet she didn't suffer much from it. Something was blunting its effects; something inside her, burning—

(Hasai!) she said as she caught up with Herewiss and Sunspark and Torve. (Is that you?)

(*Sdaha*, against the great cold of the outer darknesses, this is *nothing*. We have learned to deal with cold.)

(I'm glad!) she said silently.

Herewiss and Torve had paused at the edge of the phantom span, and behind them Sunspark stood, looking downright dubious. The Fire-wrought part of the bridge was as thick and wide as the railless metal span, but clear and as fragile as air. Herewiss knelt to brush his fingers across it and straightened quickly, as if burnt.

"Whoever did this wreaking," he gasped, "they've got more Power than I have—and they're up there *now*, fueling it!" He got to his feet and stepped out onto the crystalline part of the bridge, realized that the footing was secure, and took off after Freelorn again at a run.

Torve and the others went after, Sunspark hammering behind them at a gallop, the bridge under its feet ringing like struck crystal.

Segnbora followed, stepping out onto the bridge. *Maybe I shouldn't,* she thought as she looked down. But to her surprise, the vista of shadows and creeping fog that veiled the south—face glacier half a mile below didn't much trouble her. Hasai's Dragofire was strong in her, getting stronger as she headed after the others. *Lady grant it holds,* she thought, beginning to run.

At the Skybridge's end, between the two huge crystal doors that lay open there, a tiny figure passed into the dimness beyond and was lost to sight.

The group ahead of her slowed and came to a stop at the end of the bridge, gazing up at the chill clear grace of towers and keeps, at the awful tallness and thickness of the doors. Segnbora caught up with them, feeling their nervousness. Sai Ebássren, the place was called in Darthene: the House of No Return. What lay within, no legend told. The only certainty was that when the three Lights were gone, the place would vanish, and anyone trapped within would never emerge.

Herewiss did not pause for long. Sending a great defiant glory of the Flame down Khávrinen's length, he walked through the doors. The twilight within swallowed him as it had Freelorn. For an instant Khávrinen flickered like a star seen through fog, and then its light vanished.

Sunspark hesitated at the doors, though only for a moment. It was trembling in body, a sight that astounded Segnbora.

"Firechild—"

(I'm bound,) it said in terror. (I can't burn. I can't change—)

She reached out to it in mind, perplexed, and felt Sunspark drowning in a cold more deadly than the lost gulfs between stars that Hasai had mentioned; a cold that could kill thought and motion and change of any kind. Hasai had been shielding her. (Maybe you should stay outside,) she said.

It turned hard eyes on her. (I will not let him come to harm in there,) it said, and turned away from her to walk shaking through the doors. The dimness folded around its burning mane and tail, and Sunspark vanished.

"That's done it," Lang said, genial and terrified. "Damned if I'll be outdone by a walking campfire—" He unsheathed his sword and went after, Torve close after him.

There Segnbora stood, left alone on the threshold, trembling nearly as hard as Sunspark had.

No return.

She swore at herself and hurried in behind the others.

She was in a great hall, all walled in sheer unfigured crystal, through which Adínë and the peaks beyond it showed clear. The air was thick with a blue dusk, like smoke. She barely had time to see these things, though, before the terrible thought-numbing cold she had experienced through Sunspark came crowding in close around her, ten times worse than it had been outside.

From within her came an answering flare, Hasai and the *mdeihei* calling up old memories of warmth and daylight to fight the cold. She regained a bit of composure, looked

around for the others. They were nowhere in sight. Deep in
the twilight she could see vague forms moving far away, but
somehow she knew that none of them were those with whom
she had entered. Her companions were all lost in the blueness, with Freelorn.

(Herewiss!) she called silently. (Sunspark!) But no reply
came back, and her underspeech fell into a mental silence as
thick as if she had shouted into a heavily curtained room.
Thought was blocked here, then.

"Herewiss!" she shouted aloud. The curling twilight
soaked up the sound of her voice like a heavy fog. She set off
into the blueness, hurrying.

For all her fearfulness, the sheer greatness of the wreaking
that had made this place astonished her. Even at first entrance
the place had seemed as big as Earneselle or the Queens' Hall
in Prydon. But now, as she walked across the vast glassy floor,
the walls grew remote and the ceiling seemed to become a
firmament that not even a soaring Dragon could reach. Mir-
rored in walls, galleries, and crystalline arches, she saw vague
intimations of other rooms: up-reaching towers and balco-
nies, parlors and courts, an infinity of glass reflected dimly in
glass, too huge to ever search or know completely.

That terrible chill was part of the wreaking too, though here
inside the castle it seemed not to be biting so viciously at the
bones. It was becoming a quality of the mind: a cool lassitude,
a twilight that ran in the veins and curled shadowy in the
heart, smothering fear and veiling the desire to be out of
there. She could feel that cold rising in her, but the presence
of the *mdeihei* was a match for it. Ancient sunfire burned the
twilight out of her blood as fast as it grew. Dragonfire, painful
and bright at the bottom of her lungs, burned the sad resignation away. Frightened by the constant assault, but reassured
by the Dragon's presence, Segnbora headed deeper into the
shadowy blue.

The dead and those who had abandoned life slowly became
evident around her. There were many, but none of them were
walking together. Young men and old women she passed;
foreigners and countrymen, maidens and lords. Here and
there she recognized a surcoat-device, but afterward she was

generally sorry she had looked. The dead wandered slowly and aimlessly through the blue, eyes drowned with weary surrender; ancient wounds in plain sight, neither bleeding nor healed.

Through halls and galleries and passages she went, up and down stairs, while Glasscastle's inhabitants drifted around her, unaware, unconcerned. The feeling of sorrow in the air crushed in harder now, as if sensing her resistance. Every breath she drew seemed to have a catch in it, as if tears were about to follow.

Hasai and the *mdeihei* blazed within her, the white of their Dragonfire burning and glittering from scales of many colors. The defiance and dismay of the *mdeihei* at so many beings who had given up *being* burned them, burned her. Their appalled song, a heart-shaking weave of deep notes like the ocean speaking in outrage, fought with the song of melancholy that whispered from Glasscastle's walls.

Terrified that she might fall victim to the inward-stealing sorrow, Segnbora began breathing the litany of life and pain along with the *mdeihei* as she sought in mind for any feeling of Freelorn or Herewiss. The effort was in vain—the wreaking seemed to have shut down her underhearing almost completely.

Finally she paused at a meeting-place of three long halls, and, in midbreath of a long phrase of Dracon song, stopped.

She didn't look up. That would have broken the illusion of Hasai's great head hanging over her, defying the cool darkness. But she looked where he did. Among indistinct, wandering forms, there was a flash of light—faint, but still bright enough to be noticed in this blue gloom.

(What's that?) Hasai wondered.

(I don't know, but let's see—)

The path ahead was dark. She reached up a hand, simultaneously reaching down inside her for her little dying spark of Fire. Forcefully, she willed the one thing she had always been able to manage: a brief flash of light. For once it would be enough.

(What!) she thought a second later, amazed. Nothing had come; her Power source was blocked from her.

She tried again. Nothing happened. "Damn," she said. Supposedly it took death to separate one from one's Power, however feeble. There wasn't time to puzzle over it now, however. It was imperative that she find the others as quickly as possible.

The light glittered again, closer: a faint shimmer, there and gone. She headed toward the place where it had been—

—and went silent in shock. Not far away an outwall rose, a giddy frameless window on the evening sky and the upper peak of Adínë. And there against crystal and dying sunset stood silhouetted a small slender woman in a midnight blue surcoat.

Her dark head was bent. Her arms were folded in front of her as she gazed out into the sorrowing twilight. Her back was turned, and from her surcoat the opal eyes of an Eagle flashed at Segnbora. It was a white Eagle in trian aspect, silver wings and blue Fire for eyes—the undifferenced Darthene arms, worn only by Queens and Kings. Segnbora had seen those same arms this morning on Eftgan's back, but these were worked in an antique style, in embroidery that looked new—

"Efmaer," Segnbora whispered.

Slowly she went to the unmoving woman, and stood beside her. Efmaer took no notice, just went on staring down into the pathless air. Her face was young, and frighteningly still. Her pale gray eyes had given up their color to the twilight, and taken on its violet shimmer.

Segnbora had to swallow twice before she could speak. "Queen," she said, "you're a long time away from Darthis."

The gray-violet eyes opened a touch wider. Disbelief danced in them for just a moment, and then began to fade again, sinking back into vague sorrow. The Queen didn't move.

"Efmaer," Segnbora said, louder. In the incredible silence, her own soft voice seemed to rattle her bones.

The Queen's eyes shifted just a little toward Segnbora. "Since I came here," Efmaer said, hardly above a whisper. "no one has spoken to me. I dream, and the dreams grow vocal."

It isn't fair! Segnbora thought, losing her voice again, this time to impending tears. This woman had been one of the great powers of her time: vital, powerful, quick to laugh or fight or love. She was the woman who had fought Death and won. Yet now she was like all the others here, her spirit emptied out on the crystal floor.

"Queen," Segnbora said at last, "I'm no dream, unless I stay here too long. Have you seen a man go by here, one of the living? He was wearing the arms of Arlen."

Efmaer turned slowly, and her eyes dwelt on Segnbora's surcoat and her lioncelle passant regardant in blood and gold. "I know that charge," Efmaer said, showing for the first time a wrinkle of expression, a faint frown of lost memory. "My sister—"

"Enra," Segnbora said. "I'm of her line. You are my . . . my aunt, Queen."

"How many generations removed?" Efmaer said, and for a second the bronze in her voice went bright.

Segnbora could not answer her.

"That many," said the Queen. "She is dust, then. She walks the Shore . . ."

Efmaer's voice drifted away as she started to lose herself again in the undercurrents of Glasscastle's sorrow. Segnbora gulped. There was something nagging at the back of her mind, something that would mean a great deal to this woman. If only she could remember—

"Queen," Segnbora said, "if you haven't seen him, I can't wait. I have to find him."

"I could not find the one I sought, either," Efmaer said in that same half-dreaming voice. "I looked and looked for Sefeden, while the Moon went down and the Evenstar set. We must have passed one another half a hundred times, and never known it. Hear me: The Firework sustaining this place is greater than any mortal wreaking, and the place keeps its own. You will not leave . . ."

"My friends and I will get out," Segnbora said, hoping she was speaking the truth. "Come with us—"

Efmaer shook her head. "Only the living can leave this place . . ."

"Are you dead then, Eagle's daughter?"

For the first time, Efmaer looked straight at Segnbora. Emotion was in those eyes now, but it was an utter hopelessness that made Segnbora shudder. "Do I look dead? Would that I were. Not Skádhwë itself could kill me here!"

"Skádhwë is here?"

"Somewhere," the Queen said. "Once the doors closed, I lost it, the way I lost everything else. Yet even while the doors were open, it did me no good." She closed her eyes, and with a great effort made another expression: pain. "I fought, but I could not kill myself, and so I am less than dead . . . "

Pity and horror wrung Segnbora, but she couldn't stay. "Queen, I have to go hunting."

"He will be with her," Efmaer said. "Far in, at the place where your heart breaks. But be out before moonset . . . "

The woman didn't speak or move again. Segnbora paused only long enough to take one of those pale, pliant hands and lift it, kissing the palm in the farewell of kinsfolk of the Forty Houses. Then she turned and hurried away.

Hall after hall opened before her, all alike, huge prisms full of silence and the reflections of empty eyes. Corridor like corridor, gallery like gallery, and nowhere any face she knew. She ran harder. Through the walls she saw the treacherous Moon hanging exactly where it had been when she entered. Likewise the sunset appeared about to grow dimmer, but had not changed. Inside Glasscastle there was eternal sunset, she realized. Without, who knew how much time had passed? The three Lights could be about to vanish, for all she knew.

The thought of the others still unfound, of the awful way back to the main hall, of Efmaer's ghastly placidity, all wound together in her brain and sang such horror to her that for a few seconds she went literally blind. Trying to turn a corner in that state, she missed her footing and skidded to her knees. Desperately she tried to rise, but could not. Her leg muscles had cramped.

There Segnbora crouched, gasping, sick with shame and rage. The awareness of the huge head bowing over her, great wings stretching upward, was small consolation.

(*Sdaha.*)

(Yes, I know, just a—)

(*Sdaha.* Here's our lost Lion—)

She pushed herself up on her hands and looked. There was Freelorn, not more than ten or fifteen feet away from her. He was kneeling on the crystal floor, very still, his head bowed. The sight flooded her with intense relief.

"Lorn," she whispered, and scrabbled back to her feet again, ignoring the protests of abused muscles. "Lorn. Thank the—"

—and she *saw*—

"—Goddess." Her voice left her throat, taking her breath with it.

Her throne was wrought of crystal, like everything else in the place, but it reflected nothing from its long sheer surfaces. The one enthroned upon it seemed caught at that particular moment when adolescence first turns toward womanhood, and both woman and child live in the eyes. She was clothed in changelessness and invulnerability as with the robe of woven twilight She wore, and Her slender maiden's hands seemed able, if they chose, to sow stars like grain, or pluck the Moon like a silver flower. Yet very still those hands lay on the arms of the throne, and Segnbora found herself trembling with fear to see them so idle.

Her quiet, beautiful face lay half in shadow as the Lady's gaze dwelt on Freelorn. For a long while there was no motion but that of Her long braid, the color of night before the stars were made, rising and falling slightly with Her breathing. Then slowly She looked up, and met Segnbora's eyes.

"Little sister," the Maiden said, "you're welcome."

Segnbora sank to her knees, staggered with awe and love. This was *her* Lady, the aspect of the Goddess she had always loved best: the Maker, the Builder, the Mistress of Fire, She Who created the worlds and creates them still, Giver of Power and glory. Not even that night in the Ferry Tavern had she been stricken down like this, with such terror and desire. The Maiden gazed at her, and Segnbora had to look down, blinded by the divine splendor.

She gasped for breath and tried to think. It was hard, through the trembling, yet it was the fact that she trembled at all that disturbed her. Even as the Dark Lady, walking the night in Her moondark aspect, She did not inspire fear. Something was wrong. Segnbora lifted her head for another look, and was once more heartblinded by Her untempered glory. Segnbora hid her eyes as if from the Sun, and began to tremble in earnest.

Within her Hasai bent his head low, and spread his wings upward in a bow. (She's not as you showed me, within you. Nor is She like the Immanence. Its experience, too, is always one of infinite power, but the power is tempered—)

(It's—) The words seemed impossible, a wild lie in the face of deity, but she thought them anyway. (It's not Her.)

Segnbora cut herself off. She had a suspicion of what was wrong with this Maiden. She also believed she now knew Who was maintaining the great wreaking that had built the Sky-bridge, and Who was keeping the Glasscastle-trap inviolate. Only an aspect of the Goddess could do such things . . . Segnbora got up, anxious to be out of Glasscastle before she discovered whether her suspicion was correct—

—and was very surprised to find herself still kneeling where she was. With a flash of anger she met the Maiden's eyes again. They poured power at her, a flood of chill strength, knowledge, potency. The look went straight through Segnbora like a blade. Once before, long ago, those hands had wrought her soul, those eyes had critically examined the Maker's handiwork. Now they did so again, a look enough to paralyze any mortal creature, as flaws and strengths together were coolly assessed by the One Who put them there.

But Segnbora's soul was a little less mortal now than it had been when first created. There were Dragons among the *mdei-hei* who had had direct experiences of the Immanence on more than one occasion. The judgment of ultimate power didn't frighten them; they were prepared to meet the infinite eye to eye, and judge right back.

I am what I am, Segnbora thought, reaching back toward the Dragons' strength and staring into those beautiful, daunting eyes. She would *not* be judged and found wanting with her work incomplete, her Name still unknown!

Suddenly she was standing, surprised that she could. She expected to be struck with lightning for her temerity, but nothing happened. Segnbora kept her eyes on the fair, still face, and saw, past the virulent blaze of glory, something she had missed earlier. The Maiden's eyes had a dazzlement about them, as if She too were blinded.

"My Lady," Segnbora managed to say, "I beg Your pardon, but we have to leave."

"No one comes here," the Maiden said gently, "who wants to leave. I have ordained it so."

The terrible power of Her voice filled the air, making the words true past contradiction. Segnbora shook her head, wincing in pain at the effort of maintaining her purpose against that onslaught of will. "But Freelorn is the Lion's Child," she said. "He has things to do—"

"He came here of his own free will," the Maiden said. She moved for the first time, reaching out one of Her empty hands to Freelorn. He leaned nearer with a sigh, and She stroked his hair, gazing down at him. "And now he has his heart's desire. No more flight for the Lion's Child, no more striving after an empty throne and a lost sword. Only peace, and the twilight. He has earned them."

The Maiden half-sang the words as She looked at Freelorn, and Her merciless glory grew more blinding yet. Segnbora shook her head, for something was missing. Whatever lived in those eyes, it wasn't love. And more than Her glory, it was Her love—of creating, and what she created—that Segnbora had worshiped—

(*Sdaha, be swift!*)

(Right—) She reached out to grab Freelorn and pull him away from the Maiden's lulling touch, but as she moved, the Maiden did too—locking eyes with Segnbora, striking her still.

"You also, little sister," She said, "you have earned your peace. Here you shall stay."

"No, oh no," Segnbora whispered, struggling again to find the will to move. But, dark aspect or not, this was the Goddess, Who knew Segnbora's heart better than she did.

The Maiden spoke from within that heart now, with Segnbora's own thoughts, her own voice, as the Goddess often speaks . . . . *I'm tired, my mum and da are dead; there are months,*

*maybe years of travel and fighting ahead of us—and even if I bring
Lorn out of here, he'll probably just be killed. Isn't this better for him
than painful death? And isn't it better for me, too? No death in ice
and darkness, just peace for all eternity. Peace in the twilight, with
Her* . . .

The song of the *mdeihei* seemed very far away. She couldn't
hear what Hasai was saying to her, and somehow it didn't
matter. The cool of the surrounding twilight curled into her
like rising water. Soon it would rise high enough to drown her
life, abolish both pain and desire.

The Maiden was seated no longer. Calm as a moonrise, She
stood before Segnbora, reaching out to her. "There's nothing
to fear," She said. "Nothing fails here, nothing is lost, no
hearts break or are broken. I have wrought a place outside of
time and ruin—"

The gentle hands touched Segnbora's face. All through
her, muscles went lax as her body yielded itself to its Creator.
Her mind swelled with a desire to be still; to forget the world
and its concerns and rest in Her touch forever.

"Then it's true," she whispered as if in a dream. "There's
no death here . . . "

"There is no death anywhere," the Maiden said, serene,
utterly certain.

The relief that washed through Segnbora was indescriba-
ble. The one thing that had been wrong with the world was
vanquished at last. Impermanence, loss, bereavement . . . the
Universe was perfect, as it should have been from the beginning. There was nothing to fear anymore . . .

. . . though it was curious that one dim image surfaced, and
would not go away. In languid curiosity she regarded it,
though her indifference kept her from truly seeing it for a
long time. It was a tree, and a dark field, and brightness in the
field. Night smells—

—smells?

There were smells that had little to do with night. Ground-
damp. Mold. Wetness, where her hands turned over dirt, and
jerked back in shock. Wetness, and the liquid gleam of dulled
eyes in Flamelight. And the carrion smell of death—

In a wash of horror, the dream broke. Segnbora knew who

she was again, and Who held her. The Maiden had made the worlds, true enough, and in the ecstasy of creation had forgotten about Death and let It in. But She had never denied Death's existence, or Her mistake, in any of Her aspects. Segnbora tried to move away from the hands that held her, and couldn't. Her body felt half-dead.

She settled for moving just one hand: the right one, the swordhand that had saved her so many times before. Her own horror helped her, for she realized now that she was in the presence of a legend: the One with Still Hands, that Maiden Who has stopped creating and holds all who fall into Her power in a terrible thrall. This was a dark aspect of the true Maiden, one Who had embraced forgetfulness, and Who had taken Glasscastle as Her demesne, Her prison.

(*Hasai!*)

Struggling to raise her hand, she called him, and to her shock got no answer. Twilight had fallen in the back of her mind, and she could feel no Dragonfire there. She would have to raise her swordhand alone, even though the Maiden's cool hands on her face made it almost impossible to concentrate.

Sweat sprang out with the effort. The hand moved an inch. She would *not* be left here! She would *not* leave her *mdaha* stuck in an eternity of not-doing! She would *not* walk past Lang and Freelorn and Herewiss a thousand times without seeing them . . . ! Another inch. Another. The hand felt as if it were made of lead, but she moved further into herself, finding strength.

In the twilight, something else moved. Down inside her memory, in the cavern—not her own secret place, but the cave at the Morrowfane—stones grated beneath Hasai's plating, scoring the dulled gems of his flanks as he rolled over to be still from the convulsions at last. Horrified, Segnbora discovered that the One with Still Hands was there as well. Dark as a moonless night, she was soothing Hasai's worst pain, offering him a *mdahaih* state that would never diminish him to a faint voice in the background, but would leave him one strong voice among many. But her promise was a lie.

(*Mdaha!* Move! She can't do it. She'll trap you in here, and we'll both be alive and *rdahaih* forever!)

He could not move. Desperately, Segnbora reached all the way back inside, climbed into his body and took over—wore his wings, lashed his tail, lifted his head, forced one immense taloned foot to move forward, then another, then another. Together they crawled to the mouth of the cave, Hasai gasping without fire as they went.

(*Sdaha,* have mercy! Let me go!) he begged, agonized.

She ignored him, pushing his head out the cave entrance into the clear night. The entrance was too small for his shoulders and barrel. She pushed, ramming muscles with thought and cave wall with gemmed hide, steel bones. (Now!) she cried, and they crashed into the rock together. It trembled, but held. (Now!) Stones rattled and fell about them. The mountain shook and threatened to come down—but stone was their element, they were unafraid.

Hasai began to assist her, living in his own body again, remembering life, refinding his strength. *(Now!)* They jammed shoulders through the stone; wings smote the rock like lightning, burst free into the night. Segnbora's arm knocked away with one sweeping gesture the hands that held her. In rage and pity, and a desire to see something other than slack peace in those beautiful eyes, her hand swept back again. She struck the Maiden backhanded across the face.

Shocked, sickened by the violence she had done, Segnbora waited for the lightning . . . or at least for her own handprint to appear on Her face. Nothing came, though. No flicker of the eyes, no change in the mouth. Slowly the Maiden turned Her back on Segnbora, went back to Her throne, seated Herself. She said nothing. Segnbora found herself free.

(*Sdaha*—)

(I know, *mdaha,* time!)

Segnbora shook Freelorn by the shoulder. There was no answering movement—he seemed asleep, or tranced. *Well, dammit, if I have to carry him—* She reached down and took him under the shoulders, heaving hard. Freelorn made a sound, then. It was a bitter moan; a sound of pain and mourning as if some sweet dream had broken.

"Come on, Lorn," she said, wanting more to swear than to coax. Moonset couldn't be more than a quarter-hour away. "Come on, you Lioncub, you idiot, come on—!"

Turning, she got him up—then blinked in shock. They were all there, drifting in. Lang, looking peaceful. Dritt, Moris, Torve, Harald, all the life gone out of their movements. Sunspark, quenched in the twilight like a Firebrand dropped in water. Herewiss, his light eyes dark with Glasscastle's dusk, and no flicker of Fire showing about Khávrinen.

Despair and anger shook her. She didn't have time to go into each mind separately and break the Maiden's grip. She doubted she had the strength, anyhow. Not even the Fire, had she been able to focus it, would help her now, though sorcery . . .

She paused, considering. Perhaps there *was* a way to break them all free at once. It shamed her deeply to consider it, but then she had no leisure for shame.

(*Mdaha!*)

(Do what you must,) Hasai said, placid. (I'll lend you strength if you need it.)

She gulped, and began the sorcery. It was a simple one, and vile. These people were her friends. She had fought alongside them, guarded their backs, eaten and drunk and starved with them, lain down in loneliness and merriment to share herself with them. Their friendship gave her just enough knowledge of their inner Names with which to weave a spell of compulsion.

It was almost too easy, in fact. Their own wills were almost wholly abolished. The images of loneliness, loss of Power, and midnight fear that she employed were more than adequate. She knew less about Herewiss and Sunspark than about Freelorn and the others, but could guess enough about their natures to make them head out the door. Torve was hardest—a name and a wry flicker of his eyes was all she had. Yet she was terrified for this innocent, and her fear fueled his part of the sorcery, making up for her lack of knowledge.

As she gasped out the last few syllables of the spell, Segnbora began carefully making her way out of the construct in her mind. She slipped sideways through the final fold of the sorcery, scoring herself with sharp words in only a few places, thankful for once that she was so slim. Once out, she bound the sorcery into a self-maintaining configuration that would give her time to fight off the inevitable backlash and follow the others out.

One by one, her companions began drifting away from the Maiden's throne, out toward the great gates. She sagged a moment, feeling weary and soiled, watching them go.

Inside her, wings like the night sheltered her and fed her strength. (*Sdaha*, don't dally—)

(No.)

She looked one last time at the throne, where the Maiden sat silent, watching the others go, dispassionate as a statute in a shrine. *O my Queen*, Segnbora thought. Surely somewhere the Maiden dwelt in saner aspects, whole and alive and forever creating. But to see even a minor aspect of Godhead so twisted was too bitter for a mortal to bear for long. Hurrying, Segnbora turned away to follow the others.

They were far ahead of her, unerringly following the way out that she had set for them. The sorcery was holding surprisingly well, considering how long it had been since she had used sorcery to as much as mend a pot or start a fire. She went quickly, trotting, even though physical activity would bring on the backlash with a vengeance. It felt wonderful to move again.

(*Mdaha*, you all right?)

(My head hurts,) he said, surprised. The *mdeihei* rarely experienced pain for which there was no memory.

(It's the effect of the sorcery; you're getting it from me.)

Somehow she couldn't bring herself to be very solicitous: There were still too many things that could go wrong. They could come to the doors and find them closed. Or, if they were open, the bridge could be gone. Or—

Something moved close by, a figure approaching Sgenbora from one side. It was not one of her own people, she knew. Her hand went to Charriselm's hilt.

Summersky opals winked at her as Efmaer came up beside her and walked with her, quickly but without animation. "You are leaving," the Queen said.

"Yes. Come with us—"

Efmaer shook her head. "Gladly would I come . . . but I

never found Sefeden to get my Name back, and without it I
cannot leave . . ."

"But you *know* your Name."

"I have forgotten it," said the Queen.

Segnbora's insides clenched with pity . . . and suddenly the
memory she hadn't been able to pin down appeared in her
pain-darkened mind.Urgently, she stopped and took the
Queen by the shoulders. She had half expected to find herself
holding a ghost, or something hard and cold, but there was
life and warmth in the body, and an old supple strength that
spoke of years spent swinging Fórlennh and Skádhwë in the
wars against the Fyrd.

"Efmaer. Enra gave the secret to her daughter, and it
passed into the lore of our line. I know your Name."

Undead, the Queen still managed to show shock and dismay that a stranger knew her greatest secret, the word that
described who she *was*. But her distress lasted hardly a
breath.

"Tell me quickly."

Segnbora swallowed, looked Efmaer in the eye and whispered it—one long, cadenced, beautiful word in very ancient
Darthene. Efmaer's eyes filled with it, filled with life, and
tears.

"Kinswoman," she choked, the word carrying a great
weight of thanks and wild hope. "Go. Don't stay for me. I'll
meet you by the doors if I can. I have to see about something
before I go."

Off Efmaer went into the unchanging dusk. Segnbora
turned and ran after her friends. They were almost out of
sight, near the outwalls, where the twilight was thickest.

(*Mdaha*, what's the time?)

(There's a little left yet.)

She ran, harder than before, somehow feeling relieved of
a great burden. She could feel the backlash of her sorcery
creeping up on her, a hammering in her head and a weakness
in the limbs. But her sorcery was holding, the others were still
bound by her will. She caught sight of them now, not too far
ahead, right up against—

"Oh *Dark!*" she said in complete despair, not caring what the swearing might invoke.

The great doors were shut. The faint light of the lying Moon shone high as before, but its light looked dimmer somehow. Freelorn and Herewiss were standing there looking dully up at the doors with the others. There was someone else there too, backed up against the entrance.

She pushed passed Herewiss and stopped sharp. If her heart hadn't withered already, it would have done so now.

There was more energy bound up in that waiting figure than in anyone else she had seen in Glasscastle. It was someone slender, a blade of a woman with about as much curve; someone with a slight curvature of the back that made for an odd stance, balanced forward as if perpetually about to lunge; someone with a sword like the sharpened edge of the young Moon, and short straight hair shockingly white at the roots; someone wearing a surcoat with Enra's lioncelle on it, passant regardant in blood and gold. Her dark eyes had a dazzlement about them, a terrible placidity. The One with Still Hands looked out of them. She was not defeated yet.

"*No,*" Segnbora whispered. Her otherself gazed at her with eyes tranquil and deadly, and hefted another Charriselm, making sure of her grip.

"You're not leaving," her own voice said.

Segnbora stepped closer, fascinated by the sight of herself. The other watched her unperturbed, wearing the aura of calm that Shíhan had taught her was better than armor.

(*Mdaha,* you suppose she has you too?)

(As far as I can tell, I'm only here once. Is she truly *you?*)

Segnbora took another step forward.

"Save yourself some trouble," said the Segnbora who guarded the door, "and don't bother."

(I think so,) she said to Hasai, recognizing the line. Queasiness started to rise inside her. The backlash was starting, and that meant she would soon be unable to hold together the sorcery. The others would start to drift away. Her otherself took a step forward. There was no question about her purpose. Segnbora raised Charriselm to guard, two-handed, and for the first time eyed her own stance as other opponents must have eyed it, seeking a weakness to exploit for the kill. It terrified her. All those who had attempted what she must now attempt were all dead. They started to circle one another.

"What I don't understand," the other said in a calm, reasonable voice, "is why you're trying to leave."

"I have my reasons," Segnbora said, shuddering at the strangeness of answering her own voice. "And I have my oaths—"

"Your oaths are vain," said her otherself, edging closer in that particular sideways fashion that was Segnbora's favorite for closing inconspicuously with an enemy. "Who'll notice if you break them?"

"*She* will—"

"Oh, indeed. And what has She done for you lately, besides graciously allowing you a night in bed with Her? You know, don't you, that it was only Her sneaky way of telling you that you're about to die? You don't?" The other looked scornful. "Oaths! The way Freelorn's behaving, he'll never make it anywhere near Prydon, you at least know that! He'll get himself killed, along with the rest of you, on that cold dark ledge. Ice and darkness, that's what oaths get you—"

Segnbora slid closer, trembling. It was hard to think of this as just another fight. The necessary immersion in the other's eyes—that act of *becoming* the opponent in order to counter her moves before they happened—was impossible when those eyes had the mad Maiden's dreadful stillness in them. Her every glance made Segnbora afraid she would drown in their blank dazzle, drop Charriselm and surrender. To make matters worse, the backlash was hitting her harder now—not by accident, she suspected.

(Let us fight for you!) Hasai said suddenly.

Segnbora blinked at this, and her otherself moved in fast, striking high at her head with Charriselm's twin. Segnbora whirled out of range toward the other's right, taking advantage of her own slightly weak backhand recovery, and came about again. There was a stir of movement among the silent watchers. For a moment her will to keep them in one place wavered, and they started drifting back toward Glasscastle's center, where the Maiden waited.

(Don't answer, *sdaha*. The *mdeihei* and I have been here long enough to be able to work your body; and your memories of your training are *now* for us. Tend to the sorcery. We will deal with this other you.)

The other Segnbora was inching in again, waiting an un-guarded moment—evidently Shíhan's injunctions about not wasting time on showy but ineffective swordplay were binding on her too.

Segnbora didn't much want to give her body to the *mdeihei*, but even now the sorcery was unraveling. (*Mdaha*, you get me killed—!)

(Killed? *Here?*) Hasai said, gently ironic.

The other leaped in to the attack again. While she was still in midair Segnbora felt other muscles, other wills, strike through her body and wear it as she had worn Hasai's earlier. Without her volition she saw Charriselm twist up and slash out in the *ha'denh* move, the edge-on stroke and backstroke that opens the *ekier* sequence.

Normally, the feint of the first stroke and the vicious back-hand cut of the second would have been enough to disem-bowel her opponent, but Segnbora's sword met its mate half-way through the first cut. The two swords together sang a tormented note like a bell having its tongue cut out. Char-riselm glanced down and out of the bind, and white Darthene steel sliced air where Segnbora would have been, had not the *mdeihei* twisted her impossibly sideways.

(Ow! My back!)

(You still live, don't you? Tend to the sorcery!)

There was no more time for discussion. In the back of her mind the hard-stressed words of the sorcery were turning on one another, blades cutting blades, striving to undo them-selves from her constraints. Ignoring her roiling insides, she shoved words back into place, reinforced them, threatened them, cajoled them in heartfelt Nhàired. It was like carrying water in a sieve, for all the while the power of the wreaking wore away at her outer mind, letting the twilight seep in again.

While she stopped up hole after hole of the sieve to keep

her sorcery from running out, she watched the *mdeihei* inside her skin using her to turn and cut and thrust, attacking high and low, using all-out routines like *sadekh* and *ariud*. Nothing came of it. Every time, Charriselm met its otherself in her twin's hand and the steel cried out. Every time she felt her own leverages, her own moves, being used against her. Again and again the *mdeihei* saved her life with dives and dodges that nearly snapped her spine, but the situation got no better.

(I had—no idea you were so—difficult in a fight, *sdaha*,) Hasai said, breathing hard from Segnbora's exertion. He lunged her forward in the dangerous hilt-first "mutiny" maneuver, but her otherself twisted nimbly away.

(Neither did I.) Segnbora pushed a couple of words frantically back into the weave of the spell. As she did, she remembered something Efmaer had said. *I could not kill myself, and so I am less than dead.* Was this what had happened to her? Had she fought herself here at the gates and lost?

Hasai backed her up a step, raised Charriselm and stood poised in her body like a dancer, waiting for imprudence to tempt her adversary within range. The other Segnbora took the bait, stepping in suddenly and swinging—the *edelle* slash that could open Segnbora up like an oyster if it connected.

The Dragon sucked her stomach in and struck downward with Charriselm to stop the *edelle*, then whirled the blade up in a blur to strike at the other's unprotected throat. But her otherself came up to block, and Segnbora's stroke was slightly off angle. The two swords met, and this time there was no scrape, but rather a sudden snap that went right to the pit of Segnbora's stomach. A handsbreadth above the hilt, Charriselm broke in two. The blade-shard went spinning away through the air to fall ringing on the crystal floor.

"*No!*" she cried, staring in anguish at the broken-off stump that had once been whole and beautiful. Before the doors, her otherself relaxed into guard, knowing Segnbora would think three times about trying a passage armed with only half a sword. At the back of her mind, words began falling away from one another—

A quick motion off to one side brought her around. It was Efmaer. The Queen came to her with her hands extended, and nothing in them . . . or not quite nothing. She held a long

slim darkness, like a slice of the utter darkness beyond the
world, like a splinter of night made solid—

"You gave me my Name," Efmaer said, urgent. "This is all
I have to give you. Take it!"

Only for a second Segnbora hesitated as she stared at the
uncanny thing. It was impossible to focus upon it despite its
razor-sharp outline. Then she seized it out of Efmaer's hands,
by the end that was slightly thicker, and swung it up. There
was no weight of hilt or blade; no feeling of actually holding
anything, not even coolness or warmth or resistance to the air.

(Hasai—)

(Trust us, we will do well enough.)

"Kinswoman, be warned," Efmaer said, "it'll demand a life
of you some day—it did of me!"

Segnbora nodded absently. She was already busy with the
sorcery again, shoring it up. Her otherself dropped once
more into a wary crouch, waiting, watching Skádhwë. Hasai
saw his advantage and moved in on the other, not waiting.

"So," said the other, "now you'll kill me—"

Segnbora wrought a long word in Nhàired and wove it into
a spot in the sorcery that was going bare.

"You're in my way," she said, remotely feeling the strange
heft of the sword as Hasai lifted it. Legend said it would cut
anything, but would it work here, inside another legend?

"That's only part of it," her otherself said. "You like to
kill."

She couldn't help looking into the other's eyes then and
seeing there the placid regard of the Maiden. The power that
had almost drowned her before stirred again.

Hasai danced in close, striking with Skádhwë.

(I can't—) Segnbora whispered in mind. Her resistance
made the *mdeihei* guiding her body miss the stroke. Her otherself slipped out of range, whirling to come at her on her weak
side. The *mdeihei* spun Segnbora about too, so that the face-off
stood again as it had.

Down in Segnbora's mind a word unraveled itself from her
sorcery and slithered away like a serpent of light, followed by
another, and another. Herewiss turned away, and Freelorn,
and Lang—

(*Sdaha!*)

"Yes!" she said aloud. This wasn't *her* Maiden, not the Lady of the White Hunt, defender of life and growth. This was just her own body occupied by an indweller as committed to stagnation as Hasai was to doing and being.

The *mdeihei* felt her resolve and leaped again. The other Segnbora, perhaps thinking Segnbora wouldn't kill or hurt her, was slow about retreating. A second later she danced back with a cry. Red showed high up on her arm, pumping fast.

Segnbora flinched. She had felt nothing, no bite of sword into flesh at all.

"If you kill Me, you're killing part of yourself!" the other cried, sounding afraid for the first time.

Hasai pressed in, following his advantage. Segnbora felt tears coming, but didn't argue as she patched the spell again. Only a moment later did she realize what she was going to have to do. It would have been easiest to let Hasai win the fight, but she refused to allow him sole responsibility for that. The spell would hold for a second. She moaned out loud, took back her muscles, slid in and struck with Skádhwë at the Charriselm being raised against her.

With no more feeling than if it had been cutting air, the shadowblade sheared effortlessly through Charriselm and then downward to take off her otherself's arm at the elbow. The thick sound that the arm made in striking the floor, like so much dead meat, turned Segnbora's stomach. The agony in the other's eyes was beyond words.

Segnbora would gladly have dropped Skádhwë, but it seemed to be holding her hand closed about it. Her otherself struggled to her feet, and reached down to work the broken Charriselm out of the severed hand. She lifted the useless sword left-handed, and faced Segnbora with tears streaming down her face.

"Why couldn't you have stayed?" the other Segnbora screamed at her. "Why couldn't you just let it happen! You always wanted—"

Segnbora swung Skádhwë again, and felt nothing as her otherself's head—so much silver in its hair!—went rolling away across the crystal floor, trailing red. The slender trunk dropped, pumping out what seemed too much blood for so slight a frame.

One more body. That's all it is. One more body. Oh, Goddess help me—!

Time was short. The sorcery was unraveling, assaulted by her revulsion at what she had done.

Quickly Segnbora lurched toward the doors, aware of Efmaer off to one side, of Herewiss and Freelorn drifting away. The doors were sheer, without any latch, and fitted so closely together that a thin knifeblade couldn't have been pushed between them. There was no hope of swinging open their massive weight.

Unless, perhaps . . .

She raised Skádhwë over her head and struck down, a great hewing blow. The sword sank half its depth into the crystal, as if into air. Again she struck, and a shard of the thick glass peeled away and shattered on the floor. Again, and again—

A great prism-slice the size of an ordinary doorway leaned out toward her, slow as a dream, and fell. It smashed thunderously right at her feet.

"Come on, get out!" she shouted at the others, yanking in her mind at the compulsion-sorcery.

Like hounds on leashes they all came stumbling after her, Freelorn and Herewiss, Lang and Dritt and Moris, Harald and Torve and Sunspark, out the jagged hole into the true twilight. The Moon was telling the truth again, and frightening truth it was. Its lower curve had dipped behind the wall of the Adíně glacier's cirque. Only the crescent's two horns still showed in the sky. West of the Moon, the Evenstar balanced precariously on the ridge of the cirque, a trembling, narrowing eye of light.

Behind Segnbora, Herewiss shook his head as the wind hit him, and glanced around like a man roused from reverie. Then he glanced up at where the Moon should have been, and wasn't. "My Goddess, it's almost gone, the *bridge—!*"

Segnbora stood poised by the door, peering in desperately. "Efmaer!" she cried.

Just inside the door stood Efmaer. She was looking over her

shoulder, trying to catch a last glimpse of her loved through
the twilight.

"Efmaer!"

The Queen turned to Segnbora, reached out a hand. Segnbora took it and pulled, and Efmaer stepped through the
jagged portal—

—She did not have time to look surprised. She simply
stopped in midmotion, and went to dust: the dust of a woman
five hundred years dead. Within seconds the relentless wind
came howling down from the mountain, took her, and whirled
her away.

Segnbora stared stupidly at her empty hand, then turned
and ran through the group, who stood watching her with
confusion and fear on their faces.

"Come on," she yelled through her sobs, "the wind is back,
the bridge is going to vanish! You want to try standing on
air?"

She ran out onto the phantom part of the Skybridge, half-
hoping it would give way under her. The memory of Efmaer's
hand turning to dust in hers was sickening.

Footsteps pounded close behind her. The Moon's horns
looked across the cirque ridge at her, far apart, growing
shorter. The Evenstar wavered. Segnbora ran, gasping and
terrified. Running had never been one of her strong points.
Freelorn came pounding past her, showing off his sprinter's
stride to good advantage. Hard behind him came Herewiss,
with Khávrinen once more afire on his back. Then came Sunspark, streaming fire like a runner's torch from mane and tail.
Torve and Lang and Harald and Moris and Dritt passed her
too, wheezing.

Segnbora saw them all make the solid part of the bridge just
at the moment the Moon pulled its horns completely beneath
the ridge, and the Evenstar closed its eye and went out. With
ten yards to go, the bridge of air dissolved beneath her, and
she began to fall . . .

Then Hasai was doing something. The fall simple went no
farther, as if she had wings. In the moment of time he bought
her, hands grabbed at her frantically and pulled her up onto
the steel.

She shook them off and headed down the bridge, fast, only slowing when the angle of the arch made footing difficult. Tears blinded her, burning coldly in the icy wind. She shook them out of her eyes. Raging at heart, she plunged down to the end of the span, down to rock and snow. There she ducked down around to one side of the Skybridge, and slid on her rear end toward one of the huge supports rooted in the mountainside.

The others were out of sight. Above her she heard them calling her, confused, frightened, relieved; and she ignored them. Poor crippled One, I pity You—but You'll have no more company in Your exile. Nor am I going to let Herewiss give up a piece of his life to bind this grave closed. Enough life's, been wasted here. I have a better way—

She came up hard against the leftmost support, a pillar of Fire-wrought steel easily as thick as Héalhra's Tree in Orsmernin grove. Even in the dark it shimmered a ghostly blue.

"Segnbora." Herewiss's voice floated down to her from above. "What are you doing?"

Segnbora didn't answer. Instead, she raised Skádhwë and with a great swashing blow sliced right through the steel support. The others had had enough time to get off safely.

The Fire in the steel was no hindrance. The pillar cracked and buckled backward, groaning, peeling apart from itself like a wound in metal flesh. Segnbora sliced at it again. The groan grew terrible as the upper part of the pillar came away from the lower, and the span of the bridge began to lean away from the mountainside.

She scrabbled across rock and snow to the second support and hewed that too. Far above, the groan grew to a scream of tortured metal. Smiling grimly, taking ferocious pleasure in the sound, Segnbora made her way to the last support, swung Skádhwë back, and struck. The slim shadow of its blade flicked through the metal and out the other side. The immense shadow of the Skybridge above her, shifting, leaned faster and faster and suddenly gave way to the deepening violet of the evening sky.

The screaming stopped. Silently as a flower petal—and as slowly, as gracefully—the huge strip of steel floated down into the abyss of blue air. Then with a crash that shook all Adíně, it struck the south-face glacier halfway down its slope, shattering it. Up and out the broken bridge rebounded, falling again. The air was littered with small, lazily turning splinters of ice and steel.

The bridge came to rest beyond her line of vision. She heard it though, and when the far-off noise subsided there was only the sound of her gasping, coming through tears of anguish and triumph.

There was a long silence from above, broken after a while by Herewiss's subdued voice.

"Well," he said, "that's one thing less Eftgan has to worry about . . . "

Ten

Fear hissed at me and struck
  from beneath a stone.
I crushed its head with a rock.
  Though dead, it still squirmed.

(Darthene Rubrics, xxiii)

Segnbora came down from her room the next morning and made her way to the breakfast hall only to find it empty. There was not even a single platter or cup on the table. The great inner court, when she passed through it, however, was lively as a wasps' nest is after it's been kicked. People and horses in the courtyard clattered and shouted so loud she could barely hear Hasai's comments inside her, and the *mdeihei* were drowned out entirely. Tack was being burnished, weapons readied, and the silver chains of officers were everywhere.

(What goes?) Hasai inquired, as loudly as was polite.

(How the Dark should I know?) she said.

Up the stairs to the battlements she went, three at a time, Charriselm's scabbard bouncing at her side, its every bump a reminder of the black non-weight that was sheathed in it now. The place where her sword had been felt like the socket of a lost tooth. She was grateful when she reached the top, but not reassured at all by the sight of Freelorn and Lang and Moris and Dritt and Torve leaning on their elbows, looking over the battlements, calm of face but tense of stance.

As she came up to them, something went *rap!* through the bright morning air, a sharp sound that raised goosebumps on her arms.

"What is it?" she said, joining them at the battlement. None of them answered her, so she looked for herself. Down in the valley, looking remote, a dark blot surrounded the star-shaped walls of Barachael town. The blot heaved and moved oddly, separated into smaller pieces, consolidated again. One part of the darkness moved rhythmically backward and then forward again, toward the town's big brass-studded gates.

The forward movement arrested suddenly, and after several seconds the faint rapping *boom* of the battering ram came floating across the air.

"Damn, oh *damn,*" Segnbora said, and out of reflex reached for Charriselm's hilt in frustration. She snatched her hand away as it fell to the not-hot-not-cold smoothness of Skádhwë's end.

Torve, beside her, raised his eyebrows idly at Segnbora's swearing. "It's silly, really," he said. "The people are all inside khas-Barachael, so there's no reason for the Reavers to force the gates—if they can. I just hope they don't decide to fire the fields. It's late for putting in another crop of wheat . . . "

There was really nowhere else to put her hand. After a couple seconds of hooking it uncomfortably in her belt, Segnbora sighed and let it fall to Skádhwë's hilt. It was an odd feeling, neutral, like touching one's own skin. "The Reavers arrived last night?" she said.

Torve nodded. "Through the pass. I dare say the Queen is wishing she had had Herewiss seal the pass before taking on Glasscastle . . . "

"Where is the Queen?"

"Upstairs with Herewiss," Freelorn said, giving Segnbora a sidewise glance meant to be disciplinary. "If you'd get up earlier, you wouldn't miss so much."

Segnbora made a face at her liege and leaned on the battlement like the others, elbows-down, staring at the Reavers' futile work in the valley. "More are coming?" she said. It was a rhetorical question. There were always more coming.

"Here and elsewhere," Lang said, not looking at her, in that way he had when he was worried and didn't care to let his eyes betray it.

"What happened at Orsvier?"

"She won."

"You said 'elsewhere,' just now," she remarked, puzzled. "Where's the new incursion?"

Lang wouldn't answer her. She looked past him at Dritt. "Bluepeak," Dritt said.

Segnbora's stomach began to churn, and inside her the

mdeihei sang their own unease in response to hers. Herewiss's dream was starting to come true, then. Of all the places in the world where the Shadow's sleeping influence shouldn't be disturbed, Bluepeak was the foremost.

"How many Reavers?"

"Her scrying would not come clear on that point," Torve said. "Maybe three thousand. People, a large supply convoy, beasts . . . and Fyrd."

"Fyrd?" she whispered. Allied with humans? The idea shocked her. Not even in the ancient days of terror, between the Catastrophe and the Worldwinning, had Fyrd ever gone so far as to join forces with humans, whom they regarded as prey.

These must be the thinking kind, then; the species they had fought en route to the Morrowfane. The Lion and the Eagle had supposedly vanquished them at Bluepeak long ago, but now they were back. No doubt they were thirsting for vengeance for the times before they had gained intelligence; times when humankind preyed on them.

"Looks like Bluepeak will be our job," Moris muttered.

"Looks that way," Torve said with his usual calm. He turned his eyes back to the Reavers in the valley, who—having had no luck with the town gates—were sitting down to a late breakfast.

"Idiots," Harald said under his breath. "Torve, couldn't you sent out a sortie?"

"Without orders? The Queen would take my officers' chain and use it to hang me by my privates," he answered, only half-joking. "Besides, they're out of bowshot."

Wings whistled overhead. Segnbora and the others glanced up and saw what looked like fire flying. Feathers burning like embers, eyes like live coals, a tail like flame streaming back from a torch . . . They flinched back from the parapet as the brightness landed there. It stood still long enough to smooth a couple of smoldering feathers back into place, then ruffled itself up in a flurry of red-hot brilliance.

(Levies,) it said, (strategy and tactics, forced marches, that's all your soldiers can talk about. I'm bored.)

Segnbora raised an eyebrow at the form Sunspark had adopted. "Shame, Firechild! There's only one Phoenix!"

(What's shame?) Sunspark said. (As for the Phoenix—if it's so fond of this shape, let it come try a couple of falls with me. If it wins, I'll let it keep the form.) It peered over the battlement at the Reavers below, interested. (Are they with us?)

Segnbora gazed at Sunspark with idle affection. Its tail-feathers were like those of a peacock, but red-golden and bearing eyes like coals. They were searing the stone against which they lay. She started to get an idea. "No," she said.

The elemental turned its fiery eyes on her, glowing even hotter. The others moved down the battlement, all but Torve, who stood his ground. She felt Sunspark examining her state of mind with hot impatient interest. (This is a new kind of joke, perhaps?)

(Yes. And no. Better than a joke.)

(Something for Herewiss? Something to make him glad?)

(Yes.) She considered her thought carefully before sharing it. (Before I tell you, consider this: When he finds out about it, will he be angry, will he be in pain? If he won't . . .) She let the thought rest.

Sunspark looked down at the Reavers, considering carefully. For all its power, it knew it had much to learn yet about being human. (What are they doing?) it said, audible to the others.

Torve looked at it as calmly as if it had been one of his own people. "Breaking the gates of the town," he said, "to get inside and kill the people, or take their belongings at least."

Sunspark didn't look up from the valley. Segnbora caught its thoughts: *Herewiss doesn't care for killing, or for robbing either. He tries to prevent them whenever possible.* (And when they've done that? What then?)

"They'll come here and try to kill us, so that no one can stop them from doing as they please in this part of the country," Torve said.

(That's done it!) Sunspark said.

Leaping from the battlement in a swift flash of fire, it sent them all staggering back. Segnbora felt her singed face to find out if her eyebrows were still there. Once certain that they were, she looked around hurriedly. Sunspark had vanished. But Harald and Dritt were pointing down at the valley and laughing.

Far down in the depths of air, the group around the battering ram suddenly began to break up. One person after another jumped up to beat frantically at smoldering clothes, their yelps of consternation trailing tardily through the air.

"Can it manage a whole army, though?" Lang asked uncertainly.

Then it was Segnbora's turn to point and laugh, as a bloom of light erupted before the gates, followed by the sound of screaming. The ram—a lopped monarch pine, full of pitch as monarchs are—literally exploded in red-hot splinters and clouds of burning gas. People and ponies were flung in all directions. Then from the explosion site something like a serpent of flame went pouring over the scorched ground. It lengthened and wound right around the walls of Barachael, met its tail and kept on going, coiling around, reaching upward. In moments the town was lost behind burning walls, and the huge head of a coiled fire-serpent wavered lazily above Barachael. The confused shrieks and yells of the routed Reavers mingled with the screaming of their ponies. People and animals ran every which way. A roar of amazed laughter and applause went up from the walls of khas-Barachael.

In response the Reavers, who had moved away from Barachael town and toward the keep, raised a chorus of war shouts. But their shouts had a half-hearted sound to them, as if they had other matters in mind. Sunspark was looking down at them with innocent malice, its fiery head swaying like that of a sleepy viper deciding whether to strike.

"What the—!" someone said from a higher parapet.

Segnbora glanced up and saw Eftgan and Herewiss looking over the rail at Barachael town, very surprised.

"Your idea?" Eftgan said to Herewiss.

"No!" he said, grinning down at Sunspark.

It stretched up its flame-hooded head and blinked at him good-naturedly. (They had torches,) it said, (and might have burned the town. However, if anybody's going to do any burning around here, it's going to be *me.*)

Herewiss and Eftgan came down to the battlement together and leaned on the parapet with Freelorn's followers. "I wish that sealing the pass was going to be as simple," Eftgan said.

Freelorn glanced at her. "It really *can* be done, then?"

Herewiss nodded. "It took me a while to work out the exact method, and it'll take some hours to attune to the mountain properly . . . but, yes, I can do it."

"And survive?"

Herewiss's glance crossed with Freelorn's, gently mocking. "That's with Her, of course," he said, "but I have a few things to do yet before I go willingly to death's Door. I believe I'll live."

"It's risky, though," Eftgan said, as if resuming an argument with herself. "The earth always moves better on a night when the Moon's full, but the next time that happens there's an eclipse. The Shadow will be very strong then—"

There was a silence. Segnbora bit her lip. In a place as bitterly contested as Barachael, where the land was soaked with centuries of blood and violent death, even the simplest wreaking could be warped by the built-up negative forces. An eclipse was no help at all. And to attempt a wreaking that involved unconsciousness of the upper mind, as this one surely would—

"I'm strong too," Herewiss said.

The complete assurance in his voice made Segnbora shudder. She had heard such assurance before, and disaster had followed.

"The wreaking itself doesn't worry me; I received more than enough Power to handle it at the Morrowfane. The tricky part will be the survey of the land. That'll have to be done out-of-body, and it'll take at least a day. Moreover, it must be done today, or tomorrow at the latest, in order for me to be properly rested up for the long wreaking."

Lang raised his eyebrows. "Survey?"

Herewiss nodded and leaned on the parapet. "Can't seal the pass without checking the valley to see how its stone lies —strata, faults, underground water. Touch the wrong part of a landscape and the whole thing could be destroyed."

"This area's quite unstable," someone said, and heads turned toward Segnbora, confusing her terribly until she realized that it was she who had spoken. "There are two major faults under the valley," she heard herself go on in a voice that

sounded like hers but was somehow odd. "Eight minor vertical faults run east-west between Adínë and Aulys, and one
runs across the lower Eisargir Pass. One major vertical fault
crosses the valley mouth from Swaleback to Aulys's southern
spur—"

(*Mdaha*? What are you—)

(If he will work with stone, here, he must learn this, *sdaha!*)
said the great dark voice inside her. She held her peace and
let him use her throat.

"Then beneath those is a lateral fault that runs down the
Eisargir Pass from the foot of Mirit into the valley, past the
town, and out into the plain. It's very treacherous. We made
no Marchward here because of it. To touch it wrongly will
cause it to discharge and fold the valley in upon itself. The
mountains might come down too. Especially Adínë, whose
support-spurs are rooted close to the lateral."

The others stared at her, particularly Herewiss. He opened
his mouth, but paused a moment, unsure how to begin.
"Sir—"

"I greet you, Hearn's son," she said, and approximated
Hasai's slight bow.

"Sir, how do you know all this?"

The *mdeihei* were laughing indulgently, as one laughs at a
child. "We are Dracon," Hasai said, very gently. "We *know*.
Stone is our element."

"Sir," Herewiss said, "I'd like to trust what you say, it'd save
me a great deal of time, but—"

"—but you don't understand," Hasai said, patient. Segnbora was surprised to hear the overtones of his inner song,
calm and measured, coming out in her own voice.

"What you ask us is a great mystery. Even we aren't sure
how stone became our element. But in the world from which
we came, we were born in the stone, and dwelt in it. These
are the very earliest times of which we speak. When food and
drink failed us, stone and starlight were all we had left. We
learned to use them. Those who didn't understand stone—
how it could be moved to make shelter or melted with Dragonfire to help one find more starlight in dim times—those
didn't survive. Those of us who lived to become as we are

now, are born knowing the structure and movement of rock as we know how to use our fire to shape it. We experience stone as if it were part of us. Indeed, we *are* the foundations, the roots of the world."

Herewiss and Freelorn looked at each other. No one on the parapet spoke.

From down in Barachael valley, the hot eyes of the blazing serpent that encircled the town looked up with interest. (You're good with fire, are you?) Sunspark said, its voice lazy but full of challenge.

Segnbora gulped. But Hasai turned her head and looked down at the elemental calmly. "We know something of fire."

Sunspark glanced at Herewiss, as if considering the agreements that bound it, and then back at Segnbora. "Some day," it said formally, "we'll match our power, you and I, and see which is greater."

"Some day," Hasai said calmly, "we shall." The words made Segnbora squeeze her eyes shut against a sudden blinding headache, for they were in future definite tense, describing something that had not yet come to pass.

When the memories passed, and the sight of common daylight came back to her, Hasai lifted her head again. "Hearn's son," he said, "do you desire our aid?"

Herewiss looked at Segnbora as if trying to see past Hasai's voice. " 'Berend, what do *you* say?"

She coughed and cleared her throat, getting control back. "I say, if Hasai offers you aid, take it."

"In that case," Herewiss replied slowly, "I'd like to check his assessment of the faults—" He stopped, unwilling to complete his suggestion.

"—in my mind?" she guessed.

"Yes."

Segnbora considered the idea. "You're welcome to look in," she said finally. "When?"

"As close as possible to the hour that we begin the wreaking. Tomorrow night?"

"Wait a minute!" Segnbora said, panic rising. *"We?"*

Herewiss shrugged. "I'll need ongoing information during

the wreaking itself. I could probably do it alone, but why stretch myself thin when there's assistance offered?"

Segnbora hesitated. To participate in the wreaking itself would mean becoming involved with Herewiss's Fire. And the Fire was something she had sworn she would never touch again; she had suffered too many frustrations on its account. Besides, being unable to focus, she might become a danger to the proceedings . . .

Herewiss picked up her last thought. " 'Berend, you came out of the Precincts with everything they had to teach, less one," he said. "I doubt you'll foul a wreaking in progress. Goddess knows how many of them they put you through!"

Most of them, Segnbora thought sourly, *for all the good it did.* She had no excuse. "All right," she said. "Tomorrow night, then."

"We'll move mountains together," Hasai added in a rare show of humor. There was starlight in the cave, and behind him ran the slow quiet laughter of the *mdeihei.*

Herewiss nodded to Segnbora, and then turned to Eftgan. "Madam," he said, "we have to finish discussing the Bluepeak business."

He started back up the stairs to the tower, taking them two at a time, Khávrinen bouncing at his back and trailing blue Flame. Eftgan gave Segnbora a curious look and followed.

What have I got myself into! Segnbora thought. She put her head down onto her hands and gazed across the valley at Barachael, memories of the Precincts, and her unsuccessful attempts to focus tearing at her.

Below, the fire-serpent folded its hood and looked at her with innocent wickedness. (Tell me a joke?) it said.

Segnbora groaned.

The next day it began to seem as if Eftgan's glum assessment of the Shadow's ability to direct the Reavers was correct. It certainly seemed as if they knew the incursion route down the Eisargir Pass was threatened. They came pouring out of the valley in a disorderly but constant stream. Skin tents sprouted everywhere, and thousands of shaggy Reaver ponies cropped the green corn down to stubble. The old silence of the valley was replaced by a low, malicious whispering, like the Sea's when a storm is brewing. Dusk brought no peace, either. All the valley glittered with the sparks of campfires, around which war songs were being sung, and swords sharpened.

Segnbora sat atop an embrasure in the northeastern battlement as twilight settled in, looking down at the press of Reaver tents and people gathered around the lower switchback of the approach to khas-Barachael gates. Hasai looked with her, undisturbed. (This place is well built, for something made by your kind,) he said. (It won't fall to such as these.)

"Maybe not. But this is the strongest fortress in this part of the south, and they don't dare march away from here and leave it unconquered at their backs. Even if Herewiss seals the pass successfully, these three thousand will just sit at the gates and hold the siege."

(You're troubled, *sdaha*. And it's not the prospect of battle that's causing it.)

With a sigh, Segnbora swung down from her perch on the wall and sat on the stone bench inside the embrasure, leaning back against the cool wall. (I'm not delighted about this business of being involved in a wreaking,) she said silently. (Especially this one. And you got me into it.)

The dusky melody of Hasai's laughter rumbled inside her. (I think not. Who spoke the words, who told the Firebearer he was welcome? Did you lie to him, then?)

Exasperated, Segnbora closed her eyes and slid down into herself. Above the cave within her, it was twilight too. Stars were coming out one by one in the shaft that opened on the sky. Hasai lay at ease on the stone, his eyes silver fire, his tail twitching slightly like that of an amused cat. Segnbora walked over to him and sat down by one of his front talons, leaning her back against it and craning her neck back to see him.

The Dragon was a shadow, winged like the night, only his face glittering in the cool light of his eyes. "Very funny," she said. "*Mdaha,* I didn't lie. But I'm afraid of him depending on me. I might fail him."

"*Éssn'hh'suuóo,*" Hasai chided. "When will you accept what you are?"

"Be patient, will you? It took me long enough to find out what I'm not."

"Part of you is me," the Dragon said. "I will not fail so simple a task as examining the stone in this valley. If you wore my body more often, you would know that."

The melody of the bass viols in his voice became grave. Behind him the *mdeihei* matched his song in cadences of calm regret.

"Your memories are buried deeper under you mind's stone than ever. We are at your foundations, and still you try to keep us out. It would be so easy to become one," he said, lifting his head. "Look . . ."

In a flash of memory, Hasai showed her the building of the Eorlhowe in North Arlen—a whole mountain that had been uprooted from a remote range in west Arlen as casually as a man might pluck a flower for his hair. The mountain was taken to the tip of the North Arlene Cape, laid there upon the body of the slain Worldfinder, and melted down upon him with Dragonfire until it was only half the size it had been. Then its remains were talon-carved and tunneled and re-worked into the residence of the DragonChief, the Dweller–at–the–Howe. Segnbora shuddered at the thought of the paltry skin of stone that had been "protecting" her inner mind from Hasai and the *mdeihei*.

"Your fear cripples you," Hasai said more gently. "You fear what we are. Even our joys are terrible to you. Matings, births, deaths, the Immanence that isn't your Lady but is nonetheless real— You must give up the fear, come to terms with these and all the other things from which you cannot run away. Cease hiding yourself from yourself, be who we *are!*"

"It's not that easy," she said, taking a last glance at that distressing memory of the Howe. As she watched, storm-clouds clustered about it, hiding the Howe's rounded peak. Dragons flashed in and out of the clouds like lightning, their roars deafening the thunder. Whether this was ahead-memory, or past-memory, she had no idea.

(Hallo the heart!) came a voice from a long way up. It was Herewiss's voice, tentative but cheerful.

"Damn," Segnbora muttered.

Hasai lowered his head toward her. "Later, *sdaha?*"

"Later for sure," she said, disgruntled. She was not ready for this, but nevertheless she called up to the stars, "Come on in!"

"I brought a friend," Herewiss said, slipping sideways out of nothing as if through a narrow door. Khávrinen was laid casually over his shoulder. Fire flowed from it and caught in Freelorn's eyes as he appeared behind his loved.

"Nice place you've got here. Where's your lodger? Lorn wanted to—"

Segnbora watched in amused approval as Herewiss stopped in midsentence and looked up . . . and up, and up. Freelorn halted beside him and did the same, his eyes going wide. When Segnbora had first come in, Hasai had been indistinct, a looming dark presence. But now the gems of his scales caught the light of Herewiss's Fire and threw it back in a dazzle of blue sparks. He lowered his head to thirty or forty feet above Freelorn and Herewiss, tilting his head to look first at one of them, then at the other.

"I see the resemblance remains," he said, very low, rumbling a major chord of approval. Following the words came Dragonfire, a slow and luxuriant spill of blinding white radiance that poured from his mouth to the floor and pooled there, burning. "Greetings, Lion's Child. And to you and your Flame, greetings also, Hearn's son."

From the darkness beyond Hasai the *mdeihei* joined the greeting, recognizing the sons of two lines worthy of notice even as Dragons reckoned time. The huge cavern filled with a thunder of concerting voices, a harmony that shook the walls.

Herewiss bowed very low. Freelorn glanced around him in amazement at the noise, and then down at the spill of Dragonfire, under which the stone floor had melted and begun to bubble. Finally he tilted his head back up to look at Hasai.

"Resemblance?" he said in a small voice.

"To Héalhra," Hasai said calmly.

Freelorn's mouth fell open.

"I was at Bluepeak Marchward some years before the Battle," Hasai said. "I saw him when he was a little younger than you. You have his nose."

"I, uh . . ." Freelorn said, and closed his mouth. He looked over at Segnbora.

She shrugged. "He's been around awhile, Lorn. *Mdaha,* what do we have to do for Herewiss?"

"Come deeper inside us, *sdaha.* He will see what he needs to see when you do."

Hasai dropped his head down to Segnbora's level, his jaws opening slightly to receive her hand. Dragonfire still seethed in his mouth, so that the floor hissed and smoked where drops of it fell. For a split second she hesitated. Then, recognizing a challenge, she rolled up the sleeve of her shirt and thrust her arm into the fire. This was happening in her mind, after all. How badly could it hurt?

She found out. Jaws closed and held her trapped in the essence of burning, a heat so terrible that it transcended pain. Her control broke. She opened her mouth to scream, feeling the heat more completely than anything she had ever felt in her life. But to her utter amazement, without the sensation stopping, the pain vanished—

She felt the stone. There was no way she could *not* feel it. The sensation was like a fencer's when balance at last becomes perfect and power flows up from the earth. Connections formerly hidden suddenly became clear and specific: her body seated on stone, the bench; the bench's placement on the stone of the upper-battlement paving; the positions and junctures of the blocks of khas-Barachael's walls; the massive piers and columns of its foundation-roots in Adínë's southern spur.

She felt the whole mountain, a complex of upthrust blocks and minor stresses pushing against one another and easing again as Adínë's roots met those of its neighboring peaks. Her perception widened and spread around the valley to include Eisargir and Houndstooth and Aulys, mountains leaning on or striving against one another. The valley, too, filled with her until she felt the faults and stresses there, a surface unease like a vast itch. She felt the transverse vertical faults, lying fairly quiet now that mountain-building in the area was largely

finished. She felt the lateral fault, stretching from head to foot
of the valley and holding dangerously still.

Farther down, heat grew in the stone. Its structure and its
temper changed as her perception slid down through the
fragile skin on which continents rode and jostled. Weight and
pressure grew by such terrible strides that there was no telling
anymore whether the stone was liquid or solid: it simply
burned darkly, raging to be free, yet having nowhere to go.

Down farther still, it was too hot, too dense, for stone.
Molten metal seethed and roasted in eternal night, swirling
with the planet's turning, breeding forces for which Segnbora
had no words but which the Dragons understood. These were
some of the forces they manipulated while flying, and finding
their way.

(Enough!) Herewiss said, his voice seeming to come from
a long way off. (Sir, I see your point.)

(Look here, then,) Hasai said, redirecting Segnbora's attention to the very top of the papery layer where mountains were
rooted and the valley lay. (You see the danger of the lateral
fault. Trigger it and the vertical faults will likely collapse the
valley, bringing down the mountains. Yet the pass you pro-
pose to close has the lateral running right down it, and direct
intervention there will definitely set off the fault.)

(There's also the problem of the negative energies,) Segn-
bora said. (See how they're gathered along the lateral fault.
It's ready to have a quake. Evidently that's an option the
Shadow's been considering for a while.)

(I've been thinking about it too,) Herewiss said, sounding
grim. (The question is, what do I do about it? There's only
one possibility . . .)

He trailed off, sounding dubious.

(What's your thought, Firebearer?) Hasai said.

Herewiss indicated one of the eastern roots of Houndstooth, a colossal pier of granite and marble set a half mile
deep in the crust.

(Positive and negative attract,) he said. (If I strike there with
my Fire and cause that root to move, the negative should flow
away from the lateral fault and attack my positive Power. But
before that happens and the forces cancel out, the root itself

will move upward enough to knock the Houndstooth peak
down into the pass and block it permanently—) He broke off,
looking at Hasai's perception as if seeing something wrong.

(Yes, you've found the problem with your plan,) Hasai said.
(Watch.) As he spoke, the perception moved and changed in
response to Herewiss's suggestion. They felt, rather than saw,
the smooth peak of Houndstooth rear up and collapse westward into the Eisargir Pass. A few seconds later the lateral
fault came violently alive. Half of Barachael valley slid south
with a jerk, while the rest jumped north. Every vertical fault
went wild, one after another, some blocks thrusting hundreds
of feet upward in a matter of minutes, some sinking fathoms
deep. Mount Adínë fell on Barachael. Eisargir collapsed on
itself and buried the priceless ironlodes forever. When it was
all over, nothing was left but a broken, uninhabitable wilder-
ness.

Herewiss grimaced. (The psychic energy canceled out all
right,) he said, (but I had no idea there was so much move-
ment-energy in that lateral fault. Damn!)

(Don't berate yourself,) Hasai said. (The move was well
made for one so new at the game. Come, Firebearer, try it
again. There is always a solution.)

(Well then, how about this . . .)

For a long while afterward Segnbora's mind was filled with
the feeling of rock shifting and grinding and mountains falling over in various disastrous combinations. She got very
bored. The game Hasai and Herewiss were engrossed in was
like an extremely complicated variation of checks—and
though Segnbora enjoyed playing for the delight of crossing
wits with another player, her inability to think more than three
or four moves ahead usually kept the game short and its
ending predictable. Freelorn, to her intense irritation, looked
over Herewiss's shoulder in fascination, understanding everything.

(That'll do it!) she heard Herewiss say at last.

Focusing her attention fully on the scene she was feeling,
she found, to her amazement, a Barachael valley still relatively
intact, with both town and fortress unhurt, and the Eisargir
Pass successfully sealed. Some distance away in her mind, she

could feel Herewiss grinning like a child who had beaten a master.

(That was an elegant solution,) Hasai said. (And as I understand the Shadow from my *sdaha,* It would have to intervene Itself to foul the situation any further, which It's reluctant to do, not so? It fears risking defeat.)

(That's right,) Herewiss said. (There's one move that still bothers me, though. The next-to-last. That one root of Aulys, the one that's split up the middle—)

(Move it as a whole, and you'll be safe.)

Hasai's perception of the valley winked out, leaving them standing in her cave again. Segnbora took her hand out of Hasai's mouth and looked at it closely. There were no burns or blisters. Her *mdaha* rumbled at her in amiable mockery. "Hearn's son," he said, "when this business is over, I'd be delighted to play with you again. There are some stresses in the volcanic country in west Arlen that might stretch you a little."

Herewiss nodded. "With 'Berend's cooperation, absolutely." He turned to her. "I'll be starting the wreaking at sunset tomorrow. Lorn and Sunspark will be keeping an eye on our bodies while we're out of them, and Lorn will be tied partially into the wreaking to keep us in touch with what's happening in real time. Are you still with us?"

She felt like telling him no, but Hasai, gazing silently down at her, felt about in her memories and brought one in particular: night outside the old Hold, and her voice saying to Herewiss, "You'll find your Power, prince . . . I'll help if I can."

"Yes," she said. "Dark, it's been years since I last moved a mountain."

Herewiss, hand in hand with Freelorn, gave her an approving look. "Later, then," he said. Fire from Khávrinen blazed up and swirled about them. They vanished.

Segnbora folded her arms and looked up at the silver eyes gazing placidly down on her. "You're up to something," she said.

Hasai flicked his wings open, a humorous gesture that made cool wind a second later. "When one knows what's going to be," he said, "one tends to make it happen that way."

"So what's going to happen?"

Hasai slowly dropped his jaw at her. "Live, *sdaha,* and find out."

He vanished into a memory. Segnbora sat for a moment on the bench, listening to the amused song of the *mdeihei*—then grinned with anticipation, felt her way out of the embrasure, and went to bed.

"How are the stars?" Herewiss said from behind her.

"Almost right," said Freelorn. He was beside her, leaning on the sill of the tower window. "Another quarter-hour and the Moon'll be in the Sword."

"Great. I'm almost done."

The Moon, just past its first quarter and standing nearly at the zenith, looked down on a valley that flickered with campfires and the minute shiftings of Reavers going to and fro. Around Barachael's walls, a lazy ring of fire smoldered, flaring up every now and then when some skeptical Reaver got too close. Segnbora, feeling a touch naked without surcoat and mail, turned her back on the valley vista and watched Herewiss at work.

The tower room had been emptied of everything but two narrow pallets and a chair. Around these, in what had been the empty air in the middle of the room, Herewiss was building his wreaking—the support web that would both protect him and Segnbora and slow their perception of time long enough for his Fire to do its work. He stood in britches and shirt, as Segnbora did, with one hand on his hip. With the other hand he wielded Khávrinen as lightly as an artist's stylus, adding line after delicate line of blue Flame to what had become a dome of pulsing webwork with him at its center.

The completeness of his concentration, and the economy and elegance of the structure itself, delighted Segnbora. *Lady, he's good,* she thought, admiring the perfect match between the inner symmetry-ratios of the wreaking and the meter of the spell-poem he was reciting under his breath. It had been foolishness to dismiss him from the Precincts simply because he was male.

"If you leave my pulse running that fast," she said, noticing the brilliance of the last lifeline Herewiss had drawn, "I'll be in bad shape when we get back."

"Nervous, huh?" he said, glancing at her and lifting Khávrinen away from the description of a parabola. He touched the sword's tip to the pulse line, draining it of some Fire. "Better?"

"Yes."

"Good. Sunspark?"

Hot light flowered in one corner of the room and consolidated into a slim red-haired young woman with merry golden eyes. (They're impatient down there, loved,) she said, pleased. (They keep testing me.)

"Fine, just so long as they don't get too interested in khas-Barachael. You know what to do?"

(This being the fourth time you've asked me,) Sunspark said, folding her arms in good-natured annoyance, (I dare say I do. None of them will leave the valley. They'll find the way into the plains barred, just as Barachael town is barred to them. On the night of full Moon, immediately before the eclipse starts, I'll begin driving the lot of them back up the pass. None will die.)

Herewiss nodded, narrow-eyed, completing the interconnection of several lines. "I hate to admit it," he said, "but there's a possibility that something'll go wrong with all this. If the pass fails to seal properly, and I've exhausted myself, and they get down into the valley again—"

(Loved,) Sunspark said, (in that case I'll be very quick with them. Their bodies will be consumed before the pain has a chance to start.)

Herewiss looked gratefully at the elemental from inside the shimmering blue web of the wreaking. "Thanks, loved. I'll do my best to make it unnecessary." He rested Khávrinen point-down on the floor and gazed around at the finished spellweb. "Lorn?"

"The Moon's right," Freelorn said, turning away from the window. "Let's go."

Trembling a bit with excitement, Segnbora unbuckled her swordbelt, drew Skádhwë from it, and tossed the belt in one corner. Herewiss walked out through the web and then

turned inward to face, from the outside, the part of it specifically concerned with his body.

"A little to the left, 'Berend," he said as she moved into
position. "Lorn, you're fine." They each stood at one corner
of an equilateral triangle. "All together: *step*—"

Segnbora walked through the part of the Fireweb sympa-
thetic to her, feeling it crackle with charge as it brushed
against her face and hands. The hair stood up all over her as
the spell passed through her body and rooted in flesh and
bone. At the same time came an astonishing wave of lethargy.
Hurriedly Segnbora lay down on the left-hand pallet, settling
herself as comfortably as she could. She laid Skádhwë down
the length of her, folded both hands about its hilt at heart
level, and began relaxing muscles one by one.

Across the circle, Herewiss was settling himself with Khávrinen, while Freelorn bent over him. "My head aches," Lorn
said. "Is it supposed to do that?"

"That's the part of your mind that's slowing down to keep
up with us," Herewiss explained drowsily as the wreaking
took hold of him too. His eyes lingered on Freelorn for a
moment.

"Don't even think it," Lorn said, and bent lower to kiss
Herewiss good night. Herewiss's eyebrows went up for a second, then down again as his eyes closed.

(*Mdaha,*) Segnbora said to her inner depths, closing her
own eyes, (see you when I'm out of the body!)

(I think not,) the answer came back, faint, amused.

(*What?*) She tried to hold off the wreaking long enough for
Hasai to explain, but it was no use.

Briefly, the spell fought with her lungs, then conquered
them and slowed her breathing. That done, the Firework
wound deeper into her brain, altering her thought rhythms
toward the profound unconsciousness of wreaking suspen-
sion. For a second of mindless panic Segnbora fought that
too, like a drowning swimmer, but then everything, even
Hasai and the *mdeihei,* fell away . . .

Eleven

"Choose," She said to the cruel king. "For I am bound by My own law, and what you desire shall be given you, until you shall ask Me for something beyond My power to grant." He told her his desires, and she granted them all—until at last, alone, desolate King of an empty city, he cried out to Her in anguish, "Change my heart!"

"I shall leave you now," the Goddess said, "for you have asked a boon past My power. Only one has the power to fulfill that wish . . . and you are doing so."

from "The King Who Caught the Goddess,"
in *Tales of old Steldin,* ed. s'Lange,
rr'Virendir, 1055 p.a.d.

Segnbora was wide awake. She swung her feet off the pallet and stood up with Skádhwë in her hand. The room around her was foggy and hard to see—Herewiss's spellweb had already slowed her time sense considerably. Dust and convection currents moved around her at what seemed many times their normal speed. Her othersenses were wide awake too, and showed her strange blurs going swiftly about the room: one yellow-bright as fire, one dark with an odd tangle of potential at its heart: Sunspark and Freelorn.

Herewiss still lay in his body, the blue-white core that was his soul struggling yet with the shell that surrounded it. Tense with the sensation of his difficulty, Segnbora turned away from him to gaze down at herself where she lay on her pallet.

(*Mdaha?*) she said. No answer came back; evidently the *mdeihei* were tied to her body, and must stay there, silenced, when she left it.

Sorrowful and nostalgic, she looked down at her still form, drowned in a repose deeper than any sleep. It had been a long time since the Precincts, when she had last been out-of-body and able to see herself so clearly. A lot had changed since then. There was a wincing fierceness about the corners of the eyes now that hadn't been there when she was younger. There was also a tension in her posture, as if her body was prepared to move in a hurry. *Too much time alone,* she thought, with the curious soulwalker's objectivity. *Too much time on the run.*

(It's not that bad,) Herewiss said from behind her. She turned, and in sheer appreciation didn't move or speak for a few thoughts' time.

In general, Herewiss still looked like his body. He was still lean and tall, wearing the no-nonsense musculature of a smith: hands both powerful and delicate; a fine-featured face made handsome by sleepy, gentle eyes. But in his wreaking form shone a child's innocent joy in life. Fire, with its incredible potential for creation and destruction, blazed in him like the Sun held captive in a crystal. He was dangerous, and utterly magnificent.

(Well met,) she said, and meant it.

(You speak for me too,) Herewiss said.

Segnbora realized how oddly he was looking at her, and wondered what he saw.

(We're short of time,) he said. (But for the moment, look at *that!*)

He pointed at something behind her. Segnbora looked over her shoulder, away from the quick-flickering light of the Fireweb. Laid out along the floor, long and dark behind her, was her shadow.

(That's impossible!) she said in momentary indignation, turning to see it better. (You can't have a shadow out of the body!) Yet there the darkness lay, stretching to the wall and right through it, blandly contradicting what had been taught to her in the Precincts. Experimentally Segnbora raised an arm, and was dumbfounded to see the serrated shape of a Dragon's wing lift away from the shadow-body.

Behind her she felt Herewiss restraining his laughter.

(My *mdaha* is truly becoming part of me,) she said, amused in spite of herself.

(Where is he? I thought he'd be here with us.)

(So did I. He's with my body, it looks like.)

Herewiss felt dubious for a moment. (How are you going to tell me what's happening in the stone, then? If he's not here—)

She started to lean on Skádhwë, then aborted the gesture as the sword's point began to pierce the stone they stood on.

(Well, I have my memories of what it's like to be one of the *mdeihei*. All I have to do is live in them completely enough and we'll be fine.) She wished she was as certain of that as she made it sound. (Now, where do we have to go?)

Herewiss nodded at the room's north wall, laying Khávrinen over his shoulder. Segnbora did the same with Skádhwë, and together they walked through the wall and into the clear air over Barachael. The stars wheeled visibly in the paling sky above them, moving a little faster each moment as Herewiss's wreaking further slowed their time sense.

(How about that, it works,) Herewiss said, pausing. (A moment. Lorn?)

The answer came not in words, but in swift-passing impression of concern, relief, encouragement. All was well in the tower, though Freelorn wondered why Herewiss had waited so long to check in with him. Hours had passed.

(We're all right, loved,) Herewiss said. (The pauses may get pretty long, but don't worry about us unless the web fails.) He broke contact and walked down the air toward Barachael valley. Segnbora followed.

Their othersight was stimulated by the wreaking, and the Chaelonde valley bubbled like a cauldron with normally unseen influences. The Reavers' emotions were clearly visible, a stew of frustrated violence and fear. Barachael town crouched cold and desolate behind the invaders. As the low threshold of her underhearing dropped lower still, Segnbora heard the slow bitter dirge of the town's bereaved stones, which were certain that once more the children of their masons had been slaughtered. The other lives of the valley, birds and beasts, showed themselves only as cautious sparks of life, aware of an ingathering of Power and lying low in order not to attract attention.

The sky to the east went paler by the moment. The Moon slid down the sky and faded in the face of day, looking almost glad to do it. While they watched, the Sun leapt into the sky too quickly, as if it wanted to put distance between itself and the ground.

The ground was a problem. Dark negative energies seethed within it the way thoughts of revenge seethe within an angry mind. Though the faults weren't yet very clear, it was plain that these negative energies ran down most of them, draining toward the foundations of the valley, where they collected in a great pool of ancient, festering hatred.

(We have to get into empathy with *that!*) Segnbora said, revolted.

(I'd sooner sit in a swamp, myself,) Herewiss said, and he strode down the air toward the reeking morass. (Still, the sooner we do it, the sooner we can get out and get clean again. Come on, down here . . .)

He led the way around toward the base of the easternmost spur of Adínë. There one of the vertical faults followed the spur's contour, a remnant of a day long before when the earth had shrugged that particular jagged block of stone above the surface. The fetid swirling of emotion in the valley broke against the spur as a wave breaks, flowing around it and up the pass. Herewiss stepped carefully down onto a high ridge of the spur and waited there for Segnbora. She arrived shortly after him, and they both paused to watch the way the shadows in the valley shrank and changed. The few moments' walk down from Sai khas-Barachael had begun at sunrise, and now it was nearly noon.

(Now what?)

Herewiss lifted Khávrinen. Fire ran down from it and surrounded him until he blazed like someone drenched with oil and set alight. (In,) he said, and glanced down at the ridge he stood on.

Without further ado he stepped down into the earth as if walking down stairs.

(Show-off,) Segnbora thought affectionately. She walked down the outer surface of the ridge, seeking the way into the mountain that would best suit her. Turning, she saw her incongruous shadow against the ridgewall behind her. Reaching behind her with both hands, she grasped it and pulled it forward about her shoulders like a cloak, becoming what she couldn't be.

It was astonishingly easy. There was fire in her throat again, and she had wings to feel the air, one of which was barbed not with a claw of white diamond but with a sliver of night made solid. She dug her talons into the naked stone. Without moving, Segnbora *knew* what lay beneath her. The deep, slow, scarce-moving selfness of the rock, the secret burning at the roots, the earth's heavy veins running with the mountain's blood . . . they were her veins, her blood, her life.

It was hard to think, immersed in the ancient nonconscious musings of stone. The transience of thought, or any concern for the insignificant doings of the ephemerals at the outer edge of Being, seemed pointless.

Internal affairs were much more important. Leisurely, the conflict between the black flowing fires of the Inside, and the cold nothing of the Outside, was played out upon the board of the world. The player Outside blanketed the board close, wearing away its opponent with wind and rain; grinding it down with glaciers; cracking its coastlines with the pressure of the hungry seas. The Inside raised up lands and threw them down; tore continents apart; broke the seabottoms and made new ones; hunched up fanged mountain ranges to bite at the wind, and be bitten in return.

This particular range had hardly been in the game long enough to prove its worth as a move. Understandably, the huge nonconsciousness wondered idly—as the Sun went down again—why this area was suddenly such a cause for concern . . .

Segnbora breathed stone deeply and strove to remember herself. There was something lulling for a Dragon in this perception of stone, as there was for humans in the presence of the Sea: It was both the call of an ancient birthplace and the restful comfort of the last Shore.

(Herewiss?) she said, singing a chord of quandary around his name.

(Here,) his answer came back, darkness answering darkness.

She couldn't feel him except indirectly. He had chosen to leave his physical imagery behind for the time being, and was manifesting himself only as a mobile but greatly restrained stress in the stone, staying quite still until he got his bearings. Khávrinen was evident too, seeming like the potential energy which that stress would release when it moved.

(I feel you. Aren't you coming in?)

(I *am* in,) she sang, delighted by the truth of it. (I'm outside, too. Both at once. I can feel you inside me; you're like a muscle strain. And I can feel the other side of the world from here. What do you feel?)

(Granite, mostly. Marble. Iron—that's the mines.) He paused to feel around. (They haven't come near the great lodes, even after centuries of work. I'll have to tell Eftgan where the good metal is . . .) He trailed off, sounding uneasy.

Segnbora felt what Herewiss felt and found everything much as it had been when Hasai had done the first survey; but the assessment didn't satisfy her. (I need more precision. I'm going to narrow down a good deal and make this perception clearer. Will the valley and ten miles on all sides be sufficient?)

(Those were the boundaries that Hasai was using. Yes.)

She felt closely into the valley floor itself for ten or twelve miles down, absorbing and including into herself the sensations of pressures and unreleased strains, strata trying to shear upward or sink down.

Whole mountains she embraced as if with encircling wings: Aulys, Houndstooth, Eisargir and Adíně, then east to Whitestack, Ésa and Mirit, south to Éla and Fyfel, west to Mesthyn, Teleist and the Orakhméně range. They were a restless armful. Rooted they might be, but they were alive as trees—shifting, trembling, pushing.

The whole Highpeak region, far into the unnamed south, was shivering, about to bolt like a nervous horse. The cause of its nervousness was at the heart of her perception. With ruthless diligence she absorbed it all, missing no detail: the vertical faults lying stitched across the valley in a row, south to north, angry and frightened. The treacherous lateral fault, its line running from the pass between Adíně and Eisargir into the valley, through Barachael and out the narrow gate to lower land. And under it all, the old dark sink of negative energies.

(I see it,) Herewiss said, his thought thick with revulsion. She caught a quick taste of his perception. It was rather different from hers, and primarily concerned with the Shadow's influence. He felt it everywhere, particularly in the lateral fault, where the accumulated hatred made it appear to crouch and glare like a cornered rat. It knew who he was, what he had come for, and the whole valley trembled with its malice.

Segnbora trembled too, revolted and suddenly afraid. They were fools to try to tamper with this dynamism, so delicately balanced that a talon's weight applied to the wrong spot might bring down mountains. The Dweller-at-the-Howe had been wise to forbid the Dragons from delving here. Worse, she could feel the murky sink of hatred swell, growing aware of their presence.

(Herewiss!) she said. He didn't answer, and she began to grow angry, the Fire burning hotter in her throat. He was so damn sure of himself! *(Herewiss!)*

(What do you want?) he snapped.

Her othersenses told her that he was as angry as she was, and the knowledge enraged her further.

(Don't meddle!) he said. (I'm in the middle of a wreaking, and if you distract me—)

Typically, he was paying no attention to her; he was sunk in his own concerns. (Your wreaking has barely begun. I'm not distracting and you know it. Listen, I'm Precinct-trained, and—)

(They don't know everything in the Precincts,) he said, bitter and superior. There was a touch of jealousy in his mind, too, which caused her to start. Jealousy . . . didn't that mean something specific in this situation?

She brushed away the irrelevant thought—doubtless it was the maundering of some *mdaha* long dead and out of touch with life. Herewiss had slighted her, and her patience was wearing thin.

(Do you want my aid or not?) she demanded.

(Not particularly, no! I have more than enough Power to handle this business myself, and you know it! I thought you might have appreciated the kindness I was doing you by letting you come along on a wreaking, but I see it was wasted.)

He was a stress in the darkness, one close to release, spiteful and certain of his own utter potency. The burning began to swell in her throat, and sweet it was to let the passions rise.

She had been patient long enough.

The forefingers of her wings—the terrible black diamond razors that could tear even Dragonmail—cocked forward and down at him. (Little man,) she said, (it's time you found out what you have been toying with!)

Slowly she bent down, waiting for him to attack her. She savored the moments, wondering how she would finish him.

A quick slash? A forepaw brought smashing down? A breath of her fire? But he wasn't physical now. He dwelt in the stone as she did, and the stress he wore as form began to warp and change. He was lifting up Khávrinen to kill her.

Let him try, the fool! she thought.

The *mdaha* who had spoken before now cried out again . . . something unintelligible about not seeing, about a presence creeping up from behind, about an ambush . . . Segnbora snarled at the interruption, a sound that woke rumblings in the stone. She arched herself upward to come crashing down on the pitiful little weapon raised against her—

—and then she understood, she *saw.*

As she watched in horror, the darkness in the stone drew together to one spot. At the lateral fault it stood, staring at her. Dracon though she was—immense, terrible—she abandoned her pounce and crouched down like a bird under a serpent's eye.

The Shadow smiled at her, baleful, and waited.

Herewiss didn't waste his opportunity. Swollen with rage, he towered over her in the stone with Khávrinen upraised, ready to destroy her. (Come on!) he cried in an ecstasy of fury. (Stop me, if you're such a power! Try to stop me!)

Segnbora didn't answer. It was impossible to look away from the one Whose essence lay concentrated in the fault, waiting for Herewiss to strike and bring the valley down around their ears.

Herewiss's rage didn't diminish. He merely lowered Khávrinen a bit to savor her fear, to prolong the sweet conflict— and in that moment abruptly felt what she did. Immediately his tone changed. (Beware! We have company!)

It flowed out into the stone again, surrounding him, unwilling to give up such a splendid tool. Segnbora felt Herewiss founder and go down, and couldn't stir so much as a thought to help him. The Shadow was after her too, flowing into the dark places in her soul that had belonged to It since she was very small. Relentlessly, It inflamed them all: her anger at a life that didn't go exactly as she wished; her old feelings of impotence and insignificance . . .

She fought back. If she let It, It would enter her and cause her to trigger the fault, which in turn would bury the valley, killing her friends and enemies alike. That couldn't be allowed. Desperately, she thought of Lang, of Eftgan—lovers who had taught her laughter. She pictured Freelorn, beautiful Freelorn, who demanded so much and gave so much in return . . . She wasn't alone!

The realization was dangerous. Her opponent changed its tactics from persuasion to direct attack: a blast of hatred and pain that would have killed her in a second had she been in her own body. Fortunately, she was not. She pulled her Dracon-self closer about her, wearing it like mail. Hatred, even the vast hatred of an embittered God, meant little to a Dragon who had experienced the Immanence from the inside, with all its joys and rages regarding all things mortal and divine.

And as for the pain, Segnbora simply opened herself to it as a Dragon would. She spread her wings wide and took it all, drank it like Sunfire, made it hers as she had made the stone and the mountains hers. She was not its tool.

(Herewiss!)

A tide of blackness was almost all she could perceive of Its attack against him. Within it, however, she saw something moving—a disembodied force, the essence of Khávrinen and the Power it focused, slashing the dark into ribbons. Always the Shadow resealed Itself, but always the fierce blueness pushed It aside again, widening the breach for the man who fought his way upward out of the Shadow's heart.

I'm Hers, not Yours! he gasped, forcing the darkness aside and pushing himself higher into the stone. And even for Her, I'm not a thing to be used! ('Berend?)

(Here!)

With terrible abruptness, both attacks ceased. Segnbora reeled.

(Pull yourself together!) Herewiss shouted at her instantly. (It can't get us to trigger the fault, but It'll be glad to do that Itself!)

So It was doing. Segnbora could see all Its power, all Its hate, flowing back into the lateral fault—concentrating, burning, stinging the stone into the beginnings of movement. A low rumble spread through the strata. There was one spot in particular, a thousand feet or so south of Barachael, that was almost ready to fracture. In a matter of seconds its stone would reduce itself to powder with explosive force, releasing the vertical faults on either side of it.

(*There!*) she cried, and as she did the Shadow poured Itself fully into that spot, an irresistible blast of destruction—

—but Herewiss was already there, dwelling in the stone, *being* it, holding it together. It was granite and marble, but he was diamond, unshatterable by Goddess or Shadow—for the moment.

(I'll hold it!) he said, the thought tasting of gritted teeth. (You distract It!)

With what? she thought, fumbling desperately for an idea.

Distant as if one of the *mdeihei* sang it, seemingly irrelevant, a scrap of verse spoke itself in her. *No shadow so deep that light cannot sound it, no hatred so hard that love cannot loose it—* Béorgan's old ballad, the alliterative one. It told how she had taken the Shadow within herself, and her courage had defeated It. She had drained Its power so that her daughter could challenge the Shadow in her turn and slay It. And that gave Segnbora a mad, dangerous idea . . .

Though still wearing her Dracon-self, Segnbora brought her human nature to bear as strongly as she could, and began exposing her dark sides to the Shadow's influence. Intent on Herewiss, It perceived only an augmentation of Its power in the area, and therefore let her darknesses gather from It and grow, becoming small likenesses of Itself. Sensing a chance to turn her vulnerabilities into weapons, she missed not a one of them: hatreds, petty jealousies, desires gone sour, procrastinations; laziness that would let others languish in pain while she lay idle; envy that smiled at the misfortunes of her peers. It was a disgusting collection, but in itself presented no danger. Loss of a sense of sickness—acceptance of the state—*that* was to be feared. And that was creeping up on her fast . . .

As swiftly as she dared, Segnbora slipped close to the Shadow and let loose her tarnished parts. They melded with It, becoming part of Its substance. Terrible power rushed through them and back into her. She dared not fight it, lest she betray her presence.

As she had become Dracon, and as Dracon had become stone, she now became the Shadow.

Mortal, and therefore limited even out of her body, Segnbora could contain only a small part of Its being in herself . . . but it was enough. In a sickening flash she experienced the incalculable rage of One Who had possessed Godhead and for jealousy's sake had then thrown it away. She also experienced pain: an anguish deeply colored with blame for the Goddess Who had let the pain happen—

There was no time to look further. Segnbora didn't speak, didn't even truly think, but merely held her control as best she could and looked at the painful memories, living inside the old story, wordlessly recreating it with a Dragon's immediacy and a storyteller's skill. It was an easy story to tell. She knew it by heart. It was the same story she had dreamed that night in the old Hold: the story of the Maiden, of Death, and of Her children, the Two, Who had loved one another.

The hatred that was the rest of herself still strove without pause to destroy Herewiss—but It did so a little less vehemently. It was distracted by old memories. Gradually, the story changed, becoming less a narrative and more an invitation.

Do You remember how it was? The two of You loving outside the constraints of existence, taking eons to learn and love one another's infinite depths? Do You remember the divine passion, how Your loving invented time and space—a place to love and explore together, in all the bodies that ever lived? Do You remember the Loved, and how there was always One Who understood? Your sister, Your brother, Your beloved . . . O remember!

It was in Nhàired she sang now, as if weaving a spell, silently recalling the Song of the Lost. Normally that Song was never voiced except during the Dreadnights, in the depths of the Silent Precincts, to beseech the Shadow to remember Its ancient joy and be merciful to the world. Segnbora sang it now without the fearful intonations the Rodmistresses used, but winding poignant Dracon motifs of compassion and forgiveness around the words. She was calling to herself as much as to the other. Vile though her darknesses were, they were rooted in light, just as the Shadow's malice was founded in the pain of Its ancient loss, the memory of love discarded forever. If it could not be saved, neither could she . . .

The Shadow held still in the stone, Its malice wavering, half forgotten. A hasty flicker of perception stolen through It showed Herewiss, hanging on in the stone, shuddering with pity and also with fear for her. No one had ever before been so foolhardy as to sing the Song of the Lost in first person, and tempt the Shadow. But he didn't waste more than one shudder. He began examining the strata around him, and found the spot where the Shadow's consciousness had rooted Itself most concretely into the stone.

But yet will come that time when Time is done, the world begun again, aright, she sang, pouring herself into the promise. *And once again We shall be as We were—*

She drew away, singing. The Shadow surrounded her, towering above, about to drown her in deadly consummation. Without warning Khávrinen's essence flicked through the earth like a white-hot thought burning through a brain. Instantly it severed the linkage of the Shadow's consciousness to the stone.

There was only one wild shriek of rage and betrayal before the dark presence faded, temporarily banished, but that cry was enough. All around Herewiss an unstoppable tremor stirred in the stone. As if that weren't enough, an ominous coppery feeling with an aftertaste of blood began sliding through Segnbora's self. The Moon was eclipsing.

(*Goddess!* Herewiss, get out of there. We have to get back to our bodies or you won't be able to control this!)

(Right,) Herewiss said, sounding abstracted. Khávrinen swept again and again through the bedrock, and its unseen Fire wavered with Herewiss's alarm as he tried to cut himself loose from his empathy with the stone. (I seem to have gotten kind of attached, you go ahead—)

(Are you crazy? This is your wreaking and I'm stuck in it!)

Precious seconds were slipping by. Herewiss laid about harder and harder with Khávrinen, and didn't move. (Dammit! My own Fire won't cut my own Fire—)

(Watch out!) Segnbora said. Furiously, she whipped down one wing at the stone, a wing tipped with the black razor-diamond that was Skádhwë. Through fathoms of marble and granite it sliced, the shadow of a shadow, until it reached the rock under Herewiss.

He shot upward and out of the strata, free. Shrugging off her Dracon-self, she followed him up and out of the empathy—

They broke the surface of the valley, gasped for the dear familiarity of breath like swimmers down too long, and began running up the air in frantic haste. The Moon's face, full now, was stained half red against the early evening sky. The stain grew larger as they raced for the tower window with the light in it. Under them, red fire dove and swooped about the valley, driving massed darknesses before it. They spared the sight hardly a glance and dove through the tower wall. Segnbora threw herself down on the cot where her body lay—

—and hit her head.

No, that's just the usual headache. Up, get up! Freelorn was shaking her, worsening the agony of pins and needles that transfixed every bone and muscle she owned.

Herewiss was already up, sagging against the window. With Freelorn's help, she staggered over to join him. Segnbora was temporarily blind, but the othersight was working. Above the valley the Moon's whiteness had diminished to a thin desperate sliver, struggling with the creeping darkness as if with a poison, and foredoomed to lose.

The corroded copper taste was as hot in Segnbora's mouth as if she had been struck there. The Chaelonde seemed to run with blood. Below them the lateral fault burned through stone and earth, moving. Sai khas-Barachael began to shake beneath their feet.

"Put your scales on," Herewiss whispered, grabbing one of her hands in a grip like a vise, and with the other drawing Khávrinen. Segnbora stumbled and fell down into herself, into the cave where Hasai waited with wings outspread in alarm. There was no time for the usual courtesies. Segnbora matched him size for size, flung his wings about her as she had wrapped herself in his shadow before, and became him.

As the sensation of the stone in the valley became plain again, the *mdeihei* cried out in a song of terrible alarm. "*Shut up, the lot of you!"* she shouted in Dracon, and once more gathered the whole valley within the span of her wings, feeling it all.

The pain struck her immediately as the lateral fault came alive inside her, a black-hot line of agony running from chest to shoulder and up her left wing like a heart seizure. Her outer body gasped and clutched at the sill, missed it, and thumped down to her knees with a jolt. Inside, no less clearly, she felt the heave and stutter of the faults as they tried to move, attempting to foul Herewiss's game before it was fairly started.

Fortunately, Herewiss had not lost his grip on her hand. Half crouched over and supported desperately by Freelorn, he was beginning to shine like a vision as his soul settled more firmly into the spirit-to-body connection necessary for full Power flow. In his free hand, Khávrinen blazed like chained lightning, impossible to look at with the eyes of either body or mind. Herewiss struck deeper into his Power, tapping what seemed an inexhaustible source, and straightened with refound strength. Then he was inside Segnbora's perception, as Dracon as she.

The Fire burning in her throat was suddenly blue, an awesome counterpoint to the dark burning of the faults, and the rage of the frustrated Shadow. Stirred by Its influence, the player on the Inside made a move. But it was a poorly reasoned move, born of fury and the hope of a quick win. The lateral fault jumped an inch north and south.

Segnbora felt Herewiss smile the satisfied smile of a player whose opponent has fallen into a trap. The burning blue upflow of his Fire seared through her perception and poured in a great flood down into the valley's stone, binding together three of the vertical faults.

Like diverted lightning, the released energy of the lateral fault stitched whiplash-quick through the strata in several different directions. But Herewiss was quicker. Fire streaked through the strata too, sending fault-blocks up or down, blocking and absorbing forces, setting up piece by piece the final checkmate that would freeze the lateral forever and seal the Eisargir Pass. Two more moves and he would have it!

Bent over double by the fault-pain, which was harder to handle now than while she had been out-of-body, Segnbora heard someone a long way off shouting in thought. She couldn't make out concepts, though.

"They're not?" Freelorn said, much closer, and very alarmed. "Dusty! They're not all clear of the pass yet. Sunspark says you have to hold off if you don't want all those Reavers dead—"

Herewiss said nothing aloud, but Segnbora could feel his resolve. *No one dies of this, not even them.* Yet the position he had set up in the stone was delicate and couldn't be maintained for long.

The Shadow, sensing Herewiss's hesitation, immediately called the attention of the foiled, blocked forces in the stone to the weakest spot in Herewiss's game: the root of Aulys that was split in two. Pressure played about it like lightning. Half of the massive root twitched, about to shift . . .

(Hold your position,) Segnbora said.

Both inside and outside the stone at once, she anchored herself with rear talons and barbed tail, and reached out to sink diamond fangs into the trembling root. It struggled and tried to tear away from her, vibrating so violently that she was certain she was going to lose teeth. But a Dragon never lets go except by its own decision.

She held. Eyes squeezed closed, every muscle pulled taut as a rope, her tail desperately tightening its anchor around a lower stratum as she felt her fore-talons slipping. She held, using her mind, feeling the rock as a whole.

"They're out! They're out of the pass! *Dusty!*"

Canny and desperate, the Shadow kicked two of the remotest vertical faults as a distraction. Herewiss was having none of it. Using Segnbora's Dracon-self as she had, he descended deeper into the stone, deep enough to set his jaws around his last move, a great marble fault-block half a mile south of Barachael. This was the key to the puzzle. Diamond fangs set hard into the stone. He heaved—

The blow came at her, not at him, and took them both off-guard. Preoccupied with the immensities, neither of them expected the sudden choking darkness at their back in the

place where the *mdeihei* dwelt. A song of madness swept the
mdeihei, controlled them, sent them tearing at the floor of
Segnbora's cave. Razor talons and ruthless blasts of Dragonfire ate and sliced down through the stone of her memory,
to lay it bare and make it real. For one memory in particular
they searched . . .

(No!) she screamed at them, but they paid her no heed.

Stone crumbled away like curd. Even now the memory was
coming to birth, coming true: darkness, gravel grinding
against her face, that old anguish . . . There was no way to stop
it, except by breaking the empathy, leaving Hasai, halting the
wreaking—

Herewiss held the block of stone in jaws that ran with blue
Fire, but he couldn't move it without her. He strained at it,
tapping deeper into his Fire and deeper yet, not giving up. Yet
without her link to the Dracon perception, he could not go
further.

—stone shattered and melted. *Don't suffer, don't let it come true
again! Break the link!* the darkness sang to her, consoling, se-
ductive. The memory became more real. *A green afternoon,
under the tree . . . No, what's he doing here? What's he—no! No!*

Break the link!

(*I can't.*)

Then live in the horror, without respite, forever.

The last stone was torn away from the memory. In such
anguish that she couldn't even scream, Segnbora flung herself utterly into the Dracon-self, into Herewiss, into her own
self and her own death. Fire blazed; the terrible stresses Herewiss had been applying to the fault-block gripped, took,
pulled it up out of its socket—

The gameboard rumbled and leaned upward as if a hand
had tipped it over. Pieces tried to slide off every which way.
Lost in the pain of contact with that memory, Segnbora could
nevertheless sense Mount Adínë's shuddering as the ground
at the end of the khas-Barachael spur began to rise, first
bulging, then cracking like a snapped stick.

Sai khas-Barachael danced and jittered on its ridge like a
knife on a pounded tabletop, held secure only by Herewiss's
Fire and will. The earth on either side of the lateral fault

thrust up, then slammed together like a closing door. The fault expended its energies in a noise like the thunderstorms of a thousand summers. Hills crumbled and landslides large and small crawled downward all the length of the Chaelonde valley. The river itself tilted crazily out of its bed and rushed down into a new one as the block Herewiss had triggered shoved its way above ground, making a seedling mountain, a new spur for Adínë.

Behind them, the Houndstooth peak of Aulys seemed to stand up in surprise, look over Adínë's shoulder, and then fall back in a dead faint. The terrible thundering crash of its fall went on for many minutes, a sound so huge it obliterated every other sound and was felt more than heard. It was a sound never to be forgotten: the sound of the pass between Eisargir and Aulys being sealed by the Houndstooth's ruin.

Hours later, it seemed, the singing roar that encompassed the world began to die down. Segnbora found herself still alive, and was amazed at that. Herewiss was nowhere to be felt in her mind. She was on hands and knees on the floor of her cavern. Slowly, aching all over, she levered herself up and found herself looking at Hasai.

He was droop-winged and weary-looking, dim of eye, crouching in the middle of a badly torn-up and melted stone floor. Behind him, lurking shameful in the shadows, she could just make out the dark forms of the *mdeihei*. Many eyes watched her, but their voices for once were still as they waited to see what she would do.

"O *sdaha*," Hasai said, singing slow and sorrowful, "we betrayed you." He made no excuse, offered no explanation, merely accepted the responsibility.

She breathed in, breathed out, as weary as the Dragon before her. The *mdeihei* waited.

There were thousands of things she felt like saying to them, but what she said was, *"Ae mdeihei, Nht'é'lhhw'ae."* *We are forgiven.*

The shadowy forms drew away. Segnbora laid a hand for a moment on one of Hasai's bright talons. There were great talon-furrowed rents in the floor. They had slag piled all around them that smoked ominously like pools of magma. "Will you clean this mess up, *mdaha?*"

He looked at her as if he wanted very much to say something more. At last, he said only, "*Sdaha,* we will do that."

"*Sehé'rae,* then—" She turned her back on him and stepped back up into the outer world.

The room still jittered with little aftershocks left over from the quake, and echoed with the voices of all Freelorn's band. Herewiss leaned wearily by the window, with Freelorn supporting him on one side and Sunspark on the other. Eftgan was in front of him, and all four were talking at a great rate. Segnbora pushed herself up off the floor and rubbed her eyes, looking out the window.

Her normal sight was now clear enough to show her a Chaelonde valley much broken and changed, but with Barachael still mostly intact. The darkened Moon wore a fuzzy line of silver at its edge, first sign of the eclipse's end. The air that came in the window was astonishingly sweet to the under-senses, as if many years' worth of trapped death and pain had been finally released.

Leaning against the windowsill, she looked at Herewiss. He was drawn and tired, and all the Fire was gone from about Khávrinen for the moment. For the first time she could remember, it was simply gray steel with an odd blue sheen. But Herewiss's eyes were alive with a satisfaction too big for all of Barachael valley to have contained—the look of a man who finds out he *is* what he's always believed himself to be.

Seeing her, he reached out a hand. Across the open window they clasped forearms in the gesture of warriors after a battle well fought.

"What was it you said?" Segnbora said, thinking back to the old Hold in the Waste, and the night her sleep was interrupted. " 'There was blood on the Moon, and the mountain was falling'—?"

Dog-tired as he was, Herewiss's eyes glittered with the thought that his true-dream might not prove as disastrous as he had believed, particularly for the man who stood beside him. "Got it right, didn't I?"

She nodded, put an arm out and was unsurprised to find Lang there, wary of Skádhwë but ready to support her. "Only one problem, prince—"

"What's that?"

She grinned. "After this, people are going to say you'll do *anything* to avoid a fight . . ."

Twelve

Laughter in death's shadow fools no one who understands death. But if you're moved to it, be assured that the Goddess will smile at the joke.

—found scratched on the
wall in the dungeon of the King
of Steldin, *circa* 1200 p.a.d.

"I hate—letting them think they're driving us," Herewiss said between gasps. "But it's better this way."

He stood in the midst of carnage, the burned and hacked bodies of fifty or sixty Fyrd. Here and there in the rocky field of this latest ambush, Freelorn's band stood cleaning swords, leaning on one another, or rubbing down sweating horses and swearing quietly.

Segnbora leaned gasping against Steelsheen's flank, unwilling yet to sheathe Skádhwë. The last Fyrd to come at her had been one of the new breed of keplian, bigger than the usual sort, with clawed forelimbs and those wickedly intelligent eyes that were becoming too familiar these days.

She had had no trouble immersing herself in the other's eyes to effect its killing. The problem had been getting out again afterward. She felt soiled, as if she had stepped in a pile of hatred that would have to be scraped off her boots.

"How many times is this?" Lang said, coming up beside her.

"Seventeen, eighteen maybe—"

"I don't know about you, but *I* feel driven."

Segnbora nodded. Fifteen days ago they had ridden out of Barachael, and had had nothing for their pains ever since but constant harrying by ever-increasing bands of Fyrd. All had come from the southwest, where Something clearly didn't want them to venture. Freelorn had suggested world-gating straight to Bluepeak, where they would meet the Queen; but Herewiss, unwilling to tempt the Shadow into direct intervention by too much use of Fire, had vetoed the idea.

So they rode, and were harried. Herewiss always took them north, out of the way, after an attack such as today's. In daylight, anyway. In darkness they turned again and tacked southwest, toward Bluepeak. They were losing time with these detours, and knew it. Everyone's temper was short, and getting shorter.

"Let's go," Herewiss said, sheathing Khávrinen and turning Sunspark's head northward as he mounted.

There was annoyed muttering among Freelorn's band, and heads turned toward Lorn in appeal. But Lorn, already up on Blackmane, looked wearily after his loved and shook his head. "Come on," he said, and rode off after Herewiss.

They rode a brutal trail through country made of the stuff of a rider's nightmares. They had long since left behind the green plains of southern Darthen. Presently they were crossing the uninhabited rock-tumble of Arlen's Southpeak country. Glaciers had retreated over this land when the Peaks were born, leaving bizarrely shaped boulders scattered across scant, stony soil. Acres of coarse gravel with a few brave weeds growing out of it might be all one would see from morning 'til night.

The horses were footsore from being kept at flight-pace on such miserable ground. The grazing was poor, too. After the well-filled mangers of Barachael's stables, it was hardly surprising that the horses were in no better mood than their riders. Though no one lived in this barren country, it would be only a matter of time before they ran into Reavers, or Arlene regulars in Cillmod's pay. If not them, there would certainly be Fyrd.

"This is all *your* fault," Freelorn grumbled at Segnbora as Steelsheen picked her way along beside Blackmane.

Segnbora looked up in surprise from her contemplation of Skádhwë, which lay ready across the saddlebow. "Huh? . . . Oh, well, in a way it is. I caused the Battle of Bluepeak, too. Ask me about it sometime."

He glowered at her, and nodded toward Herewiss. "All *he* did was seal up the Shadow's favorite avenue into the Kingdoms. What do *you* do but start making love to It . . . and then jilt It!"

She started to disagree with Freelorn, and then thought
better of it. "So I did."

"You're probably in worse trouble with It now than Herewiss is."

Segnbora frowned at the exaggeration, though it was typical of her liege. "Oh? What do *you* know about it?"

At that moment Herewiss dropped back to join them, and
said, "Considering that he's read the entire royal Arlene library collection on matters of Power, he probably knows
more about it than either of us. Face it, 'Berend. The Shadow
already knew of the threat that I posed, but at Barachael It
became aware of you, too. And as they say, your newest hatred
is the most interesting.

"True," Freelorn added, becoming serious now. "No
doubt It believes you're Its deadliest foe at the moment—"

"Ha! Some foe . . ." she said, thinking of her still-unfocused
Fire.

The wreaking she had performed with Herewiss had been
successful, but now she was almost sorry she had agreed to
participate. Ever since, she had not been able to stop brood-
ing about her Fire. Over and over again, Hasai's words had
run through her mind: *Your fear cripples you. You must give it up.*

Recognizing an old hurt about which they could do nothing, Herewiss and Freelorn fell silent.

Annoyed both at herself and at them, Segnbora took the
lead for a while, riding apart and letting the quiet conversation of the others fade beneath her awareness of the surrounding country. Skádhwë's reassuring blackness soaked up
light at her saddlebow. Its weightlessness, at first unsettling,
had become second nature. It was very useful in a fight. And
certainly no other sword was all edge and no flat. Likewise,
no other sword would cut anything but the hand of its mistress, as Freelorn had discovered while handling it one morning.

Skádhwë seemed not to care for being used by anyone else.
It was delicate, but very definite, about drawing Lorn's blood.
Of her, it had demanded nothing so far, and Segnbora
thought of Efmaer's words with unease, wondering when the
weird would take hold.

Unease seemed to have overtaken everybody these days. No longer were they simply fugitives on the run from Cillmod's mercenaries; the Shadow was after them now, too, and the knowledge that their souls were in peril had them all on edge.

Segnbora could feel the Shadow working on them even now, driving the group apart, subtly sapping its effectiveness. Even Herewiss was short of conversation these days. He had drawn closer to Lorn, pulling away from the others. As for Freelorn, although every step toward Bluepeak brought the reality of his true-dream closer, he had a haunted look. His followers turned to him for answers, but as often as not came away with a strong sense of his inner distress. At this rate, she thought morosely, they'd never make it to their rendezvous with the Darthenes, at the place where they were massing to take the Shadow's attack.

The afternoon dragged the Sun down to eye level and turned the western horizon into a blinding nuisance.

(*Sdaha,*) Hasai said from way down, (we smell water.)

(You've been quiet today. Where?)

(West and south. A league as the Dragon flies.)

She nodded and thumped Steelsheen's sides, bringing her about in order to inform Herewiss of a place to camp. Hasai had been quiet much of the time since Barachael—a sentient silence with satisfaction at its bottom . . . and something else she couldn't quite underhear.

(You're finally becoming properly *sdahaih,*) he had said one evening as she drifted off toward sleep. (Anything can happen now.)

There had been an ominous overtone to his musing. (What do you see, *mdaha?*) she had asked sleepily.

But he and the *mdeihei* had turned their attention away from her, singing wordless foreboding with strange joy woven through it. *They're crazy,* she had thought, and gone to sleep. Dragons were always ambivalent about their foreseeings, as if they couldn't—or wouldn't—decide what was good or bad.

The camp they found three leagues ahead was in a stony, scrubby canyon: shattered, green-white cliffs above, and dry watercourse below. Scant rains kept alive the brush and several little spinneys of warped ash and blackthorn, but nothing else. "Where's the water?" Herewiss said to Segnbora, annoyed.

"There," she said, speaking Hasai's words for him, and gestured at the face of the cliff. Herewiss gave her a look and dismounted from Sunspark.

"No rest for the weary," he said, and advanced on the cliff with eyes closed, checking her perception. Then he opened his eyes, picked a spot, and brought Khávrinen around in a roundhouse swing. Splintered stone shot in various directions, trailing Fire. Water followed it, bursting from the rock in a momentary release of pressure and then subsiding to a steady stream down the cliff's face.

They watered and fed the horses while Herewiss stood gazing around with a wary look, as if expecting trouble. Segnbora went away feeling thoughtful herself, and led Steelsheen to the most distant of the ash spinneys. *This place has a bad feeling about it,* she thought, and then realized why.

The trees were warped and bent, as if by the wind. But the real cause was something less healthy, a something snarled among the ashes' branches. She threw the reins over Steelsheen's head so that the mare would stand, and pulled some of the stuff out. The long strands were white and soft as spun silk, though as unbreakably strong as any rope when she pulled it between her hands—

From behind her, Herewiss reached in and pulled down the main mass of the material. As the white stuff came away from the tree, a whole mort of things came tumbling out to thump or clatter to the ground.

"Look at that," he said conversationally, bending down to poke with Khávrinen at something jutting from the white swathing. "The point-shard of a sword. Darthene Masterforge steel, see, Lorn? Look at the lines in the metal."

"It takes a lot to break a sword like that," Freelorn said from beside his loved, but sounding nowhere near as composed.

Why now? Why now! Segnbora thought, as Herewiss bent to pick something else out of the whiteness. He came up holding a piece of pale wood, badly warped: It was smoothly rounded at one end, broken off jaggedly at the other. "A Rod," Herewiss said. "Or it used to be."

Dritt and Moris had come up and were staring nervously at this spectacle. "I thought the only thing that could break a Rod was the Rodmistress's death." Moris said.

Without looking up, Herewiss nodded. He used Khávrinen's point to turn over other oddments tangled in the haphazard white weave: bits of broken jewelry, tatters of what might have been brocade. A bone from a human forearm poked out of the mass, ivory-yellow and scored by toothmarks. It had been cracked for the marrow, and sucked clean.

"Mare's nest," Herewiss sad, turning to the others and glancing at them one after another. "And recent. We're probably right at the heart of her territory."

"Then this is no place for us," Freelorn said. He turned to go take the hobbles off Blackmane, but Herewiss didn't follow him. Freelorn looked back over his shoulder, confused.

"Lorn, it's sunset," Herewiss said. "We'd never make it past her boundaries before nightfall without giving away our position to the Shadow with our noise."

Freelorn stared at Herewiss as if he had taken leave of his senses. "Loved, that's a busted Rod there! Fire obviously doesn't do much good against a nightmare!"

"There are other defenses," Herewiss said absently. It was as if he were reading about the problem from a book rather than seeing it in front of him. He looked up at Segnbora. "How about it?"

Segnbora walked around to the other side of the spinney as if to examine the whole nest, waiting until the tree hid her before she swallowed, hard. Nightmares—minor demonic aspects of the Goddess's dark side—typically nested in barren places like this. They fell upon travellers, sucked them dry of the spark of Power they possessed, then fed the dead flesh to their fledgling nightfoals. Since they were Shadowbred, Fire was food and drink to them. A Rodmistress's Rod was thus useless against them. They could only be killed with bare hands, and then only if those hands were a woman's.

Segnbora walked around to face the others. "It's getting toward Midsummer," she said, amazed at how calmly her voice came out. "Her brood will be gone now, and she'll have eaten the nightstallion—"

Freelorn's face twisted. "They—*eat* their—!"

"They are the Devourer," Segnbora said, very low. "That aspect of the Dark One trusts nothing She hasn't consumed." She glanced over at Herewiss, forbidding herself to tremble. "Well, I broke Steelsteen with my bare hands. I think I can manage this."

Behind Herewiss, Lang's face was white with shock. She refused to watch it after that first glance. "I'll make a circle," Herewiss said. "You'll have warning. What else will you want?"

Last rites, probably. "A fire," she said.

Herewiss smiled slightly. "I think I know where to get some. Sunspark!"

Segnbora walked toward the sudden campfire, wishing there were such a thing as luck, so she could curse it.

For once, night came down too suddenly for her taste. Segnbora sat with the others beside Sunspark's blazing self, looking out toward the stony darkness. Here and there, at a hundred yards' distance, a flicker of Herewiss's Fire showed blue between the boulders, indicating the ward-circle he had laid down. Firelight danced on the face of the cliff. Under a gnarled little rowan bush Segnbora sat and tended to herself in the huge silence, which even the horses, hobbled and tethered inside the circle, didn't break.

Segnbora was running out of things to do in order to get ready. She had gone through all the small personal bindings that a sorcerer would perform to further the larger binding she intended. Her swordbelt's hanging end was tucked in. Her hair, too short to braid, she had tied with a thong into a stubby tail and bound close to her head. Her sleeves were rolled up. The buckles on her boots and her mailshirt were tight. She would have tied Skádhwë into its sheath, but it had no peace-strings as Charriselm had had, and all her attempts to bind the shadowblade with cord had been useless. It cut them all. Finally she had just taken it out of the scabbard and stuck it into a handy rock.

Now she thought of one more binding to add. Rummaging around in her belt-pouch for a bit of thread, she bound it around her left thumb nine times, thus forming a soul-cord that would keep her soul within her body until a pyre's blaze freed it. She tied the ninefold knot and glanced up as she bit it off. Freelorn was holding a cup for her. It was of light wood, with a design of leaves carved around it below the lip. She recognized it: his and Herewiss's lovers'-cup.

"Hot wine," Lorn said, sitting down. Warmed by the gesture, she took it and drank, hoping the shaking of her hands wouldn't show too much.

"It shows. Forget it," Herewiss said, sitting down beside Freelorn. She extended the cup to him, leaning back against the knobby little rowan as Herewiss drank in turn. Afterward, he poured some wine into the fire, which had acquired eyes, and then passed the cup back to Freelorn.

Lorn leaned back against a rock, and Herewiss leaned back too, resting his head against Lorn's chest. "You *sure* there's nothing you can do?" Freelorn said, sounding sorrowful.

Herewiss glanced up at him. "Swords don't bite on nightmares, loved. I'm sorry."

Freelorn nodded, still looking uneasy. "This business of the Lady's 'dark side,' " he said, "I've never really understood how She can *have* a dark side . . ."

"It is this way," Segnbora started, mostly out of reflex, and then stopped herself. Embarrassed, she took the cup back and drank again.

"No, go ahead," Herewiss said, with a wry look. "If you're going to become something's dinner tonight, we might as well get one more story out of you. Tell it as they tell it at Nháirëdi. I've never heard their version."

She sighed, suddenly amused by the surroundings. This was no cozy inn or palace hall, for once, but rather a huge night in waste country. Who'd have thought she'd ever play to an audience of kings-by-courtesy, part-time princes, and outlaws?

"It is this way," she said. "Because the Goddess bound Herself at the Making into everything She had made, the great Death became bound into Her too, and She into It. Though

She had brought It life, the Shadow still hated Her and did Her all the harm It could, causing each of Her fair aspects to cast a dark shadow of its own. Therefore the Devourer exists, and the One with Still Hands . . ." She shivered. ". . . and the Pale Winnower. Their Power is terrible, and the Goddess cannot banish them; in this Making, They are part of Her.

"But in the south of Steldin, people explain our Lady's dark side differently. They tell how, on the plain north of Mincar, there lived an austringer and her wife. The austringer was a placid woman, easily pleased and as calm as one of her hawks after a feeding. The austringer's wife, on the other hand, was never content with anything, and sharpened her tongue continually on her spouse.

"There came a day when the austringer took a good catch of pheasant and barwing. The next morning she set out for Mincar market to sell the game.

"Now, while on her way to the market, passing through the wealthy part of town, the austringer saw a sight that was stranger and more lovely than any she had ever seen. Tied to the reining-post was a great, tall silver-white steed, shining in the morning. When she drew near to it, it turned its head to gaze at her with eyes as dark as the missing half of the Moon. It was tethered with a bridle of woven silver.

"She recognized it then. It was one of the Moonsteeds, aspects of the Maiden that mirror the Moon in its changes, and which cannot be caught by any means except with a bridle that is wrought of noon-forged silver in such a fashion as to have no beginning and no end. Some lord or lady had caused the bridle to be made, and had managed to catch the Steed. And as the austringer stood there and pitied the poor creature, once free from time's beginning and now bound, it lowered its head and said to her, 'Free me, and I'll do you a good turn when I may.'

"So she cut the bridle with her knife, and the Moonsteed reared and pawed the air and said, 'If you want for anything, go out into the fields and call me and I will be with you.' And it vanished.

"The austringer thought it well to vanish from the area herself. She went to market and sold her birds, and then went home in a hurry in order to tell her wife what she had seen. That was a mistake. 'Surely,' her wife said, 'the Steed will grant you anything you want. Go out and ask it to make us rich.'

"She nagged the austringer unmercifully until at last she gave in and went out into the night, under the first-quarter Moon, to call the Steed. It came, saying 'What can I do for you?'

" 'My wife wants to be rich. Wants *us* to be rich, rather,' said the austringer. 'The first was closer to the truth, I think,' the Steed said, 'but go home, it has happened already.' And the austringer went home to find her wife happily running her fingers through bags of Moon-white silver, chuckling to herself about the fine robes and elegant food she would soon have in place of her brown homespun and coarse bread.

"For about a week things went well. But folk nearby began to ask questions, and then the tax collectors arrived, leaving with more silver than pleased the austringer's wife. 'This isn't working,' she said to the austringer. 'Go ask the Steed to make *me* the tax collector. And I want a house befitting my station.'

" 'No one will talk to us anymore!' the austringer objected. Her wife gave her no peace, however, and sent her off to the fields at nightfall. The austringer called the Moonsteed, and there it came in a white blaze of light, for the Moon was near to full. 'What can I do for you?' it asked. 'Though I have a feeling I know.'

" 'My wife wants to be a tax collector, and have a tax collector's fine house,' the austringer said.

" 'Go home, it's done,' said the Steed. And the austringer went home and found their thatched cottage changed to a tall house of rr'Harich marble; and her wife was twenty times as rich as she had been before.

"After that things went as you might imagine. A week later the austringer's wife wanted to be mayor, and so she was. Afterward she became bailiff, and Dame, and Head of House, one after another. Her house became golden-pillared and roofed with crystal, filled with rich stuffs and things out of legend—feather-hames and charmed weapons and even the silver chair that later belonged to the Cat of Aes Arádh—but none of it gave her joy for more than a day. Each night she sent the austringer out to ask for another boon, and the austringer grew sad and pale, seeing that her wife loved her possessions more than she loved *her*.

"And as the days passed the aspect of the Moonsteed grew darker, for the old Moon was waning. White-silver the Steed had been at first, like moonlight on snow. Now it waxed darker each night, and frightened the austringer.

"The boons grew greater and greater. Head of the Ten High Houses, the austringer's wife became; then Chief of them, then High Minister, then Priestess-Consort. And still she wanted more.

"Finally the night came of the dark of the Moon—"

Segnbora broke off for a moment, fumbling for the wine cup. Her mouth had gone suddenly dry. It was only three nights from Moondark now, that time when a nightmare would be strongest.

"—the dark of the Moon, and the austringer went out to the fields to call on the Moonsteed for the last time. It came, burning with awful dark splendor and wrath, and said in its gentle voice, 'What is it now? Your wife has asked, and I have granted, even to the last times when she asked to be Queen of Steldin, and then High Queen of all the Kingdoms. What more might she want?'

"The austringer trembled, and said, 'She wants to rule the Universe.'"

Segnbora lifted the cup again and finished the wine.

There was silence. Freelorn glanced down expectantly at Herewiss, whose eyes were turned away, then back at Segnbora. "So?"

"So She *does*." She handed back the empty cup. "Now you tell one."

Suddenly Blackmane screamed. Herewiss jerked upright as if he had been kicked. All around the camp heads turned out toward the darkness.

The nightmare stood for a moment among the boulders that had fallen from the cliff, and then stepped forward delicately. It was small: the size of a seven-months' filly. Its silken mane and tail hung to the ground. Slim-legged and clean of line, it seemed at first as elegant and graceful as a unicorn. But its eyes were evil: red and bottomless, full of old cruelties and insatiable hunger. From a coat the color of the rolled-up whites of a dead man's eyes, it cast a faint yellowish corpse-light that illuminated nothing.

Segnbora got up, dry-mouthed again. She took a few steps forward and folded her arms, staring right into those ancient, burning eyes.

"Be thou warned," she said in the formal manner reserved for the laying of dooms, "that I am well informed of thee and thy ways, of thy comings and goings, thy wreakings and undo-ings; and that it is my intent to bind thee utterly to my will, and confine thee to the dark from which thou came'st at the birth of days. So unless thou wish to try thy strength with me, and be compelled by the binding I shall work upon thee, then get thee hence and have no more to do with me and mine."

She held very still. The nightmare now had the option to retreat. It could also answer ritually, or it could attack.

"How should I fear *you?*" the nightmare said, lifting its head to taunt her sweetly. The voice it used was that of Segn-bora's slain otherself, not piteous as it had been during those last moments in Glasscastle, but mocking and cruel. "Rodmis-tresses in the full of their Power have passed this way, and you see what has happened to *them.* You, however, have retired from sorcery, afraid of failure."

"*Silence!*" Segnbora said in a voice like a whipcrack. But no power was behind the order, and the nightmare laughed at her, a sound ugly with knowledge.

"You make a fine noise," it said, flicking its tail insolently. "But all your years' studies have left you with little but knowl-edge. Mere spells and tales and sayings. You have no Power. Or rather, what Power you possess you are afraid to focus."

Burning with shame, Segnbora clenched her fists and took a step forward, then another, seeking control. (Hasai—!)

"Oh, call up your ghost," the nightmare said, stepping forward too. "You don't dare give *him* the Power he needs, either. You walk on water, and complain that you can't find anything to drink! Face it, you will never find what you seek. You are too afraid. You are dead!"

Behind her Segnbora could feel Freelorn getting ready to move, and Herewiss holding him still with that same vise-grip in which he had held her at Barachael. The others were frozen, eyes glittering, muscles bound still. Even Sunspark's flames flowed more slowly than usual.

"Some heroine you are!" the chill voice taunted. "Dead on your feet. A rotting corpse. You are a Devourer, like me."

Her head jerked in surprise.

"You don't believe me? Then look at your slug of a lover there!" The bitter eyes dwelt on Lang with vast amusement. "He no more dares open himself to you than you do to him. He knows that what you call 'love' is mere need. If permitted, you'll suck him dry of his own Power, his own love, and he knows it! Eftgan knew that too . . ."

Humiliation seared Segnbora, and terror. She had no problem holding her peace. Her mouth refused to work.

The nightmare chuckled maliciously, enjoying her growing victory. "No wonder you're such a good storyteller. Everything that comes out of your mouth is a story, especially when you speak of yourself. You haven't really opened to another person since that day when you became big enough to be taken out in back of the chicken house—"

Segnbora took another slow step forward, drowning in the bitter truth, hanging onto the ritual for dear life. "I may warn thee again—get hence, lest I lay such strictures about thee that from age to age thou shalt lie bound in the never-lightening gulfs—"

"Say the words of the sorcery," the nightmare said, baring her yellow teeth in scorn. "They'll do no good. You cannot control another aspect of the Devourer, being one yourself! Consider what lies hidden under stone in your heart . . . you hate the one who plundered you, and that hate poisons every act of 'love' you attempt. You will never properly be able to employ your Power!"

She shook her head, but the awful words of truth would not go away.

"Listen to what I say; to what you know to be fact. Even your friends pity you. Freelorn, for example. He found out what happens to someone who gets closer to you than a sword's length. You stabbed his heart with something sharper than a knife. No wonder that when you were once faced with yourself, you killed—"

Segnbora leaped at the nightmare head-on, grabbing great handfuls of its mane. Desperately, she attempted to hold its head away from her, but the nightmare plunged, reared and fastened its teeth into Segnbora's mailshirt, cracking the links like dry twigs and driving them excruciatingly through padding and breastband, into the soft tissue of her breast beneath. Jaws locked, it shook her viciously from side to side, as a dog shakes a rat.

With every jerk of its head Segnbora cried out in pain, yet she managed to hold on for some seconds. Finally, in agony, she released her right hand and grabbed the nightmare's nose, digging her thumbnail deep into the nostril. Now it was the nightmare's turn to scream—once as she let Segnbora fall, and once again as a great handful of its silken mane came away in Segnbora's hand.

Segnbora scrambled to her feet. Her pain was awesome, but she concentrated on twisting the long hank of mane into a rough cord between her hands. The opponents began to circle one another again.

"It was foolish to hold me so close for so long," she said, gasping. "I know how to bind you, child of our Mother. I know how to make an end of you, Power or not. Shortly you're going to be seeing more of the dark places than you'll like—"

She sprang again, this time for the nightmare's flank. It danced hurriedly to one side, but with a second leap Segnbora found herself astride the nightmare's back.

The nightmare bucked, kicked, and reared, leaping in the air and coming down with all four feet together, as a horse does to kill a snake. But Segnbora hung on, legs locked, hands twined in the long mane. She got one hand down over the nightmare's nose again, and stabbed it in the nostril. It screamed, and as it did she whipped the corded length of mane down and into its mouth. Quickly she brought the ends under its chin and up around its muzzle, and knotted them tight, binding its mouth closed.

The nightmare made a horrendous strangled sound that would have been a scream. It turned and raced headlong toward the jagged face of the cliff, intending to buck Segnbora off against the stone. The onlookers scattered out of the way, and Segnbora jumped from its back, rolled, and was on her feet again before it had time to realize what had happened. Turning to face her again, it reared, menacing her with its hooves. Segnbora ducked to one side and fastened her hands in its mane, pulling. The nightmare grunted and, as she had hoped, pulled away. Segnbora fell down on the ground again, but this time with her hands full of mane.

The nightmare turned and reared. By the time its hooves hit ground, Segnbora had rolled out from under them, and was afoot again. Her breath came hard, and beneath her mail-shirt her breast was bleeding freely, white-hot with pain. But her fear was gone. Nothing was left but wild anger, and the urge to destroy.

"I told you," she said, winding the length of mane between her fists like a garrote. "First the binding—"

The nightmare turned to flee, but as it turned tail Segnbora vaulted up over its rump and onto its back. Frenzied, the nightmare bucked wildly, but it was no use. This time the cord went around its throat and was pulled mercilessly tight. It plunged and slewed from side to side and tossed its head violently, trying to breathe.

Segnbora hung on, and twisted the cord tighter. The nightmare began to stagger, its eyes bulging out in anguish. Its forelegs gave way, next, so that it knelt choking and swollen-tongued on the ground. Segnbora held her seat even at that crazy angle, and pulled the cord tighter still. Finally the rear legs gave, and the nightmare fell on its side. Segnbora slipped free, never easing her stranglehold. The nightmare moved feebly a few times, then lay still.

Holding that cord tight became the whole world, more important even than the agony of her torn breast or the hot blurring of her eyes that she had thought at first was confusion and now proved to be tears. She blinked and gasped and hung on as Herewiss and Freelorn and the others ran up and kneeled around her.

Lang reached out to her, but Herewiss stopped the gesture. "Is it dead?"

"I don't know. Probably not." She could still feel a pulse thrumming feebly through the cord.

"Are you all right?" That was Lang with the same stupid question, as usual.

"No. Let me be." The nightmare's pulse was irregular now, leaping and struggling in its throat like a bird in a snare. How can they look at me, she wondered? It's all true. How can they bear to—

One last convulsive flutter ran through the nightmare's veins. Then there was stillness under her hands. Slowly and carefully she stood up, shrinking away from any hand that tried to help her. The pain in her breast was intense, yet she barely felt it.

She walked away, then, and her companions stared after her. Their eyes on her retreating back were as unbearable as sun on blistered skin, but still she ignored them. The darkness beyond the camp began to swallow her.

(A nightmare has no weapon to use but your own darkness.) Herewiss's thought burst into her mind, cold and passionless as a knife. (Resist, and it only cuts deeper.)

She kept walking.

(One night, 'Berend,) he ordered. (One night's pain is all we can spare you. We've lost too much time already. Be finished by dawn, or we won't wait.)

She shut him out and went off into the cool night, looking for an end.

Thirteen

"Well," the Goddess said, "your heart didn't heal straight the last time it broke. So we'll break it again and reset it so it heals straight this time."

Children's Tales of North Arlen, ed. s'Lange

How long she walked, she had no idea. The stony valley all looked the same. Eventually, she simply sat down and began to weep for life wasted.

Sometime later, the rocky night turned into the night that lay inside her, with stars showing through the great shaft in the roof of her cavern, and the much-muted song of the *mdei-hei* rumbling in the shadows. She didn't care about them in the slightest, or about the starlight, or the sound of the Sea, or the huge obscure shape of Hasai towering over her in the darkness. She sat hunched up and waited for life to go away.

It wouldn't, annoyance that it was. A solution occurred to her, but she had no energy for it. And anyway, everything she had ever done, she had botched—surely she'd mess up a suicide too. A life of study without use, learning without wisdom, action without satisfaction, Power without focus, lust without love: What use was it? She sat there and tried to bleed to death through the wound above her heart.

"You will not achieve death for some days yet," said the subdued voice of the Dragon above her, using the precognitive tense.

Annoyed, she leaned back against the great forelimb gingerly, careful not to disturb the blood clotting on her breast. She closed her eyes, squeezing out useless hot tears. "Drop dead," she said.

"We have done so."

"Try it again. You missed something the first time."

"Speak for yourself, *sdaha*," the voice of thunder said. It had her own annoyance in it.

Tonight, as occasionally happened, she didn't have to look

up at Hasai in order to see him. His eyes burned silver, but they burned low. His talons clenched the stone floor in a painful gesture that made her remember the cave at the Morrowfane.

"The nightmare spoke some truth," he said. "As with your Lovers, you will not permit us to have what we need, so that we, in turn, may give you what *you* need. You believe you must do everything yourself. But there is no such thing as perfect self-sufficiency, even among humans."

She shook her head, confused, thinking of what her father used to tell her: *You'll never be able to depend on others, if you can't first depend on yourself.*

Hasai winced at her in Dracon disagreement. "You cannot depend on yourself if you cannot first *trust* others."

Segnbora sat still, trying to understand, but the words made no sense. Hasai gazed down without moving for a long while, and at last shuffled one huge forelimb back and forth along the floor. *"We are you,"* he said with terrible intensity. "If you cannot trust us, your trust of yourself will be betrayed every time. *Sdaha,* hear me!"

It was no use. It made no sense.

"Sdaha," Hasai said, so low it could have passed for a whisper. "What lies beneath your stone that you dare not lay open? What terrifies you so much that the Shadow would resurrect the memory in the hope that you would die of it?"

That got her attention. "It brought forth that memory because it sees me as a threat. In a way that's good, I suppose. It means I may be able to do it some real harm at Bluepeak."

She leaned sideways and put one hand upon the stone at the bottom of her mind. It burned hot as flesh beneath a half-healed wound, warning her off. Her insides flinched at the touch of it, and she began to tremble.

Pain experienced stops hurting, she knew. The *mdeihei* had taught her that. There was another reason to look below the stone, too: The Shadow had found her weak spot. If she didn't deal with it now, it would strike her there again, perhaps at Bluepeak. And how could she betray Lorn at a moment when he would need her the most? She couldn't. She couldn't see her friends' lives lost, her liege-oath broken, the Kingdoms foundering for lack of the Royal Bindings . . .

She smashed one fist down on the stone. Damn! Damn!

"Taueh-sta 'ae mnek kej!"

"Mdaha," she said, shaking all over. Slowly, she leaned forward until she was on her hands and knees over the stone. *"Mdeihei—"*

They leaned in close, the huge form above her, the many indistinct forms in the shadows. She reached behind her, toward Hasai. Wings reached down to shelter her, but it wasn't shelter she was interested in. Her hand found the burning mouth, and jaws closed over it. She pulled those wings down around her, into her, wore them and their body and their heart.

Under the stone, darkness burned. She cocked forward the terrible diamond razors of the wings' forefingers, intent on the place where her deepest anguish lay. "My *mdeihei*, this is what you wanted. And what I want now. If we die of it . . ."

A roar of defiance and challenge went up from the gathered generations. *"Mnek-é,"* she whispered, *I remember*. Her talons raked down and laid her soul bare at last. Stone peeled away, and her control went with it. Night fell . . .

Her nuncle, of course. Nuncle Bal was in and out of the old house at Asfahaeg all the time, busy around the land—gardening, cutting trees, planting new ones. She had watched him about his business often enough, and sometimes she had noticed him looking at her for a long time. She wondered sometimes whether he was lonely and wanted to play, but she never quite got around to making friends with him. There was too much else to do.

She had the Fire, a lot of it, and pretty soon they were going to send her away to a real school where you learned to do magic with it, instead of just simple body-fixings and under-speech, which were all the Rodmistress down in town would teach her. At the school they'd make her a Rod of her own, and she'd be able to do all kinds of things.

In the meantime, there were lessons and exercises to make the Fire grow, and she was busy with those. In fact, she had stumbled by herself on one special exercise that gave her the same tingling excitement that the Fire did, though in a slightly different way. When she showed her new method to Welcaen, her mother had laughed and praised her and told her it was fine to enhance the Fire thus, but that she shouldn't forget to be private when she did it. The most private spot she could think of was the hiding place behind the old chicken house, where the willows' branches hung down all around, making a dusky green cave. And that was where she had spent most of that warm spring day, delightedly touching herself in that special secret place—until Nuncle Bal came brushing through the downhanging branches and stopped in surprise, and stood there staring at her . . .

Her mother had told her that usually it was not polite to be naked with someone unless you had agreed on it beforehand. Not knowing how Nuncle Bal felt about it, she pulled her smock back down and smiled at him.

"Hi," she said.

He smiled back, and all of a sudden she felt really cold inside, because there was something wrong with the way he was smiling. Confused, she put out her underhearing and listened.

What she heard made her so scared that she couldn't pull it back again, couldn't even move. She never heard anything like *this* before. Her mother and father when they shared . . . she knew that feeling. It was warm: a filling-and-being-filled feeling. She wasn't sure what they were doing, exactly, but it wasn't *this*. The feeling that went with *this* was cold: a wanting, and wanting-to-be-in-something. It was hungry, just hungry enough to *take*—

He was letting the rake fall against the willow truck, and she was getting really scared now, so that she started to jump up and run away. But he was right in front of her already, and he grabbed her hard around the throat with one hand, and covered her mouth with the other. She couldn't breathe. She tried to scream, to cry, but there wasn't any air. Her ears started to ring and everything went red in front of her.

Nuncle Bal seemed to be saying something, but she couldn't tell what it was through the red, the black, the roaring. She fell backward into the darkness, silently begging *oh please, let it be a bad dream. Let me wake up, please!*

After a while the roaring went away some. *It was a dream,* she began to think, and then heard his voice, thick, low and hungry. "You want it," he said. Her eyes came open. She saw his twisted smile, shuddered, and squeezed them shut again. "You want it. Sure you want it."

He was doing something to her smock. What was he—

"Mamaaaaa!" she started to scream, tears starting to her eyes. But before she could get the scream out that hand came down on her throat again. The red, the roaring, *oh no, pleeeeeeease* . . .

. . . her back was cold. She was on the ground again, and her smock was off. So were Nuncle Bal's britches, and she squirmed and fought but couldn't get out from under his hands. His breath was on her face and he leaned in and pushed her legs far apart, too far. It hurt, and what was he doing, he was rubbing her secret place, the wrong way! And what, what—

NOOOOOO!

The scream wouldn't come out of her throat. It was all inside her head, a shrieking pain, but not as bad as how he was hurting her down there. He was in her secret place that was supposed to be for her to share with her loved some day, and he was pushing himself inside. There was a horrible burning pain, again, and again, until she felt herself being torn open. There was a white-hot line of relief, then, and new agony stitching itself through the rest of the burning. It was sickening. She wanted to retch but couldn't, his hand—

Tears rolled down the sides of her face, into her hair. After a while she couldn't feel them or anything else, it hurt so bad— Inside she yelled and yelled for help, but no help came. They weren't sensitives and they couldn't hear her, any of them! He was pushing it in and out, hard. It hurt worse and worse, and he was breathing fast and hot right in her face. She was breathing his wet stale breath and that made her want to be sick too—and it hurt, it *hurt, somebody make it stop!*

Somebody, Mama, Daddy, Goddess, please, please make it stop!

He slumped forward, and she thought she felt something

shoot inside her, but she wasn't sure because of the pain, the way it burned, her secret place that had always felt so nice. Broken, torn, she'd never be able to use it again. No one would love her, ever, *hers* was broken—and the Fire, when he hurt her, it came out, it was in the pain, *no more, never, it hurt, horrible—*

She lay there and sobbed for air, all the screams in her stifled by horror; and when he came around and knelt over her face and pushed the hard thing, all bloody, into her slack mouth, and rubbed it in and out, she let him. At least he wasn't hurting her anymore. But when he turned her over and started to put it against that other place, she realized that he was going to hurt her even worse this time. No one was going to come help her now, either. She pushed her face down against the cold harsh dirt and tried with all her might to die.

It didn't work. When her first scream broke free, he strangled it again. The terrible strength of his hand turned the world red and then black once more. The last thing she heard as she pitched forward into blackness was, very remote, the sound of some little girl screaming as the size of him tore her open the other way, too . . .

Eventually her hearing came back. She heard him pick up his rake and hurry away, pushing the rustling branches aside. Some while later, lying as she was with her face on the hard ground, she felt-heard hoofbeats, cantering, then galloping. He was gone. Very slowly she got up. It hurt, especially between her legs, when she moved them at all. She pulled down her smock and scrubbed at her face to try to get the dirt off: Her father didn't like her to be dirty.

That roaring stayed with her all that day, as confusion and rage sounded all around her. It was her thoughts now, dazed, shocked, going around and around in her head and coming back again to that which she had felt tangled with the agony —the Fire.

When they finally put her to bed, full of some bitter herbal potion the Rodmistress had made her drink so she'd sleep, her head still roared behind the steady flow of her tears. Only later, after she had been staring for hours at the vague circles the candles made on the ceiling, did the tears flow more slowly. Gradually, the pain between her legs began to feel far away. The roar died to a whisper. But the whisper said the same thing she had been hearing all day . . . *No more. Never again.*

And there was a quieter whisper beneath that. One so soft that she hadn't heard it then, never heard it afterward; only heard it now with a Dragon's impossibly sharp underhearing —a seed of rage, taking root in blood and battered flesh, burning dark with hate: *Some day, when I'm big, I'll kill him.*

The pain, experienced at last, fell away and left her among her *mdeihei* with the fiery tears running down her face. They held their silence, waiting to hear what she would sing before beginning to weave counterpoint or dissonance about it.

She was exhausted. It was fifteen years since that afternoon under the willow. Fifteen years since she had shown herself any more than Balen's terrible smile, or thought of the experience as more than "the rape." She had thought she was over it, past it all.

What idiocy.

As she grew, she had quickly given up thinking much about sharing her body with others. Her agemates indulged in all the delightful anticipation of adolescence—the feeling that something magical awaited them when sharing began. But when the time came she had plunged into an experience that had about it nothing of magic. Instead, every sharing had a touch of the sordid about it, a taste of fear which made her want to have it finished quickly. Afterwards, she would inevitably plunge into another sharing, in search of what had been missing. She never found it. Nor, as she got close to the brink of focusing, had she ever managed that, either. How could she, when sharing felt so much like Fire?

Slowly Segnbora lifted her gemmed head, and sang relief and grief and weary regret at the walls. From the shadows her *mdeihei* took up the dark melody and shared it with her in compassionate plainsong. "Oh Immanence," she sang, "I'm full of Power, and in danger of running forever dry; I've shared a hundred times, and I'm virgin still; I walk on water, and yet thirst . . ."

She brought her wings down against the floor in a gesture of bitterness.

"And the nightmare was right, too. I'm a killer. The Shadow has merely to touch that memory ever so lightly, and I kill one more time. Is this my destiny, then? To be a clockwork toy that can be set to killing by any fool who happens to find the key?"

Gentle and ruthless, her *mdeihei* answered her in one long note that shook the cave. "*Yes!*"

"Or so it seems," Hasai said kindly.

She looked over at her *mdaha*, catching for the first time the unease that had always been in his voice. She had never before been Dracon enough to hear it. He gazed back, gentle-eyed, huge, terrible as a thundercloud with wings. And yet, to Dracon eyes, he was also frightened, crippled, shadowed.

"*Mdaha,*" she said, bending her head down close to his. "Your discomfort bears looking at, for haven't you often told me that the *mdeihei*, and you, are me?"

"Often."

"That being the case," she said, "it comes time now to deal with *your* stone, *sithesssch.*" He looked at her almost sadly, knowing—as he had always known—that it was true. "For you are me, and at Bluepeak the Shadow will strike at you too. If you succumb, I will too. Then Lorn dies, and the Kingdoms founder, and I'm forsworn. And more than that: The green place you fought for, the world you treasure so, will fall under the Shadow's domination, and not even Dragons will be safe."

Hasai was still as stone, except for his tail, which lashed nervously. Segnbora leaned closer, flipped her own tail around to pinion it and hold it down. The sight of her tail briefly surprised her. It wasn't like Hasai's. It was scaled in star-emeralds as fiery green as new spring growth. It was spined in yellow diamond.

"It has to do with me somehow, doesn't it?" she said. "With going *mdahaih* in a human—and with something older than that, even. Hasai, it must be settled, or the Shadow will settle it for us!"

He started to draw downward, away from her touch. "There is yet time—"

"No there's *not!*"

Hasai lashed free of her tail, began to rise slowly from his crouch, wings lifting, the diamond sabers of the forefingers coming around to threaten her.

Segnbora gazing up, unmoved. "I am you, *sithesssch,*" she said. *Beloved.*

Hasai moved not a muscle. As the momentary anger slowly ran out of him, his eyes changed. They were no less afraid, but now there appeared in them room for something else.

"Now," Segnbora whispered. "Quickly."

The fluid, black-glittering splendor of him made itself into a curve, a pounce, a terrible striking downward, a living knife. Stone sliced open like parting flesh, the blood was memory, it leaped—

Their Sun ate their world. They saw it happen. They had had warning—both ahead-memory of the actual incident, and years of wild starstorms, during which the Sun's light was too intense to drink without dying, and every Dragon had to leave the Homeworld for a time, and wait far out in the cold for the Sun's fire to die down.

Shell-parents grew infertile, and eggs that should have hatched roasted in the stone instead. At last came the final storm they had dreaded. In haste, all of Dragonkind streamed off their red-brown world and hung helpless in space, watching their star swell to a hundred times its size and devour their Homeworld.

They were orphans.

But they weren't homeless. Wisely, the older Dragons had looked to the youngest Dragoncels to see what they ahead-remembered of their own going *mdahaih.* What they had found was the place they'd know as *mdeihei*—an odd, cool little world, greener than theirs, covered with a strangeness called *water* and inhabited by life of bizarre and fascinating kinds.

One Dragoncel, however, remembered more than the others. He knew the way, and would die upon reaching their goal. His name was Dahiric. The Dragons gave him another name: Worldfinder. They put him at their head and he led them out into the Great Dark.

How long they travelled there, none of the Dragons were

ever sure. Many died along the way—starved for Sunfire in the empty wastes—but Dahiric, a doomed and purposeful green-golden glimmer at the head of ten thousand others, never veered from the memory he followed. Born only to die, and to make this journey, he was determined to succeed. Finally, after what might have been ages as humans reckon time, they found the place. It was all that the *mdeihei*-to-be had seen: strange-colored, but alive; a home at last; stone to sink their claws into. They dropped down toward it—

—and found what Dahiric, and many more, were to die of. From the dark side of the world, where it had been hiding, a black foul air came boiling out toward them. It was blacker than the space in which they hung, and it was alive. It hated thought and light and any kind of life but its own. It was also vast enough to swallow the bright little planet whole: a project on which it had been working for eons. It didn't relish the Dragons' interruption.

Dahiric knew his duty. Gripping a double wingful of the little planet's field of forces, he dove down into the roiling blackness, flaming. The Dark drew back, and the Dragons saw Dahiric drive a long tunnel down into it. At the tunnel's bottom his light blazed like a falling star. But Dahiric was young. His fire was limited by his immaturity. His flame went out, and the Dark closed behind him. After a little while he came floating out of the boiling blackness, dead.

Had there been air to carry the battlecry the Dragons raised, stone would have shattered across the world. Ten thousand strong, they dove at the Dark from every angle, flaming as best they could. Their fire was in short supply, however, since they had been out in the night so long, and ten thousand Dragons were not enough. The Dark opened before them, swallowed them, spat back the dead.

Soon there were nine thousand, seven thousand, fewer. Many had no offspring yet and went *rdahaih* in a second, without time to make their peace with the Universe from which they were departing. Some went mad from the strain of having so many relatives become *mdahaih* in them in so short a time. Others so afflicted flung themselves into the Dark and were lost too.

A few simply fled, and lived.

One of these was the youngest of the Homeworld's Dragon-cels. He had never been quite normal. When he had become fully *sdahaih* at last, and his shell-parents and relatives had asked him when and where he would go *mdahaih,* his answer frightened them all. What he foresaw was darkness and cold and terrible pain; and then the odd, crippled body of an alien . . . one who was certain she would go *rdahaih* and take with her all the *mdeihei.* It was a terrifying vision, and all rejected it.

He grew, and yet the vision did not change. Therefore, he slowly became resigned to being a curiosity among his own kind. As befitted a Dragon, he came to make light of the difference, submerging it in placidity. But he did not realize that the way he did this—by learning to stand a little aloof, even from his *mdeihei*—also encouraged other Dragons to stand aloof from him as well.

Hasai became estranged from his own kind. He took no mate. He held his peace. He flew alone. And when he finally found himself facing that same awful blackness that in min-utes had killed half his race, Hasai failed. With no comrade who would admit to fear, and so support him toward courage, he became nearly blind with terror. He fled.

The rest of Dragonkind, fortunately, had not exhausted their options. There in empty space they convened in body and mind, and held Assemblage—the last full Assemblage that would be held for a generation or two, until the Advo-cate summoned them again two thousand years later. They paid the price of Assemblage—the lives of the DragonChief and the Eldest—and then all those left alive turned their hearts inward and gave their will and power over to the Im-manence.

Few of them saw where the Messenger came from. She was a Dragon in shape, but even the webs of Her wings burned intolerably bright. Her every scale was a star, a point of power so terrible it could be felt through Dragonhide. The Messen-ger wheeled and dropped through the massed Dragons, scat-tering them—then halted above the raging, boiling immensity of the Dark. Through their othersenses, the Dragons could feel the Dark's alarm as it reached up to snuff out this trouble-some intruder. Likewise, they heard its silent scream of pain as the Messenger flamed, letting loose a torrent of Dragonfire as potent as a star's breathing.

The Dark writhed convulsively, ripped away from the world with a jerk and a soundless howl of rage. It streamed toward the Messenger to engulf Her utterly, but the Messenger only spread wings and claws and seized it. Working at the forces in space with fiery wings, She drew the Dark away from the world, screaming and struggling. Together they dwindled, drawing farther away from the little blue world, until all that could be seen of them was a light like a dwindling star. Those who dared to follow came back and reported that the Messenger had plunged, together with the Dark, into the heart of the nearby yellow Sun. Neither came out again.

Later, the survivors found Dahiric's body among those of the slain. The others they burned in Dragonfire, as was the custom on the old Homeworld, but Dahiric they bore down to the surface of the new world. There they found a fair place at the endpoint of a great spur of land, where water washed it. They uprooted a mountain, as had been done on the Homeworld for Phyiril and Saen and others of the Parents, and they laid it over him, melted it around him, and made a dwelling there for the new DragonChief. Thereafter, the Dragons settled into their new young world, and watched humankind come slowly out of the caves into which the baleful influence of the Dark had driven them . . .

. . . and behind the rest of the Dragons, a silver-and-black Dragoncel drifted to earth like the last leaf of autumn. His shame at his cowardice gripped him like the pain of giving-up-the-body, and would not leave. True, no other Dragon accused him of fear, but no one comforted him, either. He was alone, as always. Alone with a new shame, and with the old hidden terror of the day he would go *mdahaih* in a human.

All these burdens he buried under layers of Dracon placidity. The centuries went by. He maintained his dignity, flew alone, and kept silent. Then finally his life became reduced to waiting for the stars to assume the proper configurations. This they did. At last, his luster dimming, Hasai spiraled down to the Morrowfane by night and crept into a cave there, to wait for the seizures, and to wait for the one who would come . . .

* * *

He looked across the cavern at her now, head held high, waiting for her to disapprove of him and pronounce a sentence worse than death: eternal imprisonment with a *sdaha* whose opinion of him was not passive placidity, but active scorn.

Behind him, the *mdeihei* were strangely silent.

"You ran," Segnbora sang.

He said nothing.

"And you are of value nonetheless," she said, weaving around the words a melody that attributed importance to her words. "You did what you did, and here you are. And here am I, too . . . or should I say, here are *we.*"

Hasai looked at her in amazement. She sighed a little fire and unfolded one emerald-strutted wing, laying it over his back in a gesture of affection.

"So where do we go from here?" she asked.

He opened his mouth, and nothing came out for a moment. " '*Sithesssch,*' you said," he sang in dubious tones.

She flipped her tail in agreement.

"Then only one matter still troubles me . . . "

"What?"

"The *mdeihei,* and their opinion. As you know, they do not judge, but merely advise. Still, I would like to know that they are not ashamed."

Segnbora considered the matter, listening to the utter silence in the background where the *mdeihei* usually sang. "*Mdaha,* don't worry. If they are truly of the Immanence, as they claim, they will understand."

The doubt fell out of his voice, but Hasai still looked at her strangely. "You're truly *sdahaih* at last," he said. "It's very odd."

"How so? You knew how it would be."

He dropped his jaw, smiling. "Sometimes, for the sake of surprise, we forget a little."

Segnbora spread both wings high and curved her neck around to look at them. "Well, I certainly feel *sdahaih.* Shall we go test it?"

"There's more to being *sdahaih,* and Dracon, than flight,"

Hasai said, and his song trembled with the joy of one who's found something long lost. "Memory. And its transformation."

She shook too, thinking of all the painful experiences she could accept, or remake if she wished. Now that she was *sdahaih,* the ever-living past was as malleable as the present. There were some things she wouldn't change, experiences that had made her what she was now. *Balen,* she thought. *He stays. There's unfinished business there, somehow. But as for other matters—*

For the first time since that afternoon under the willow, her love was clean—and now more than ever before she wanted to give it away. "I remember a place," she sang quietly, looking at Hasai, "where stars swirl in the sky like a frozen whirlpool, and the Sun is red and the stone is as warm as your eyes—"

He met her glance with eyes that blazed. *"I'ae mnek-é,"* he sang. *We remember.*

Wings lifted and beat downward, and the cave was empty.

The soaring began at the Homeworld, and never quite ended. They made the Crossing all over again, together this time. Other Dragons looked curiously at the one who in fore-memories had been alone, but who now went companioned by some child of the Worldfinder's line, green-scaled and golden-spined, with eyes the fiery yellow of the little star to which they journeyed.

They saw the Winning again, not with guilt this time, but simply as one of the events that would eventually bring them together. Afterwards, they fell to earth like bright leaves drifting, and lay basking in the Sun. They glided together through long afternoons, taking their time so that the people below would have something to marvel at. They matched speed for speed in the high air, and tore it to tatters of thunder. They went bathing in the valleys of the Sun, and chased the twilight around the world for sport. He made her a present of the sunset, and she made him one of the dawn, and they both drank them to the dregs until the fire of their throats was stained the red of the vintage.

They lived in fledgling and Dragoncel and Dragon, in child and girl and woman—found memories that were lost, discovered past and future. Gazing into one another for centuries, they also found completion. And at the bottom of *that,* they found Another gazing back. One Who became them as They became It. Goddess-Immanence and peers, Made and Maker, the two Firstborn, They flowed together. Not merely One, not simply the same. They *were.*

For that, even in Dracon, there were no words.

Eventually they remembered the way home, and—living in it—were there. Segnbora, leaning back against the immense forelimb from which she had not moved all night, looked up at her *mdaha*'s silver eyes.

"I have to be getting back," she said. "They'll be wondering where I am."

"Best hurry and tell them. *Sehé'rae, sdaha.*"

"*Sehé* . . . "

Halfway out the entrance to the cave, she paused, touching her breast in confusion. In the place where the nightmare had bitten her, there was nothing but a pale, crescent-shaped scar.

"Dragons heal fast," Hasai said from behind her.

A quiet joy like nothing she had ever heard sang around his words. She knew how he felt.

"*Sehé'rae, mdaha,*" she said, and went out.

She opened her eyes on a dawn she could taste as well as see. When she stood up to stretch, she saw the Moon, three days past third quarter, the phase under which she had been born, hanging halfway up the water-blue sky like a smile with a secret behind it.

Picking her way back toward the camp, she came across someone waiting for her with his back to the rising Sun. His long black shadow stretched out toward her, the stones within it outlined brightly by the Fire of the sword he leaned upon.

"Welcome back," Herewiss said as she approached.

Skádhwë was struck into a nearby rock. She raised a questioning eyebrow at Herewiss as she plucked it out and resheathed it.

"I didn't touch Skádhwë," he said. "I asked it politely, and we reached an accommodation."

"Thank you," she said. She glanced down at the cracked and broken links of her chainmail. "This whole thing was a setup. You knew the nightmare was here. You knew twenty miles away. You couldn't *not* have known."

He caught the merriment in her voice and grinned. "I'm on other business than just Lorn's and Eftgan's," he said. "There's all kinds of power in this world, looking to be freed. I do what I can."

"I could have died," she said, "of what it said to me. I understood it, it spoke the truth, and yet I killed it anyway. The despair could have finished me."

"I know," Herewiss replied. "My decision was not made lightly. If you hadn't been strong enough . . . yes, you would have died. And I would have taken responsibility for it."

She looked at him, pitying and loving him, both at once. "Thanks," she said.

"I didn't do much of anything," he said, half-bowing graciously. "You seem to have found your own solutions."

He looked past Segnbora with great interest. Turning, she was just as interested to see the long-necked, long-bodied, short-legged Dracon shadow that lay behind her. It was positioned as if the creature that cast it were standing on her hind legs. Experimentally she pointed a finger, and saw the shadow of the forewing barb cock outward.

"Is it true," Herewiss asked with a gentle smile, "what they say about Dragons and maidens?"

She turned back and shrugged slightly. "You'll have to ask someone who'd know," she said. "I'm not a maiden any-more . . ."

She started back toward camp to saddle Steelsheen and hummed a chord.

Fourteen

... the Goddess could not spend all Her time persuading the Kings and Queens of the world of the idiocy of war. Therefore She invented tacticians . . .

(source unknown)

As they topped the crest of yet another line of foothills they paused, silent in the dusk, and looked down upon ancient history. Forest patches lay on the wrinkled fells and hollows of the land below. Although it was just two nights before Midsummer, the wind ran chill over the land, rustling trees and grass so that the earth seemed to shudder like the flank of a troubled beast.

South of their position the foothills became rougher, their bare stones turning brown, red, and hot gray in the fading light. Farther south still rose the Highpeaks. Off into the crimson distance they marched, mountain after mountain. At their forefront, frozen like a white wave of stone about to break, stood Mount Nómion, which overshadowed Bluepeak.

"The weather's changing," Freelorn said.

He was looking uneasily at the filmy banner of windblown snow that stretched southward over the Peaks from Nómion's major summit. It had a distinct downward curve to it that indicated it was a south wind fighting to get past the mountains and slide under the warmer northland air.

"Storm tomorrow, loved. Can't you do something?"

Herewiss's eyes were elsewhere—searching the country west of them for any sign of the Darthenes. Eftgan's last message had said that she and her troops would bivouac a league-and-a-half west of the mouth of Bluepeak valley two nights before Midsummer, well out of the sight of the Reavers encamped in Britfell fields around the town. But the land beneath them had a trampled look, and was empty.

"I could," Herewiss said, reaching over his shoulder for Khávrinen to better sense what had been happening there. "It would be unwise, though. Eftgan may already have done something."

"Or Someone else might have," Segnbora said. She was as troubled as Lorn, for different reasons. Her undersenses clearly brought her a feeling of haste and disruption from the land below, as if plans had gone awry and many minds down there had recently been in turmoil. Worse were Hasai's memories, and those of some of the *mdeihei* who knew this area well. Something dark and threatening lurked under this land, and was ready to rise up in menace.

She shuddered, as did the *mdeihei* inside her. Herewiss was sitting still with Khávrinen flaming in his lap, its Fire subdued.

"Someone else *has* been meddling, I think," he said, glancing over at Freelorn. "There's will behind this weather, and I'd sooner not probe it more closely than that, since I'd be leaving myself open to be probed back. Better to stay low for the moment." He looked down at the Bluepeak highlands. "Eftgan came at this site from the north a day and a half ago—"

"Were they driven back by Arlenes?" Freelorn said, anxious. Cillmod had been raiding across the Arlene-Darthene border for nearly a year now, in violation of the Oath. It was unlikely that he would allow a Darthene incursion into his territory to go unchallenged.

"No. Reavers—and they were here first. Eftgan had a skirmish with them and went north again. The Reavers went west. No sign of Arlenes; they must not have received word that Eftgan's in the vicinity."

Dritt looked confused. "Eftgan's a Rodmistress, though. Shouldn't she have been able to sense that the Reavers were here, and avoid them?"

Herewiss nodded.

There was uneasy shifting among Freelorn's followers. Lorn himself was bewildered. "How can a Rodmistress's scrying go wrong?"

Herewiss swung down from Sunspark and began loosening the girths of its saddle. "The same way mine can, I imagine," he said. Segnbora could feel the great effort he was making to conceal the trouble in his mind. "I can't feel where she is

—my range has been steadily diminishing for the past day. Something's settling down over this whole area. Power."

No one had to ask Whose power.

Sunspark looked sideways at Herewiss. (I'll find her,) it said. There was unease in its thought over Herewiss's sudden anxiety.

Herewiss laid a hand on its burning shoulder, where the fiery mane hung down. "Go, loved. But burn low. Don't advertise us."

It tossed its head and was gone in an oven-breath of wind, leaving only wisps of smoke to mark where it had stood.

Segnbora dismounted from Steelsheen in silence, thinking that the tai-Enraesi house luck was certainly working as usual. Of all the places she had never wanted to be in a battle, this led the list! Since Earn and Héalhra had first set the bindings here a thousand years before, this land had slept uneasily. It was steeped in Power—not beneficent power like the Morrowfane's, but a dangerous potency that could be manipulated easily by whatever lesser force moved there. Sorcerers and those with the Fire stayed away from Bluepeak, afraid to trigger unwelcome influences. Yet here they were, merrily riding into this unstable land with the clear intention of arousing those influences in order to bind them. Segnbora would sooner have kicked a sleeping lion awake, then tried to tie it up.

"How far from Nómion would you say we are?" Herewiss asked his loved.

"Eight miles, maybe." Freelorn was chewing his mustache absently, an old nervous mannerism. "We'll be there by tonight if we push the horses a little."

They stood together, Herewiss playing with Khávrinen's hilt, Freelorn looking out over the darkening land toward a remote ridge that stood away from the foothills in front of Nómion. That ridge was Britfell, the White Height, which partially hid the mouth of Bluepeak valley.

There was nothing white about the fell this time of year. Its barren curved ridge was a brown wave rising over the green land below it. Here and there it was dotted with blackthorn that had managed to take root in its sheer stones.

On the hidden southern side of that wave, within Bluepeak

valley, the tiny combined force of the Arlenes and Darthenes had—one thousand years before—been hunted up against the cliffs of Britfell's inner side by Fyrd. Seeing them trapped there, the Shadow had taken a hand, climbing down out of the Peaks in the shape of the Gnorn, a form so fearsome that just the sight of it would kill.

Earn and Héalhra, trapped together on a height near Britfell's end, faced with the slaughter of all their people, took the option offered them by the Goddess. They sacrificed their mortality to undergo that Transformation by which mortals become gods. Together, as White Eagle and White Lion, they attacked the Gnorn and destroyed it—slaying the Shadow and being slain, and leaving their people free to move north and found Arlen and Darthen.

There was hardly a child in the Kingdoms who hadn't played at Lion-and-Eagle and fought that battle in dusty village streets or empty fields. Segnbora had done it herself, usually insisting (for loyalty's sake) on being the Eagle to someone else's Lion. For Freelorn and Herewiss it must have been a little different, of course. The inventors of the game had been the founders of their houses; their Fathers many times removed.

"Goddess help us if the Reavers are holding the mouth of the valley!" Freelorn said.

"Probably they are."

He looked sidewise at his loved. "You should have let me buy those mercenaries, dammit."

"Lorn, the point of this excursion is winning back your throne, *not* having battles. And buying yourself mercenaries *guarantees* you'll have battles. Everybody in the neighborhood assumes you're going to start something with them, and so they start something first. Besides," he said, smiling wryly at Freelorn's exasperated look, "it seems there aren't enough mercenaries available right now to make a difference. Someone else has been hiring. Cillmod."

Freelorn shrugged, still chewing his mustache. "You miss my point. What I mean is, I'm going to have a hard time getting into the valley to do the Royal Binding; that is, unless we try something obvious, like using Sunspark."

"Where did you have in mind to do it?"

"Lionheugh."

That was the little island-height at the end of Britfell's curve, well inside the valley's mouth.

"Since the Transformation took place there, it's favorable ground. Every place else has too much blood."

Herewiss looked grimly amused. "So all we have to do is get you past a whole army of Reavers, and probably Fyrd," he said. *And keep you alive afterward.*

Segnbora caught his worried thought, but Freelorn merely raised his eyebrows.

"Problems?"

"I think we'll work something out," Herewiss said in his lazy northern drawl. Under his hands Khávrinen swirled momentarily with a confident brilliance of Flame, then died down again.

A hot whirlpool of air set dried grass smoldering on the ridge. The vortex darkened as if with smoke, spread horizontally and solidified into Sunspark's blood-roan shape. Herewiss reached up to lay a hand against its cheek.

"Well?"

(I found Eftgan's soldiers busy with more of those Reaver-folk we had trouble with at Barachael,) it said, pawing the ground modestly, and leaving a scorched place. (They're busy no more. I drove them back down into the valley to play with the rest of their people.)

"Oh, no!" Herewiss covered his face with one hand. "Loved, I thought I told you to be circumspect!"

Its burning eyes were merry. (So I was. I don't need to show fire to burn something. Things just became, should I say, too hot for them?)

Segnbora couldn't suppress a chuckle, at which Sunspark beamed.

"Don't encourage him," Herewiss said as he bent to pick up the saddle again.

(I did have a little trouble,) Sunspark added, in a tone of thought that said it was making light of the problem. (For some reason I wasn't able to make things burn as easily as usual. Something there was slowing me down.)

Herewiss nodded, and kept his voice equally light. "We'll

keep an eye on it. Well done, loved. Did the Queen have any word for me?"

(Yes indeed,) Sunspark replied, and said one.

Segnbora exchanged amused glances with Lang, who stood beside her. It was not a word one usually associated with Queens.

Herewiss looked sternly at Sunspark. "Did you burn *her?*"

(Oh . . . just a little . . .)

Fastening the girths of the saddle, Herewiss kneed the elemental good-naturedly in the belly. It developed a surprised look, then a searing hot breath went out of it—*whoof!* Herewiss pulled the girth tight.

"You and I," he said, "are going to have a talk later. Meanwhile," he mounted up, "let's join Eftgan before the Reavers figure out that the, ah, heat's off . . . "

The camp seen from above looked like any other bivouac that Segnbora had ever seen: squares set out with tents at their centers, picket lines of horses tethered nearby, men and women sprawled around campfires tending to their weapons or their dinners.

Britfell rose up a mile south, a looming blackness from which the occasional hunting owl came floating down in search of small game disturbed by the activity thereabouts. The owls weren't getting much business, though. It was a quieter camp than most Segnbora remembered. Evidently the Darthenes, too, realized that there were forces about that it would be better not to disturb.

They passed the outer sentries and shortly thereafter were met by a dark-haired rider on a Steldene dun gelding, bearing a torch, the light of which danced off the bright chain of a major.

"Torve!" Freelorn said, pleasantly surprised. "Well met. You seem to have made better time than we did from Barachael."

"Barachael's secure," Torve said with his usual calm cheerfulness. "The Queen's grace wanted me here, so here I am. She asked me to bring you in."

"She felt us coming?" Herewiss said, sounding somewhat relieved.

"You were close," Torve said, his unassailable calm strained a little. "There have been problems with scrying of late."

"We noticed."

The Queen's tent was little different from those that the rest of the army used—slightly larger, perhaps, but of the same patched canvas. All that identified it as hers was the Eagle banner on its pole outside the door. On the other side of the doorway, however, the diamond-studded haft of Sarsweng was thrust into the ground up to its hook. Its diamonds glittered restlessly in the torchlight. Eftgan was sitting in shirt and britches on a low folding chair, surrounded by a scatter of maps and parchments and papers. She was tapping one map idly with her Rod while talking to a man who squatted beside her chair.

She rose to greet Herewiss and Freelorn and the others, tossing her Rod aside. "I'm glad to see you," she said, sounding as if she meant it. "Come in and be comfortable. Everybody, this is my husband Wyn—"

The group murmured greetings. Segnbora caught Wyn's eye and traded smiles with him. It had been ten years since she had last seen him, and (as she had suspected) the years had left no sign of their passing. Short and compact, Wyn s'Heleth was in his early fifties and looked perhaps thirty. His face was like a handsome hawk's. His eyes were so merrily threatening it was sometimes a strain to meet them.

Segnbora had herself introduced Wyn to Eftgan back in Darthis, when the old King had been looking for a wine merchant who wouldn't charge him exorbitant prices. Not too long thereafter the Darthene Court had found itself with not only good wine at reasonable prices, but with a future Prince Consort. Connoisseurs were still talking about the rare vintages that had been uncorked for Eftgan's wedding.

"There's stew in the pot and dishes beside it," the Queen said, sitting down. "Wine and water in the jugs. Sit, friends. We have trouble." She dug about in the welter of maps and pulled out a large one of the whole Bluepeak area.

Trouble's a gentle word for it, Segnbora thought as Eftgan talked and pointed. The Reavers had a considerable start on the Darthenes, and there had been nothing the Queen could do about it. Worldgating would have been impossible, when so many people were involved. Eftgan had therefore been forced to march westward from Orsvier slowly enough to allow for musters and pick-up levies along the way. The Reavers seemed to have handled all such matters a long time before, on the other side of the mountains, for here they were, four thousand strong, arrayed in siege around Bluepeak town and holding the mouth of the valley from Nómion's flank to Britfell's outer curve. Lionheugh, as Freelorn had feared, was well inside their lines.

"They have three thousand foot and a thousand horse," Eftgan said, "and the fact that they got here first gives them the advantage of the ground, too. They've taken stand on both sides of the Arlid, and to dislodge them we're going to have to attack uphill. I don't like that . . . "

"How do you stand?" Herewiss said.

"Fifteen hundred horse and four thousand foot," Wyn said in his sharp voice. "Eighty sorcerers, fourteen Rodmistresses—"

"Fifteen," Eftgan said. "You always forget to count me. However, sorcery hasn't worked since yesterday—or, when it does work, you don't want to be anywhere near the consequences. As ranking Mistress here, I've advised my sisters to keep their Fire to themselves unless I—or you, Herewiss—order otherwise. By the by, have you heard anything from the Precincts?"

"No."

"Neither have I. It's disturbing. I asked them for advice on this matter two weeks ago, while it was still possible to bespeak as far as the Brightwood. I suppose the Wardresses started debating the subject and are taking too long about it, as usual." She sighed. "It's too late now; we'll have to make do with our own advice. Meanwhile," she said to Freelorn, "there's the business of the Royal Bindings to consider. I brought the Regalia."

Freelorn nodded. "I know the ritual. But the Arlene Regalia

is in Prydon . . . all of it but Hergótha, anyway." He looked annoyed as he said it. Hergótha the Great—Héalhra's ancient sword—had been missing since Freelorn's father died. If there was anything Lorn wanted back as much as the Arlene kingship, it was that sword. "And I remind you, I'm not an Initiate. My father never took me on the Nightwalk into Lion-hall."

Eftgan nodded. "We'll take our chances, Lorn. You're the Lion's Child, and Héalhra's blood is what's required here. The problem is," and she pushed at the map of Bluepeak with one booted toe, "I'm reluctant to do even so minor a Gating as would put us down on the Heugh—that was the spot you were thinking of, wasn't it? The Shadow's influence is building by the minute. Any use of Power from now on could be terribly warped." She frowned. "Did I tell you that the valley is crawling with Fyrd? A new kind—"

"Thinkers?" Dritt guessed.

The Queen looked at him glumly. "Yes."

Freelorn reached for the map and pulled it closer to where he sat cross-legged on the floor. He studied it for a few breaths, then indicated the mouth of the valley. "The Reavers are drawn up here, under several of Cillmod's mercenary-captains."

"A little more north," Wyn said. "About a quarter-mile north of the Heugh, stretching right across to the Spine."

"Uh-huh. They're on the other side of the Spine too?"

"It seems a safe assumption, though we haven't confirmed it. They've got a small force at the Spine's northern end; we've left it alone."

Freelorn nodded, leaning over the map. "I doubt they're paying much attention to their rear, then, since the besieging force is holding it secure, and the Fyrd are back there too. I suspect no one will notice if we go in the pantry door instead of the great-hall entrance." He pointed at Britfell, indicating a spot near where the fell joined the northern massif of Kemana. "Here."

Now it was Wyn's turn to look shocked. "You're crazy! There's no going up Britfell, it's too sheer! Maybe a climber could do it in a day or so, if there were time . . . "

Herewiss was looking at Freelorn with an expression compounded of worry and dawning hope. *For once,* Segnbora thought, anticipation rising in her, *maybe one of Freelorn's crazy strategies is going to pay off*—

"I've done it on horseback," Freelorn said. "With my father. There's a path. We went up the north side and down the south in about six hours, coming out on the far side of the curve about a half mile north of the Heugh. And if two people did it, so can ten." He glanced around at his own group. "Or a hundred," he said to the Queen. "Or five hundred."

"That path must not be very visible from either side," Eftgan said, sounding uncertain, "which suggests it will be rough to ride."

"If the Shadow had built it, it could hardly be worse. But it's a way over. And everybody, even the Reavers, knows there's no way over the fell. That's what brought our ancestors to grief." Freelorn tapped the map again. "So. We take a few hundred of your horse—Why be stingy? Make it five hundred—and go over." He scrunched up his forehead in thought. "Allow sixteen hours for the whole passage. You order your main force to draw up north of the valley's mouth. The Reavers won't move; they're not such idiots as to attack downhill and give up the advantage of the ground. If they draw back and try to tempt your forces to come after them, fine. Meanwhile, you and I and five hundred horse are *here*" —he tapped the inside of Britfell's curve—"where we can't possibly be. We come down around the Heugh and do our binding there, while the cavalry takes the Reavers in their unsuspecting flank and rear, attacking downhill and driving them against your main force to the south. Hammer and anvil." He grinned.

Wyn was beginning to look interested despite his doubts. "That still leaves the cavalry with an unfought force at its back: the besieging force. If they leave the city and come down on you—"

"How many are holding the siege?"

"About a thousand foot."

Freelorn shrugged. "If they send enough people to make a difference, won't the garrison inside try a sally?"

"So they've said," Eftgan said. "That'll make no difference to the cavalry, though."

"So." Freelorn tapped the Spine. "Once your main force engages the Reaver force, you send a good-sized party to secure the ground between the Spine and Nómion and clear the Reavers off that side of the river. There's our bolt-hole. We ford the river and go up behind the Spine, then rejoin the main force."

Eftgan sat silent for a little while, studying the map. "We're fifty-five hundred to their four thousand," she said at last. "I don't have the leisure for strategic victories. I need conclusive ones. This at least gives us a chance to do what we have to without using Power and risking a disaster. And the surprise of taking them from the rear would be tremendous. It should disorganize them wonderfully. And, since organization was never their strong point anyway . . . "

Eftgan glanced over at Wyn for his opinion. He nodded at her. She paused to give the map one more long look.

"The last scrying I managed," she said, "gave a hint of something that might be coming from the northwest, from upper Arlen. Help or hindrance, I couldn't tell. And I don't dare delay to find out. The Bindings must be reinforced soon. A delay could turn loose forces I don't care to contemplate."

Standing, she bent to pick up her Rod from among the papers on the floor. "No matter. We'll work with what information we have. Freelorn, I'll ride with you regardless of the uncertainty. Wyn will handle the main force in my absence. Meanwhile—"

The tent flap was thrust aside. In peered a tall, rawboned woman in the Darthene royal blue, with somewhat disordered dark hair and a captain's chain around her neck. "Ma'am," she said, breathless, "the Reavers are attacking the north side of the camp again. Maybe a hundred or so."

"Oh, damn," the Queen said. She tossed her Rod away and reached to the side of the tent, where Fórlennh BrokenBlade lay sheathed. "They love trying to draw us out," she said, buckling on the scabbard. "Any trouble handling it, Kesri?"

"Not really."

"Good. Of your courtesy, go call the other captains and the

captains-major. I have something to tell them." The captain vanished and the tentflap fell. Eftgan turned to Freelorn and Herewiss. "Midnight's coming on. We'll start an hour after midnight, and give the Reavers a surprise tomorrow afternoon."

Lorn and his people began heading out of the tent to see to the horses and to their own bedrolls. Eftgan flicked a wry glance at Segnbora, an outward indication of mixed concern and anticipation. "Just like old times, 'Berend."

Segnbora thought of Etáchnë and other such fields that lay behind the two of them, victories and defeats equally frightful. "Not *just* like, I hope."

"No," Eftgan said, looking thoughtfully at Skádhwë in its scabbard, and at Segnbora's odd shadow on the floor. "I suppose it won't be."

Fifteen

Mn'An'dzát kchren'rae ëhwiss thaa'-
seth:

(The Five Truths, terrible and
joyous:

Stihé hë-stihé.
Stihú hë-stihé.
Whrn'thae najh'stihëh.
Ousskh'thae najh'stihëh.
Mda't'dae bvh-sda't'dae mnek-é.

What is, is.
What was, is.
Matter is an illusion.
Meaning is an illusion.
The Door opens both ways.

Rui'í'rae-sta haa'ae!

Believe none of these!)

Ehh'ne Ihhw'i'ae (What Dragons
Say), vii, 14

Full night, when it came, was starless. A heavy overcast hung like a roof just above the highest peaks: Nómion and Kerana. In that stifling silent darkness, a long column of riders picked its way to the foot of Britfell's northern slope and came to a halt.

The prospect was daunting. Sheer walls of cracked cliff-face rose up uninvitingly. Around them were strewn rubble and boulders brought down by the annual flux of heat and cold. Eftgan, on her tall bay gelding Scoundrel, shook her head as she looked upward.

"Lorn, if the road isn't still there—"

"Then we're no worse off than you were before," Lorn said.

Ahead of Segnbora and the others, he, Herewiss, and the Queen were shadows among shadows. Everyone in that riding had made sure there was nothing bright about their gear; faces and hands and buckles and swordhilts were smeared with a mixture of grease and soot. Even so, Segnbora's Dragon-sharpened vision saw movements and expressions clearly enough.

Freelorn pulled up Blackmane's head and headed him off to the left. "Let's take the adventure the Goddess sends us," he said, "and go as far as we can."

He urged his dun straight at the cliffside. Blackmane snorted mild protest but went where his rider directed him, climbing a slope of talus and scree and not stopping until they reached a narrow ledge fifty feet or so above the cliff's foot. "This way," Lorn called softly to the riders waiting below, and put his heels to Blackmane again. The horse took him leftward past a rounded outcropping of stone, and out of sight.

"This is crazy," Lang said, beside Segnbora.

"Maiden's madness, I hope," Eftgan said, and shook Scoundrel's reins. He stalled, snorting, until Eftgan laid her crop gently below his left ear and touched him with heels again. Up Scoundrel went in a nervous rush, scattering pebbles and small stones. One by one they followed him, reining their horses in to keep them stepping lightly and minimize the damage done to the path.

The ride was like something out of an old tale or a bad dream, full of long terrifying pauses during which Freelorn lost the way and found it again, dismounted to heave fallen boulders off the narrow track or to lead Blackmane where he thought it too dangerous to burden a horse with a rider's weight.

The path, if it could be dignified with such a name, wound back and forth along the face of the cliff, switching back at wildly irregular intervals, the switches often barely enough for one horse to negotiate. Always there were heartstopping drops below.

Segnbora kept her elbows in as she rode, once again very glad of Steelsheen's breed. Steldenes were bred in mountainous country and were frequently accused of being part goat. The mare picked her way delicately along ledges of rotten, sliding stone with only an occasional snort of protest at the poor quality of the trail. Other horses behind, flatland breeds, weren't doing as well. The sound of whispered swearing came drifting up from riders down below.

As they climbed, the night got blacker, if that were possible. A feeling began to grow among the riders that Something with no good intent was watching the silent climb. Tense minutes stretched into an hour, then two and three. Segnbora began to feel as if she had been climbing up this miserable wall forever, as if her whole life had been spent fighting with eggshell-fragile stone, squinting at it, terrified of every step.

At the same time, she had to admit that this feat would be sung of for years, if any of them finished the climb and survived the battle that waited just the other side of Britfell. She maneuvered Steelsheen cautiously around another treacherous switchback, not looking down.

Inside her, in their own darkness that now seemed bright by comparison, Hasai and the *mdeihei* hissed laughter at her fear of heights, and then began singing (in sixteen-part harmony of the kind Dragons used when feeling playful) their memory of the ballad which the bards would indeed later write for Freelorn: *When Fyrd came over the Darthene border / and Reavers moved at the Shadow's order* . . . Segnbora almost felt like smiling, until she remembered that just because her *mdeihei* had a memory of the ballad, that was still no guarantee that any of them would survive this venture.

One of Sheen's hooves slipped, and Segnbora's heart seized as she leaned with the mare so she could regain her balance. For an instant they came close to a perilous drop, but Steelsheen recovered and went on, sweating and trembling, but knowing what her mistress wanted. Unconcerned, the *mdeihei* were singing in unison now, a calm chorus. *They climbed the Fell and they crossed the water, the Lion's Son and the Eagle's Daughter—*

Several hours before dawn it began to snow. The wind rose, and became a howling blast. Snow that grew blizzard-fine drove stinging into faces, numbing hands on the reins. The horses whickered in complaint and tried to walk with eyes averted toward the cliff, which only caused them to miss their footing all the more. Forewarned, their riders muffled themselves up as best they could. Even in Midsummer snow often fell in the high South, though usually more lightly than this. The sky got infinitesimally lighter as day broke above the storm, though not enough to lighten anyone's spirits.

There's will behind this weather, Herewiss had said. That will could be felt watching them more strongly every minute. The head of the column was fairly close to the top of the fell now, but that was no comfort. The thought of having to take a similar path downhill, on an icy trail, was on everyone's mind. The storm was blowing from the south, and had been abated somewhat by striking the fell and having to pour over it. Matters would be much worse on the other side.

The trail leveled so abruptly that Segnbora was taken completely by surprise. It led westward here, going around the edge of a west-pointing backbone of the fell. A pause to look

west would have been pleasant, but there was no time for it
—the column was still coming up the far side of the fell, and
there was little standing room. Besides, they had entered the
cloud cover, and visibility was low. Even so, Eftgan dismounted long enough to stretch her cramped arms and legs
and look ahead hopefully.

Herewiss, beside her, looked unhappy. "Can you feel anything?" he said.

Eftgan shook her head. "I can hardly hear myself think in
this wind, let alone anyone else. That one"—she glanced
upward at the slate-dark cloud cover—"has settled Itself
down snug. It's muffling all thought but Its own. The main
force is going to have to rely on riders for messages, and
there'll be no way for us to know what's going on until we
rejoin it."

"Sunspark can assist," Herewiss said. But he sounded uncertain. "When will they move?"

"Noon. We should be well finished with our business at the
Heugh by then, and they can go ahead and have a battle
without worrying about what it might raise." She bit her lip,
a sign of hidden fright that Segnbora recognized.

Segnbora had no time to indulge her own nervousness,
however. There was barely enough time to dismount and feed
Steelsheen some grain. By the time she got back in the saddle,
Lorn was already picking his way down the trail on the other
side, with Eftgan in back of him and Herewiss behind her.

"Let's move, slowcoach," Lang said as he nudged his dapplegray, Gyrfalcon, past her. "Going to lose your place up
front."

Dubious honor that it is, she thought, swinging up into the
saddle and following him.

Now the pace of the climb slowed to an agonized creep, for
the stone was not only iced, it was rotten. Rock crumbled
maddeningly under foot, and the horses rebelled—shaking
their heads, snorting, testing the footing at every step. The
blinding cold snow turned the world into a featureless gray
room through which vaguely seen figures led the way. The
ordeal was endless.

In front of her, Gyrfalcon shied, and then Steelsheen did

too. Segnbora had another of those terrifying long looks down. *Ice and darkness. Oh, damn!* The mare recovered her balance. Segnbora squinted at Lang's shadowy back and then squeezed her eyes shut for just a moment, looking down among the *mdeihei* for an answer to her growing terror.

The cave was full of memories, much easier of access than they had been before the evening with the nightmare. Overlaid on her perception of the trail as it was now she saw Bluepeak valley as it would look from Britfell on a clear day toward sunset.

The season was fall, not summer, and some of the fields below, yellow with wheat, stirred in the south wind. Other fields burned, and the black smoke was carried north, occasionally obscuring the bodies of the slain, and the trampled, bloody ground.

High in the surrounding peaks, on scarps and steeples of rock, winged figures watched, frozen with horror, as the frightful dark shape of the Gnorn went tottering about the battlefield, killing with Its look. Scrabbling Fyrd came after It in hungry terror to devour the dead. Behind It, Bluepeak town was burning. And westward on a lone height at Britfell's far end, two men with drawn swords stood watching the terror with tears running down their faces. A Dragon's eyes, keener than any hawk's, could make them out plainly: One man was huge and broad as a bear, with a shaggy mane of fair hair, hazel eyes, and Freelorn's prominent nose. The other was tall and angular, with dark hair threaded with silver, and kind downturned eyes as blue as Herewiss's, blue as Fire.

She saw them throw down their swords at practically the same moment, desperately making the Choice; saw them take hands there, while the Gnorn came weaving toward them through the screams and death of Bluepeak; saw them give up what they had been and gaze into one another's eyes to find out what they could be—

—and she fell out of that memory and into another one: this time, the memory of some nameless *mdaha* in the ancient time on the Homeworld, one who sat perched on a dark red stone in a violet twilight with another, while the starpool came up over the horizon. The Dragon turned to look into the other's eyes, which were silver fire set in a hide of turquoise and lapis. The Dragon fell a great depth into those eyes, into a timeless, merciless, fathomless love which held the whole Universe within it as a person awake holds the memory of a dream—

Our line often soared with the Immanence, she remembered Hasai saying. *One gets used to It.* But no Dragon ever got used to the Other's regard. The more one looked into that Other's eyes, the more powerful, and the more unbearable, the experience became.

In a blinding moment of realization, Segnbora understood what she had seen in Hasai's eyes on the night of unearthed memories. She understood, too, why she always averted her gaze after looking too long into the eyes of another human being—

The agonized joy of the discovery threw her out into the world again, back into whirling snow, ice and darkness. But the cold didn't matter anymore. Not even her own exhaustion, nor Steelsheen's panic, bothered her now. All she needed was a moment to put it into words, and the secret would be hers forever . . . Ahead of her, hearing Steelsheen's hooves scrape and clatter on the slippery rock, Lang twisted around in the saddle to look at her.

" 'Berend?" he called anxiously through the screaming wind.

Their eyes met.

She *saw* him . . . saw *Her.* Lang looked no different. His voice still came out in a drawl. She could still underhear his mind lurching back and forth between indecision and placid acceptance. He still hated some things without reason, and loved others unreasonably. He still judged and criticized by provincial standards. He still smelled from not washing enough . . . *yet he was She.* The *One.* And when Segnbora looked ahead at Herewiss or Eftgan, or back at any of the nameless five hundred following behind, or even at their horses, the result was the same. *All of them, everyone who lives. Every one the Goddess—*

"Lang," she said. It was almost a whisper, for she had little breath to spare in the grip of this painful ecstasy. This was the man whom she had used with casual cruelty, to whom she had refused intimacy when she felt disinclined to it. Yet there within him the Goddess looked out at her—not judging, as She certainly had the right to do, and not angry, either— simply loving her totally, without hesitation. She had always known that the Goddess indwelt in every man and woman, but *experiencing* it this way, now, was something else again.

Joy, laced with bitterness at her years of callous disregard of the One she loved, rose until it choked her. Tears spilled over and froze on her face in the icy wind. Her voice wouldn't work anymore. Knowing it was useless, and driven by an overwhelming need to communicate somehow, she bespoke him. (Lang!)

He stared at her in sheer disbelief. " 'Berend?"

He had heard her!

The pain fell away from her joy like a cast-off cloak. Segnbora sobbed, sagging in her saddle, and drew in a long breath. She had a great deal to tell him. (Loved—)

—and Gyrfalcon missed his footing, going down on his knees on a patch of ice. His hindquarters slipped off the path to the left, and the rest of him followed. Segnbora had a quick glimpse of Lang reaching for the ledge, more surprised than frightened, and that was all.

"LANG!" she screamed.

Almost before the scream had left her throat, Sunspark had leaped away from the ledge and sunk down into the snow- swirling emptiness like a thunderbolt, streaming fire. The line of riders behind her halted as she, like Freelorn and Eftgan in front of her, peered down into the whiteness, dumb with shock. A long time they waited there for the bloom of fire through the snow. Then, slowly, the brightness came walking up through the air and stood again before the ledge. Herewiss was alone on Sunspark's back.

('Berend,) Herewiss said, and had to pause. She could feel his eyes filling. (It was quick. I share your grief.)

All behind her, starting with Dritt, Moris, Harald, and the foremost of the Darthene riders, she could feel sorrow and fear spreading like ripples in a pool. She was numb, having fallen from such a height to such a depth so quickly. Yet still she could see Who consoled her as she looked at Herewiss.

(May our sorrow soon pass,) she said silently. A knife turned slowly within her at the memory of the last time she had said those words.

Herewiss broke their gaze. With a thoughtful look, he reined Sunspark about and took the path again.

It took two more hours to complete the rest of the ride down. The slope grew gradually less steep, and the ledges a bit wider, but the snow continued. Lang was not the only rider who was lost. Just minutes after his death, another horse and rider came plummeting down past Segnbora. The falling rider's glance locked with Segnbora's in the second of her passing. Still weeping, Segnbora could do nothing but pour herself into the look, see Who was falling, and aid Her in accepting what was happening. In that second, the woman's fear-twisted face calmed. Then she was gone.

Segnbora rode on, trembling. She turned a switchback and suddenly found herself at the top of a long skirt of scree and rough stones, which lead down to a slope carpeted in snow-covered grass. Glancing at the sky, Segnbora knew the storm wasn't going to let up. In front of her, Eftgan was checking her saddlebags to make sure the Regalia were safe. Herewiss had drawn Khávrinen and was pointing at the snow. There were prints in it: the big splayed tracks of a horwolf, and a keplian's pad-and-claw set. Both trails were only minutes old. Both led to the cliff's foot and away again, westward.

"We're expected," Herewiss said. "I'm done with being circumspect, Queen." Fire flowed down Khávrinen's blade in defiant brilliance. "We've got to stay alive. Meantime, we had better get to the Heugh fast. The Bindings are slipping from the pressure of so many beings in this area."

Eftgan nodded. "Can you shore up the Bindings until we complete the ritual?"

"I can," Herewiss said. "I've been doing it for several hours. But its' tiring. How long I can hold out, I've no idea."

"Once we begin, the blood-binding won't take long," Eftgan reassured him. Thumping Scoundrel's sides, she wheeled westward. "The ground between here and the Heugh is smooth. Let's make time."

They had to go slowly at first, so that the Darthene riders

still on the slope would have time to catch up. It was about fifteen minutes into this process that the first cohort of Fyrd found them. There were only twenty or thirty: horwolves and keplian who had been patrolling the heights and thought it wise to attack before the main force was down off the Fell.

It was a mistake. Like lightning dancing a death-dance, Khávrinen rose and fell in the forefront of the skirmish. What its blade didn't slay, Herewiss's Fire did. Sunspark was incensed; any Fyrd at which it looked became ashes in seconds. Fórlennh and Súthan flickered red and blue in Firelight and flamelight. Segnbora swept Skádhwë's blackness about her in an utter calm that felt very strange. Shortly, nothing moved but Darthenes and the wind. Drifts began forming around the bodies in the snow.

The Darthenes had a few wounded, none seriously, and none lost—a small miracle for which everyone was thankful.

"What's the time?" Freelorn said.

"Three hours past noon." Eftgan looked around and saw the last of her riders coming down off Britfell. "Wyn will be moving the forces forward at four. Let's get up that Heugh."

It was only a mile to Lionheugh, but they bought every furlong of the distance dearly. The fourth cohort of Fyrd was the biggest, some three hundred of the creatures. There were not many nadders, because of the coldness of the weather. There were, unfortunately, many maws and keplian, the worst Fyrd breeds for riders to handle. There were also four death-jaws, three of which Herewiss dealt with, and one of which Eftgan destroyed with an astonishing blast of blue Fire.

By the time this attack was over, no one was quite as lively as they had been. Nearly everyone had a wound of one type or another. Eftgan and Freelorn were unhurt, but Herewiss had a long set of slashes from a keplian's claws, and Moris and Dritt and Harald all had maw bites. But no Fyrd had been allowed to get away and warn others of what had happened.

"You and I were lucky," Freelorn said to Eftgan.

"Luck has nothing to do with it. If *our* blood falls on this land and we have the brains to do a binding right away, that One would lose a great deal of its Power." Eftgan whipped blood off Fórlennh. "Herewiss?"

He was sitting astride Sunspark with a look on his face that was either annoyance or strain. Khávrinen in his hand was flaring with a wild glory of Fire as he healed himself. "It's putting on pressure," he said. "Things are trying to return to the way they were before the Binding, and this Fyrd blood isn't helping matters."

"Let's go. 'Berend?" She glanced at Segnbora as they began to move through the blinding snow. "You all right?"

"Fine." Segnbora held Skádhwë over her knee at the ready.

"You always used to be so noisy in battles! I keep looking around to see if something got you."

"My lodgers are doing my hollering for me," she said. The Dragons didn't care for Fyrd, and her *mdeihei* had been singing martial musics laced with Dragonfire ever since she came down from Britfell. Battlecries seemed superfluous with that inner thunder going on.

Eftgan met her glance with an odd expression, as if seeing some stranger who was Segnbora's twin. " 'Berend, you've become *more* than your lodgers, somehow. What *happened* up there?"

It was a poor time to explain. "I'm not sure," Segnbora said. "Nothing of the Dark One's doing, that's certain." She knew it to be true as she said it.

If there was anything the Shadow didn't want mortals to know, it was what Segnbora had learned. Once one knew Who one was, It lost Its power over that person. She shook her head and kicked Steelsheen into a gallop, getting Skádhwë ready. The realizations were coming too close together. The hugeness of them was dazzling her. She needed something concrete upon which to fasten her mind . . .

Unfortunately, she got it. To their right, the crest of Britfell had been getting lower as they headed west. With little warning the fell simply stopped in a sheer cliff. Out of the falling snow their destination loomed: Lionheugh.

To the west, not even the snow could muffle a great confused roaring—shouts and battlecries, the bray of Reaver warhorns and the thin silver cries of trumpets. As they drew rein under the shadow of the Heugh, Eftgan waved Torve over, putting up Fórlennh and unsheathing her Rod.

"Leave me fifty," she said. "Take the rest and hit them hard wherever it seems best. My compliments to my Consort when you see him, and tell Wyn I'm sorry we're late, but we were detained. Ride!"

"Madam!" Torve said, and rode off hard with four hundred fifty of the Darthene cavalry behind him.

The snow swallowed them.

Freelorn rode up to join the Queen, with Moris and Dritt and Harald close behind.

"I have to do something about this weather, even if it's only temporary," said Eftgan, shaking the Fire down her Rod. "Then we'll do our business. Herewiss, how are you doing?"

He was holding Khávrinen before him in both hands, his eyes fixed on it. A frightening brilliance of Fire streamed about man and sword. "I'll hold," he said, but there was strain in his voice, and the feeling of malicious intent in the air hung closer than it had before. "The Shadow's pressing, though. There's much bloodshed going on and It's feeding on that. I daren't be distracted long—"

"Up with us," Eftgan said.

Punching Scoundrel, she rode at a gallop up the path to the Heugh. No one was surprised by the Fyrd waiting for them there. They dropped from rocks and leaped up under the horses' hooves. Eftgan's Rod crackled with Fire as she laid it about her like a whip. Whatever she struck didn't move again. Segnbora and Freelorn galloped behind her, watching the Queen's back, slicing down with Skádhwë and Súthan. Behind them came Herewiss, with Moris and Dritt and Harald about him as guard.

Very quickly, it seemed, they made the top of the Heugh and gathered there on the level ground, the Queen's riders and Freelorn's followers circling around in case any more Fyrd should attack uphill.

"No Reavers yet, and none of Cillmod's people," Eftgan said, dismounting hurriedly and raising her Rod. "That's a mercy; maybe they don't know we're here. *E'hstírre na lai'tehen ándrastiw vhai!*"

Eftgan cried into the wind in Nhàired, lifting her Rod two-handed and pointing it at the roiling sky. She sighted along the Rod's length as if along the stock of a crossbow. At the last word of her wreaking, another piercing line of blue Fire lanced upward and struck into the underbelly of the cloud above them.

The wind screamed, the cloud tore away from the ravening Fire like flesh from a wound. It tore, and tore—ripping backward and dissolving, revealing blue sky and afternoon sunlight. The snow stopped as the clouds retreated, until a great patch of sky the width of Bluepeak valley was clear.

Standing on that height, for the first time they could see what was happening. The Reavers and the main Darthene force were locked in battle in the pass, and the Darthenes were already well ahead of the position at which Eftgan had intended them to start. Even as they watched, the Reavers lost some ground, pushed uphill by heartened Darthenes who knew why the weather had suddenly cleared up. A sudden blot of darkness from the east—the riders who had followed Eftgan over the fell—smote into the Reavers' uneven right flank and scattered it.

"The clearing won't last," Eftgan said, breathing hard and leaning against Scoundrel. "I have to save some Power for the binding. Lorn, the Regalia, quickly!"

Freelorn had already undone Eftgan's saddle-roll, and now unrolled it before her. It contained an odd assortment: an old knife of very plain make, black of hilt and blade, and a rough circlet of gold that looked as if it had been hammered out by an amateur. It had, Segnbora knew, for this was Dekórsir, the Queen's Gold—the crown that each Darthene ruler hammered out unguarded in the open marketplace, once a year, to give the people a chance to dispose of an unfit ruler if there was need. There was also another circlet, this one of exquisite workmanship, woven as it was of strands of linked and braided silver.

Freelorn lifted the circlet up with a blaze of angry delight in his eyes. It was Laeran's Band, the crown of the kings and queens of Arlen. *Where did you get this!*"

"I had it stolen several days ago," Eftgan said, kneeling down beside the saddle-roll. "In the middle of last week, when Cillmod took it out of Lionhall."

Freelorn stopped still as death and stared at Eftgan. "When he *what* . . . ?" he said.

His voice failed him. No one but the members of the royal line of Arlen could set foot in Lionhall and come out alive. And Freelorn was an only child. Or had thought he was.

"It occurs to me that your father may have had a sharing-child he didn't know about," Eftgan said, setting Dekórsir on her head. "Or one he didn't care to legitimize. No matter right now. I'm just sorry we couldn't find Hergótha."

Freelorn turned the supple strip of metal over in his hands. "The thought of Cillmod wearing this—"

"I couldn't stand it either. Shut up and put it on, Lorn. Herewiss can't hold the Binding by himself much longer."

It was true. Herewiss had dismounted from Sunspark, unable to spare even the small amount of concentration needed to stay astride, and was sitting with his back against a rock. Khávrinen lay across his lap, clutched in both hands. He had begun to shine, growing almost translucent, as he had at Barachael, and the stones of the Heugh sang with the Power that was poured out of him. He was holding his own, but just barely. Segnbora looked around her and found that under-hearing was no longer necessary to feel the strain in the earth and the air.

Eftgan's riders and Freelorn's followers were all looking over their shoulders, hunting the source of the strange feelings inside them. Herewiss's will could clearly be felt battling with the One that poured Its rage into the valley. He was keeping away the ancient reality, as if he had his back braced against a closed door. But the pounding on the other side, the rhythmic throb of rage and hatred, was getting stronger—

"We are the land," Eftgan and Freelorn were saying in unison. They knelt before one another, knee to knee, holding the black knife together, Lorn wearing the strip of silver, Eftgan the circlet of gold. Their joined voices—Freelorn speaking the ritual in Arlene and Eftgan in Darthene—made an uncanny music. The hair on Segnbora's neck rose at it, hearing in human voices an echo of the *mdeihei*. "Its earth is our flesh; its water our blood; its well-being our joy; its illness our pain . . ."

The ritual continued, speaking of mysteries particular to the royal priesthood. Many of the riders turned away, trying not to listen to a ceremony that no one of common blood had heard since the founding of the Kingdoms. Segnbora stood by with Skádhwë in her hand and listened fearlessly, in wonder, hearing once again the Goddess speaking to Herself: one Lover speaking to the Other in solemn celebration of Their eternal relationship.

She saw Lorn take the knife and cut Eftgan's upheld left wrist with it, crosswise and careful. Both of them paused a moment, trembling. At the stroke of the ritual wounding the hammering of hatred in the air grew more savage. It was almost physically perceptible. Eftgan took the knife from Freelorn and reached for his left wrist—

—the Fyrd came up the hill in a wave, horwolves and maws together. Behind them came two-legged forms in rough skins and crude metal and leather corsets, bearing leaf-shaped bronze swords and bows of horn, howling like the beasts they followed.

Eftgan pitched forward gasping from a black-fletched Reaver arrow lodged between her shoulder and throat. Horrorstruck, Segnbora watched helplessly as Lorn sat her up straight, breaking the fletching off the arrow and pulling the point end out of the wound with brutal efficiency. He snatched up the black blade and something else—then there was a Reaver in front of Segnbora, blocking her view.

She met the man's brown eyes, sank into them as Shíhan had taught her, felt the move he was about to make. A second later, Skádhwë had countered and sliced the man's chest through from side to side. As he died she didn't break that gaze. She knew Who she had killed, and let the Other know Who had killed him. She grieved for his death and accepted it as her own, completely. Then she looked up at her next opponent—a nadder this time—saw Her there too, and killed again, out of necessity, in love.

She killed again. And again. And again.

The Darthene riders encircling the hill knew immediately what Segnbora didn't have leisure to notice for some time: there were too many Reavers and Fyrd. If they attempted to hold this position, they'd be killed off slowly. Most of the riders had pushed to the side where the worst attack was coming from, the west side, so that behind them Eftgan and Freelorn and Herewiss could get away.

Freelorn shoved Eftgan up into Blackmane's saddle and fastened Scoundrel's reins to the stirrups. Rushing over to Herewiss next, he literally picked him up from where he sat, snapping orders at Sunspark. The shocked elemental knelt to take Herewiss on his back.

Segnbora had her hands very full of Reavers and Fyrd for a few wild minutes, until slowly they began to give her breath. Their first charge was exhausted. In addition the Reavers, ever wary of sorcery, had begun to stay clear of Skádhwë's uncanny blade. There was a madwoman wielding it, her face streaming calm tears.

" 'Berend!" Freelorn shouted at her.

Segnbora took a moment before answering to look with her sharpened vision at the battlefield. The sight was a shock. More forces were pouring into the valley's mouth from behind the Spine—not Reavers, and not Darthenes, certainly. They were falling on the Darthene right flank and crushing it as easily as a stone falling on an egg.

"*Damn* him!" she cried, and turned away from the hill-crest, running for Steelsheen and the others. The Queen's scrying had been accurate after all. Cillmod had gotten wind of the upcoming battle, and had evidently decided that this was an expeditious time to both distract the Darthenes from retaliation on his borders and exterminate their fighting force as well. There were none of the Royal Arlene army down there. Such loyal Regulars might have been persuaded to turn against Cillmod since Freelorn was in the field. All these were mercenaries.

Flinging herself into Steelsheen's saddle, Segnbora rode down the trail to clear a path for Freelorn, swearing all the way. It was very obvious now why there were so few unattached mercenaries for hire in the Kingdoms. The Darthenes down there were badly outnumbered.

Behind Segnbora, Sunspark was doing some swearing of its own. (What's the matter with him? Did they hurt him somehow?) It danced a little as it cantered down the trail, obviously wanting very badly to let its fire loose. (If he doesn't come out of this shortly, the whole lot of them are going to make a very nice cloud of smoke!)

Freelorn, holding the bleeding Eftgan in front of him on Blackmane, looked as haggard as if he had been shot himself. Remembering Herewiss's true-dream, the thought made Segnbora's heart turn over. "Firechild," she said, "he's all right, he's just keeping things from getting much worse. For the love of him, *save it for later!*"

The Power Herewiss was pouring out was astonishing. It frightened Segnbora. She had witnessed great wreakings in the Precincts in which fifty or more Rodmistresses had worked in consort, and all of them together hadn't let out a flood of Fire like this.

Khávrinen struck razor-sharp shadows from everything its light touched, and Herewiss's flesh burned transparent as an imminent dawn. Some of the Reavers were turning away from them even now, frightened by the sight of the statue-still rider with the thunderbolt in his hands. One Reaver, though, got up the nerve to fire an arrow. The instant it touched the writhing aura of Flame that wound about Herewiss, it flared and fell away in ashes.

"Can you gallop without dropping him?" Freelorn shouted at Sunspark as they made it down off the Heugh onto the plain again.

It bared its teeth at him in scorn. (Gallop! Is that all? Where do you want him?)

Freelorn looked from west to east, and got a look of sudden recognition on his face. He flung out an arm, pointing. "There!"

East and a little south of the Heugh, one of the spurs of Kerana came down in a little scraped-away scarp, sheer on all sides except for one shallow approach where riders could go up. It could be defended without too much trouble.

(Done!) Sunspark said. It leaped cat-smooth into the air, shooting southeast so fast the air behind it thundered in shock.

Freelorn and his band and the Darthenes went after at full

gallop, not sparing the horses. They couldn't: If they didn't make it up that scarp, there would be no later to save them for. They had a mile or so to cover, across snowy ground, and they had hardly been galloping more than a half minute before they lost the sunlight and the clouds closed up again. With unnatural swiftness it began to snow again. The wind rose to a scream once more, and darkness began to fall. It was the darkness Segnbora feared most, for above it and within it the voice of the Shadow could be heard, howling with enmity.

On the scarp a mile off, a light shone as if a star had fallen there, bright enough to cast shadows at even this distance. But the brilliance of Herewiss's Fire was no great comfort. A fresh group of Fyrd and Reaver riders were hot behind them, perhaps a half mile back. Eftgan, clutching Blackmane's saddle and hanging on as best she could, looked back at their pursuers and moaned softly. Freelorn's face was grim.

"They're catching up, Lorn," Segnbora shouted.

The group rode like hunters, whipping their horses into a lather. Onward they rode into the screaming, stinging night. The scarp was right before them, lit with a pillar of blue Fire that flickered eerily on the cloud-bottoms and turned the wind-whipped snow to a blizzard of blue sparks.

The riders went up the scarp like a breaking wave, the horses stumbling, foundering, finding the path by luck or Goddess's love. The way up was none too wide and could easily be kept clean of Reavers—for a while. Behind Freelorn and the Queen, the others closed ranks. Overhead, the daunting blows of the Shadow's hatred became suddenly audible. There was thunder in the snow clouds, and the wind shrieked furiously around the steeples of the cliff-wall behind them.

Freelorn threw himself out of the saddle, pulled Eftgan down and helped her over to shelter behind a rock at the foot of the cliff. He pulled out the knife, put it into her clutching, shaking hand. Crying with the effort, she braced herself against the stone and reached up to cut—

Shouts and the clash of steel rang out on the plain, where some of the Darthenes were holding the approach to the path up the cliff. Sunspark, who had been bending over Herewiss

in concern, jerked its head up and stared down at the Reavers
and Fyrd in rage.

(This is *your* fault!!) it cried in a thought that not even the
smothering darkness could muffle.

It leaped like a skyrocket down to the foot of the scarp,
reared, and brought down its forefeet with a crash that split
stones. Wildfire burst up from where its hooves struck, and
ran madly to either side in front of the scarp. The fire ignored
the Darthenes, but any Reaver or Fyrd it touched blazed like
tinder and was blown away across the snow, ashes, a breath
later. The Reavers drew back in panic from the apparition that
suddenly stood between them and the scarp: a huge, crouching cat of swirling fire that stalked forward with blazing eyes,
pausing to raise one flaming paw.

—the blood ran down Freelorn's arm, and he pressed it to
Eftgan's wound. "And we who are One—come on, Eftgan!
—One and not-One say to the land which is us, and of us, be
not—"

The earth began to tremble. From the south, visible in this
unnatural black as something blacker yet, a great wave of dark
Power rose and rose above the mountains, leaned, and fell
with a crash that couldn't be heard, only felt. Like death, like
drowning, it rolled over them, past them, and in that wave's
wake ten or twelve Darthenes dropped and Sunspark's fire
went out.

Even Herewiss's blaze dimmed and shrank, failing like a
candle placed under a cup. But he did not surrender. When
the snuffed-out stallion clambered up the rocks to his side, it
found him clutching Khávrinen. He was forcing it to burn,
pouring out everything he had. It was not enough. In the
darkness where the blade's Firelight didn't reach, forms
moved and grew solid. Eagerly they lifted long-rusted swords,
bared long-rotted fangs, and looked hungrily up toward the
little shelf where the Darthenes stood.

(I can't change, I can't burn,) Sunspark cried in anguish,
(*what do I do now?*)

Segnbora could feel it straining mightily, trying even to
trigger that last burning in which a fire elemental ends its

existence as an individual . . . anything to hold the threat away from its loved. *He can't hold off the Shadow alone,* Segnbora thought, almost choking with the sheer hate that filled the air. There was nothing the Shadow hated so much as the Fire, except perhaps those who wielded it. Herewiss couldn't last forever, and when his reserves gave out, he would simply be dead.

The first man in a thousand years to have the Fire, the Queen of Darthen, the rightful King of Arlen, most of the forces that Darthen could field—all dead at once. The Shadow, imagining a world all to Itself, darkened.

Inside Segnbora the *mdeihei* were rumbling deadly threats that seemed absolutely empty to her. *What can* they *do? They're* dead!

DeathFire—

When someone with the Fire died, regardless of whether they had ever been focused during their life, their death focused the Fire for one final moment. Even those with just the spark of Flame that most men and women have managed to focus then. That was what gave one's deathword its power.

Segnbora stared with sudden cold purpose at the rising tide of dark malice. Suddenly she understood why Lang had died when he did, and why her parents were murdered. The Shadow had wanted to stop her before this moment, this realization. She held up Skádhwë and looked at it. *One life it will demand of you,* Efmaer had said, and now Segnbora was sure which life the dead Queen had meant. The Shadow was betting she wouldn't dare kill herself.

A lethal wound would be enough. She could add enough Fire to what Herewiss had to aid him in holding the Shadow off until the Binding was done. And afterward, he'd heal her—

—or not–

It was a terrible chance she'd be taking. She didn't want to die. But if the Fire she had trapped inside her could be of use here, then . . .

Behind her Freelorn held up one bleeding arm and with his free hand reached into the unwrapped saddle-roll for what

she had seen him grab before: a fistful of stones and dirt from
Lionheugh. He held it to Eftgan's arm; her blood trickled
down.

A crash like sudden thunder rocked the scarp and sent men
and horses sprawling. Freelorn and the Queen fell apart.
Herewiss pitched forward on his face, his Fire all but darkened. More than just hatred pressed down on them from the
darkness now. The Shadow was invoking the worst fears of Its
enemies, and on all sides men and women screamed and
cowered from painful deaths suddenly lived in their own
flesh, losses of loved ones, shames that formed darkly in the
influence-ridden air. The Dark One still didn't walk among
them openly, but was having no trouble driving the defenders
to death or madness, one by one.

Out in the darkness, Segnbora saw the hralcins rear up.
Ugly unearthly shapes lurched across the scarp at her, singing
hungrily and reaching out at her as they had in the Hold.
Crabbed claws sought to tear, but Segnbora's screams were
frozen in her throat. Only escape was left. Frantically, looking
around for a route, she saw Freelorn stand up, cursing with
fear and shaking his wounded arm. It wasn't wounded anymore: the cut made by the sacral knife was just a white seam
of scar. The Shadow could heal for Its own purposes.

Leaving Eftgan, Lorn stumbled over to Herewiss and shook
him conscious with savage efficiency. Segnbora stared at him,
confused. He wasn't the same Lorn. There was purpose in
those eyes. When she met them, Segnbora saw Her in them
as she had been seeing Her in everything today. But there was
a difference. There was knowledge, foresight. Freelorn knew
now what Herewiss had dreamed in the Hold. He had seen the
arrow in his back, and had seen himself turn toward death's
Door . . .

Stunned, Segnbora watched him turn away from her with
awesome purpose; watched him turn away from the gasping,
shaken Herewiss, and rise out of his crouch. The hiss of an
arrow whispered through the screaming wind. Slowly, slowly
Freelorn sat down with the barbed Reaver shaft standing out
from behind his right lung, and pressed a fistful of dirt already

stained with Eftgan's blood to the entry point. Then he fell back against Herewiss, and slapped the blood and dirt against the ground—

The terrible pressure of hatred grew suddenly much less as the Royal Binding took hold on the land, quieting the unquiet ghosts, banishing the phantoms of Fyrd and slain Reavers and hralcins. Herewiss's Fire blazed up again as if someone had taken the cup off the candle. But now his mind wasn't on the battle.

"LORN!!" Herewiss cried, and without hesitation went limp and fell over again. He had gone out-of-body, gone after his loved to catch him at the last Door, and to prevent him from passing it.

Off on the southern horizon, another darkness began to take shape. This was a more solid one, a heaving black shape that Segnbora had seen before, but didn't dare look upon now, being in a human body. The Shadow had become enraged enough to take on a physical shape and come after them Itself. And It had adopted a form It knew, from past history, to be very effective.

"Don't look!!" she cried to the Darthenes.

They hardly needed the warning. Those still alive and conscious after the assault by their worst fears were already hiding their faces from the hideous prospect.

No time to wait for Herewiss to come back, Segnbora thought, shaking all over. *Just have to do it myself—* Hurriedly she knelt and took Skádhwë two-handed, resting the point a shade to the left of her breastbone. *Mdaha,* she said, and in that moment was informed by her ahead-memory that Herewiss was *not* going to be healing her . . .

Oh wonderful! Sithesssch!

Sdaha—

Sehe'rae!

She pushed the sword in, hard. The greedy shadowblade slid into her with shocking ease. At last she found out what it was like to be run through, and tried to scream past the terrible feeling of her heart fibrillating around the intruding blade, trying to beat, trying to beat, failing. All that came out of her throat was a choked cough.

Inside, she felt her Fire leap together with her heart's blood and burst outward. Blind with pain, she groped for support, willing herself to stand and do what she had to. But she found no support. The darkness went red, and then black, and she fell forward . . .

. . . a long fall, the longest one, but it had an end. There was a voice crying *Get up! Get up!,* the voice of someone familiar. Her mother perhaps, or Eftgan. Had she overslept again? The Wardress would be furious—

She was lying on something hard. She rolled over to push herself up on her hands and knees, feeling the sword in her fist. Probably one of those rocks the Dragon's thrashing had dislodged had hit her in the head. She felt weak and stumbly. She pushed upward, shook her head to clear the daze out of it, looked up.

A pang of terror twisted in her heart like a knife of ice. This was no cave. True, there was empty darkness all around, but before her stood two doorposts blacker than any night, going up and up forever, out of sight. Between them stars blazed. Endless depths of them, a patient silent glory she had seen before in dreams and visions, but never for real. This was the last Door, the Door into Starlight.

No, I'm not ready! she cried, staggering to her feet. But her protests made no difference to the insistent forces shoving at her back. They were stronger than she. They impelled her, whispering to her that it was over, that her struggles were done.

The Shore! she thought with longing. *Mother and Father. Lang!* Tears rose at the thought of him, at the image of his last confused grab for the ledge. *Loved, I have a great deal to tell you. Maybe it's not too late.*

There was a great silence in her mind that shouldn't have been there.

"*Hasai?*" she said, letting herself be pushed toward the Door as she searched in mind for him. *You're dead. Are you there too?*

No answer.

I'm not going! Segnbora thought, on the very threshold. But she had no way to stop herself. She was being pushed too hard, and she was holding something in one of her hands. A darkness . . .

Swift as thought she used the last-chance block that Shíhan had taught her was for emergency use only. One hand on the hilt, the other bracing the steel from behind.

She screamed with agony in that eternal silence as Skádhwë, ramming against the impermeable blackness from which it had been torn, sliced deep into her hands. The darkness shoving at her back was merciless, and cared nothing about her anguish. Through her sick pain, Segnbora realized who was pushing her closer to the Door. She fought back, feeling her blood flow from hands and heart. There was something she needed to remember. Something—

I am Who I am. And knowing that, It has no power over me.

Dismay ran through the force that urged her forward. She forced it back, and back, arching herself, and then fell backwards, gasping. Skádhwë fell soundlessly to the invisible floor. Slowly and painfully, she got to her knees, picked Skádhwë up, and stood. It might indeed be her fate to die after she had finished what she had to do.

She turned. Had she been breathing, the breath would have caught in her throat. He was huge, looming above her, dressed in the old clothes he wore while gardening. The big hard hands stained with leaf-mold and rough with calluses reached out to her.

"No!" she whispered, and almost turned to flee. But there was only one way to run—through the Door and out of life.

That terrible smile leaned closer.

"No!" she said. It was a squeaked word. A little girl's voice, terrified, but still defiant.

The smile lost some of its assuredness.

"No," she said again, more strongly, her voice sounding strange in the utter silence. She raised her head, met those hungry eyes, held them . . . held them . . .

He was not as large as he had been. Certainly he was no larger than any other man. He was smaller, in fact, than many she had killed at one time or another.

Raising Skádhwë, she took a step forward and watched the

fear spread across his face. Balen had used brute strength to overwhelm the child she had been, but she was a child no longer. He was unarmed, and she was armed with a weapon against which there was no defense. Another step she took, and he backed away. She almost took the final step, but paused. It would be easy to kill him, yes. Possibly enjoyable.

But for how long? Would this be just another form of running away? If she should she instead accept him—

Kill him! her heart said to her.

I give him into your hands, her heart said to her. *Do with him what you will.*

The great silence on this side of the Door surrounded her.

Even he *didn't kill me,* she thought.

She lifted her eyes to Balen again. Trembling, he shot her a terrified glance. In that blunt and brutal face, she saw again what she had seen in Lang, and Herewiss, and Freelorn, and even the Fyrd. Her. HerSelf.

She tossed Skádhwë away.

Very slowly, even with fear, she went to the man, reached out to touch his shoulders. He winced at the touch, as if gentleness burned him.

"Goddess," she said. "Shadow. I know Who You are."

Balen looked at her face, and then looked away again in anguish. Segnbora couldn't bear such terror. She reached out to take his face in her hands.

"Balen," she said, speaking the name aloud for the first time in her life.

He blinked in confusion.

"I seem to be getting a lot of practice at being others, these days," she said. "First Dragons. Then . . . Myself. I see that this is what the practice was for. To see You for what You are. Just Her, in another suit. A tool to make me what I am, no less than the beautiful face and the ever-filled cup were tools. You were a little rougher on me than you might have been, perhaps. You were the sword. But *my* hand was on the hilt. *I* destroy. And I create . . ." She gulped, feeling tears start. "Time I got started. I've bound you into my life all this time, my poor 'rapist.' Enough of it. Go free."

He squinted at her in terrified disbelief.

"Beloved," she said. "Go free."

Drawing him close, shaking all over, she laid her lips on his, once and gently. Then she hugged him tight. When she opened her arms, he was gone.

Weak from the sudden release of so much emotion, she sat down hard on the invisible surface and wiped her eyes, then realized that the wetness on her hands was more than tears. The weakness, too, probably had something to do with her heart's blood running down her surcoat.

Oh Goddess, I forgot, she thought, getting dizzier by the moment. *Blood loss. I have to get back there. Where's Skádhwë, I can't leave it . . .*

Fumbling, falling to hands and knees again, she began feeling around for the blade. Against the dark floor, this was rather like looking for clear glass in water. The dizziness got worse. She reeled; her sight forsook her. Perhaps she was starting to die.

The sudden pain, an infinitesimally thin line of it, told her she had found Skádhwë again. Grateful for the hint, she grabbed it hard, using the pain to shock herself awake, although she was half dead already.

She pushed herself upright . . .

. . . on the cold snow, and opened her eyes. All around her men and women were covering their faces in horror of something that was coming. She had to get up. Where was Skádhwë? . . . still sheathed. Good.

Left-handed she fumbled for something with which to support herself, and found a stone. She levered herself up to her knees and managed to stand, though a wobbly stance it was, and probably very temporary. She drew Skádhwë, and saw with dismay that it was covered with blood. Shíhan, were he here, would be scandalized! Never go out with an unclean blade, he had taught her. She whipped the blood off the blade in a quick downward slash, third move of the *edelle* maneuver—

—and Fire whipped down after it.

I am *dead,* she thought in absolute disbelief, and lifted the sword to stare at it. Fire, raging blue and as impossible to look at as sunlight, trickled down Skádhwë's black edge. Just a

double-thread at first, and then more. It grew quickly, a
torch's worth of Fire, a Firebrand's worth, a lightningbolt in
her hands, burning like a star, throwing her shadow long and
black against the cliff.

I have it! she thought in fierce joy, for that one mad moment
not caring that she was about to die. She stared backwards at
her shadow, the proof of the light—shortlegged, long of neck,
wings where she had arms. *I'm whole,* she thought, and
laughed, raising the hand that held Skádhwë. The right wing
stretched upward, huge. *No!* We're *whole!* The left arm up
now; the wing reached up in response. *Sithessch, we'll die, but
we'll do it together!*

—and abruptly, with a deathpain that shot down her right
arm to her heart, that wing-shadow tore away from the cliff,
casting a shadow of its own, impossibly coming *real.*—

The second wing tore free, another pain. She saw webs that
gleamed like polished onyx and struts rough with black sapphires. Then came the terrible length of tail, the deadly spine
at the end of it whipping free, lashing outward, poised above
her to protect. And after the tail, the taloned forelimbs, their
diamonds flashing in the blinding Firelight. A neck, the great
head, glowing eyes burning not silver now but blue, leaning down over her and glaring past her with impartial challenge at Reavers and Fyrd and the dark something that approached—

"*Hhn' ae mrin'hen,*" said the voice of wind and storm from
right above her. "Whole at last, *yes!*"

She stared up at Hasai, so torn between wonder and terror
that she couldn't tell anymore whether her weakness came
from impending death or sheer astonishment. Her *mdaha*
gazed down at her, tilting his head in a gesture of greeting,
and turned his attention again to the field and the forces
attacking the scarp.

She had heard Dragons roar in her mind. But in the open
it was something else. Rocks fell down from the cliff, and the
ground shook almost as hard as it had before. Not just one
voice roared, but two, ten, a score, a hundred. The *mdeihei*
were there too, not as solidly as Hasai, but present enough
to be a host of shifting wings and deadly razor-barbs and

glowing, glaring eyes, all looking down at the attackers. They sang of a solution to this problem, one that was not to be feared. *Death. Death. Death.* Hasai reared his head back, bared the diamond fangs that few had ever survived seeing, and flamed.

The Reavers fled, panicked. Hasai's blast of Dragonfire melted the ground where they had been standing. Even the slow-stalking shadow at the southern edge of the field halted at that, as if stunned. Fyrd scattered in all directions but eastward, where the Sun seemed to be coming up.

The scarp was fenced with fire again, but this time the consuming white of Dragonfire, with a tinge of blue to it; and inside the circle a tremendous shape with wings like thunder-clouds was rearing up against the cliff, burning in iron and diamond, ineluctably real. And down by one of his hind ta-lons, hanging onto it for support, a tiny figure bleeding Fire from a wound in the heart stared up and up at what had been, and now *was.*

Segnbora thanked him politely for her defense—then she turned to look with grim, delighted purpose out at the field, at the fleeing Reavers and Fyrd, and down at the thing in her hand that burned with Fire.

"Sithessch'tdae," she sang to Hasai and the other *mdeihei* who stirred in shadow along the ledge, "untidy to leave them running around like this, don't you think?"

The *mdeihei* sang angry assent in a thunder that echoed from the surrounding mountains, causing a bass obbligato of avalanches to follow.

"Must we send them *rdahaih?*" Hasai said in an ominous baritone solo.

Segnbora stepped forward to the edge of the shelf where they stood, only partially aware of Herewiss's and Freelorn's prone forms. Breathing or not, they'd have to wait until later. "I don't know," she said, and raised Skádhwë, thinking hard.

It can't be done, they say—a gating for more than fifty. However . . . She closed her eyes, not needing the physical ones to see at the moment, and drew up a great flood of Power from the tremendous supply they had always told her she'd have. In mind she saw them, every Fyrd in the valley and for miles around. She hated them, and loved them, and did what was necessary. She poured the Flame out of her as if opening a floodgate, until the valley was awash with it.

It was simple to gather up the minds of every Fyrd in the area and hold them all under the surface of that Flame until they drowned. *Stop showing off,* she told herself severely. *You may drop dead in a moment, and there's business to be done here.* Yet she laughed in pleasure as she thought it, and Hasai and the *mdeihei* went off in a thunderous accompaniment of hissing Dracon laughter. Whether she lived or died, she was going to enjoy this. She had waited a lifetime for it.

The Reavers and the Arlene mercenaries at the other side of the field were fleeing, and she stared across at them, angry and pleased. She could easily kill them all, but she knew Someone Who would prefer it otherwise, if at all possible.

So, she thought, and reached out in heart to feel them all, every last one, mind and soul together. The Rodmistresses had said it was impossible, but behind her she had a supporting multitude who would testify otherwise if she asked them to. She *was* that multitude. She could contain universes.

Immersing herself in the minds of her enemies, she became them. Before they had a chance to recover from being *her,* she stepped to the cliff's edge and lifted Skádhwë. With it she drew four great slashing lines of Flame that fell onto the darkened field, and grew, and grew—

Suddenly the ground within the lines was missing, replaced by five thousand different images blurred together—some of them of the Arlene countryside, or of Prydon city, some of them of the strange cold country beyond the mountains from which the Reavers came. Into the crammed-together vistas fell men and women who cried out in terror and were gone. She closed the door behind them with a word and a sweep of Skádhwë, and glanced up in thanks at the glowing eyes that hung over her. Then she turned south.

There, something dark stirred in its mantle of blackness and glared utter hatred at her. She looked back at It calmly, having loved It before, and unafraid to do once more what was necessary. She reached out to grasp the forces that Dragons could manipulate, and took one more step forward, right off the edge of the cliff. There she stood on empty air.

"Come out and meet us if you dare!" she cried, The song

winding around the words held in it the ultimate challenge: inescapable love. Behind her the *mdeihei* echoed the song in perilous harmonies. Trembling, Segnbora stood there while the darkness gathered Itself up into that terrible crushing wave she had seen before, full of screams and blood and ancient death. It rose higher and higher above her. She lifted up Skádhwë's flaming length and stood her ground, letting her eyes sink into the Shadow's darkness, becoming It, accepting It for her own, her dark side, Her other Shadow.

It trembled toward her—then gathered Itself down into a shuddering ball of fear and thwarted hatred, and vanished.

The wind died abruptly, and the sky began to clear. Four thousand Darthenes stood in an empty field with no one left to fight.

Segnbora took a last gasp of breath and walked back onto the cliff, beginning to feel mortal again for the first time since she had turned Skádhwë against herself. Behind a rock Eftgan lay breathing shallowly. Beside her, two forms struggled to sit up, helping each other. One of them had an arrow in him, but it didn't seem to be paining him much. As Segnbora came up to them, the taller of the two reached out to his loved and touched the arrow's protruding shaft. It vanished in a flicker of Fire, as did the place where it had gone in.

She knelt beside them and laid Skádhwë over her knees— a burning shadow, a piece of the night set on Fire. They stared at it.

"You did it," Freelorn whispered. *"You did it!"*

She smiled at him. "All your fault, my liege."

"But what did you *do?*" Herewiss was looking at her with such a mixture of joy and perplexity that she could have both laughed and cried at once. "I saw what you did to yourself," he said. "Why aren't you dead? And where did Cillmod and all those Reavers go?"

"I sent them home, for the time being." She looked down at her surcoat, brushed at it. There was a neat tear where Skádhwë had gone in through cloth and mail, but that was all. The scar was a faint white seam just to one side of the nightmare's bite.

"I told you," said a great voice above her. "Dragons are quick to heal."

Silver-blue light fell about her as someone else bent low to look curiously at the place where the shadowblade had gone in. She gazed up at him—her shadow casting a shadow of his own now—and at last, the tears came. She reached up to the tremendous jaw as it dropped open, and very gently laid her hand in the Dragon's mouth, as she had feared to do, as she would never fear to do again. The jaws closed, and self joined with self.

"Now what, *sda'sithesssch?*"

"Now, *mda'sithesssch,*" she said, gathering him close and laughing through the tears that fell on the sapphire hide, "there's a King to escort to his throne. Let's get busy!"

Sixteen

Some gifts are so great that the only way the recipient can express his gratitude is to immediately give the gift to someone else. A dangerous business, this, among fickle humankind, who often see such generosity as indicative of a thoughtless heart. But in such a matter, do as your heart directs you. In the last reckoning, She is both giver and receiver, acting both parts to increase the joy of both—and if humankind doesn't understand, She does.

(Charestics, 118)

They leaned on the walls and looked down into the dark streets of Darthis. No light burned anywhere—not so much as a hearthfire or candle or lamp. Below them the city dreamed in a silver pallor of moonlight, though there was a shifting and stirring in the Square under the walls of the Black Palace.

A few thousand people stood down there, quiet or murmuring, waiting for the Queen to strike the first sparks of the Midsummer needfire and distribute it among them. Most of those waiting were only concerned with their part in the festival—lighting the candles and lamps they carried from the new fire and racing through the city with it, spreading luck and laughter. But a few looked up toward the palace walls and stared fascinated at something strange.

Blue Fire flickered there, dancing about a long slender shape that seemed to be too dark to be a Rod. And there was another light there, a pair of silver-blue globes that looked uncannily like eyes staring downward. The more perceptive in the crowd had even noticed that the moonlight didn't fall on them. It was blocked away by a huge winged shape that seemed there when one looked away from it, and not there when one looked at it straight.

Whatever they saw, no one seemed particularly bothered by any of these oddnesses. This was, after all, Midsummer's Eve, when magic was loose in the world.

Down in the square, flint struck steel, and a spark nested in tinder and began to grow into flames. The cheering began. Viols and trumpets and kettledrums struck up a jubilant music that echoed off the walls, and effectively drowned out a deeper music several stories up. *"Hn'aa'se sithesssch mnek-kej-stá untúhë au'lhhw't'dae,"* the music said, a voice like a trio of bass instruments playing a lazy, cheerful processional.

"Ae, mdaha'esssch," sang a softer voice, in a raspy alto. "We may as well enjoy the rest while we can . . ."

"There won't be much of it," Hasai said, unfolding and folding his wings in resignation. He spoke in precognitive tense, but with good humor; the melody woven about his words said plainly that he preferred action to peace and quiet. "Arlen will be astir like thunderstorm air for months. If Cillmod doesn't already know who was responsible for what happened at Bluepeak, he will very shortly. The war with Darthen will soon open."

"And the Queen forges her new crown tomorrow," Segnbora groaned. A formal occasion first thing in the morning was the last thing she needed. "All I want is to sleep late."

"You may, if you please. I will teach you how, now that you have a *sdaha's* proper timesense. Will a month or so be enough, *sithesssch?"*

The steps on the battlement were no surprise. Two hours ago Segnbora had remembered hearing them, and she had been waiting for them ever since. "If he *did* know," the shorter of the two approaching men said on reaching the top of the stairs, "it explains why he made the bastard Chancellor of the Exchequer."

"To keep an eye on him?"

"Sounds like something my father might have done. This also explains how he managed to get the backing of the High Houses. But even if he can go into Lionhall, he doesn't know the Ritual, he's no Initiate—or if he is, he's messing up. Arlen is ready for me now."

Freelorn and Herewiss looked strange out of surcoats and mail. They leaned on the wall, one on either side of her, in softboots and britches and shirts. Herewiss looked up at the dark shape that blocked-but-didn't-block the Moon away. "How much are you there, *lhhw'*Hasai?"

"As much as my *sdaha* needs me to be. Or as I need to be. Since we're one, there's little difference . . ."

"Where were you an hour or so ago?" Herewiss said to Segnbora. "Eftgan was looking for you. Wanted your help with the needfire, or something."

"I was flying," Segnbora said, nodding at the sky.

Herewiss nodded soberly. She shared a gentle look with him, understanding now from her own experience how complete his underhearing must be, reaching even to others' most private thoughts. "I have to thank you," she said.

"You don't have to anything. You did it yourself."

"So I did. And you mediated some of that doing with me, saw me into the situations I'd need to get where I am. You had little reason to give me such a gift, either," Segnbora said. "I tried to move in between you and your loved, a while back. You must have noticed."

Herewiss nodded, looking grave. But not too much so. "These days, I don't let old reasons interfere with what I want to do. And maybe, even when I was angriest at you, maybe I saw something . . ."

"Who I was?" she said.

"Yes. A liaison. There's a whole race sharing the Kingdoms with us that not even the human Marchwarders understand properly—they have the language, but not the body that forms it. But there was more. You were a catalyst. And will continue to be. Things will be happening that need me— things I couldn't do without you and your Dragons. Likewise there are things you couldn't manage without *me*. I'm part of a solution. And more—"

She fell silent, nodding, already having hints of what the "more" was. This was a small problem. Sometimes the ahead-memories came too fast, and she had trouble deciding what to share, what to keep to herself.

She shrugged. The future was merely another kind of present to a Dragon, malleable as the past, part of the game. What mattered was what the player intended to be.

In one word, her newfound Name, she told them.

"We'll keep your secret," Freelorn said just above a whisper.

Segnbora smiled at them, knowing that the One she meant to hear her Name had heard it through them, then waved

good night, and headed for the stairs. Along the upper parapet, Hasai lazily put out a single forefoot—all he needed to
do to keep up with her.

"No more words?" he said.

"What should I say?"

Slowly Segnbora lowered her head to gaze back down the
parapet, where Freelorn took back from Herewiss the lovers'
cup she had left them, and drained it—and found it still full.

"*That,*" Hasai said. "Forever."

Lost between laughter and tears of joy, Segnbora nodded,
reached out to her *mdaha,* and led him off into their future,
and to bed.

ON TIME, CALENDARS, AND RELATED SUBJECTS

The motions of the Middle Kingdoms' world around its Sun match those of Earth around Sol (except for negligible variations, such as those caused by sister planets missing in their solar system and present in ours). Their year is therefore the same length as ours—365 days, 5 hours, 48 minutes, 48-odd seconds. Though in Segnbora's time clocks still have only hour hands, the astronomers of the Kingdoms have evolved their own methods of handling the year, and the little pieces of it that tend to pile up as time passes and throw calendars out of alignment with the seasons.

Both Arlen and Darthen use a 360-day "year" of four 90-day "seasons" that correspond to our winter, spring, summer, and fall. Days are counted straight through each season, and spoken of as "the fifth of Winter," "the thirty-eighth of Summer," and so forth. In addition, the First of each season is always a major holiday, tied to solstice or equinox—Opening Night for Winter (the only one of the holidays that doesn't fall directly on solstice or equinox), Maiden's Day for Spring, Midyear's Day for Summer, and the Harvest Festival (either Lion's Day or Eagle's Day) for Fall. The five remaining days are intercalated and belong to no season: they are placed between the end of Fall and the beginning of Winter, and during these cold days at the bottom of the year, the Dreadnights as they're called, no enterprise is begun, no childnaming or marriage celebrated. They are the Shadow's nights, and unlucky. Every fourth year a sixth intercalary day (in Arlen **Endethnë,** *"Lady's Day," in Darthen* **Aerrudéj,** *"the Goddess' Joke") is added between the Dreadnights and Opening Night, to deal with the need for a leap-year day.*

However, this still leaves a significant fraction of time out of the reckoning. The addition of the leap-day to compensate for the 5h-48m-48s leftover at year's end is in fact an overcompensation. If left uncorrected, each year will be 11.2 minutes short. This may not sound like much, but in our world in the past has led to awful misalignment of the calendar year with the seasons—the first day of spring falling in December, for example. But this backward drift of dates is preventable by any number of methods. The astronomers of the Kingdoms found that the eleven-minute deficit will amount to a full day's error

*in 128y-208d-13h-38m-21.125s. Therefore, once every 128 years, that
208th day (which by our calendar would be July 19th) is dropped from the
year entirely, or rather converted to July 20th; that date in turn becomes the
29th of Summer rather than the 28th, and is called the Festival of the Lost
Day. (The festival is devoted to pranks, pratfalls, drinking sprees, and attempts
to lose things, usually unwanted ones. There are also lying contests, with prizes
for the best explanation of where the Lost Day went.) This system of adjustment
runs independently of that for leap-year days. Though it would probably be
more efficient to combine the adjustment systems, as our culture does, the
Kingdoms' astronomers are quick to point out that this would mean one less
holiday.*

*It is quite true that even this adjustment is not totally sufficient to keep the
calendar in line with the seasons and the Sun. There is still an unadjusted error
that makes the year too long by 0.0003 day, which will pile up to three days
in each 10,000 years. However, in the words of Talia d' Calath, the Grand
Royal Astronomer to King Berad of Darthen, "It is possible to worry too much,
too far in advance." The Dragons have promised to remind human beings to
insert another one-day intercalary day every 3300 years—though there is still
disagreement over why they laughed so hard when they promised.*

*There are of course many minor local holidays not mentioned here. But
neither Arlene nor Darthene calendars include anything like weeks or months.
One may indicate a given day by season and number: or say "four days ago,"
or "six days from now," or "a month and three days," etc. "Months" (actually
the word is* isten *in both languages, very like the Greek* λυκάβασ *which we
translate as "lichtgang" or "Moonreturn") are sometimes broken down to 29
days for counting purposes, but this is rare. Mostly a month is reckoned from
a phase of the Moon to its next occurrence, most frequently full to full. This
might be expected in a largely agrarian culture, where the times of planting are
important. But to the people of the Kingdoms, the Moon is the living vigil of
the Goddess, mirroring Her changes in its own as it slides from Maiden's slim
crescent to Bride's and Mother's white full to Crone's waning sickle to Moondark perilous and hidden; and for the most part people have a fondness for the
Moon and enjoy reckoning by it, without resource to numbers.*

*Astronomers—and, of course, sorcerers and people with the blue Fire—are
cognizant of such lunar functions as node crossings and regression of nodes,
apogee and perigee and advance of the perigee point, librations and nutations,
and eclipses both lunar and solar, such being important to their work. But (and
very sensibly) no one has ever particularly cared about what the lunar calendar
does in relation to the solar one. The only real notice taken of alignment between
the two is in mention of Nineteen-Years' Night, when the Moon is full on
Opening Night and wreaking with sorcery or Fire is particularly potent.*

There is a tendency for Moon cycles to be referred to by name, the names differing from area to area. For example, the first full Moon of Spring, and the days following it from waning to dark to new crescent to full again, is usually called the "Song Moon" in Arlen, while some Darthenes call it the "Unicorn's Moon," and some others, the "Maiden's Moon" or the "Mad Moon." Special note is taken of the Harvest Moon in most places, both because of the shortening of its rising time and in memory of the bloody harvest cut at Bluepeak during one of its risings an age ago; the full Moon that follows the Harvest Moon is always the Lion's or Eagle's Moon, in Earn's and Héalhra's memory.

Since the memory of the times before the Catastrophe has largely been lost, years are counted from the coming of the Dragons and the destruction of the Dark, and noted by number and the abbreviation for pai Ajnedäre derúwin, *"after the Arrival." Example: Segnbora's birthday is Spring the 57th, 2098 p.a.d.*

ON DRACON ANATOMY AND PHYSIOLOGY

The Dragons are perhaps purposely vague about their very beginnings. "Thinking about a time before their own consciousness," d'Welcaen reports, "makes them nervous." But the earliest Dracon memories recall a time when the Homeworld was populated by plant-analogs and other life forms. There was a food chain, and Dragons had use for the internal organs which now exist only in extremely debased vestigial forms.

Somewhere along the line—possibly due to changes in the Homeworld's orbit, or in its star's characteristics—the planet's seas began to evaporate, and its atmosphere to strip off. The Dragons report this as taking many thousands of their lifetimes. Converting this time to human standards is difficult, and gives answers ranging from one to six million years. This may seem like quite a while, but it isn't really, for an organism whose average generation is from four to six thousand years. The Dragons had to adapt in a hurry to the changes in their environment.

Already silicon-boron based—and what their atmosphere and "seas" consisted of is still a matter for conjecture—the Dragons' evolution went in the most efficient possible direction. Their anatomy began adjusting itself toward extreme lightness, for maximum efficiency in soaring in search of food. As food got scarcer due to increased irradiation, wild mutations got more common—including one that became most successful: the alteration of silane rings in the black wing-membranes, so that they became in effect giant solar cells, using the already-existing neural pathways for conduction of generated bioelectricity. Dragons born with this mutation, needing no normal food, thrived and multiplied, and soared further and further sunward for food. The increased irradiation induced more gene changes and mutations in brain physiology, so that the "highflyers" found themselves able to manipulate "force"—magnetic fields, gravity wave-fields, and other instrumentalities less classifiable to humans. Organs used for digestion, respiration, and elimination slowly went vestigial, until finally the "late model" Dragon was left— an efficient, flying energy-storage machine, spaceworthy, tolerant of extreme high and low temperatures (as had become commonplace on the Homeworld), *and able to express that energy as Dragonfire and use it as tool and weapon.*

The reasons for that particular manifestation are debatable, but d'Welcaen suggests that Dragons feel about their mouths as humans feel about their hands. Dracon psychology says that language is the primary means of effective survival: which perhaps explains why, even after their development of underspeech, the Dragons never gave up communication by way of vocal speech. Even their tongues still work after all these centuries—though they're not necessary: Dracon sound generation long ago went over to non-acoustic mechanisms like those of whales. Fluid-filled or stressed-solid-filled cavities stimulated by "muscle" contraction, or catalytic chemical reactions, or neural/membrane synergies, or all three, allow Dragons to communicate with precision and stunning variation in almost any medium except empty space, and also permit the super-prolonged hisses, three- to eighteen-tone chords, and choral-verbal speech for which they're best known.

Dragonfire, according to d'Welcaen, is strictly a "psi" phenomenon allied to "manipulation of force," and as complicated for a Dragon as breathing for a human—a Dragonet can flame before it can talk. The skill is almost wholly a constructive one these days; the times when a Dragon would have to melt several tons of lead-bearing stone over itself to protect it from a starstorm, or blast its way out of the covering again, are long past. A Dracon name for the Sun that shines on the Middle Kingdoms is hh-Aass'te're, *"the Shallows" —a pale, cozy little star, tame and safe compared to the mad fire of the Homestar in its last days. These days Dragonfire is for show, and for* nn's'hraile, *in a particularly heated argument; for building; and, when words fail at last, for mating fights, when hottest fire decides who will reproduce, and who will go very suddenly* mdahaih.